The author delivers both with panac
that is easy to follow and peppered v
aplenty.

Filled with action, drama, romance, and political intrigue, Margot de Klerk's intricately woven young adult adventure tale is bound to entertain lovers of the supernatural genre.

Pikasho Deka, *Readers' Favorite*

I loved this book! It's been such a long time since I read a book that has kept me on the edge of my seat ...*Wicked Magic* was such a unique novel that I couldn't put it down.

Tiffany Ferrell, *Readers' Favorite*

Filled with suspense and action, this is a phenomenal book that is spellbinding from start to finish. The storyline moves at a fast pace, building to a dramatic and thrilling finale...

Susan Sewell, *Readers' Favorite*

The plot moves quickly, and the creative details bring this entertaining world to life, making this witty and weird novel full of potential for a new series.

Self-Publishing Review

BOOKS BY MARGOT DE KLERK

VAMPIRES OF OXFORD SERIES

Wicked Magic
Wicked Blood (2022)

WICKED MAGIC

A VAMPIRES of OXFORD NOVEL

Margot de Klerk

MdK

COPYRIGHT

Copyright © 2022 Margot de Klerk

First paperback edition 2022

ISBN
978-1-9196213-1-9 (paperback)
978-1-9196213-0-2 (ebook)

Map by Joshua Schnalke

Book Cover Design by www.ebooklaunch.com

Dedicated to my mother, who never stopped believing in my crazy pipe dream of becoming an author.

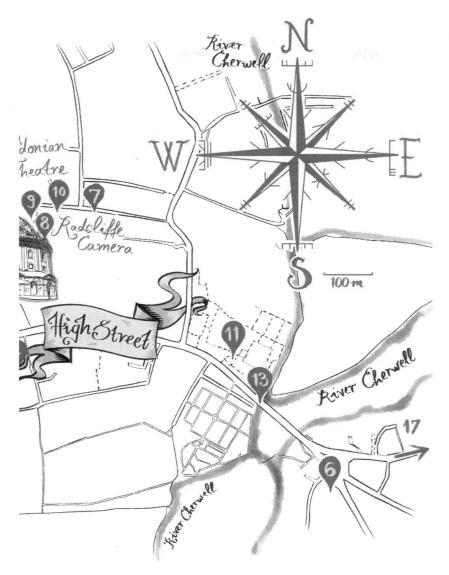

11 MAGDALEN COLLEGE
12 WESTGATE SHOPPING CENTRE
13 MAGDALEN BRIDGE
14 SHELDONIAN THEATRE
15 HUNTER HEADQUARTERS

16 TO DAMIEN'S HOUSE AND
   UNIVERSITY PARKS
17 TO CYNTHIA'S HOUSE
18 TO NATHAN'S HOUSE

CHAPTER ONE

'MAN, THAT NEW GIRL Cynthia Rymes is seriously hot,' Matt said. 'That level of hotness in one girl should be banned or something.'

Banned or something. Yeah. Nathan squinted at the girls playing lacrosse in Uni Parks and thought that if anything was going to be banned, it was him and Matt hanging out and ogling the girls from Headington School in the park.

'Which one's she?' he asked, nicking Matt's bottle of coke because he'd finished his own.

'Mate!' Matt whined. 'The blond one with the two plaits. Front and centre. Seriously!'

'Yeah, hot,' Nathan agreed. He peered at her again. Maybe it was because he was exhausted—he'd been up half the night trying to finish his bio homework—but she had a bird in her aura. Like, a swan or something, but black. Nah, couldn't be.

'Nice legs,' he said, flopping back on the grass and staring at the trees.

'What time did you go to bed last night?' Matt sniggered. He lay back beside his friend and shoved a handful of crisps in his mouth. Matt always ate like a pig.

'Dunno, maybe four AM?' Nathan thought for a moment. 'Late. I forgot about bio, and Mr Jackson's homework literally killed me.'

'Didn't think it took that long,' Matt said, spraying crisps everywhere.

Yes, but Matt didn't have self-defence six days a week, nor all manner of supernatural drama. Monica had wailed on Skype for half an hour about how she was sure that the witch she was training with in Morocco was trying to kill her and make soup out of her entrails, or something. Then Dad had called to cancel Nathan's trip to London this weekend because he was going on an urgent hunt in Liverpool, or maybe Newcastle. And between everything, he'd just forgotten that bio homework was still a thing.

'Lucky,' Nathan said. One of the girls scored, and he watched as Headington's team did a group hug. Girls were nice to watch. Try and talk to them, and it was a whole different game. He seemed to be surrounded by them, but it never got any easier. Everything he said was wrong, somehow. Even when it was right, it was still wrong.

Monica was Nathan's closest friend, and her definition of advice was 'just sleep with her and get her out of your system'. That had not helped Nathan in the slightest when he'd had a terrible crush on Suzanne Ecclestone last year. What Monica failed to understand was that humans did not just sleep with people to get it out of their system. Monica didn't see any differences between being a witch and being human.

It was completely different.

Maybe he should ask Adrian for help?

But Nathan could just picture how that would go. It wasn't hard to imagine, actually. Adrian would laugh so hard they'd hear him in Mexico. And then Nathan's cheeks would explode from blushing so hard, or something.

Not the way he planned on going.

'Nate, are you even listening to me?' Matt asked.

'Sorry,' Nathan said, not sorry in the slightest. 'I think I fell asleep for a second. What were you saying?'

'I was asking if you wanted to catch the new *Maze Runner* movie on the weekend, but I reckon the only thing you're going to be catching is forty winks.'

'I'll be fine by Saturday,' Nathan said. 'We can do the movie. Will you check the screenings?'

'And dinner at the Noodlebar,' Matt demanded. 'You owe me dinner.'

'I do?' Nathan asked.

'I paid last time!'

'Shit, I totally forgot.' Nathan sighed. 'Fine, dinner at the Noodlebar, but we have to do the late screening because I'm probably training Saturday.'

'You and your karate shit, man, so boring,' Matt said.

'Shut up!' Nathan reached over and hit his friend. Matt tried to roll away, but if there was one thing being a vampire-hunter-in-training was good for, it was hitting bratty mates who had exceeded their daily witty quip quota.

'Oi!' Matt sat up suddenly. 'Hey, match's over. Looks like Headington won.'

They supported the Headington team, mostly because Matt found Cynthia Rymes hot. Well, also because they were playing some Witney team, so Nathan supposed that he had some loyalty towards the local girls. With reluctance, he sat up.

'What would Poppy say if she knew you were checking out the lacrosse team at the park?' he asked, watching idly as the girls shook each other's hands.

'Poppy and I aren't together,' Matt replied. 'We're taking a break.'

'For what, the fifth time?'

'No!'

'Maybe the sixth,' Nathan said.

'Nate, don't be a dick.'

Nathan was considering pointing out that Matt should just break up with Poppy, but then Cynthia looked over at them and waved, and he forgot what he was planning on saying.

'Mate, wave back!' Matt hissed, elbowing him hard. Nathan obediently waved, trying not to wince. Matt had sharp elbows.

Cynthia beamed and jogged over to pick up the cones on the edge of the field near where they were sitting. Was she exaggerating the way she bent over a bit? Damn, she had nice legs. Wait, wasn't it rude to stare? Shit.

Cynthia picked up the last cone, hesitated for a moment, then stepped towards them. 'Hey, you guys are from MCS, right?' she asked shyly.

'H—hi,' Nathan said. Was he blushing? His cheeks felt hot. Damn!

'Aren't you Poppy Wiggen's boyfriend?' Cynthia asked Matt.

'Matt,' he called back cheerfully. Matt was very suave when it came to girls. Nathan theorised that this had something to do with having a girlfriend or losing his virginity, probably the latter, because it was a recent development. Matt of his youth had not been suave. He added, 'My friend Nate's a big fan of lacrosse, actually.'

Nathan's cheeks heated up even further. Hello, death-by-exploding-cheeks. 'Um, uh,' he stammered, searching for an excuse.

'My sister plays lacrosse.'

'Oh, cool.' Cynthia smiled. She shifted the orange cones under her arm then came over and held her hand out to him. Nathan stared at it with extreme panic for a second, until he received another elbow to the gut from Matt and remembered that human beings shook hands when they met. He stood, awkwardly, and grasped her hand.

'I'm Cynthia,' she said.

'I know,' he blurted out. Fuck. He was too tired for this; his brain was on holiday or something. 'I mean, uh... your name's on your jersey.' *Nate, shut up!*

Cynthia's cheeks went pink. It was adorable. At least she was blushing too. Solidarity in blushing—or wait, did that mean he'd embarrassed her? Shit, he didn't mean to embarrass her!

'I guess it is,' she said wryly. 'And you are... Nate?'

'Nathan,' he said. 'Um, Nathan Delacroix.'

'Nice to meet you,' she replied. 'Our next match is next week. You could bring your sister, I guess?'

Nathan nodded like the idiotic nodding dog his sister had stuck on the rear dash of his aunt's car when she was six. 'Sure, why not?' he asked, forcing himself to stop nodding. 'I'll, um, see you then?'

Cynthia beamed at him. 'Cool!' she said. 'I'd better, um, get these back to our teacher.' She pointed at the cones. 'And, you know, go home and shower. Gosh, I probably smell.' And then she blinked at him, went scarlet, and turned and fled. Nathan stared after her, completely bemused.

'You're a wanker,' Matt said cheerfully from behind him.

'Why?' Nathan complained.

'You embarrassed her.' Matt looked way too happy. 'I think she likes you.'

'Sure, I'm likeable, right?' Nathan asked.

'No, you're awful.' Matt smirked. 'Ask her out.'

'Not in this lifetime,' Nathan said. He looked over his shoulder at Cynthia, in time to see her bury her face against a friend's arm. 'Girls like her don't date guys like me.'

'What, hot sporty girls don't date athletic guys with stuttering problems?' Matt teased. 'You don't say!'

Nathan slugged him hard on the arm. 'Come on, arsehole,' he said. 'I'm exhausted, I have training, and I still gotta write that economics essay for tomorrow. Let's get home.'

Lily von Klichtzner was sitting on his doorstep when he got home from training that night.

Well, not literally. She was waiting two doors down, on the low wall in front of number seven's garden. But Nathan had to walk past her to get to his aunt's house, and there was no way she was waiting for the batty couple who lived at number seven.

He drew level with her. 'No. Lily, I have homework.'

'I need one ward, please,' she begged. 'Damien is being such a control freak since the whole thing with the Council.'

The Thing with the Council—name pending patent—had taken place in May, now around five months ago. Nathan was surprisingly sketchy on the details, despite having been present for most of it, because no one told seventeen-year-olds anything. He knew it had involved a kidnapping attempt.

'Don't you have any witch friends for this stuff?'

'Monica's in Morocco.' Lily pouted.

'I know.' Nathan sighed and scuffed his toe against the ground.

Lily peered at him from her position on the wall and said the magic words. 'I'll pay.'

Nathan pretended he was thinking about it, he honestly did, but Lily's father was a billionaire or something, and Nathan owed Matt dinner. 'How much?' he asked finally.

'How much do you want?'

'Depends on the ward, I guess,' he replied.

'It's an anti-scrying ward,' Lily said.

Nathan's heart sank. Wards were protective talismans, sort of a hunter speciality, but Nathan wasn't a proper hunter yet. Anti-scrying wards were hard because they weren't rooted in one spot. Wards that went on a person were always trickier.

'You know he'll probably just call Adrian back to follow you around if you stop him from scrying you, right?'

'Adrian's a better deal,' Lily said. 'Adrian gets bored easily.'

'Truer words,' Nathan said miserably. When Adrian got bored in Oxford, he did one of three things. Savaged the locals, had sex with the locals, or annoyed Nathan. The latter had become his favourite activity, of late. 'Travelling wards are tricky, Lily.'

'Five hundred pounds,' she said. 'If you can do it before the weekend.'

Five hundred pounds for another sleepless night. Nathan sighed again.

'I'll be in town to watch a movie Saturday night; can I give it to you then?'

'Oh, sure,' Lily said. 'But I don't mind coming to you.'

She didn't get it at all.

'Lily, if you keep coming here, Aunt Anna's going to notice,' he told her patiently. 'And I'm going to be a dead hunter, for doing deals with vampires.'

Lily pouted. It was the same look she used on Damien and Adrian, and they both gave her whatever she wanted. Nathan stared at the house behind her.

'Okay, Saturday,' she agreed in a sing-song voice. 'I wouldn't have to come here if you gave me your phone number, you know!'

It was the age-old debate. What was worse on the cavorting-with-the-enemy scale? Clandestine meetings or having their phone number? Nathan pulled out his phone and let her put her number in.

'I'll text you when I know what time I can meet,' he said. 'You have to pay into my bank account, kapeesh? I can't carry that much cash.'

'Text me the details!' Lily bounced off towards her car. Nathan scuffed his shoes against the ground all the way back to his house. A travelling ward. Fuck.

Wards were tricky business, despite looking simple. It wasn't about the runes and symbols you drew to make them work, though those were essential. What they were really made up of was belief and magical power. Nathan was human and tired. He had zero percent of either.

What went for static wards counted double for travelling wards. Wards liked being in one place, because they could feed off of ambient magic. There was plenty ambient magic in an old city like Oxford, particularly because there were quite a lot of witches around these parts. Witches liked old cities. Vampires also liked Oxford, although they didn't usually love small cities because if there was an accident when they fed it was harder to cover up. Anyway, with all the witches who had lived in Oxford over the years, the city was filled to the brim with ambient magic.

Travelling wards could suck that up too, as long as you were in an area with lots of it, but it was harder because they were moving and not carved into walls—walls soaked up magic and transmitted it into wards very well. Also, as soon as you left an area with ambient magic, the ward would start getting unhappy, which either meant it would go on the fritz or it would die altogether.

It was fine for witches; they were a walking, talking power source.

Lily was a half-vampire, though. Vampires were created through magic, but they didn't have magic.

Nathan pondered the problem whilst he did his maths homework. By the time he had, probably wrongly, calculated all of the equations on page seventy-eight, he had a mental checklist.

- Wood that conducted magic, to carve the runes on
- Carving tool—what were they called again?
- Power source
- Symbols that both of them believed in—though Lily would probably believe whatever Nathan told her to believe
- A good night's sleep

The last one was the most essential, seeing as he was going to have to infuse the thing with his own belief in order to power it enough to travel. Why had he agreed again?

On Friday, Matt ribbed him the whole day about Cynthia, and he got a D on his econ homework.

The day could not get any worse.

By the time he got home, he had fifteen text messages from Monica.

Monica: Fuck me

Monica: This woman

Monica: She's killing me

Monica: Also, it's fucking hot

Monica: I'm English. I don't do hot

Monica: I'm sweating my makeup off

Monica: Can I retire from being a witch

Monica: Baby Delacroix, donde estas?

Monica: Ew, she wants me to chop mouse entrails

It went on like that. Clearly, someone else was spotting Monica's phone bill for her. Nathan ignored all of her messages and sent one of his own.

Nathan: If I were to make a travelling anti-scrying ward, what would be the best wood to use? And what runes?

Monica must have been epically bored because the reply came about two seconds later.

Monica: You want *blindaz*. The fuck you need that for?

Nathan: Not for me. It's for Lily

Monica: Don't do it. Damien will

Monica: Fucking

Monica: Kill

Monica: You

Monica: When he finds out

Nathan: Not my problem. Wood?

Monica: Depends what you can get. Hazel, if you can get it. It carries magic best. Also good for vision/clairvoyance spells. If not then cedar=protection, maple=wisdom

Nathan: Will have a look, thanks

Monica: If Damien kills you, can I have your PlayStation?

Nathan rolled his eyes and went to raid his aunt's supply cupboard.

Aunt Anna was not a hunter, but Uncle Jeff was, although it was an ill-kept secret that Aunt Anna did all the technical stuff for Uncle Jeff because she was something of a ward specialist. If Nathan thought he could get away with it, he would have asked her to make the ward for him.

She'd want to know why he needed an anti-scrying ward though, seeing as only witches could scry, and then he'd have to explain everything.

Aunt Anna kept everything in a cupboard in the garage, which was locked with a very large padlock. This did not take into account that lockpicking was taught to young hunters at about the age of seven. Nathan helped himself to a chisel and a runic dictionary but got stuck on the wood. She had several, and none were labelled. He snapped a picture and sent it to Monica with a panicked 'which one?'

Monica: The leftmost is hazel I think. I hope. If not, you're screwed

Nathan: It better be or you're never getting the PlayStation

Monica: Noooooo!

Monica: It's defo hazel, I googled it

Blindaz was a nice small rune in the runic dictionary, so he grabbed a vaguely round piece of wood and stole sandpaper from his uncle's

DIY supplies.

It took Nathan an hour of painstaking work to sand the hunk of wood into a passable amulet and carve the rune into the front and back. That was the easy part; he'd done that quite a few times in training. The bit that movies and books always managed to wuss-out of showing was the real hard work: imbuing the amulet with magic. Real magic wasn't clean or quick or efficient. It was messy and imprecise and involved a lot of believing in yourself.

Believing in yourself was a surprisingly tricky skill to master.

Nathan's believing involved lit candles, filched from the bathroom where his aunt kept a supply with strange scents. It also involved closed eyes and chanting. He did it at two AM so no one would walk in on him, and it took a clean two hours before the rune looked even slightly gold to his magically sensitive vision.

A witch would have dipped it in some kind of tincture and waved their hands and chanted in Latin, but none of that was an option for humans. Exhausted from two hours of intense self-belief, Nathan collapsed into bed and slept through his alarm.

CHAPTER TWO

'WAKE UP! AUNT ANNA SAYS TO WAKE UP! YOU'RE LATE FOR TRAINING!'

'Jess?' Nathan rolled over and peered sleepily at his eleven-year-old sister. 'What time is it?'

'Seven-fifteen.'

'Crap!' Nathan tumbled out of bed, taking half the bedding with him and landing in a tangle on the floor. Jessica laughed.

'Get out!'

'Don't be rude, Nathan!'

Nathan trained at his mentor's house, a fifteen-minute cycle from home. That Saturday, he arrived sweaty and out of breath. Grey was unimpressed.

'If I had been late to training, my mentor would have sent me home again.'

'Graham, please,' Nathan said between pants. 'It won't happen again.'

'I'm sure I've heard that before.'

Nathan groaned. 'Fine, well, I could do with another, oh, six hours sleep, so—'

'On second thoughts, maybe it's more of a punishment to let you stay.'

Should have kept my damn mouth shut, Nathan thought sourly. Rumour had it that Grey was capable of being nice, once a year on Christmas day. Seeing as Nathan got Christmas day off, he had never had the privilege of experiencing it.

Saturdays, the Saturdays when Nathan didn't go to London to see his parents, were dedicated fully to training: self-defence in the morning, followed by weapons training, finishing off with skills in the afternoon. The latter included the warding he had done the night before, as well as all manner of other tricks for tracking vampires.

'Dad said he's on a hunt in Liverpool,' Nathan said when they sat down for lunch. Mrs Larson had made sandwiches. 'Is it an important target?'

'If it were, do you think I'd tell you?' Grey replied.

'Course not,' Nathan said dejectedly. He didn't even have to know who it was—he was just curious what his father got up to. But, of course, no one told him anything.

'Eat your lunch,' Grey said. 'We're working on languages this afternoon.'

Brilliant.

Most other teenagers would probably think it was cool to be able to speak five languages fluently, but they didn't have to do push-ups every time they made mistakes.

'Can't we do more knife work? Or start on guns? I'll be eighteen in October. It's not that far off.'

'No guns until you're eighteen,' Grey replied sternly. 'Your parents want you to start on Arabic.'

Another language? Seriously?

'What do I even need Arabic for? No vampire worth their salt is gonna live in the Middle East—they'd fry!'

'Don't question orders, Nathan.'

Nathan wanted nothing more than to fall into bed by the end of it, but he had to shower and dress to head to the cinema. He cycled into town and locked his bike outside Pembroke College. Matt was waiting for him, wearing chinos and a shirt.

'You're looking smart,' Nathan said dully.

'Do you mind if Poppy joins us?' Matt asked. 'I promise if she starts making a fuss we'll leave.'

Nathan thought longingly of his bed. 'If you want to postpone…'

'No! No! Don't leave me alone with her! She might start crying again!'

Nathan had zero interest in Matt's relationship drama. He sighed. 'Fine.'

Lily texted as they were walking up Cornmarket.

Lily: Are you in town yet?

A really wicked idea occurred to Nathan.

'Hey, Matt, you mind if I invite a friend as well?'

'As in a female friend?' Matt asked.

'Yeah, but not a girlfriend, just one of Monica's friends. I have to give her something, so I said she could meet me.'

'Wait,' Matt said. 'You have female friends?'

'*Focus*, Matt.'

'Ooh, I want to meet her!'

Nathan: Do you want to join me and my friend for dinner and a movie? He invited his girlfriend and I need moral support

Lily: Yes, please :)

Okay, maybe it was a little cruel to take advantage of Lily's desperation for friends, but she was the only person Nathan knew who was more socially awkward than he was.

Nathan: We're going to the Noodlebar now.

Lily: See you there!

By the time they got to the restaurant Lily was waiting outside, looking cute as a button in a blue dress. She beamed at Nathan, and Matt gawked.

'*She's* your friend? Are you serious?'

'Matt, meet Lily,' Nathan said, feeling very cool. 'Lily, this is Matt. He goes to school with me.'

'Hi,' Lily said sweetly and shook Matt's hand. Matt was still staring. Nathan tried to see Lily through his friend's eyes—untainted by the knowledge that her father was eight hundred years old and probably ate Lily's suitors for breakfast. Yeah, she was cute. Lily was petite, with generous curves and very long blond hair. She had blue eyes and pouty lips and perfect skin.

Of course, she would look perfect. It hid the bloodsucking monster inside. Nathan wondered what Matt would think if he realised the girl he was drooling over drank human blood as the price for beauty and eternal youth.

That was when Poppy arrived, which basically set the tone for the entire evening.

Poppy was pretty too. Actually, Nathan used to have a bit of a crush on her, which had been killed stone-dead when Matt started dating her and she turned out to be a massive psychopath. She had black hair and very green eyes, and she liked to wear short skirts. She kissed Matt like she was trying to eat his face, then frowned at Lily.

'Who are you?'

'Nathan's friend,' Matt said, having apparently got over his tongue-tied-ness.

'I'm Lily.' Lily smiled.

'Charmed,' Poppy replied coolly. 'I'm Poppy.'

'Shall we get dinner now?' Nathan asked.

'What are we watching?' Lily asked once they were sitting down.

'The latest *Maze Runner* movie,' Matt replied. Poppy latched herself onto his arm.

'I checked, there's a viewing of *Sleeping with Other People* at the same time...'

'No way.' Matt rolled his eyes.

'Oh, come on, you never want to watch the movies I like!'

'Because *Maze Runner* is great, and chick-flicks are lame!'

Leaving them to bicker, Nathan reached into his pocket and pulled out the ward. He'd wrapped it in tinfoil to stop it from absorbing any foreign magics before it got to Lily.

Lily's smile grew as he handed it over. She unwrapped the foil immediately. 'Oh, it works!'

'You could not sound so surprised,' Nathan said. 'I stayed up to four AM making that.'

'Monica said she didn't think you could get it to work.'

'Monica's a bitch.'

'What's that, then?' Matt asked. 'You giving each other gifts already?'

'It's ugly,' Poppy observed.

'It's a magical amulet to keep away the supernatural,' Nathan said, which got him wide eyes from Lily but, predictably, sniggers from the other two. What would they do if they knew he wasn't joking? But Matt loved laughing at Nathan's vampire jokes.

'I think it's cute,' Lily said. She strung the leather cord around her neck then stood up. 'I'm just going to the bathroom. Nate, will you order a sweet and sour chicken for me?'

'She's cute,' Matt said as soon as Lily was out of sight. Nathan covered his face with his hands.

'Matt, shut up.'

'Oh, come on. I think she's into you.'

'Lily is not 'into me',' Nathan said. 'And even if she was, I am not into her.' He was quite attached to living, after all. 'Anyway, you wanted me to ask Cynthia out just the other day.'

'Cynthia Rymes?' Poppy asked. 'When did you see her?'

'At her lacrosse game,' Nathan said.

'You were at the lacrosse game?' Poppy demanded, her voice going shrill.

'Nathan, you traitor,' Matt said.

When Lily came back, the ward was pulsing a bright, vibrant red to Nathan's magical sight. That meant it had successfully imprinted on her when she added her blood. Nathan pretended he wasn't relieved that it had worked. Lily didn't need to know he doubted his own skills.

After dinner, they headed to the cinema. Poppy kept up a litany of complaints, but Matt was a good friend and sat between her and Nathan so that he got the worst of the tirade. When the movie was over, they stood outside the cinema and contemplated what to do next.

'Dang, if we were eighteen, we could get a drink,' Matt said.

'Babies.' Lily grinned.

'Don't be mean, Lily,' Nathan told her.

'Oh, that's Adrian's fault, he says I'm too nice and he told me to practice on you.'

'Adrian's such a prat.' Nathan groaned. He could imagine his uncle's face if he realised Nathan had wrangled Lily into a double date, too. Considering that, he really ought to do the gentlemanly thing. 'Should I, uh, walk you home or something?'

'You can walk me to Oriel, Damien should be done with his fellows' dinner by now.'

At the High Street, they separated from Matt and Poppy, who were taking the bus home.

'It was nice to meet you, Lily,' Matt said.

'And you,' Lily replied shyly. She looked like she was blushing, though that might have been because Poppy was trying to set her on fire with her eyes.

Once the two had boarded their respective buses, Nathan and Lily headed for Oriel College, which was tucked away behind Christ Church.

'You really didn't have to walk me,' Lily said.

Yes, he did, because when Adrian found out he'd made the anti-scrying ward, he was going to murder Nathan. Nathan didn't say that, though. Trying to be cool, he said, 'I was walking in this direction anyway. Show me the inside of Oriel College and we'll call it quits.'

'Sure,' Lily said. The porter was just closing up the front gate, and they ended up running for it.

'Cutting it fine there,' he told Lily, then frowned at Nathan. 'No visitors after hours.'

'Please, can't I just show him the quad quickly?' If cuteness were a superpower, Lily would have it. The porter caved.

'Quickly,' he said. 'Or you'll get me in trouble.'

'Thanks!'

Monica had shown Nathan enough of Oxford University to have worn down the mystique. Oriel College was quite pretty, though, and Lily explained its history to him as she let him peek into the two quads and the hall.

The hall was silent, so they headed up a staircase to Damien's office instead. The door opened before Lily could knock.

'Good evening, Lily, Mr Delacroix.'

'Hello Damien,' Nathan said breathlessly. His sixth sense, the one that picked up magic, was going wild, screaming 'Vampire! Vampire! Vampire!' at him. Damien always seemed to suck all of the air out of the room.

Damien was a good two inches taller than Nathan, about six foot one. He had buzzcut blond hair and a sort of old-fashioned militaristic air around him, like soldiers in the old portraits Nathan had seen of his ancestors. Damien would have fit right in. When he smiled, it didn't reach his eyes.

He was dressed in one of the long gowns fellows sometimes wore, over a grey suit.

'Are you ready to go?' he asked Lily.

'Yes,' she said brightly. Damien locked the door before Nathan could glance into his office. He'd never seen inside—in his head there were coffins and gothic arches, and the décor tended towards skulls and bloodied knives. Adrian swore it was just filled with old books, though. Nathan had seen Damien's house, which had turned out to be disappointingly normal, so Adrian was probably right.

'Did you enjoy your film?' Damien asked as they descended the stairs. It was a completely normal thing for a dad to ask his daughter, which made it utterly jarring coming out of Damien's mouth.

'Yes,' Lily answered. 'We watched the *Maze Runner*.'

'I take it that is one of those dystopian futuristic films with a high ratio of explosions per minute,' Damien said. 'Did Mr Delacroix pick the film?'

'I think his friend did,' Lily said. 'You don't need to be so disdainful. You know, girls can like movies with a... *high ratio of explosions*, too.'

Nathan grinned to himself.

They crossed the quad and Damien held the door for them at the gatehouse. Outside the streets were mostly empty.

'Do you need a lift somewhere, Mr Delacroix?' Damien asked.

'No, I came by bike,' Nathan said. 'It's locked over on St. Aldates.' He turned to Lily. 'Thanks for keeping me company. Sorry Matt's a bit of an idiot.'

'It's alright,' Lily said. 'He's a charming idiot.'

'Hah, that's just because you don't know him that well,' Nathan replied. 'When you get to know him, he becomes a dumb idiot.'

Lily smiled.

'Goodnight,' Nathan called, heading for St. Aldates. He'd barely rounded the corner when a little kid came flying out of a backstreet and barrelled straight into him.

'NO!'

Then the girl was off again, sprinting towards St. Aldates. Two men emerged from the same direction she had, and they were covered in ugly, stinky dark magic. It clung to them like tar, invisible to anyone who wasn't magically sensitive, but clear as day to Nathan.

'Did you see a kid?' one demanded. 'Where'd she go?'

'There she is!' the other yelled. They took off. Nathan made up his mind in a split second. He dived in front of them, swiping one's legs out from under him and wrenching the other's arm in a way which probably dislocated the shoulder.

The man screamed in pain. The other staggered to his feet and began chanting in some guttural language. Nathan grabbed him and drove his head against a wall, hard enough that when he dropped the man, he didn't get up. The other one pulled out a knife, but he obviously had no formal training. Nathan disarmed him swiftly and knocked him out the same as his mate.

The knife was pulsating with black magic and covered in strange markings. He pocketed it to examine later and set off to look for the little girl.

She was smart. Nathan found her at a bus stop, huddling close to a group of lost-looking tourists. He might have missed her, if it wasn't for her aura.

She had a bird in her aura.

It looked like a swan, only black. *A black swan. That looks familiar.* He'd thought he'd imagined it, with Cynthia. Maybe he'd been bone tired last time, but with adrenaline coursing through his veins, Nathan couldn't have been more awake now.

'Hey, kid,' he said. She spun around and gasped, throwing her hands up in defence. She couldn't have been older than seven or eight. Her clothes were a mess, a school uniform for sure, but it looked like she'd slept in them. Nathan wasn't sure which school, but then there were tonnes of primary schools in Oxford.

'I'm not going to hurt you,' he said softly. 'Can I call someone to get you?'

Her eyes filled with tears. *Uh oh.*

'Or I could take you somewhere.'

'No, you have to go away,' she whispered. 'You're going to lead them right to me.'

Nathan snorted. 'Those guys aren't going anywhere fast, 'cept maybe a hospital. I knocked them out.'

'Do you know, like, kung fu or something?'

'Nah, I'm a vampire hunter,' he joked. Her eyes widened.

'Vampires don't exist,' she said seriously, which was honestly the most unexpected thing she could have said. She was managing to be a bird and a human at the same time, but she didn't believe in vampires?

'Okay,' Nathan replied slowly. 'Well, I know krav maga, and I knocked them out, I promise you that. I have a phone—do you want to call someone?'

She bobbed her head uncertainly. Nathan passed her his phone. If she tried to nick it, he was pretty sure he could catch her.

She plugged in a number and pressed the call button. The phone rang a few times, and then the tension drained out of her body when it was answered.

'Mummy, Mummy, I need you to come and get me,' she wailed. In about two seconds flat, she was full-on sobbing. 'I don't know, I just ran away! I don't know, a nice man lent me his phone!'

'Why don't you let me speak to your mum?' Nathan asked. 'I can tell her where you are.'

The girl peered at him through teary eyes, looking distinctly distrustful. After several moments, she held out the phone.

'Hello?' Nathan said cautiously.

'Hello? Hello? Emma?' asked a frantic-sounding female voice.

'This is Nathan Delacroix,' Nathan replied. 'I lent your daughter my phone. She seemed to be in some trouble.'

'I—I—' the woman gasped. She paused and Nathan heard her breathing loudly. Then she collected herself. 'So sorry,' she said. 'We've been terribly worried. I don't suppose you could tell me where you are?'

'On St. Aldates. Oxford,' Nathan replied, in case they weren't locals. 'Do you want me to bring your daughter anywhere?'

'No, stay there,' the woman said. 'I'm on WhatsApp. Can you send me a pin with your location? I'll be there in about fifteen minutes.'

Nathan had to end the call to do that, which made Emma cry harder.

'Just let me send our location to your mum,' he grumbled. 'Then you can call her again.'

Around twenty minutes later, a grey Renault estate pulled up beside them and double parked. Before the engines had cut, a girl jumped out of the passenger side and ran to Emma. Nathan watched with interest as the two girls embraced. Two black swans. Colour him unsurprised.

The mother joined them a moment later and, dang, she was a different animal—a dog, maybe? She hugged both of her daughters in one go, and there was a whole lot of crying. Nathan was beginning to put a picture together in his head of what had gone on here, and it wasn't pretty. Who was kidnapping bird girls in Oxford? How long had Emma been held in captivity? Did he need to report this to the Council?

The group hug separated, and the older girl turned to Nathan.

'Thank you so—Nathan?'

It was Cynthia.

'Hey,' Nathan said tiredly. 'So, long story short, I think I just saved your sister.'

Cynthia hurled herself at him, hugging him and kissing his cheek, and it was literally the most awkward thing ever. He was going to have dreams about this forever, because for someone who seemed so awesome at sports, her body was soft in all sorts of places that he hadn't expected, and her lips were warm, and her hair sort of tickled against his cheeks where it brushed him, and—

Cynthia Rymes was kissing him.

Oh, wow.

She pulled away, still clinging to his arm, and flushing as red as a tomato.

'Thank you so much!'

'You know him?' her mother asked. Now that she'd calmed down, she was eyeing Nathan suspiciously.

'Oh yeah, Mum, Nathan goes to MCS. He's one of Poppy's friends— you know Poppy Wiggen, she's in upper sixth—and I met him at our last lacrosse game.'

Okay, Nathan wished she had left that last one off, because it probably made him sound like a pervert.

'Um, hi,' he said, thoroughly embarrassed. 'I'm Nathan Delacroix.'

'Thank you,' said Mrs Rymes. She pursed her lips. 'Will you let me drive you home?'

'Oh no, I have my bike—'

'You should come with us, we can explain what happened,' Cynthia said.

'Cynthia, no,' her mother said.

'But Mum—'

Mrs Rymes shook her head and Cynthia sighed. 'Sorry,' she said to Nathan.

'It's okay.' Nathan was no stranger to keeping secrets. Anyway, he had the information to figure this one out tucked in his pocket. 'You should take Emma home. I think she's been through an ordeal.'

'Are you sure we can't drop you?' Mrs Rymes insisted.

'No, no, it's fine,' Nathan replied.

'Mum,' Emma said, 'He said he knocked out the bad men.'

Nathan covered his face with his hands. Between his fingers, he saw that Cynthia looked vaguely impressed. Her mother looked horrified.

'Excuse me?' she demanded.

'Your daughter was being followed by a bunch of guys,' Nathan said, dropping his hands again.

'How?' Cynthia asked.

'I do MMA,' Nathan muttered.

'Wow,' Cynthia said.

'And you just happened to be there at the right time?' Mrs Rymes asked. 'That's lucky.'

'I walked my friend back to Oriel College. We were at the cinema.' Nathan's phone buzzed in his hands. He shoved it in his pocket; whoever it was could wait.

Mrs Rymes studied him for a moment, frowning. 'I really think we should drop you home,' she said. 'You're not injured, are you?'

'Nope, not a scratch,' Nathan said. He sighed. 'I really don't want to leave my bike in town overnight. I've already had two stolen round here.'

'We can put it in the back of the car.'

And so Mrs Rymes brought the car around whilst Cynthia and Nathan went to grab his bike.

'MMA's pretty rough, isn't it?' Cynthia asked as they walked.

'I guess,' Nathan said hesitantly. Was that cool or not? 'I like martial arts.'

'That's kind of epic,' Cynthia told him.

'I suppose,' Nathan said. 'The bruises are certainly epic.'

'Ever broken any bones?' she asked.

'My left arm and my right ankle,' Nathan said.

'Wow,' said Cynthia. 'Never would have thought it, seeing you hanging out with your friend in the park.'

'Do I look that incapable?' Nathan asked, wondering whether to be offended or not.

'No! I meant, uh, oh.' Cynthia hesitated. 'I meant, you just looked, uh, like a normal guy. And I guess you have hidden depths, or whatever.'

'Or whatever,' Nathan repeated dubiously, but he was grinning. Cynthia thought he had hidden depths! Matt was going to die when Nathan told him about this. If Nathan told him about this. It might be better to keep quiet about it. The last thing Nathan wanted was to involve Matt in something dangerous.

'Where are we going?' Mrs Rymes asked once they'd loaded his bike into the car.

'Straight down the Abingdon Road, I'll show you where to turn off.'

By car, the trip was only five minutes. Soon they had found Aunt

Anna's four-bedroom redbrick. It was quite a plain house, but Nathan was kind of glad for that right now, because at least it didn't scream vampire hunter. Mrs Rymes already seemed suspicious of him.

Aunt Anna came hurtling out the door the moment the car stopped. She stared at them, frowning. Nathan sighed and opened his door.

'Hey, Aunt Anna. My friend gave me a lift home.'

'Nathan, do you have any idea what time it is? You were supposed to be home by eleven-thirty!'

'Oops...'

'Damn, did we get you in trouble?' Cynthia whispered behind him.

'Nah,' Nathan said. 'I'll be fine.'

'Get in the house!' Aunt Anna said.

'Alright, but can I get my bike?'

Cynthia climbed out to help him, except that she didn't do much helping. Once he had his bike on the ground, she touched his arm. Nathan looked at her in surprise.

'Um, thanks,' she whispered. 'I don't know what we would have done if you hadn't been there.'

'You're welcome,' Nathan said. 'See you soon?'

'We should meet up sometime,' Cynthia replied.

'I'd like that.' Nathan smiled at her, though she probably couldn't see because their streetlight was out. 'Thanks for the lift, Mrs Rymes,' he called into the car, then he gave Cynthia a little wave and headed to put his bike in the garden.

Aunt Anna met him in the kitchen.

'You should have called. I texted you twice. I was worried.'

'I'm sorry, Aunt Anna,' Nathan said. 'It honestly didn't occur to me. I, uh, ran into Cynthia after Matt and I split, and we got chatting.'

'Don't let it happen again,' she warned. 'Or I'll tell your parents.'

That threat carried weight. Dad valued discipline above all else. He'd be furious if he found out Nathan was violating curfew and hanging out with girls.

'I'm really sorry,' Nathan said, trying to look as contrite as possible.

'Just go to bed.' Aunt Anna sighed.

That night, Nathan fell asleep with a smile on his face.

Cynthia thought he was cool. *Hell yeah!*

CHAPTER THREE

MONICA: BORED!

Monica: Entertain me

Monica: Lily said your amulet works

Monica: You scumbag, when did you learn magic?

Monica: You hunters have so many tricks

Monica: Stop ignoring me!

Monica: NAAAAAAAAAAAAATEEEEEEEEEEEEEEEEE!

The knife Nathan had picked up was definitely magical, so it called for a witch to identify it. Fortunately, Nathan knew one who was never more than a snarky text message away.

> **Nathan:** Good timing, can I send you a pic and you see if you recognise it?
>
> **Monica:** You bitch, my mentor could have cooked me in a cauldron in the time you took to reply
>
> **Monica:** And now you're just using me for info
>
> **Monica:** What am I, your witchy booty call?
>
> **Monica:** Go on tho, I'm curious

In the light of day, the knife looked even more evil than it had last night. It felt wicked in Nathan's hands, like it wanted to bleed someone dry, so he'd wrapped it in a hoodie last night and hidden it in his cupboard. Now, he laid it carefully on his bed.

The symbols were not runes he'd ever worked with before—hunter runes were mostly Germanic in origin, but these were unfamiliar. The knife had a strange, curved blade and a serrated edge. It was weird. Nathan had never seen anything like it before.

He snapped a picture and sent it to Monica, then hid the knife again and went downstairs for breakfast. She took the better part of fifteen minutes to reply.

> **Monica:** Where TF did you get that????

Monica: That's serious black magic!!!!
Nathan: What is it tho?
Monica: Old folk tale in Middle East about Sahir. Dark magic practitioners. I'm not an expert but Noura is freaking out

Noura was Monica's witch mentor. Nathan had only a vague idea of what she was teaching Monica, but it involved an alarming amount of animal sacrifice, which put it solidly in the moral grey area that all hunters hated.

Nathan: She recognises it?
Monica: She says don't cut yourself, it'll drain the life out of you!

Well, shit. That officially put a dampener on Nathan's mood.

Nathan: Should I report this to someone?
Monica: I dunno? Tell Adrian? Your call

Nathan sighed into his cereal. Jess, sitting opposite him and doing homework, gave him a weird look.

'What's up with you?'

'None of your beeswax,' Nathan replied automatically. Except, he had to call his uncle. His vampire uncle. The person he was supposed to have absolutely nothing to do with, ever, unless he shoved a stake between Adrian's ribs and shuffled his (im)mortal coil.

He put his cereal bowl in the sink and told Aunt Anna, 'I'm going for a walk.'

'Don't be long, I know you haven't done your homework yet!'

Damn, and he had a tonne of work for geography.

Still, he pulled on his shoes and headed out, eventually settling on the swings in the park. From there, he called Adrian.

'Nate? What a shocker.'

'Hi, Adrian,' Nathan said. 'You free to talk?'

'I'm guessing this isn't a social call. Just let me evict the pretty blond from my bed.'

'Ha-ha, and here I thought you liked brunettes.' Nathan rolled his eyes. 'Need to ask you something. Have you ever heard of people who have, like, a bird in their aura?'

'A what?'

'Like a black swan!' Adrian was sniggering. 'Adrian, I'm serious! Alright, I saved this little kid from being kidnapped in town last night, and she had a bird in her aura, and the guys who were chasing her were seriously soaked in black magic. The one guy dropped this knife—I got

Monica to ID it and she said it belongs to a group called the Sahir.'

Adrian was silent for a second. Finally, in a significantly more serious tone, he said, 'Start from the beginning.'

Nathan narrated the events of the previous night to his uncle, starting from after he'd split from Lily and Damien. No need to mention he'd been anywhere near Lily last night. He finished with, 'The strangest part is their mother was kind of suspicious of me. I mean, I'm not that dodgy, am I? I'm seventeen.'

'I'd be more suspicious that you were going to steal someone's TV than kidnap their kid,' Adrian said.

'Oh, shut up.'

'Come on, it's fair.'

Nathan rolled his eyes. 'Anyway, Monica said I should give you a heads up.'

'You want me to come down to Oxford?' Adrian asked. 'I could probably swing it.'

'Only if you have to.' It would be nice to have backup, but the thought made Nathan uncomfortable. If Adrian came here, there was a risk of him being found out. Or rather, there was a risk of their family finding out that he and Nathan were hanging out together.

'I'll see what I can find out about bird people from here, then,' Adrian said. 'But the supernatural library in Oxford is better. And, of course, Damien might know.'

'I'd really prefer not to involve Damien,' Nathan said. 'Adrian, whatever else this is, Cynthia and Emma are just ordinary schoolgirls. Don't put them on the Council's radar.'

'Alright, well update me if you find out anything.'

'Will do.' Nathan began to say his goodbyes, but Adrian interrupted him.

'Before you go, have you thought about what's going to happen next month?'

A cold feeling crept into Nathan's stomach, despite the fact that it was still quite warm for September.

'Not really,' he said with forced calm.

'Don't let them push you if you're not ready,' Adrian said. 'Eighteen is young.'

'Yeah, sure,' Nathan replied. 'Listen, I gotta go. I have a tonne of homework.'

'Sure, see you around.' Adrian hung up. Nathan pocketed his phone, but he didn't immediately get up, even though a mother was glaring at him for blocking one of the swings.

Next month was his birthday. He'd be eighteen. At eighteen, he could become a fully qualified hunter.

Was he ready?

He didn't feel ready.

Sighing, Nathan got up and headed home. He didn't have to figure this out for a few weeks, yet. It could wait.

Homework, however, could not.

Over the course of the next few days, Monica sent Nathan a steady stream of information about the Sahir. It was information which Nathan could have better done without.

Objectively, he knew that there were plenty of dark magic practitioners in the world. In the UK, and most of western Europe, the Council kept an eye on that sort of thing. It was pretty illegal to do anything involving death, for example, be it using magic to take life or to bring someone back to life—although it was debatable whether true necromancy was actually possible. Other parts of the world tended to hold different views on that sort of thing. And then there were a huge number of moral grey areas, such as the slaughtering of animals for magic, which was necessary in a large number of spells—according to Monica, at least—but considered illegal in many countries.

'Sihr', or black magic, was forbidden in the Middle East. What it boiled down to was taking the life of others to make yourself stronger. The knife was the tool of the trade, so to speak.

That meant Nathan was very definitely in possession of a highly illegal artefact, which he should hand over to the Council, ASAP. In fact, he should let the Council handle this whole thing.

The Council—made up of three witches, three vampires, and three hunters—was the supernatural authority for the whole of Europe. This was definitely under their remit. It was not the responsibility of Nathan Delacroix, seventeen-year-old trainee hunter who was failing two subjects at school.

And he would have gladly left it on the Council's doorstep, possibly bound up with a pretty ribbon and a card saying, 'you're welcome', if it weren't for one thing: Cynthia and her sister.

How could a person be a bird and a human at the same time?

Nathan had done a bit of digging. There were, of course, the weres.

The most common was a werewolf, though weres could technically be any predator. The hunter database had records of lions, tigers, and leopards, as well as coyotes and a bunch of others. Even weredogs were possible, although the last sighting had been about fifty years ago. Most importantly, though, weres tended to like the natural habitat of their animal: jungles or savannahs. Okay, you might get a werefox in an urban area, but it was unlikely. In any case, wereswans did not exist. There were no records whatsoever of the phenomenon.

The other mystery was the aura. Weres had auras, but they looked like a sort of buzzing energy around them. You could tell they were supernatural, but not what kind of animal they turned into.

What he really wanted to do was talk to Cynthia about it. He just didn't know how.

Hey, I've been meaning to ask you, can you secretly turn into a bird?

Yeah, it just didn't have the kind of vibe he was going for.

On Thursday, Nathan cycled to Uni Parks again, determined that he'd at least speak to Cynthia. He laid on the grass with his head cushioned on his school blazer and watched the Headington Girls lacrosse team get slaughtered. Matt hadn't been able to make it—he was still making nice with Poppy, who had apparently got it into her head that Matt had a thing for Lily, or something.

Girls were confusing.

Between the mass of people on the field, it took him several moments to notice something was different.

Cynthia's aura had changed.

Nathan squinted at her. No swan, but there was a different animal. Was that... a cat? Not a big, predatorial cat. It looked like a silver tabby, like someone's pet. It was hard to see, though, because it didn't stand out well against the cloudy sky and the grass.

A short while later, Headington Girls trudged to a miserable defeat. They shook hands with the Didcot team and wandered off the field, looking thoroughly disheartened. Nathan watched them and hoped that Cynthia would notice him, but it was one of her friends who finally pointed in Nathan's direction. Cynthia turned and caught sight of him.

Then she jogged over.

Nathan's heart raced in his chest like he was running sprints for Grey—which, thinking about it, he'd be doing later. Fun times.

Stick to the plan, he reminded himself. *It's a good plan.*

It was a good plan. He'd hopefully thought through every variable.

If only it didn't hinge on his ability to ask a girl out on a date.

'Hi,' Cynthia said brightly. She looked really nice in her lacrosse uniform. 'I wish you'd come any other week. We're down our best player and we were terrible today.'

'I thought you were brilliant.'

Cynthia beamed at him. 'You're sweet.'

'Hey,' Nathan blurted out. 'I was wondering if—'

'I was hoping to see you—' Cynthia started at the exact same time. They both stopped.

'Uh, go on,' Cynthia said.

'No, um, you first,' Nathan replied.

Cynthia blushed. 'I was hoping to see you. Actually, I tried to get your number off my mum, but she wouldn't give it to me.' She paused. 'She's a bit, uh, overprotective. Sorry. I wanted to say thank you and sorry we were weird the other night. You must have thought we were, like, the Addams Family, or something.'

Nathan had to laugh at that. He knew the Addams Family, and Cynthia was not it.

'Seriously, no way,' he said. 'You should meet my family. They're complete whackos.'

'You seem normal,' Cynthia said. She rethought it immediately. 'I don't mean that in a bad way!'

Nathan had a sudden and very relieving epiphany: Cynthia was just as uncomfortable as he was. It put everything into perspective, like the sun coming out from behind the clouds on an overcast day.

'You can relax,' he told Cynthia. 'I don't think you're weird or anything. I'm glad your sister is okay. And, um, actually, I've been wanting to talk to you. Do you want to… hang out in town sometime?'

Cynthia shifted her weight. 'I—I'd like that,' she said. 'A lot.'

'Well,' Nathan said. 'I train most of Saturday, but I'm free Sunday? We could get lunch.'

'Sunday,' Cynthia breathed. 'Sunday's great.' And she smiled, and it was like the sun did break out from behind the clouds.

'I'll see you on Sunday,' Cynthia added. Then, 'Give me your phone. I'll put in my number.'

A moment later, she was jogging back to her team. Nathan clutched his phone to his chest, grinning like a lunatic. Cynthia paused halfway across the field and turned to wave at him. Nathan waved back.

That had gone great.

CHAPTER FOUR

FOR THE NEXT TWO DAYS, Nathan floated on cloud nine, and not even Adrian's ribbing could bring him back to Earth.

Sunday was a wakeup call.

He had a date. He actually had a *date*.

'What's wrong with you?' Jess asked over breakfast when Nathan dropped his fork for the third time. 'You have butter fingers today.'

'None of your beeswax,' Nathan told his sister, but with none of his usual heat. His aunt frowned at him.

'Are you alright?' she asked. 'You were pretty happy yesterday— and you did your homework without prompting. Today you seem miserable.'

'I'm fine,' Nathan replied automatically. 'I'll be out for lunch. I'm meeting, um, Matt.'

'Ummatt?' Aunt Anna asked facetiously. 'Is this a new friend I haven't met yet?'

Nathan felt his cheeks burning. Aunt Anna zeroed in on him immediately.

'Is Ummatt a girl?' she asked.

'Maybe?' Nathan answered in a small voice.

'Nathan!' Aunt Anna said. 'Are you going on a date?'

'Maybe?' he said. 'I mean,' he added hastily, 'We didn't exactly call it that.'

'Is anyone else going to be there?' Aunt Anna asked.

'Nope.'

'And where are you going?'

'Not sure yet.'

'Who's paying?' Aunt Anna asked, a knowing look in her eyes.

'We didn't discuss it.'

'Maybe you should get a clue before you go,' Jess said snootily. 'Or it's not going to be a very long date.'

'You shut up,' Nathan told her. 'You're too young to be talking about dating.'

'Am not!'

'Are too!'

'Both of you stop,' Aunt Anna said. 'Take her to the Turl Street Kitchen. It's a nice café, you can find it on google maps. It's not too pricey, either.'

Nathan sighed in relief. That solved one problem.

'If it's a date, you have to offer to pay,' Aunt Anna added sternly. 'I hope I raised you with enough manners for that.'

'Yes, Aunt Anna.'

'Good,' Aunt Anna said. 'Please wear a pair of jeans without holes in the knees.'

'Um,' Nathan said sheepishly. 'That's a big ask, Aunt Anna.'

His aunt just sighed.

A bit later, Nathan cycled into town. Cynthia was waiting in front of the McDonald's on Cornmarket, and Nathan almost stopped dead when he saw her. She was wearing a denim skirt and a black long-sleeved top, with her blond hair loose around her face, and she looked very cute.

Nathan hauled his brain back before it could dive off the cliff into incoherency and strolled over to Cynthia.

'Hi.'

'Oh, hey,' Cynthia said.

'Um, sorry I'm a bit late. Did I make you wait?' Nathan asked.

'Nope, I just got here.' Cynthia smiled. 'Where do you want to go?'

'Well, are you hungry yet? I thought we could walk around for a bit and then eat when we're ready.'

'I could eat now.' Cynthia flushed. 'Are you hungry?'

'I'm a guy—I'm always hungry,' Nathan pointed out.

At that, Cynthia's shyness seemed to melt away a little bit. 'I wouldn't know,' she said. 'No guys in my family.'

'Your dad?' Nathan asked, then realised how insensitive that question could be. 'I mean—'

'It's alright,' she said. 'I never met him. He left before I was born. There was Emma's dad, for a while, but he died when she was three. It's mostly just been us and my mum.'

'Oh,' Nathan said. What did you say to that? 'I'm sorry.'

'It's okay, you can't really miss someone you've never known,' Cynthia said carelessly. 'Mum's great. A bit overprotective, but she's really good to us. Lunch?'

'My aunt told me about a place that's good.' Nathan pulled out his phone and showed her the menu.

'Ooh, all-day breakfast,' Cynthia said. 'I'm sold.'

They meandered through central Oxford. The usual tourists were out in force, but the university didn't start up for another week or so. The city seemed oddly bereft without its usual hoard of students.

'Oxford's really pretty, hey?' Cynthia asked.

'Yeah, I guess,' Nathan said. 'I'm not sure I've ever really appreciated it, but then I've lived here since I was seven.'

'Really?' Cynthia replied. 'You have a London accent.'

'Born in London, somehow never lost it,' Nathan explained. 'You?'

'We moved here over summer,' Cynthia explained. 'I'm still finding my way around. We were living in Sweden before, in the south. Malmo. But Emma and I were both born in England, and I guess Mum wanted to come back here.'

'That's cool,' Nathan said. 'I've never been to Sweden. It's cold, right?'

'Not all the time!' Cynthia laughed.

They settled in the café and ordered lunch. Once they were waiting for their food, Cynthia said, 'Can I ask a kind of... personal question?'

'Sure.' Nathan ran through any number of possibilities in his head, hoping she was about to reveal some kind of arcane knowledge of the supernatural. That would be convenient.

'You live with your aunt?' Cynthia asked delicately.

'Oh,' Nathan said. 'Oh, yeah. But it's not like... I mean... My folks live in London. They just... there was this thing that happened when I was a little kid, and they decided they'd rather my sister and I grow up out here. So we stay with our aunt and go into London on weekends. Some weekends, anyway. Mum and Dad have been pretty busy lately, I guess.'

'Oh,' Cynthia replied. She seemed relieved. 'I thought, well, I hoped they weren't dead, obviously, but it just seemed...'

'Kinda weird?' Nathan asked. 'Told you we're whackos. Military family.'

'Have you moved around?'

'No, that's part of the reason why we stay out here. Means that Jess and I can get through school without having to move.'

'How old is your sister?' Cynthia asked, and they moved on to safer topics, at least safer in the sense that Nathan was no long skirting around the we're-vampire-hunters issue.

When lunch finished, Nathan offered, 'I'll pay.'

'Really?' Cynthia asked. 'I don't mind splitting.'

'No—I mean—I don't mind,' Nathan said. Should he insist? Monica would say that was anti-feminist. Monica would be laughing her arse off at him right now. Okay, he was on a date. He wasn't thinking about Monica right now.

His phone buzzed. Great. That was probably Monica, right there.

'I'll pay,' he said. 'You could get us coffee later, if you want to?'

Cynthia was smiling, so hopefully he'd made the right decision. How far into a relationship did you have to get before you could stop overthinking everything?

After lunch, they wandered the city centre and Nathan showed Cynthia the Radcam and St Mary's Church. They peeked through the gates of Brasenose College, then headed down to Hertford so she could see the Bridge of Sighs.

'It's so beautiful,' Cynthia enthused. She turned around and pointed at a round building. 'What's that one?'

'The Sheldonian Theatre,' Nathan replied, and the familiar discomfort crept in. The Sheldonian Theatre doubled as a meeting point for the Vampire Council.

'You wanna go look? We might be able to peek inside.'

Cynthia nodded, so they headed over there. The theatre was closed, but Cynthia enjoyed taking pictures on her phone anyway.

Nathan showed her into the courtyard of the Bodleian Library so she could snap more photos.

'Have you seen the Covered Market?' he asked. 'It's like an indoor market, I think it's like a historic landmark or something. There are coffee shops and souvenir shops, and there's this occult-themed café that I've hung out at a few times. We could have a look around?'

'Sure.'

On the walk to the Covered Market, Nathan decided that—seeing as everything might be about to go alarmingly pear-shaped—he may as well take advantage of the moment. Heart in his mouth, he reached out and gently took Cynthia's hand. She glanced up at him, then closed her fingers around his.

'Okay?' Nathan asked hesitantly.

'Okay,' Cynthia agreed.

They wandered through the Covered Market until they got onto the east-most corridor.

'I think the occult café was down here,' Nathan hedged, walking slowly down the hallway. The thing about the witching level was that most people couldn't see the entrance. They saw a high-level illusion: a blank stretch of wall with a staff-only door on it. If you had the sight, you could see through the illusion. The door became glass-fronted, and there were false exposed bricks and spooky signs with cauldrons and runes on them surrounding it for the full witchy experience.

'Is that the place?' Cynthia asked, pointing to the doorway.

The Witching Level, read the sign above the door in spiky letters. Nathan's heart dropped to take up residence somewhere around the basement. *Well, that's that, then*, he thought.

'You can see it,' he said softly, and Cynthia whipped around to face him.

'See what?' she demanded. Her eyes were very wide, her expression angry. Oh shit, he'd blown it now.

'Cynthia,' he said warily, raising his hands in a placating gesture. 'We should talk.'

'You tricked me!' she shouted and slapped him, hard.

Then she ran.

Nathan was a master at compartmentalising pain. Bruises, bumps, cuts, scrapes. Just part of a day's work. He could deal with those later. Being slapped in the face? A worry for another time. He raced after Cynthia. She was a decent runner, but Nathan was about four inches taller than her and he caught her before she'd even reached the High Street.

He grabbed her wrist, trying very hard not to hurt her.

'Cynthia, please, just hear me out.'

'Let go of me!' she hissed, sounding like a cat. 'I can't believe you!'

'It's not what you think!' Nathan said. 'Please!'

'No!'

People were starting to stare.

'Please don't make a scene,' Nathan said. 'I just want to talk.'

'Oh, wow, does that line actually work on anyone?' Cynthia gave up trying to pull away and went for offence instead. 'What was the plan? Get me to trust you, then lure me off like your mates tried to do to my sister?'

Nathan stared at her.

'I don't work with them!'

'Like I'd believe that!'

'I don't,' he protested. 'Cynthia, it's not what you think. Look, there's a place just here. Let me buy you coffee. I'll explain!'

'I really don't want to hear your explanation,' she said. 'You're a dick!'

At a complete loss, Nathan let go of her wrist. 'I really did just want to talk.'

'Yeah, right,' Cynthia replied. Then she ran off. Nathan didn't follow her. He slouched off to the Starbucks on Cornmarket and bought a latte. Then he sat upstairs and contemplated how epically he'd just messed up.

Great first date. Adrian was going to piss himself laughing when he heard.

May as well get all the misery out of the way at once. He pulled out his phone and rang Adrian.

'Aren't you supposed to be on your hot date?' Adrian asked by way of greeting.

'Yeah, it didn't go so hot, funny enough,' Nathan muttered.

'Did you screw up?'

'No, you arse. The test was a positive.' Shit, he sounded like he was talking about pregnancy tests. He rephrased, 'She could see the witching level. Then I tried to talk about it, and she freaked out and ran off.'

'Well, shit,' Adrian said. 'Sorry, kid. Better luck on the second date?'

'Not sure there's going to *be* one.'

'Hey, look on the bright side. She obviously knows about the supernatural world. Seems to be scared shitless of us, but she is in the know. Which means you can just ask her about the animal thing.'

'Yeah,' Nathan replied dejectedly. 'Except she might never talk to me again. She thought I was working with the guys who nabbed her sister. I mean, leap of logic, much? We went from holding hands to her accusing me of kidnapping.'

'What can I say? Girls are psychos,' Adrian said. 'Especially teenage girls. Just avoid 'em, to be honest. You'll have more luck dating when you're twenty.'

'If you were here right now, I'd punch you.'

'Bring it.' Suddenly Nathan was hearing an echo. 'Seeing as I'm right behind you.'

Nathan was on his feet in milliseconds. His uncle was standing right behind him. Nathan threw a punch, but Adrian caught his fist.

'Ah, ah, ah, Nate,' he said. 'We're in Starbucks. You'll get us kicked out.'

'Okay, one, what the fuck are you doing here?' Nathan asked furiously. 'Two, how the fuck did you find me?'

'Two's easy. I've been following you for the past three hours.' Adrian slouched into the seat opposite Nathan and stole his latte. 'As for one, funny story, Damien's witch friend seems to be having trouble scrying for Lily lately, so he asked me to come by and keep an eye on her. I don't approve of him having his daughter followed, obviously, she's a big girl, but I just couldn't resist the mystery. After all, Monica's in Morocco, so who whipped up an anti-scrying amulet for Lily?'

Nathan sagged back into his armchair and glared at Adrian.

'You already know the answer to that.'

'Getting mixed up in vamp business? Tut, tut, little nephew.'

If looks could kill, Adrian would be dead. Re-dead. Whatever. Ugh, Nathan hated him.

'I must say, colour me surprised, turns out you have an unusual talent for anti-scrying wards,' Adrian remarked, sipping the coffee. 'It works, even when she's at home, and Park Town hardly has ambient magic compared to the city centre.'

Nathan felt a thrill of pride, which he viciously tamped down. He did not need praise from a vampire, and he told Adrian as much.

Adrian laughed. 'Oh, you haven't changed at all over the summer.'

'Was I supposed to?'

'Well, maybe you've grown an inch or two.' Adrian squinted at him. 'Nah, not yet.'

Nathan wished he could tip the coffee over his uncle's smug face. 'Five-eleven is not short!'

'I never said it was.' Adrian leered at him. 'Did they train you over summer, though? You really ought to have caught me tailing you. Sloppy, sloppy.'

'I knew you were there,' Nathan lied petulantly.

'*Sure*, you did.' Adrian smirked. 'Shame about your girlfriend, though. She was pretty.'

'You have literally no redeeming characteristics,' Nathan said. 'I hate you so much. And you're paying me back for that latte.'

Adrian leaned back in his seat, his posture screaming arrogance. Sitting opposite each other, the family resemblance was painfully clear—same tanned skin, same brown eyes, same jawline—and it only made Nathan hate Adrian more. 'I could help you get her back.'

'Over my dead body are you compelling her to trust me,' Nathan said. There were ethical grey areas, and then there was vampire mind control. Nathan hated the idea that vampires could force someone to do something against their will. Worse, vampires could make them want to do things against their will.

It was just *wrong*.

'Ah well, I figured I'd offer,' Adrian said carelessly. 'So, you got a plan, then?'

'Yes,' Nathan lied, 'and it doesn't involve you.'

Adrian sniggered.

'Hey, if push comes to shove, you could always make her another one of your amulets. At least that's something you're good at.'

Nathan wanted one friend, just one, who wouldn't make fun of him ruthlessly for literally everything. It might be easier to figure out what he was doing wrong if everyone could just leave him alone to do it.

He pressed his head against the back of his armchair and stared at the ceiling.

'What amulet would I make?'

'A protection ward? Monica reckons those sell for in the thousands, if they're done well.'

As unwilling as Nathan was to admit it, that might be the best option he had.

He started with plan A, though, which meant doing the normal human being thing and texting Cynthia.

Nathan: Hi

Nathan: I don't really know how to say this

Nathan: I'm really sorry about how today went

Nathan: I didn't mean to scare you or give you the wrong impression. I was trying to find a way to show you that we have something in common, but I definitely mucked it up and I'm really sorry. I probably ruined everything, but will you at least give me the chance to apologise in person?

Nathan: In case it wasn't clear, I can see magic. It would have been nice to get to know someone else who can

Cynthia did not reply.

At dinner that night, Jess asked, 'So, how did your date go?'

'I don't want to talk about it,' Nathan told his plate.

'Ooooh, that bad? Did you even kiss her?' Jess cooed.

'I don't want to talk about it.'

'Did she hit you? You have a bruise.'

Nathan's hand flew to his face. The skin felt hot. Jess laughed a horrible, jeering laugh.

'Jessica, that's enough,' Aunt Anna said. Nathan pushed his chair back.

'I'm not hungry,' he said. 'I'll eat later, Aunt Anna.'

'Nathan—' she started, but Nathan was already marching out of the kitchen.

CHAPTER FIVE

'MR DELACROIX,' MR JACKSON said ominously in bio the next afternoon. 'Please stay after class.'

Nathan's heart sank. He'd spent the better part of last night researching which woods were best for protective amulets, and he really wanted to take a nap before he had to go down to Grey's this evening and get beaten up.

'Yes, Mr Jackson,' he mumbled.

Once the classroom had cleared out, Nathan collected his bag and slouched to the front of the classroom, lingering unobtrusively beside his teacher's desk. He'd stand there all night if it meant the man would just forget about him, but sadly Nathan only managed to be invisible when he didn't want to be.

'Have a seat, please,' said Mr Jackson. 'Mr Delacroix, I'm a little concerned about your performance this year. Your marks have slipped quite a bit from last year, and it doesn't seem like you're planning on applying to university?'

'I—uh—' Nathan said, his mind going blank for a moment. 'Um, I'm supposed to join the family business.'

'And you're... happy with that? Is everything alright at home? You used to be a reasonably diligent student.'

Teachers had a way of being cutting without actually saying anything nasty. In two words, Mr Jackson had condemned six years of Nathan's academic performance. He had never been special—the most he had ever achieved was *reasonably diligent*. His cheeks burned with shame.

'There's nothing wrong at home,' he said furiously. 'I'm just training—for the family business—and sometimes it's hard to balance everything. I'll work harder.'

'I rather fear that might be the problem,' Mr Jackson said. 'I think you're working too hard. You look exhausted.' He frowned. 'You live with your aunt and uncle, yes? Perhaps I should have a word with them.'

Oh no.

'Please give me a chance. I'll pick my marks up again.'

'Well, at least you remembered this weekend's homework,' Mr Jackson said. 'Let's see how you do, and we can have another chat next week.'

Bloody fantastic.

Cynthia was still ignoring his texts, and Nathan didn't want to beg her. By the time he hopped off his bike and locked it at Grey's house, he was feeling decidedly dejected.

'Late,' Grey sneered. He was leaning against the wall of the double garage. The roller doors were open, showing the makeshift gym within.

'I'm sorry,' Nathan said. 'I was trying to finish my homework.'

'Do you think vampires will care about excuses? You can't kill me because I haven't finished my homework?'

Nathan sighed again. 'Just tell me what the penalty is so I can get on with it.'

'That'll be a double, for insubordination.'

Nathan groaned. He spent the next hour running sprints and doing push-ups in between sparring bouts. By the end, he felt about to drop.

'You need to get your head back in the game,' Grey told him, standing very smugly over where Nathan had collapsed in a heap of noodle-like limbs. 'You're almost eighteen. I can't, in good conscience, support your initiation when you're like this. You'd get yourself killed.'

Nathan wasn't entirely sure Grey had a conscience. He'd probably never met an ethical quandary he couldn't beat into submission.

'Grey,' he said before he could stop himself. 'Did you ever, uh, have doubts before you initiated?'

'Are you doubting the path of the hunter? Or are you doubting your own ability to follow it?'

The honest answer was the first, but Nathan wasn't stupid. Down that path lay permanent excommunication from the family. 'The second. I just... feel like I'm being pulled in every direction.'

'You need clarity,' Grey said, with understanding, if not with empathy. 'On Saturday afternoon, I'll take you to the prison.'

The prison was where they experimented illegally on feral vampires to try and find a cure. It was something everyone knew existed, but no one ever spoke about.

As though this week couldn't get any worse.

'Brilliant,' Nathan moaned into his hands.

Grey kicked him in the ribs. 'Now get off my garage floor. Your aunt's going to be expecting you for dinner.'

By the next morning there was still no reply from Cynthia, and Adrian was starting to get impatient.

Adrian: Any update on bird girl?

Adrian: Don't tell me you haven't spoken to her yet

Adrian: Don't you have a spooky knife illegally hidden at home?

Adrian: Time is of the essence, kid

When had Adrian started getting so chatty and casual? Nathan's parents would kill him if they ever found out... and yet, Nathan felt like he was nothing like other teenagers anymore. Adrian was so easy to talk to. And Nathan had more in common with Lily, who was a half-vampire who had once tried to chow on his neck when she went too long without a snack.

He sought out Matt, the last bastion of normalcy in his otherwise crazy life. Because everything else in his life was going *absolutely perfectly*, Matt was acting kind of cold, too.

'Where were you this weekend?' Matt asked. 'I looked for you at the park.'

'Were we supposed to meet?' Nathan replied, wracking his memory to try and find when he'd made that commitment.

'Oh, come on, we always play footie. You could have at least texted me.'

'I went out with Cynthia,' Nathan said, mostly as a defence, and he regretted it immediately when Matt's jaw dropped. His friend's icy demeanour vanished instantly.

'Are you serious? You asked her out?'

'Before you ask, it was a disaster,' Nathan said. 'Listen, I need a favour. D'you suppose Poppy knows where Cynthia lives?'

'She might, why?'

Matt made Nathan come along to ask. Poppy and Matt appeared to be on the outs again, although Nathan was finding it hard to tell the difference between them getting along and them hating each other these days.

'Why do you want to know?' Poppy demanded.

'I want to apologise to her.'

'So you're going to go round her house like a lurker? Why don't you just text her?'

'I have tried that, actually,' Nathan said. 'She's ignoring me.'

'Maybe she doesn't want to talk to you?' Poppy said. 'Going to her house isn't going to help.'

'I just want to talk to her.' Preferably where she was comfortable, with her family around her, so he could restore his reputation as not-creepy.

'Yeah, well she doesn't want to talk to you.'

'You don't understand,' Nathan said in frustration. 'Can you get the address for me, or not?'

Poppy rolled her eyes and stalked off in a huff.

'Mate, seriously?' Matt asked before hurrying off to placate his girlfriend.

Honestly, Nathan just did not get girls.

Still, on Wednesday morning Matt handed him a scrap of paper with an address written on it in neat, rounded handwriting. The dots over the 'i's were hearts.

'No fucking comment, mate,' Matt said.

'Shut up,' Nathan replied.

Cynthia lived all the way up the Headington Hill. Adrian asked three times whether Nathan wanted a lift, and he said no each time. So, of course, when it came to actually cycling up the hill on Wednesday after training, he hated himself all the more.

'Stupid—fucking—hill,' he cursed, dismounting two thirds of the way up the steep part. Cars whizzed by.

The house was small and compact, but very neat. Nathan could see a swing set in the back garden, through the open gate. He locked his bike against the wall—you never left a bike unlocked in Oxford, not even for a second—before ringing the doorbell and wondering whether it would be worse if Cynthia or Ms Rymes opened the door.

Ms Rymes opened it and peered at him with a frown. Yep, that was worse.

'Nathan.'

'Hi, Ms Rymes, I was wondering if I could speak to Cynthia?'

Her eyes darted over him, his bike, back to him. He must look a mess. 'Did you cycle all the way up here to see her? There's a bus.'

Nathan shrugged. 'I'd really like to apologise to her.' Monica's advice had been apologise-apologise-and-apologise-some-more. He prayed it would hold true.

Ms Rymes sighed. 'Cynthia, there's someone here to see you!'

'Coming, Mum!'

Footsteps pounded on the stairs, and Cynthia appeared. She noticed him, and her face fell.

'What are you doing here?' she whispered. Then, to her mother, she added, 'I've got it, Mum.'

Ms Rymes gave Nathan one last suspicious glare before retreating into the house. Cynthia stepped out onto the front step but didn't shut the door behind her.

'What do you want?'

'I really just want to apologise,' Nathan said.

'How'd you get my address?'

'I traded my immortal soul to Poppy Wiggen.' Cynthia let out a surprised laugh, then pursed her lips in frustration.

'Stop it.'

'Stop what?' Nathan asked, confused.

'Being cute and funny,' she snapped. 'You're not allowed to make me laugh. You tricked me!'

'I didn't mean to.' Nathan couldn't help but feel a little bit triumphant. She thought he was funny! 'I just didn't want to start nattering on about magic if it was going to scare the crap out of you.'

'How do you even know about that stuff?' Cynthia demanded. 'And what is that place? The witching level? Are you a witch?'

'What do you know about witches?' Nathan asked cautiously.

'Nuh-uh, you can go first,' Cynthia said. 'I think you should start explaining.'

So much for feeling out the situation.

'I'm a vampire hunter.' To his shock, Cynthia laughed. 'What?' he asked.

'It's funny,' she said. 'You say it with such a straight face!'

She didn't believe him.

'No, really,' he insisted. 'I'm a vampire hunter. It's been in my family since, like, the 1300s.'

'Wait, you actually believe in vampires?' Cynthia asked. 'Like

Dracula? Or like… *Twilight*?'

'They're not really like either,' Nathan said. 'Ten times scarier, though.'

The smile ebbed away from Cynthia's face. 'Vampires,' she said. 'That's not funny.'

'What do you believe in?' Nathan asked uneasily. 'And can we not have this conversation out on the street? It's going to get dark soon and anyone could overhear.'

Cynthia shifted her weight a few times. 'Fine, you could stay for dinner. Uh. Let me check.'

She darted inside and left him there on the front step. Nathan considered entering, but that would be kind of rude, so he stayed where he was. That was also awkward. He pulled out his phone and texted Aunt Anna that he was maybe getting dinner with a friend, friend unspecified.

Anna: Fine, but don't forget your homework

'I haven't forgotten,' Nathan grumbled.

The furious whispers from inside abated and Cynthia reappeared. 'You can stay,' she said. 'Do you like tacos?'

'I eat everything,' Nathan said. 'Also, I just came from training, so I would literally eat a horse right now.'

Cynthia smiled tentatively.

The house was small and compact inside, too, with mismatched furniture. Nathan was shown straight to the kitchen, which looked out on the swing-set in the back garden.

'Sit here,' Cynthia said, pointing to the seat beside her. Emma was already sitting opposite, working on what looked like maths homework. She looked up at him and gave him a big gap-toothed smile.

'Hello, Nathan!'

'Hi, Emma.' At least one person in the building didn't think he was the antichrist.

'Tell me about vampires,' Cynthia said pointedly.

'Uh,' Nathan hedged. He'd been hoping to have this conversation in private. 'Blood drinking immortal creatures of sin? Able to hypnotise humans into carrying out their will. Killed by piercing their heart with a wooden stake.'

'And you do the staking bit,' Cynthia said.

'Well, not yet. I'm in training for it, though.'

'So the MMA story was bull?'

'It's a cover story to explain why I do martial arts. As is the military family thing. Can we do an answer for an answer?' Nathan asked.

Cynthia glared.

'How'd you know where Emma would be, that night?' she demanded.

Clearly he wasn't getting a fair trade of information.

'That really was just luck,' Nathan said. 'I was out with Matt, Poppy, and Lily. I walked Lily back to Oriel College to meet her father, and then I was just heading to get my bike when Emma crashed into me.'

'And you just decided to help her?'

'Two adult guys chasing a little kid? Sure. Anyway, they were soaked in black magic.' Before Cynthia could fire her next question at him, Nathan added, 'Do you know who those guys are?'

'They're evil witches,' Cynthia said. 'I'm asking the questions.'

Nathan crossed his arms and raised an eyebrow at her. It was an action he had copied from Adrian. To his surprise, it had the intended effect. Cynthia looked a bit unnerved.

'Fine,' she said. 'We don't know much about them, except that they're very persistent. And they use this... creepy knife to kill people and steal their magic.'

'They steal a bit more than that,' Nathan said, thinking of the evil knife in his cupboard back home. 'They're called the Sahir. They steal people's lifeforce to strengthen themselves, and they believe that if they get powerful enough they can bring back the dead.'

Cynthia looked horrified. 'How do you know that?'

'My witch friend told me.'

Nathan put his peace offering on the table. None of the protection wards he'd tried had worked. This was the same ward he'd made Lily, with an extra rune for safety from evil. He had slaved over it for ages, but it would be worth it if Cynthia forgave him. Cynthia unwrapped the little tinfoil bundle and stared at the oval amulet.

'What's this?'

'It's a hunter ward,' Nathan said. 'It'll protect you from being scried—witch tracking spells—and it has a safety from evil rune, too. That's a kind of wishy-washy way of saying that you'll have a better chance of staying hidden if someone wants at you for nefarious purposes.'

'You can do magic?'

'Not really. Amulets invoke magic, but they're not made with magic. The best way to explain it is, um, it's made of blood, sweat, and tears, I suppose.' Nathan grinned sheepishly.

Cynthia traced the runes carved into the amulet. 'It's glowing gold.'

'That means it's primed,' Nathan said. 'It'll power itself from ambient magic, the magic in the environment around you. But you need to imprint it.'

'How?' Cynthia asked.

'Trust me?' Nathan asked carefully. Cynthia frowned. 'You just have to prick your finger.'

'No,' Ms Rymes said.

Cynthia scowled. 'What's the worst that can happen?'

'That amulet could do anything, Cynthia.'

Nathan had anticipated that. He handed over his runic dictionary. 'I've marked the runes I used,' he said. 'And black magic wouldn't glow gold, I swear.' Only protection magic was gold. And Cynthia didn't need to know that this was a test, too. Once she imprinted, it would change to match her innate magic, whatever colour that was. Humans tended to associate with an element—Nathan's was earth, which was a brownish-green. Vampires went blood red. Witches could be a range of colours.

While Cynthia plied the runic dictionary, Nathan got up to help Ms Rymes.

'Where'd you get this?' Cynthia asked. 'It's amazing.'

'Borrowed it from my aunt,' Nathan replied as he set the table.

'Is she a hunter, too?'

'No, Uncle Jeff is. Aunt Anna isn't from a hunter family, but she has a very weak witch gene. Enough to be a good enchantress. She makes amulets for the family.' Nathan pulled his own out of his shirt to show Cynthia. She studied it for several seconds, before turning back to the dictionary.

'Protection,' she translated as Nathan laid out knives and forks. 'Safety, immunity from harm... and healing?'

'Fast healing,' Nathan explained. 'It slightly offsets the advantage vampires have over puny, fragile humans.'

Cynthia hummed. 'If vampires really exist, can I meet one?'

'You really don't want to. They have different standards of acceptable behaviour to us. And that's the ones who don't go chowing on random peoples' necks and erasing their memories after.'

'Do you even know any vampires?'

'A few,' Nathan said reluctantly.

'Real vampires?'

'You still don't believe me?'

'I don't really have proof,' Cynthia said.

Nathan looked out into the darkness of the garden. 'I can take you to meet a vampire. But you have to tell me the truth first. What are you?'

Cynthia traced her fingers over the amulet and sighed. 'What do you think I am?'

'I don't know,' Nathan admitted. 'I've never seen anything like you. There's nothing in the hunter databases about people who have animal auras.'

'You can see my aura?' Cynthia asked.

'You're a dog today. A golden retriever, maybe?'

'Dinner's up.' Ms Rymes put a pan of taco mix on the table with a thud, but neither Cynthia nor Nathan moved. Cynthia frowned, still fiddling with the amulet.

'Mum, can I?'

'I'd prefer you didn't,' said Ms Rymes, 'But I know you're going to tell him as soon as I'm out the room.'

Cynthia smiled weakly. 'We're shapeshifters.'

'Like werewolves?' Nathan asked. Cynthia shook her head, making a few loose wisps of blond hair fall in her eyes. She brushed them away again.

'Do werewolves exist, then? We can shift whenever we want, but only into the form of the last animal we laid eyes on.'

'Shapeshifters,' Nathan said, dumbfounded. Shapeshifters were a myth. Like, probably even Damien had never seen one. They were mentioned in old texts, but none had been seen in centuries, and most people didn't really believe they'd ever existed.

'There's a dog living in the house across the road,' Cynthia said. 'Usually, I try and look at our cat every day, because a cat is a good form to have if you need to run away and disappear. No one looks at cats twice on the streets.'

'When I first saw you—and your sister—you were swans,' Nathan recalled.

'Gosh, yeah, I'd taken Emma to the duckpond.'

'So it's always the last animal you saw?' Nathan asked. 'And if that was… a tiger?'

'Then I could become a tiger in the middle of the High Street,' Cynthia said. 'But it would be amazingly inconvenient. Also, I couldn't maintain it, unless there was a zoo with a tiger nearby.'

'Wow!' Had he just discovered an extinct species? Adrian was never going to believe this.

'You believe me?' Cynthia asked anxiously. 'You're not even going to ask for proof?'

'I mean, I'd love to see you shift,' Nathan said. 'But I'm guessing the clothing situation would be… not ideal.'

Cynthia went scarlet. 'No, clothes tend to get damaged. That's the other reason I like having a small form.'

'Fair enough.'

'How's it that easy for you?' Cynthia pressed. 'I can't believe— vampires? But you believe me.'

'My folks hunt vampires for a living,' Nathan pointed out. 'Pretty sure I'll believe anything.'

Cynthia smiled weakly at him.

'I'm sorry I thought you were going to hand me over to the witches,' she said.

'It's alright. In hindsight, I was kind of creepy,' Nathan said.

He took his seat at the table, and they started assembling their tacos. Cynthia commented, 'Must be rough, having a whole family who can beat you up.'

'They can't all,' Nathan said. 'My aunt can't fight, neither can my sister.'

'Isn't your sister training to become a hunter, then?'

'She is, but she's only eleven. It's like, training lite version.' Nathan considered that. 'I think my dad was a bit stricter on my training when I was younger, because I'm the oldest, and, well…' Because no one wanted him to go the way of Adrian. He didn't want to admit that, though. 'There's more pressure on the boys, in general. Not a lot of women become hunters, even if they do the training, because you have to be really fast and strong to stake a vampire.'

'Women can be fast and strong, too,' Cynthia argued.

'Sure,' Nathan agreed thoughtlessly. 'You'd make a good hunter.' The comment just slipped out. Cynthia made a noise of surprise, and when Nathan looked at her, she was avoiding his eyes.

'I don't know a first thing about self-defence,' she said.

'The principles are pretty easy,' Nathan said. 'I've taught people before. I can show you, if you want.'

Cynthia was blushing. She shook her head and mumbled under her breath.

'Pardon?'

'I said, you'd probably think I was really bad at it.'

'Everyone's bad when they start,' Nathan said. 'I just have the advantage of having started younger.'

Cynthia still looked embarrassed. 'If you really don't mind.' She nibbled on her lip, looking at him from behind a few strands of hair that were in her face again, and Nathan thought that she had the same cuteness superpower that Lily did.

He really didn't have the time to take on anything else right now, but he found himself saying, 'I'd be happy to.'

CHAPTER SIX

'YOU DIDN'T TAN AT all,' Nathan said when he opened the door for Monica on Friday. She'd flown in from Morocco the previous day.

'Hi Nathan,' Monica said airily. She was a strikingly pretty, skinny redhead, who was almost as tall as Nathan. 'Nice to see you too. You're so much more polite than you were back in July.'

'Monica!' Jess hurtled out of the lounge and shoved Nathan into the wall in her desperation to hug Monica. Nathan had always privately thought that his sister would happily get rid of him and be related to Monica instead. Monica was cool. Jess did not think Nathan was cool.

'Jessie! You grew up!' Monica said. 'Are you wearing makeup?'

'Don't mention makeup,' Nathan pleaded. Aunt Anna and Jessica had rowed for hours about whether Jess was allowed it now that she was in secondary school, and the only time they had managed to agree on the subject was when they united forces to inform Nathan that, as a man, he was not allowed to have an opinion on the subject.

Girls were strange creatures.

Monica, of course, knew all the right things to say to Jess so that she disappeared back into the lounge post-haste, with a big smile on her face. Nathan wondered if he ought to take notes, but it seemed unlikely that Monica's tricks would work for him, anyway.

'I was thinking we should go out,' Monica said significantly. 'And I want to meet your girlfriend.'

'For one, she's not my girlfriend,' Nathan said. 'We're taking it slow. And you'll meet her on Sunday.'

'Why wait?'

'How did I forget how impatient you are?' Nathan asked. Monica made a face.

'Let me get my stuff.' He ushered Monica up to his room to wait for him. She was the only girl, apart from Jess, who had ever set foot in his bedroom. He'd never really been one for posters or anything, so the walls were pretty bare. There were a few odd knickknacks that his father brought back when he travelled, and the bedcovers were blue with stripes. A matching blue beanbag sat in front of his TV, to which the PlayStation was hooked up. That was pretty much it.

Monica shut the door and said, 'Can I see the knife?'

'Just be careful.'

Nathan pulled the wrapped bundle out of the cupboard. Monica took it like she was afraid it would bite her.

'Fuck—that's—how can you stand to have this in your room?' she asked.

'I don't spend much time in my room, except when I'm sleeping,' Nathan pointed out. There wasn't really a moment spare, in between school, training, and homework. He didn't have space for a desk, so he did homework downstairs at the kitchen table.

'Still,' Monica said. Nathan let her have her private moment with the knife whilst he changed. October had started and, like clockwork, the seasons had shifted. The leaves were turning, and a perpetual drizzle had started up. Even though autumn could be absolutely miserable, it was usually Nathan's favourite time of year. His birthday was in October, it was sports season, and he just enjoyed being outside no matter the weather.

It was just this year that was different. If only he could postpone turning eighteen for another year.

'M, do you think I'll make a decent hunter?' he asked as he laced up his trainers.

'Huh? Why wouldn't you? You can kick Adrian's arse.'

'Yeah, but…' Nathan struggled to put his thoughts into words for a moment. 'It's not that I can't. Should I, though?'

Monica stared at him. 'Nate, when that kid needed help, did you think twice about jumping in?'

'What? No, of course not!'

'Then that's your answer,' Monica said. 'It's part of you. If you can't imagine not doing it… then you have to do it.'

How did everyone manage to make it sound so simple?

Nathan sighed and straightened up. 'Alright, let's go,' he said. 'Are we heading to your place or into town?'

Monica wrapped up the knife and handed it back to him. 'Into town,' she replied. 'I don't think you should be keeping this thing in your cupboard. It's like it's literally trying to suck the life out of everything around it. At least wrap it in something sturdier.'

'I'll try and think of something.' Nathan shrugged. 'Shall we? We can't be out late. I have training at half seven tomorrow.'

Monica was too lazy to fetch her own bike, so she sat on the back of Nathan's bike, and he cycled her up the Abingdon Road.

'You need to get your license,' Monica said, gripping his shoulder for balance as they climbed off on St. Aldates.

'I'll put it on the list for when I finally learn how to bend time.' Nathan locked his bike to the fence that ran beside St. Aldates's Church, and they started to walk.

'We could go to G&D's,' Nathan suggested hopefully, but not optimistically. Monica wasn't the kind of friend he got ice cream with.

'Live a little,' Monica replied. 'Let's go to TWL.'

Nathan's heart sank.

By day the witching level was a café and market geared towards witches. His aunt bought her warding supplies there. By night it served alcohol and became a bit racier. At the end of the day, it wasn't the worst possible place they could go, but Nathan had to be up early for training tomorrow.

He reminded Monica of that, and she told him, 'You're so boring. You should take this opportunity to have one last illegal drink before you turn eighteen.'

'I have drunk alcohol illegally before,' Nathan said patiently. 'It's not going to taste any different after the thirteenth.'

'I don't know how I'm friends with you. You are appallingly responsible.'

'I don't know how I'm friends with you, either,' Nathan replied. Monica didn't take offence, which was annoying because her comment had stung him. Nathan wondered if having your parents brutally slaughtered by vampires made you somehow immune to rude comments for the rest of eternity.

That made him feel guilty. 'Fine, let's go to TWL.'

The supernatural world generally didn't care too much about legal ages. If a human wandered across their path, they were considered fair game for any number of hijinks, irrespective of age. Luckily, there was a way for Nathan to not become potions ingredients. They hid in the night entrance to TWL, and Monica took Nathan's wrist between her slender, bony fingers. She chanted a few words in Latin that Nathan should probably have understood, and then he felt the smoky, strange brush of her magic against him. His wrist stung for a moment, and a black mark in the shape of a lightning bolt hitting a stone appeared on his skin. It was Monica's witches' mark.

'You have to remove that before I go home,' he said. 'If Aunt Anna sees it...'

'You'll be dead, I know,' Monica said. 'I'll take it off, don't worry.' She smirked at him. 'Worry about what I'm going to do in the meantime.'

'Yeah, not really worried about that,' Nathan said. 'Because you have standards and shagging a kid probably contravenes them.'

'Shagging you would,' Monica said. 'It'd be like incest. Ugh.'

Then she kissed his cheek but, unlike when Cynthia did it, there was no heart-racing, sweaty palms, or mad panic. Nathan elbowed her lightly, grinning, and they headed upstairs.

The witching level was crowded with Friday night drinkers. Mostly, they were young witches and warlocks, of whom there were a surprising number in Oxford. The university tended to attract them, partly because it had an excellent supernatural library, partly because it was old and filled with ambient and ancestral magic, and partly because the Council was here. Everyone secretly wanted to be noticed by the Council, because it meant you were powerful or special.

'So, full disclosure,' Monica whispered once they were seated with drinks. 'I figured we might do a bit of digging while we're here on the Sahir.'

'Should we?' Nathan asked warily. 'I was sort of hoping to hand this over to the Council.'

'Why haven't you?'

'...Cynthia,' Nathan said reluctantly.

'Cynthia,' Monica echoed smugly. 'Thought so.'

'Couldn't we keep her out of it?' Nathan's voice sounded whiny and pleading to his own ears. 'Couldn't we just tell them I don't know who the kid is that I saved?'

'You know what will happen, though,' Monica said. 'The Council will worm their way into the issue and find out everything. They're on high alert now, especially, because of what happened with Damien and

Christian.'

There were times when Nathan wished he had never heard the name Damien von Klichtzner before. He sighed. 'Have they replaced Christian on the Council yet?'

'Yes, with some pseudo-Roman guy or something,' Monica said. 'Not sure who he is, but the witches aren't loving him. Par for the course, I guess.'

Witches didn't love anything to do with vampires. Nathan theorised that the only reason the hunters were allowed on the Council was to mediate between the witches and the vampires. It was certainly about ninety percent of their job.

'Anyway,' Monica said, 'Did you manage to get off tomorrow to go to my graduation?'

'What do you think?' Nathan asked glumly.

'Nathan! Can't you, like, make up the hours some other time?'

Only as long as he went without sleep for the next month.

'Grey will never go for that, Monica.'

'You promised to try!'

'I did try! But Grey wants to take me on a field trip tomorrow, and he's having doubts about letting me initiate, so I sort of need to be on the ball this next week. I'm sorry.'

Monica huffed. 'Now I have to take Adrian as my third guest.'

'Take Lily.'

Monica curled a strand of hair around her finger. 'Yeah, that's not a bad idea…'

'How are you celebrating?'

'We're getting dinner at the Cherwell Boathouse,' Monica said. 'Okay, but if you're bailing on me tomorrow, then you have to promise that I'll have your undivided attention on Sunday. And you have to get celebratory drinks with me.'

'No drinks on Sunday, I have school in the morning.'

Monica made a face.

'I'm serious,' Nathan said. 'Kyle Saunders came in hungover one morning and Mr Wilkes put him in detention for a week!'

'I can't wait 'til you finish school,' Monica complained. 'We'll have one drink on Sunday. But I'm taking you out for your birthday.'

'Not if I have initiations the next day…'

'Nathan, shut up!' Monica said. 'You're acting old!'

Nathan put his drink down. 'No, you're acting like a five-year-old!' He recognised that his temper was fraying rapidly. 'Bathroom,' he added. 'I'll be back.'

Monica frowned. Nathan made a beeline for the toilets. His breaths were coming too fast. His heart raced. Hunters were supposed to be able to handle anything with a level head. Grey tried to shock him sometimes in training, and Nathan never lost his cool. Why did Monica get to him so easily? What was wrong with him today?

He ducked into the hallway that led to the toilets and leaned his forehead against the wall, taking several deep breaths. Damn, what was this? Nathan had never been prone to panic attacks. He'd never really lost control of his temper, either. Okay, except when Adrian was involved, but that was different. Adrian deliberately tried to provoke him. Monica was his friend.

Someone bumped into him, and he jerked his head up. A girl was standing next to him, clinging to him. She stared up at him with wide eyes, looking completely strung out. Her hair and skin were so pale that at first Nathan thought she didn't have any colour at all, but no, that was a trick of the light and the fact that she was wearing black. She was thinner than Monica, even, and wearing a very short denim skirt, the kind girls seemed to like that looked like it was going to fray away to nothing any minute. Her top was long-sleeved, but scrunched up at her elbows, showing off thin, tattooed forearms. Her heels made her almost Nathan's height.

'Please,' she said in accented English. 'Please...'

'Are you alright?' Nathan asked. Wait, her accent might be Russian. 'Vy v poryadke?'

'Da, da,' the girl said. 'Please... help...'

'Nate?' Monica asked, entering the corridor. She hurried over.

'Hey,' she said, taking the girl's arm gently. 'Are you okay? What's going on? Can we call someone for you?'

'No...' The girl wobbled on her feet, no surprise, her heels were freaking high. When Monica saw her face, her eyes went wide with shock.

'Kseniya? Kseniya Krovopuskova?'

The girl staggered back as though Monica's touch had burnt her. 'No! NO!' she shouted, her accent growing even thicker. Then she turned and ran, surprisingly fleet-footed. Nathan hurried after her, but she vanished behind a group of giggling twenty-somethings and when they moved, she was gone.

Damn. How had she disappeared like that? He turned back to Monica, who looked shaken.

'You knew her?'

'Kseniya... she joined my old coven—the London coven—for a couple of months before I was excommunicated,' Monica said. 'Last I heard, she didn't stay long. They kicked her family out again. I haven't seen her since I was fifteen.'

'Weird,' Nathan said. He recalled her eyes. 'She looked like she was on drugs.'

'Maybe,' Monica said grimly. 'But there's magic that can do that, too.'

Dread seemed to pool in Nathan's stomach. 'Should we try and find her?'

Monica shook her head. 'She had an invisibility ward on her arm. She'll have activated it. Must be hiding from someone.' She frowned. 'I'll keep an ear to the ground, this next week. I might have to report her. Listen...' She laid a hand on Nathan's arm. 'I'm sorry. I shouldn't have pushed. It's... is it the initiations? Is that's what got you so... upset?'

'I'm not upset,' Nathan said.

'Worried, then.'

Nathan shifted his weight. Her fingers were cool against his skin. Kseniya had been all skin and bones, but Monica wasn't much better. Three months in Morocco had given her a bit of colour, but she still resisted putting on weight.

'A bit, maybe,' he admitted, and it felt like a load off his shoulders. 'I don't know. It's just. Lily. And Adrian, too, I guess. Killing ferals is one thing, but...'

Monica pulled him into a hug.

'Can't you postpone your initiation?'

'Yeah, but you shouldn't. It reflects badly on you.' Nathan sighed. 'If my family weren't so important...'

The Delacroix family was pretty much one of the original hunter families. All eyes would be on Nathan to continue the legacy. His parents and cousins all seemed to be incredibly successful—and apparently unburdened by fits of conscience.

'Hey,' Monica said, rubbing his back and bumping her chin against his shoulder. 'You'll figure it out. Sometimes things just need time and they come clear.'

If only he had time. But his birthday was a week and a half away.

'Yeah,' Nathan mumbled.

'Want another drink?'

'Yeah,' he repeated.

Monica bought them Devil's Brews, which sounded much creepier than they actually were. Witches loved their occult-themed cocktails. Nathan sipped the hot fruity punch, sitting on a sofa in the common area, and Monica leaned against him. Her magic curled around him like wisps of smoke. Witches acted human, so it was easy to forget that they weren't. They were dangerous and exotic, just like vampires, but Monica had never felt that way.

'Can I stay at your place tonight?' Monica asked sleepily.

'As long as you don't complain when I get up early.'

'Promise I won't,' Monica said, but Nathan knew that she probably would. Monica didn't like early mornings.

Nathan slept on an air mattress on the floor and was up before his alarm. He prodded Monica awake before he left, and she peered around like she didn't know where she was.

'Happy birthday.' Nathan gave her a one-armed hug. Monica's birthday was exactly ten days before his own.

'Oh, it's you.' Catlike, she rolled out of bed. 'Are you leaving now?'

'Yep,' Nathan said, pulling on his trainers.

'Mmm... okay.' Monica put her jeans and jumper back on. Her hair was in two plaits, because she always wore it that way for sleeping, and her makeup had smudged overnight. She looked about fifteen. Nathan waited for her while she washed her face in the bathroom. It was light out, but on a Saturday the neighbourhood was still sleepy at seven AM.

Aunt Anna gave Monica a surprised look when they came downstairs. 'Monica, hi. I didn't know you were here.' She frowned at Nathan. 'What about that other girl?'

'It's not like that with Monica. I slept on the air mattress.'

'Oh, good,' Aunt Anna said. 'Because I'd hate to have to have the Talk with you. People are having sex too young these days.'

'Aunt Anna!' Nathan cried. Monica sniggered, but she'd been sexually active since she was about fourteen, so she had no right to talk.

Nathan frowned at her, and she smirked back.

'Monica, do you want breakfast?' Aunt Anna asked. 'Nathan has to go, but I'll make Jessica eggs in about half an hour, if you want to hang around.'

'That's alright,' Monica said. 'I have to head home and get ready for my graduation ceremony.'

'Oh yes, that's today, isn't it? Congrats.'

At seven-fifteen, Nathan hugged Monica goodbye. 'You'll be great today.'

'All I have to do is say 'do fidem' and not trip over my gown.'

'Seems about your speed.' Nathan laughed when Monica tried to hit him.

CHAPTER SEVEN

THE PRISON WAS HALFWAY between Oxford and London. After leaving the M40, they bounced along ever smaller roads until they finally reached a tall metal gate which blocked the entrance. A man in a hunter uniform climbed out of the gatehouse and came over to the car. Grey rolled down his window.

'Agent Larson,' Grey said. 'With Nathan Delacroix. Training visit. Benjamin Delacroix called ahead.'

His dad knew they were coming? That was news to Nathan.

'ID?'

Grey handed over his hunter ID and Nathan passed his provisional driver's license over. He'd never taken a driving lesson, but the ID came in handy occasionally. The gatekeeper checked his list, then handed them back.

'You're good to enter.'

Nathan wondered if talking in monotone would be part of hunter training, or if it was something you just learnt after a couple of years on the force.

Grey handed Nathan a sheet of paper, before pulling the car through the gate and up the drive. The building ahead looked like an old-fashioned manor house from the outside, and the signs made it out to be a private hospital. Only hunters knew better. When Nathan read the paper, he understood. It was a non-disclosure agreement. Breach of the NDA could mean expulsion from the force or even termination.

Wow.

As though Nathan would risk initiating as a hunter on this. He hadn't even told Monica or Adrian where he was going. He scribbled his signature as they pulled into a parking space to one side of the front door.

Grey paused before getting out, his hand on the door handle. 'Look,

Nathan, when we get inside… what you see might shock you. Stay with me at all times, and don't try to speak to the subjects, okay? And don't look in their eyes.'

Rule number one about vampires: never look in their eyes.

Nathan wanted to say, *I know that.* He said, 'Yes, Sir.'

'Good,' Grey replied.

They entered the reception. It was a funny trick of the imagination that even though everything was sterile and white, it somehow looked grey. Even the receptionist looked grey. Nathan gave her his NDA and she handed over an access badge without saying a word.

Grey led the way through security doors and down sterile corridors. It was very like a hospital: cheap yellow paint on the walls, rubber floors, plain white doors. They descended a flight of stairs into the basement. Everything changed. Suddenly, the hospital atmosphere was replaced with a prison. Reinforced steel doors. Nathan could guess they had a high enough silver content to repel vampires. The same sort of lights that you got in lightboxes, which mimicked the sun, because vampires were weakened by sunlight.

And wards.

Magically sensitive people, who made up a good thirty percent of hunter forces, could sense wards. Being magically sensitive was conventionally called 'the sight', and it did sometimes involve seeing magic as colours, but sensing wards had nothing to do with vision. Wards that were rooted in buildings had an almost physical presence which seemed to wriggle under your skin. It was tolerable for a short time, but being around powerful wards for too long drove Nathan crazy.

These wards were incredible. Every inch of the building had to be slathered in them. How did they even power this many wards? These had to have a tangible power source, some sort of magical well or spring, so to speak.

Nathan had no idea how you could power a ward apart from through ambient magic, and he wished he could ask Monica. Monica loved wards; she was obsessed with them. When they were younger, she used to sneak warded keychains into his school bag, give him wristbands with wards embroidered on them, sew warded patches onto jackets, all sorts of things. If it could be warded, Monica had figured out how to do it.

Monica was obsessed with the idea of the people around her dying.

Nathan closed his eyes and focused his mind, trying to block out the sight for a short time. Grey had trained him to do that, but it wasn't easy with millions of wards all screaming, 'I'm here! Look at me!'

He took a deep breath and caught up to Grey again.

'The wards?'

'Yes, it's an impressive piece of work, isn't it?' Grey said. 'I understand that to vampires it's quite torturous.'

'Wow,' was all Nathan could think to say.

They walked to the end of the corridor, passing no one. Finally, Grey scanned his card and punched in a security code at the last door. There was a little beep and the door unlocked.

'Are you ready?' Grey asked.

No.

'Yes.'

Grey opened the door. Inside was an observation room. There were several armchairs, a desk and a utilitarian desk chair. On the far side was a window, which looked down onto another room that reminded Nathan of his school sports hall.

The room below might have been furnished, once. The furniture had been shredded and shattered, but Nathan thought that it might have contained bunk beds.

'Are those ferals?' Nathan asked.

'Yes,' Grey said. 'You can observe that in some the decay process is less pronounced than others.'

He said it so clinically, like this was all just a science experiment. Nathan felt sick.

The thing with ferals was that it was easy to forget they had once been human. It was a tricky sort of irony, because feral vampires were what happened when humans were turned, and the change was rejected.

There were two reasons why it could go wrong.

Reason one: the vampire who did the turning got the process wrong somehow.

Reason two: the human couldn't deal with their new existence as a bloodsucking parasite.

Whatever the reason, the result was a creature that turned against itself, went completely mad, and then went on a rampage. If they were left to run wild, they would kill and drain every person they came across, until eventually they could drink no more. The final stage was usually tearing themselves apart.

This happened worryingly often. In fact, official hunter estimates stated that forty percent of all attempted turnings ended up going feral.

The creatures in the room below didn't look like they'd ever been human. Their skin was decayed, and their hair hung in limp clumps. Most of them only wore rags, and their forms no longer adhered to anything resembling human biology. There were bits visible that shouldn't have been. Nathan had read accounts in hunter records of zombies. These creatures looked like zombies.

Worse, every one of them knew he was there. As he and Grey approached the window, they all turned as one to look up at the two hunters.

'That's creepy.' Nathan shivered.

'In the beginning, we isolated every subject,' Grey explained. 'It was considered expedient to house them together for observation. The truth is, despite in-depth research, we are no closer to understanding the how or the why of the vampiric need for blood.'

Nathan thought many things. He thought:

- *These experiments are kind of inhumane*
- *Is there any point in experimenting on ferals, the vampires gone wrong?*
- *Wait, does that mean that they're experimenting on actual vampires, too?*
- *How come doesn't the Council know about this?*
- *Does the Council know about this?*
- *Holy shit*
- *Fuck-fuck-fuck-fuck-fuck*
- *This is messed up*

He said, 'I never realised this place existed.'

'It's necessary to keep this close to our chests,' Grey replied. 'But the breakthroughs we could make here could revolutionise human safety. Toxins, for example, that are harmless to humans, but fatal to vampires. Humans could effectively be given inoculations against being bitten by vampires. Perhaps even an immunisation against being turned.'

'Hunters are working on that?' Nathan asked, curious despite himself.

'Many things are in development,' Grey said. 'Once you're initiated, you will be inducted into the experiments on a need-to-know basis. I know you're interested in science at school. There may be a chance that you could end up working here.'

Never in a thousand years, Nathan decided on the spot. *Not for all the money in the world.*

'Wow,' he replied. 'This is... incredible.'

'Of course,' Grey added, 'I can't show you the whole facility. Even my security clearance isn't high enough for that. But your father gave me permission to show you one or two other things, if you're interested?'

Nathan tried to look enthusiastic. 'Sure, that'd be cool.'

'This way, then.'

Before they left the observation room, Nathan couldn't help but take another look. The ferals still watched him, every last one of them. They didn't have human gazes. Their eyes were red, but more importantly, they were hungry.

Adrian had never looked at Nathan like that.

He forced himself to look away from those hypnotic red eyes and trailed after Grey.

The next few rooms he was shown into were laboratories, not dissimilar to the chemistry lab at Nathan's school.

'The important work all takes place below ground,' Grey said as they walked. 'This is only one level of the operation, really, but I wouldn't dream of taking a trainee any deeper. There's plenty to see up here.'

Nathan nodded along and managed to feign interest in the scientific experiments. Some of them were genuinely interesting, like the attempts at creating artificial blood. So far, none of the results had been able to sustain vampires, although they appeared to meet the basic dietary requirements.

'We think there might be a magi-scientific component that we are missing,' Grey said. 'But, of course, it's quite difficult to get the Council's buy-in to study this any further. Witches don't like sharing magic, and vampires appear to enjoy the savagery of sinking their fangs into human flesh. Perhaps the idea of a substitute is simply too sterile to them.'

Nathan nodded along, but he wasn't sure he agreed. He was pretty sure it was the sexual aspect that vampires enjoyed, but he wasn't sure someone as square as Grey was capable of comprehending that drinking blood was sexual to vampires.

Did that mean that forcibly taking someone's blood was like rape? He'd have to ask Adrian. Then again, if the answer was yes, maybe it was better not to know.

Some of the experiments were less savoury, such as the various different ways of weaponizing silver.

Adrian carried a silver knife. He was a vampire who armed himself against other vampires. Had Adrian ever killed a human? Had Adrian killed other vampires since he'd been turned?

Nathan had so many questions all of a sudden. There were so many things he hadn't thought of.

Grey had brought him here to make things clearer, but Nathan was pretty sure that they were only getting murkier.

The piece de resistance of the trip was their final stop.

'Your father requested that the subject be moved up here for the day so that you could see him without breaching security clearance,' Grey said as they headed down a narrow corridor. There were almost no doors here, and Nathan was starting to feel claustrophobic. When they finally reached the end of the hall, there was only a pair of doors on the left side. The first one was vaulted and reinforced, made of almost solid silver. It was the brightest thing Nathan had seen since they'd come underground.

He studied the runes on that door whilst Grey unlocked the other door. Silver didn't take runes very well, because by nature silver repelled anything magical, but these runes were active. Nathan could feel them.

The room he followed Grey into was another observation room, but there was no window. Glass was almost impossible to ward, because all you had to do to break the wards was smash the glass, and even a human could do that. Instead, there was a bank of monitors on one wall.

Nathan felt the dampening effect of the wards the moment he entered. He had no magic, but even he felt like he was suffocating. Monica, Lily, any of his friends—none of them could have entered this room.

'Magical null,' he said, impressed.

'There are several rooms like this,' a voice said. 'I apologise in advance. If you are wearing any wards on your person, they may become dysfunctional for a time after leaving here.'

Nathan looked around in surprise and saw a man with snow-white hair sitting at a desk, watching the monitors intently.

'This is Doctor Bourne,' Grey said, shaking the man's hand. 'Doctor Bourne, my trainee, Nathan Delacroix.'

'You're Benjamin's son,' Doctor Bourne said. 'It's a pleasure. I've worked with your father. He's an impressive man.'

What did you say to that? No one was interested in what Nathan really thought. He said mildly, 'He is.'

'You must be proud to be his son.'

'Oh yes, very,' Nathan agreed without emotion.

'Are you interested in science, then? We're always looking for bright young minds.'

'Oh no, you're not stealing this one just yet,' Grey put in with a laugh.

'Shame, shame.' Doctor Bourne shook his head. 'Well, you're welcome to take a look, but I'm afraid the subject appears to be sleeping, or at least feigning sleep. He does show a limited response which means he can probably sense that we're close to him, though.'

'Can we show Nathan the interview?' Grey asked.

'Of course, give me a moment to put it on screen.'

In the meantime, Grey ushered Nathan over to the bank of monitors. They all showed the prison cell next door. It was a plain grey room, literally a stone box, and every stone was crawling with anti-vampire wards.

It was fairly well known that it was virtually impossible to keep vampires in prison. If they were at peak strength, they could snap steel bars and punch through walls. There were ultra-high security supernatural prisons built for them, but mostly if the Council wanted to punish a vampire, they killed the vampire. Game over.

Nathan had never realised that hunters were any different.

The creature in the cell wasn't a vampire. Its skin was greyish and decayed, which made it a feral. And yet, it was clothed and sleeping, and it seemed almost human.

It had shackles on both wrists and ankles and a collar around its neck. The chains ran to loops on the wall. They were all silver.

Nathan couldn't look away. It was the most horrifying sight he'd ever seen. Silver burnt vampires. The feral's skin was charred and blackened around the shackles.

Bile rose in Nathan's throat, and he swallowed hard.

Wasn't it more humane to just put ferals down, like rabid dogs? This didn't seem right.

'Alright, I've got it on the righthand screen,' said Doctor Bourne.

Nathan forced his gaze over to that screen. It was a clip of the feral, but now it was awake, its red eyes darting around frantically.

'Hello,' said a disembodied voice.

'H—hello?' The feral's voice was scratchy with disuse.

'Do you know where you are?'

'I—I'm hungry,' the feral groaned. 'So hungry.'

'Yes,' the disembodied voice said soothingly. 'That's natural. Do you remember your name?'

'I—I remember…'

'What is your name?'

'I—' The feral shifted more erratically. 'Please—I—please—' It began to tug wildly on its chains. 'Please! Please! Please!' It couldn't seem to say anything else. What was it begging for? Nathan watched in horror as it thrashed, wilder and wilder.

'Enough, I think,' Grey said. The video froze. The feral's eyes were wide and it was frothing at the mouth.

'Fascinating, isn't it?' Doctor Bourne asked. 'It's the closest we've come to a breakthrough, truly. It's almost as though this feral retained just enough of its humanity to interact. It seems to understand its circumstances.'

That's because it's an animal, Nathan thought, *and animals understand when they're trapped.*

He couldn't get his mouth to form words. He forced himself to breathe. From the depths of his terror, he managed to summon some kind of sense. 'It's amazing,' he said. 'Why—why is this one—different?'

'We're not sure yet.' Doctor Bourne smiled gently. 'But with patience, we'll certainly find out.'

'Wow,' Nathan replied. His heart was racing, and he was sweating like mad.

'I think we should probably be on our way,' Grey said. 'Thank you for the demonstration, Doctor Bourne.'

'Yeah—thanks,' Nathan added.

'Any time, any time,' Doctor Bourne said cheerfully, walking them to the door. 'Always good to have people take an interest in my work.'

How strange, thought Nathan, that Doctor Bourne looked so grandfatherly, and yet his smile seemed utterly cruel.

Then they left. They walked briskly through the facility and back upstairs. Nathan emerged, choking and gasping, into the sunlight. Grey watched him dispassionately, and Nathan realised distantly that he ought to control himself, because Grey was probably going to report his every reaction back to his dad later.

He couldn't stop himself from turning to face the sun, though. He closed his eyes and absorbed the weak warmth of the autumn sun. It was close to setting, turning the sky red.

Nathan was, and would always be, a creature of the light.

'Are you ready to go home?' Grey asked finally.

'Yes, please.'

They hardly spoke in the car. Nathan hoped that Grey assumed he'd been shocked at how awful the ferals were, not at the fact that hunters were keeping them captive. Please, please let Grey not realise that Nathan thought the whole facility was abhorrent.

That night, after everyone else had gone to bed, Nathan fetched his hoodie from his cupboard and laid it on his bed. He unwrapped the knife and stared at it. The serrated edge was starting to catch a bit on the fabric. It looked wicked. He knew it was his second sight, but somehow it seemed to be absorbing all of the light around it.

It was selfish. It absorbed light and gave nothing back.

This knife wasn't designed to be used on humans. Humans were petty creatures with no magic, no power. They weren't like witches and vampires. No, this was a knife designed by supernaturals to be used on other supernaturals.

Nathan studied every inch of it that he could see without touching it, committing it to memory. Finally, when he couldn't take the evil anymore, he wrapped it up again and put it back in his cupboard.

Hunters thought the most noble goal was to protect humans from supernaturals, but what if there was another, more important goal?

Who protected the supernaturals who couldn't look out for themselves? Who protected the supernaturals from each other?

Who would protect the Monicas and Cynthias of the supernatural world? Who protected kids like Emma?

Maybe hunters had it all wrong. Maybe the monsters weren't just the supernaturals. Maybe the monsters were the ones who locked ferals in the basement and experimented on them. Maybe everybody was capable of being a monster.

Nathan took a long time to fall asleep that night.

CHAPTER EIGHT

THE SUN SHONE BRIGHTLY on Sunday. Nathan had had a weird night, filled with strange, unsettling dreams. The sun made everything feel a bit more real and grounded. He almost wanted to go and sit in it and just bask in being human.

The doorbell rang just as he finished breakfast. Jessica managed to get there first. *Damn.*

'Nathan, your girlfriend's here!' she shouted.

'Coming!' Nathan called, adding under his breath, 'And she's not my girlfriend.'

Cynthia was clad in leggings and a sports hoodie. She had her pigtail plaits again, and Nathan felt an almost violent desire to kiss her.

'Hey,' he said, trying to remember how to sound like a functional human being.

'Hey.' Cynthia grinned shyly. 'You gonna invite me in?'

Nathan steered Jessica out of the way and gestured for Cynthia to come in. She stepped over the threshold with no trouble. He shut the door behind her.

'We're not staying,' Nathan said. 'I'll just put my shoes on. Jess, scram.'

'Don't talk to me like that!'

Nathan sighed. He sat on the stairs to tie his laces, then led Cynthia out again.

'Sorry about Jess, she's in this annoying phase where everything everyone says is wrong.'

'Don't worry about it, I'm quite familiar with that actually.' Cynthia grinned. 'So, what's the deal about inviting people in?'

'You noticed that?' Nathan smiled at her. She had a freckle on her nose. He could see it in the sunlight, and he wanted to poke it. 'We don't invite anyone in verbally, ever, because vampires have to be invited through the wards. Once they're invited in, they can't be uninvited without redoing the wards.'

'Oh wow,' Cynthia said. 'I was being tested for vampirism?'

'Nah, I didn't think you were a vampire.' Her aura was a cat again today, the same silver tabby as before. She had the amulet he'd given her on over her jumper. It pulsed with a sort of brown-green-blue-red mixture. All the elements. 'What's your cat called?'

'Coco.'

'Cute,' Nathan said.

'Girly,' Cynthia corrected. 'You can say it, it's girly.'

'Nah, I don't think that.'

Cynthia rolled her eyes. 'Where are we going?'

'Well,' Nathan said, 'I was sort of hoping to kill a few birds with one stone. Monica wants to meet you, for starters.'

'Monica is…?'

'It's complicated.' Nathan grinned. 'Monica's a witch. She was also Jess's babysitter for a few years, which is how we met. And she happens to be the pet witch of one of the Council members. So our lives are pretty entangled.' He shot Cynthia a sideways look. She was frowning. 'There's nothing between Monica and me,' Nathan promised. 'She's like a sister to me.'

'Okay,' Cynthia said hesitantly. 'And what else?'

'Well, I promised you a self-defence lesson, and I promised you could meet a vampire, and as it so happens, I know someone who's a vampire and an expert in self-defence, so I figured I could introduce you.'

'It's broad daylight.'

'Yeah, don't take the whole 'creatures of the night' thing too literally,' Nathan said. 'As long as vampires drink blood, they can go out in sunlight.'

Cynthia's eyes widened. 'What does work against vampires? Crosses? Garlic?'

'The cross thing is a misappropriation. Vampires aren't afraid of crosses, they're afraid of the Cross family.'

Nathan paused significantly and waited for her to figure it out.

'…As in Delacroix?' Cynthia asked.

'Exactly. We're one of the original hunter families in Europe. We've been going strong a long time, so we got a bit of a reputation. Vampires are fine with garlic; holy water is just water. Silver burns all magical creatures, but I'm guessing you already know that.'

'Yeah,' Cynthia said. 'No silver for me.'

'Weres and witches are also repelled by silver,' Nathan said. 'Most old buildings, especially churches, are warded, and that'll keep the majority of vampires out, but don't count on it.'

'So nothing stops them?' Cynthia asked.

'No, but the Council controls them,' Nathan said. 'It's illegal for vampires to kill their victims.'

'You mentioned the Council before,' Cynthia said. 'Is that a hunter thing?'

'We call it a triumvirate. Three vampires, three witches, and three hunters make up the Council. They sit here in Oxford, and they oversee all supernatural activities in Europe.'

'Wow.'

They turned down Monica's street, and Nathan gestured to her house. 'This is it.'

Cynthia looked at the house. It was perfectly normal, not dissimilar in design to Nathan's house. Monica's was a little smaller, with only three bedrooms instead of four, and a single garage instead of a double. 'A witch lives here?' she asked dubiously.

'Three witches live here,' Nathan corrected. 'Well, two witches and a warlock. Come on, I promise Monica will be mostly nice.'

'Reassuring,' Cynthia said under her breath, but she followed him up to the front door. Nathan rang the bell and a moment later the door flew open.

'Hiya!' Monica said with a grin. She was back on form from the last time Nathan had seen her, in her expensive skinny jeans and oversized pullover. She hugged Nathan, then turned to Cynthia. 'So, you're Cynthia.'

'Hi,' Cynthia said.

'Wow, I see what you mean about the cat,' Monica said. She stepped back. 'I don't invite in, for obvious reasons.'

Inside was also perfectly normal. Monica's foster parents were witches by night, but by day she was a writer, and he did market research. Cynthia was cross-examining everything, looking for signs of the occult, and Nathan caught Monica grinning.

'Don't tease,' he said.

'Aw, I'm the nicest of your friends.'

'No way, Lily wouldn't hurt a fly if it hit her first,' Nathan said.

'She'd hurt a fly if it hit Damien first,' Monica replied. Game, set, and match. Nathan had no argument for that.

'You can relax,' Monica told Cynthia. 'If I wanted a human for spell ingredients, I'd use Nathan. He doesn't have magic.'

Cynthia's eyes went wide, and then she scowled. 'You're pulling my leg.'

'Sorry,' Monica said. 'It's just a little tease. You want something to drink?'

'I'm alright,' Cynthia said.

'Kay, just let me pop upstairs.' Monica took the stairs two at a time. Cynthia turned to Nathan.

'She's tall,' she whispered.

'I know, for ages she was taller than me and she used to make fun of me all the time,' he said.

'This place is so normal.'

'Witches aren't doing spells all the time.' Nathan shrugged. 'They have normal lives, too.'

'I'm not sure the ones I've encountered before do,' Cynthia replied.

Nathan didn't have an answer for that. He took Cynthia into the lounge, and they sat on the sofa. The lounge had a bay window looking out to the front, which had been added to the house after it had been built. Nathan had always liked it because the sun shone in in the mornings, warming the whole lounge.

Monica returned wearing ankle boots and with her hair in a messy bun. 'Here,' she said, thrusting a wrapped package in Nathan's face. 'I forgot to give you this the other day. From Morocco.'

Inside was a Berber basket in black, red, and white. As was typical of Monica, it had wards worked into the middle.

'Nice.' He traced the wards. They were live, but not strong. 'Not sure the wards liked flying.'

'No,' Monica agreed. 'I've never met a ward that likes flying.'

Nathan stashed the basket in his bag, and they headed out.

'Where are we meeting the douchebag?' Monica asked.

'Hinksey Park,' Nathan replied, well used to Monica's hatred of Adrian.

'I can't believe you invited him.'

'The only other vampire I know is Damien.'

Monica made a face. 'I guess that's true.'

'Who's Damien?' Cynthia asked.

'Lily's father, terrifically dangerous, also the oldest vampire I know,' Nathan said. 'Whilst we're on the topic, I doubt Adrian's going to try anything funny with you, but as a precaution—don't look in his eyes.'

'Why not?'

'Spooky mind control powers,' Monica said. 'Hey, do you think that we're wildly in breach of Council regulations, telling her this stuff?'

'I don't think the Council have regulations on educating species that were formerly considered extinct,' Nathan pointed out.

'Hmm, that's true,' Monica said thoughtfully. 'It just occurred to me that I might have to make a report to Jeremiah.'

'Can you postpone that?' Nathan asked worriedly.

Monica shrugged. 'I'm not supposed to see him whilst I'm in town. If he doesn't ask, I won't tell.'

They turned into Hinksey Park. The back of Nathan's neck tingled, and then Adrian was there. Old jeans and tee-shirt, leather jacket, sunglasses. Adrian's dark hair curled around his ears and flopped over his forehead, and his eyes glinted with mischief. Adrian never changed.

He couldn't change because he had died in 1974.

'Adrian,' Nathan greeted.

'Hey, kid,' Adrian said. 'Long time no text. Thought you had forgotten me.' His eyes flitted to Monica, and his gaze turned wary. 'Monica.'

'Adrian,' Monica said coolly.

Nathan glossed over the moment by adding hastily, 'This is Cynthia. Cynthia, Adrian. My uncle.'

Cynthia gaped. 'What?'

'Yeah,' Nathan said. 'Though if anyone asks, we're cousins. But actually, he's my dad's older brother, and he's been officially dead to the family since 1974.'

Cynthia's shoulders drooped.

'Nate, you're a git,' Adrian said. 'You should have warned her.'

Nathan put his arm tentatively around Cynthia's shoulders. She was shaking a bit.

'Vampires,' she mumbled. 'Like, actual vampires.'

'Unfortunately, yes,' Nathan said.

'Oh my God.'

'Please don't panic,' Nathan said. 'I promise Adrian isn't going to hurt you.' He shot the man a glare, just in case. Adrian snorted.

'Lucky you, teenage girl isn't really my type,' he said carelessly. 'Thought I'd sink my fangs into more feisty prey today.' He gave Nathan a pointed look.

'Over my dead body.'

'You should stop invoking death so often,' Adrian said. 'Might come back to bite you.'

Nathan couldn't stop himself from thinking of the ferals he'd seen yesterday. He shuddered. 'I'd kill myself before that happened, and I'd kill you if you bit me. Keep your taint away, thanks.'

Adrian leered. Cynthia trembled. She took a couple of deep breaths and steeled her shoulders, before pulling away from Nathan.

'Do you really have fangs?' she demanded.

'Sure,' Adrian said. He opened his mouth and showed them off. Vampire fangs could elongate when they needed to drink, but otherwise they just looked like particularly sharp canine teeth. Adrian let his slide out and flicked his tongue against one of them, before shutting his mouth.

'You're a vampire,' Cynthia said.

'Yup,' Adrian replied.

'You were a hunter before.'

'That too.' Adrian's gaze darkened visibly. Nathan had a vague idea of what precisely had caused Adrian to be turned. The Delacroix family had tried to strike above their paygrade, so to speak: they'd gone after Damien. Adrian, twenty-seven and one of the best hunters in the family by a wide margin, had led the attack. Damien had a sense of humour. The details of the actual event were sketchy, which was not surprising. Adrian had probably had the sense not to approach his family again after he came back from the dead, or he'd have ended up with a stake in his heart.

'You're not still a hunter, are you?' Cynthia asked.

'It's not possible to be both, love,' Adrian replied.

'Oh.'

'He still has his training though,' Nathan said. 'The same training I do. I figured we could give you a practical demonstration.'

Cynthia nodded. 'Okay.'

They ended up breaking into University College's sports ground, which was just down the road. Cynthia watched in alarm as Nathan picked the padlock on the gate.

'Is this okay? And how do you know how to do that?'

'Standard part of the hunter oeuvre,' Adrian said flippantly.

'It's fine,' Monica said. 'University term only starts next week.'

'Oh.' Cynthia still looked worried. The lock opened.

'So, hunter life is kind of complicated and full of semi-legalities,' Nathan said. 'You don't have to do anything you're not comfortable with, though. Just tell me, and we'll leave.'

Cynthia shook her head. 'It's fine.'

'Too nice, Nate,' Adrian said. Nathan slugged him in the kidney and smiled when Adrian winced.

'Lesson number one,' he told Cynthia airily as they entered the sports field. 'Vampires feel pain just the same as humans do. They just recover quicker.'

'Which means kicking them in the balls is still effective,' Monica said darkly.

'Don't teach her bad habits,' Adrian protested.

Nathan dropped his bag on the ground and pulled his jumper off. Adrian followed suit. Then Nathan put his gloves on and pulled out one of his knives. Adrian's eyes glinted.

'If I get that off you, you're toast.'

'You'll never.' Close combat with knives was Nathan's best form. He sank into a ready position. Adrian rushed him, and then they were fighting, a jab here, a slice there, Nathan drew first blood.

Adrian hissed in pain. Nathan's mind filled with the image of the feral crying for help. He missed an easy parry, and Adrian slammed him on his back hard enough that his ears rang.

'Fuck!' Nathan snapped. What the hell had happened there?

Adrian stood over him, confused. 'You're off your game, kid. I never get you that easily.' He had blood on his arm, but the cut was already healed. Usually, Nathan had a good chance of doing Adrian actual damage.

'Again,' Nathan said, and let Adrian pull him up. Adrian was still peering at him in concern. Nathan knew he wanted to ask, so he hurriedly took up a fighting stance. This time, he threw the first punch, catching Adrian under the chin. He ducked Adrian's return and managed to kick his knee. Adrian landed a blow on the side of Nathan's neck, and he staggered. He saw Adrian coming and parried with the knife; blood; Adrian kept coming and he wasn't fast enough, and then Adrian had thrown the knife away and driven Nathan to his knees, locking his arms behind his back.

'What the hell?'

Nathan glared at the grass. 'It's none of your business, okay?'

'Like fuck it's not. You never go down this easy. Is this over initiations? They're not going to pull you out. They never pull our family.'

'It's not about initiations,' Nathan said. He wrestled himself free of Adrian and clambered to his feet. 'And they are considering pulling me.'

'Are you joking?' Adrian asked. 'Who're they gonna pick over you? You're probably better than I was. You train hard. I don't know how you're even passing school; I swear you spend all your time training.'

'I'm not passing school,' Nathan said uneasily.

Adrian stared at him. A dozen different expressions passed over his face. Nathan's whole body seemed to burn with shame.

'What happened?'

'I can't talk about it,' Nathan said.

'Is it hunter business?'

'I guess,' Nathan said nervously. Adrian frowned. He picked up the knife, spinning it so the silver blade was in his hand. His skin began to redden. He held the knife out to Nathan, his gaze on Nathan's. Nathan was human; he could be compelled. He made a habit of looking at Adrian's nose or forehead, but today he couldn't seem to look away from Adrian's eyes. They didn't turn red. He didn't use any kind of power. Nathan wanted to tell Adrian the truth because, well, he just wanted to.

He took the knife.

'Again,' he said weakly.

'Take five,' Adrian suggested, showing his burnt palm. Nathan nodded. Adrian wandered off. Nathan sat down and pulled out a towel.

'You okay?' Cynthia asked, crouching beside him.

'It's not my best day,' Nathan said.

'Because of your initiations?' she asked. 'What are initiations?'

'We're not supposed to talk about it,' Nathan said. 'It's basically the test you have to pass to become a hunter apprentice, the next step up from trainee. You take it when you turn eighteen.'

'Oh,' Cynthia said. 'Your birthday's next week.'

'Yeah,' Nathan said. In that one word, he summed up the whole situation: his birthday approached. He was consorting with vampires in secret. His family wanted him to be a hunter. He was certainly capable. The trouble was… he didn't know if he wanted to.

Adrian was over by the fence, looking out at the Thames.

'I'll be right back, okay?' Nathan said. Cynthia nodded. He got up and jogged over to his uncle. Adrian didn't turn around. Nathan stood behind him, which somehow made it easier to ask, 'Did they have the prison in your days?'

'They had prisons,' Adrian said. 'They weren't amazingly effective. We mostly just killed troublesome vamps, rather than locking them up.'

'There's a facility down the M40, in Buckinghamshire,' Nathan said.

'The old Wedley Manor?' Adrian asked. 'That was a lab in my day.'

Nathan doubted it. That place had been operational longer than anyone would ever admit to.

'You ever go there?'

'Sure, we used to take them dust samples and stuff. Weapons that had blood on them. They were always collecting things to analyse,' Adrian replied.

'You go into the basement ever?'

'Didn't know it had a basement.'

'Grey took me there yesterday,' Nathan said. 'Downstairs. They're keeping ferals there and doing experiments on them.'

Adrian tensed. He squeezed the links of the fence, and Nathan watched the metal buckle.

'One of them,' Nathan added, 'It was almost… okay. It kept begging for help.' He closed his eyes and heard the litany —*please, please, please.*

'Fuck, Nate,' Adrian said. 'You're only seventeen.'

'Grey doesn't think I'm ready,' Nathan admitted, and it felt cathartic to finally say it out loud. 'I don't think I'm ready.'

'No one's ever ready. You think no one else ever had doubts? We all have doubts.'

'Did you doubt?'

'Did I doubt that I was capable of driving a stake through a vampire's chest—an intelligent, capable, almost human vampire—and snuffing out their life? For sure,' Adrian said.

'Did you ever doubt whether it was right to kill vampires?'

Adrian turned around, and there was bitterness in his eyes. 'No,' he said. 'But look where it got me.'

Nathan couldn't meet Adrian's gaze. 'You could make me want it,' he said. 'You could make me forget my doubts.'

'No,' Adrian said. 'No way would I ever do that to you.' Nathan still avoided his gaze. 'Nate, look at me.'

Nathan looked.

Adrian's eyes were human and filled with sympathy. Nathan hated it.

'If you're not ready, don't go for it,' Adrian said. 'Fuck what anyone else says, this isn't something you want to get into for the wrong reasons.'

'I don't know what the right reasons are,' Nathan said miserably.

'The right reasons are reasons that you can live with,' Adrian said. 'Because in the end, you're the one who's got to live with them.'

'What were your reasons?' Nathan asked.

'I thought I was ridding the world of evil,' Adrian said. 'I saw what happened to Sebastian, and I wanted to protect other people from dying like that.'

Sebastian had been the oldest Delacroix sibling, another person who had met a brutal end.

'I don't know if vampires are evil,' Nathan said. 'You're not. Lily's not. I don't even think Damien is, really. He does bad things—but humans do too, and we don't kill them for it.'

'Oh, Nate.' Adrian sighed. 'You're an idiot.'

'Hey!'

'This is my fault,' Adrian added. 'I should have stayed away from you.'

'Yeah, you did sort of muddy the lines,' Nathan said.

'Sorry.'

'Yeah,' Nathan said thoughtfully. 'Well, I'm sort of stuck now. Don't suppose you could be evil for the next two weeks?'

'No more than I want to compel you.'

'That's… annoyingly ethical of you,' Nathan muttered.

'Look, forget sparring,' Adrian said. 'Let's go teach your girlfriend how to throw a punch.'

'She's not my girlfriend!'

'She wants to be your girlfriend. Just kiss her.'

'That's harder than you think.' Nathan scowled.

'Oh no, you're the one making it hard.' Adrian grinned. 'Come on, Prince Charming. Your Cinderella awaits. No, wait, I suppose she'd be, uh, what was the princess in Swan Lake?'

'I have no idea, you ponce.' Nathan slugged him on the arm.

They were still sniggering when they re-joined the girls. Monica was lazily turning over one of Nathan's knives, letting it catch the sun every so often.

'You done?' she called to them. 'Hey, Nate, I had an idea on how to hide that Sihr knife you lifted.'

'What, you still have that?' Adrian asked, alarmed.

'What was I going to do with it?' Nathan asked.

'He shoved it in his cupboard, wrapped in a jumper,' Monica said. 'Typical guy. What would you do if Jess grabbed it by accident?'

Nathan's heart sank. 'Oops. Okay, we can go back to mine later and you can fix it up.'

Monica held up the knife in her hands. 'Silver blocks magic, and don't you hunters use those boxes to store old artefacts? Could you get hold of one of those?'

'Maybe,' Nathan said, 'But it would take time. I'd have to request it from HQ, and then they'd want to know why.'

'Wouldn't wards do the same thing?' Adrian asked.

Monica beamed. 'That's just what I was thinking.'

'One more bout, first,' Nathan said, confiscating his knife from Monica.

'You ready?' Adrian asked. 'I'm not going easy just because you've got jelly for brains today.'

'I can't believe I'm related to you,' Nathan gripped the knife and swung at Adrian. Adrian crouched and, using a judo move, neatly flipped Nathan over his shoulder. Nathan rolled and came up on his feet. Before he even turned around, Adrian was there. This time, they were both on form. Adrian had a knack for finding pressure points. Nathan ended the bout by stabbing the knife into Adrian's thigh.

'Oi,' Adrian groaned as he sank down to sit. 'Now I have to get back to Damien's with blood all over me.'

'Should have worn black,' Nathan said cheerfully. 'Two out of three, though. You did better than usual.'

'You're such a brat. I wish Benny had never decided to have kids.'

This banter was much more their usual speed. Nathan smirked. 'Wait 'til it's Jess stabbing you. That will hurt twice as much.'

'Ugh.' Adrian sprawled out on the ground.

Cynthia approached tentatively. 'Is he alright?'

'Already healed.' Adrian chuckled.

'Ignore him,' Nathan said. 'He's a drama queen.'

'If I'm queen, then you're my bitch,' Adrian sang. Nathan kicked him in the ribs. 'OUCH, NATE!' Monica and Nathan both laughed.

'Alright,' Nathan said, turning to Cynthia. 'You want to learn?'

'I doubt I can do that,' she said.

'No need for you to fight like I do,' Nathan said. 'Seeing as you're not in the business of killing vampires. Let me put the knife away.' He returned it to its sheath, then stood opposite Cynthia.

'Alright, hands up here,' he said, 'Guard your face.' Cynthia copied him, and he reached for her hands automatically to correct the position and realised this was going to be a problem. Her skin was soft.

Nathan backed up and cleared his throat. He'd never known hands could be sexy. 'Okay, try and punch me.'

'Won't I hurt you?'

'If you're lucky,' Nathan said. Then he replayed that sentence in his head and realised how cocky it had sounded. Shit. 'I mean—'

Then Cynthia punched him.

He didn't have his guard up. He brought an arm up on instinct, catching her arm and twisting it until she was forced to stagger into him. Her body collided with his. Nathan let go.

'Uh.' Cynthia stared up at him.

'Sorry,' Nathan said. He caught her cheeks in his hands and kissed her.

Kissing Cynthia was easy and natural. All that worry over nothing! She opened her mouth and her tongue tangled with his. She got braver, wrapping her hands around his biceps. Nathan was pretty lost in the feeling of her tongue in his mouth, and the little noises she made in the back of her throat.

Something smacked him in the back of the head.

He pulled away from Cynthia and spun around. Adrian and Monica were both leering at him, and Adrian's shoe was lying on the ground behind him. Nathan stared at it. Adrian had lobbed his shoe at him!

'You heathen,' he said, picking it up. 'I ought to chuck this in the river.'

'Oi!' Adrian lurched to his feet. 'Don't you dare!'

Nathan threw the shoe as hard as he could towards the river. It would never make it the full distance, not that it mattered because Adrian, in defiance of every secrecy law in the history of ever, shot lightning-fast across the field and caught the shoe before it hit the ground.

Cynthia made a noise of fright. Nathan turned to look at her.

'Yeah,' he said sheepishly. 'Sorry.'

'He's so fast.'

'That too,' Nathan said. 'All the sparring, the training, most of it is irrelevant. The truth is, if you're hunting a vampire, you only get one chance. Stake them on the first go, or you don't live to take another shot.'

Cynthia looked a bit pale. 'But no vampires are going to come for me, right?'

'No, I'll look after you,' Nathan said. *At least, I hope not.*

'Good.' And then Cynthia went red. 'Um, I liked the kiss.'

Nathan felt his cheeks heating up too. 'Good, uh, great,' he replied. 'Coz I was kinda hoping for a repeat?'

'We could repeat,' Cynthia said tentatively. 'Maybe when your friends aren't watching?'

'Deal.'

CHAPTER NINE

NATHAN'S HOUSE WAS EMPTY when they got back, and Aunt Anna had left a note on the kitchen table.

'Free house 'til four,' Nathan reported to Monica once they were upstairs in his room. Cynthia was studying everything with curiosity, and Nathan felt disconcertingly uncomfortable. He fetched the knife from the cupboard.

Monica made his bed, which Nathan wished he'd thought of earlier, and then she spread her supplies out on it. 'This would be better done on the kitchen table, but the magic will leave a residue your aunt will notice.'

'Yeah, better not,' Nathan said. 'I'd prefer she didn't catch wind of my extracurricular activities.'

'Well, the residue will disperse in about two days,' Monica said. 'But, Nate…' Her voice turned gentle. 'You know… if you're going to get yourself kicked out of the hunters for this… don't do anything stupid, yeah? Because, believe me, I know what that's like. I mean, I don't hate working for Jeremiah, but getting chucked out of my coven sucked.'

'I'm not a hunter yet,' Nathan pointed out. 'So I can't get kicked out. Anyway, you worry about your shit, and I'll worry about mine, M.'

'Just saying,' Monica said. 'Because you're not exactly… impartial in this.' Her eyes flicked to Cynthia.

Nathan scowled. 'Let's just get on with it. The sooner that thing is sorted, the better.'

Monica nodded. 'Put it here.' She pointed to the side of the bed. Nathan carefully lowered the knife onto his bedcover.

Cynthia swore under her breath. 'Where did you get that?'

'I nicked it from the guys who were chasing your sister.'

'Matches,' Monica said.

Nathan pulled a lighter from his chest of drawers. Monica raised an eyebrow.

'It's not what you think! I've just been making a tonne of amulets lately, feels like.'

'Oh yeah, Lily's giving Damien the runaround. She reckons she should have paid you double.'

'I should have charged her double for it,' Nathan said. 'Normal hunter rates are in the thousands for travelling wards.'

'Try getting one from a witch for less than two grand. There's a reason why we always learn to make our own. You undercut the market.'

'Fifty percent discount because it'll probably die at an inconvenient moment.' Nathan handed Monica the unscented white tealights he had hidden in his drawer, and she balanced them on the five points of the pentagram she'd just drawn with salt on the floor.

'What are you doing?' Cynthia asked.

'I'm going to ward this box with an anti-magic ward,' Monica said, lifting a wooden box up. 'That way we can store the knife in there and it'll be reasonably safe. First, though, I'm going to spell it to only open to you, Nate. You're going to need one of your hunting knives.'

Magic was not nearly as impressive in real life as movies made it out to be. For one, Monica was lazy, and she drew the wards onto the box in sharpie. It was probably quicker that way, anyway, because Nathan wasn't sure how well the plywood would hold up against the chisel, and Monica practically covered the insides of the box and lid in rows of identical runes. Then she flipped the lid and drew one single rune on the outside. That one was *druhtinaz*, meaning master. The same rune went on the top of each of the sides of the box.

'How much blood?' Nathan asked.

'Cut your finger and smear it over the five runes. Don't get any on the inside,' Monica instructed.

Nathan very carefully pricked his left ring finger and smudged blood over the *druhtinaz* runes. Amazing the power of blood, really. The giver of life, the binder of slaves, the bringer of death. Once he'd covered the runes adequately, he sucked his finger. Monica had him hold the box, and she chanted for at least five minutes, then dripped wax on each rune. There was an acrid, smoky smell, and when they scraped the wax away the runes had burnt into the surface of the wood.

Monica squinted at the box and then at Nathan. 'You'd better burn the box when you're done with it, because no one else is ever going to be able to get it open.'

'Isn't that the point?' Cynthia asked.

'Yeah, but no point in leaving the evidence lying around,' Monica said. 'Let's get the other spell done. It's going to take longer.'

Monica had to consult her spellbook for the second one. Made sense, Nathan supposed. Most witches didn't usually whip up anti-magic wards in their free time. Cynthia asked all sorts of questions, so Monica ended up explaining as she went along.

'Wards draw on the power of the elements to protect,' she recited as she lit the tealights. 'Anyone can craft them. You don't actually have to have magic yourself to harness the magics of the earth, but it does help.'

'So Nathan or I could do this?' Cynthia asked.

'Yes, but I wouldn't advise either of you to mess with this ward,' Monica said. 'Stick to petty amulets.'

'Why's this one so hard?'

'Because using magic to create a ward that blocks magic is sort of counterproductive,' Monica said. 'Think of it like a nuclear fusion reactor. If the plasma touches the side, the reactor overheats. Same thing in this spell. If the magic touches the anti-magic... kaboom.'

'Please don't blow up my house,' Nathan said.

'It's more of a metaphysical backlash.'

'Nuclear reactors have fail-safes in case the plasma touches the side,' Cynthia pointed out.

'No fail-safes in magic,' Monica said cheerfully. 'At least, not my branch of magic.'

Cynthia looked a bit worried at that. Nathan took her hand and squeezed it, and she looked up at him and smiled.

'Monica knows what she's doing, right?' she whispered.

'She's never got it wrong yet,' Nathan replied.

Monica walked them through the spell. First was the invocation of the elements. A little metal bowl went on each point of the pentagram, one with soil from the garden, an empty one for air, one with burning oil, and the fourth filled with water. The bowl on the point of the star that reached towards Monica was the last one she filled. Witches believed in a fifth element, which went by different names—spirit, soul, the intangible element, magic, purity. Every witch had a different name for it, and there were different ways of invoking it. Monica uncapped a tiny vial and poured a few drops of blood into the bowl.

'Don't worry, it's just pig's blood.'

Nathan made a face at Cynthia, who stifled a giggle.

'I'm never going to be a witch,' she said. 'I hate blood.'

'You kind of get used to it as a hunter,' Nathan said.

Step two was to smear some kind of ointment, meant to channel the magic, onto the insides of the box. Monica laid it in the middle of the pentagram.

'Okay, you two need to be quiet,' Monica said. Then she began to chant.

Witch chants were almost always in some dead language. Nathan had no idea what language this was, but it sounded Greek, and Monica had to read it out from her book.

She said the whole chant several times through. Each time her voice grew lower, her body became slacker, she fell deeper into a trance. Finally, she was only mumbling, and then she fell silent altogether, just mouthing the words. The lights flickered. The hairs on Nathan's arms prickled, and he could smell smoke.

Cynthia squeezed Nathan's hand nervously, and he wrapped an arm around her.

The candles went out. Monica took a deep breath, like someone surfacing after swimming underwater. She got up from where she was kneeling, shaking out each of her limbs as though she'd been sitting for hours.

Then she picked up the box and held it out to Nathan. The ointment was gone, and the runes were burnt into the plywood.

'Should I open the window?' Cynthia asked.

'Yes please,' Nathan said. 'Watch out, the lock sticks.'

With the window open, the smoky haze of magic began to seep out of the room. Nathan didn't want to touch the knife, so he found an old pair of socks and wrapped them around it, stuffing it into the box. He put the lid on and held it out to Monica to test.

She tried tugging the lid off, and so did Cynthia, but neither of them could lift it. For Nathan, it came away easily.

'Whew,' Monica said. 'Right, I need a drink.'

'And lunch,' Nathan said. Monica rolled her eyes.

They took the bus into town and got lunch at a pub. The normalcy felt weird after the morning they'd had. Monica and Cynthia discussed hairdressers and what their favourite clothing brands were, and how annoying it was to wear high heels.

'You're lucky, you're so tall,' Cynthia said enviously. 'I'd love to be that tall.'

'Oh, don't,' Monica replied. 'Guys think shorter girls are cute and delicate. I'll never have a guy think that about me.'

Personally, Nathan thought Monica was double as fragile as Cynthia, but when they looked to him for an opinion, he shook his head stubbornly. 'No, not a chance. I'm not stupid, there's no right answer when girls talk about this stuff.'

Monica and Cynthia both laughed. By the end of lunch, they had exchanged phone numbers, and Nathan deduced that they were probably going to be best friends forever. Just his luck; whatever way you looked at it, this was going to result in even more teasing.

Afterwards, Nathan walked Cynthia to her bus stop, with Monica trailing behind to give them privacy.

'I had fun today,' Cynthia said. 'Your life is pretty whacky.'

'Yeah, I don't fight vampires and do backroom magic every day,' Nathan said. 'Mostly it's just homework and training.'

'It's still more interesting than my life,' Cynthia said. 'Um... do you want to come over to my place? Sometime this week? If you have time?'

Nathan sincerely hoped this was an invitation to get up to more kissing.

'Friday? Then we won't have school the next day.'

Cynthia nodded. 'Great. I'll see you then.' Her bus pulled up.

'Can I kiss you goodbye?' Nathan blurted out.

'Yeah,' Cynthia breathed.

Nathan cupped the back of her head. Her hair was soft. He kissed her gently. Cynthia took the flaps of his jacket and tugged him closer. When they parted, Nathan's heart was beating just a bit faster. He gave Cynthia what was probably a totally goofy smile.

'See you Friday.'

Cynthia grinned cheekily, pecked him once more on the lips, then darted into the bus. As it pulled away, Monica stepped up beside Nathan.

'Who knew little Nate had it in him?'

'Shut up.'

Monica clucked her tongue at him. 'Anyway, you better get sex off your brain. Are you coming with me?'

'With you where?'

'I need to report Kseniya to the Witch Council.'

Nathan groaned.

'What do you need me for? I thought you weren't seeing the Council whilst you were here.'

'I'm not seeing Jeremiah, but this is different.' Monica tugged him down the High Street. 'Kseniya is a marked dark mage, and she was excommunicated from a coven. If I don't report she's here, and they find out I didn't report her, then I could get done for collusion.'

'Well, shit,' Nathan said. He ought to have said, *yeah, but you don't need me for that.* He really ought to have said, *I have to get home and write my econ essay.* 'Fine, let's get it over with.'

Witches were flashy and annoying. The Hunter Council had an office in a boring sixties office block. The Witch Council just had to be *different*.

They walked to Magdalen Bridge and then down the access road that led to the punt rental. A whiskery old man was sitting there, guarding his punts.

'Closed,' he called out.

Monica pulled her jumper up and showed him her witches' mark: a bolt of lightning splitting a stone in two, and below that a triskelion. They were tattooed above her right hip. The man stared at Monica's skin for an inappropriate length of time, before getting up and leading them to a punt.

'The river's a bit swollen. Mind you don't knock your heads on the bridges.' He pushed a token into Nathan's hand, a little hunk of metal which had been hammered flat like a coin. Raised ridges on each side formed the triskelion symbol, which was the insignia of the Council. Nathan pocketed the token.

They never actually reached the first bridge. Monica directed Nathan, and he steered the punt through a blank stretch of wall which belonged to Magdalen College.

There was a brush of powerful magic, and then they were inside a tunnel. The water made a hollow noise as little waves splashed against the walls. Flame torches lit the way. At the landing platform, Nathan jumped out to tie the punt up. By the time he'd helped Monica out, a guide was there.

'Monica Walker, you are not welcome here,' said the guide. His voice sounded male. He was otherwise featureless, hidden behind a long burgundy robe which covered him from head to toe.

'I have an issue to report,' Monica declared. 'It's witch business, but of course I can take it to the vampires if you'd prefer.'

The guide vacillated a moment. Magic flickered and wavered in his aura, making Nathan's eyes hurt. Finally, he said, 'I have consulted with the elders. You may enter. Your companion is unmarked.'

'Nathan is under protection from the Hunter Council.' Monica's tone was utterly uncompromising.

If this surprised the guide, he didn't show it. 'Very well, follow me.'

They were led up a flight of stairs, and they should have been in Magdalen College, but this was definitely not in Magdalen College's floorplan. It was a grand hall with stained glass windows down the two long sides. The light filtered through them in that strange way it often did in old buildings, lighting up the dust motes in the air and filling the room with a gentle glow. They had entered at the bottom of the room, where a platform sat with three gold seats for the Council elders and a row of less ornate wooden chairs behind it for their aides. One Council elder was in attendance at the moment, with three of the nine aides. Rows of pews extended to the back of the hall, and high above was a gallery with more seating.

'Pay your respects,' the guide ordered. Monica made a face but knelt at the feet of the Council elder. He—she—it—it was impossible to say—was shrouded in a pure white robe, underneath which Nathan caught a glimpse of a gnarled, ancient face as he knelt beside Monica.

'Elder Rowan,' Monica said.

'Monica Walker, mage of the Vampire Council,' said the elder, who turned out to be female. There was something about her; the moment she spoke, Nathan felt it. She was so old, it robbed him of breath. No living creature should be that old.

'What news do you bring before me?' asked Elder Rowan. 'Will you beg forgiveness of your sins?'

Ouch. Nathan winced in sympathy. Monica scowled but ignored the jab.

'I have encountered a marked dark mage in the city,' she said. 'I believe she goes by the name of Kseniya Krovopuskova.'

'Kseniya of the Bloodletting Family?' Elder Rowan inquired. 'We are not aware that she is in residence. Such a mage should have registered when she entered the city.' The elder paused and held out a hand to an aide. The hand looked like a tree branch on an ancient oak tree. The skin was almost like bark, and white as paper. 'Fetch me the register.'

A boy not much older than Nathan shot to his feet and darted off through a side door. He returned moments later, lugging a book almost the same size as he was. Another aide appeared with a table, on which the book was set down, and they both paged through it.

'There have been no dark mages registered in the city since January 2014,' the aide blurted out. 'Basil of Cresterbury, entered January, exited January 19—'

'Yes, yes,' the elder said impatiently. 'There is no Kseniya Krovopuskova in the city?'

The aide chanted over the book. It glowed red.

'No, Elder Rowan.'

'You are certain you sighted this girl, Monica Walker?'

'She bumped into my friend in the witching level,' Monica said. 'I would have thought someone else would have seen her.'

'And yet no one did. Do you bring me lies, Monica Walker? This will not ingratiate you with the Witch Council.'

'I'm just doing my duty,' Monica said, tense and irritated. 'Come on, Nate, this is useless. Let's go.'

'You should mark your friend, Monica Walker. He should not wander on witch territory unguarded,' the elder said in the tone of someone scolding a small child.

'Nathan Delacroix is protected by the Hunter Council,' Monica repeated as she stood up. 'I shouldn't have to.'

'Is he?' the elder asked innocently. 'My mistake, then. He does not... seem it.'

'Come on,' Monica snapped. She grabbed Nathan and dragged him to his feet with surprising strength, then marched him out of the hall without waiting for their guide. The guide chased after them, catching them when they got to the landing platform.

'Please hand your token back to the gatekeeper on the way out,' he panted.

'Yeah, yeah,' Monica said impatiently. 'Come on, Nate.'

'You want to go faster, you help.' Nathan untied the rope and supported Monica down into the punt, and then he turned them as fast as possible and steered them out of the tunnel. He was feeling kind of creeped out, too.

It wasn't until they'd returned the punt and handed back the token, and were walking in broad daylight up the High Street, that Nathan asked, 'What did she mean, I don't seem it?'

'I don't know,' Monica said. There was note of panic in her voice. She turned to Nathan and her expression was grim. 'I don't think I want to know.'

Nathan was inclined to feel the same way.

CHAPTER TEN

NATHAN MADE A POOR SHOWING on his homework the next week. His latest econ essay came back with a D-, and he sensed that imminently the teachers were going insist on meeting with his guardians to discuss academic performance. That was bad.

Even with that weighing on him, Nathan still couldn't forget that his birthday was looming over him, and with it the decision about hunter initiations.

On Thursday morning, he dutifully filled in the registration form that Grey gave him. Grey hesitated very pointedly, before adding his own signature.

'I'm not absolutely certain you're ready,' he said. 'You haven't been as focused lately. But I'm willing to write that off as stress and nerves. Take this as… an expression of trust.'

'Thank you,' Nathan said, not feeling better in the slightest. Ever since Grey had taken him to the prison, he found he didn't want the man's approval as much as he had before.

It was a relief when Friday came. Nathan endured a gruelling day at school, including a bio test that he really, really hoped he'd passed. After school, he cycled up the Headington Hill. Cynthia was waiting for him at the gates of Headington Girls' School, wearing her school uniform. She managed to make the button-down shirt and knee-length skirt look cute, too. Nathan stopped next to her and leaned against his bike until she was done chatting to her friends.

'Nathan,' she called, grinning. 'How are you?'

'The day's looking up,' Nathan replied casually. 'You?' She didn't need to know that he'd practiced that line in his head on his way up. It was worth it for her answering smile.

'I'm alright,' Cynthia said coyly. She went up on tiptoes to kiss the edge of his mouth, then asked, 'Do you want to meet my friends?'

'Okay,' Nathan said, even though he could see Poppy Wiggen glowering at him.

After fifteen minutes of enduring giggling girls and snide comments from Poppy, Cynthia finally decided they could head back to her house. They walked with his bike between them into Headington proper, until they reached her house.

'Monica has been texting me all sorts of stuff about wards,' Cynthia said. 'I didn't realise she was so knowledgeable.'

'Obsessed might be a better way of putting it,' Nathan said. 'Oh yeah, that reminds me, she gave me something for you.'

'Really?'

Nathan locked his bike outside her house and fished in his bag for the paper packet. 'I'm sure it's more wards,' he said. 'She's given me about fifteen already this week.' He showed Cynthia the keyring Monica had forced on him, and the ward sign drawn onto the inside of his belt. 'I have another one in my bag, and she sewed a patch onto my one jacket, but that's about as many as I can take in one place without them driving me crazy.'

The rest were in the back of his cupboard at home, although he'd snuck two onto Jess, just in case. You could never be too careful.

Cynthia unwrapped her package and pulled out a metal bangle.

'Bloody hell,' Nathan blurted out.

'What?' Cynthia asked. 'What is it?'

Nathan bit his lip. Should he tell her?

'Uh, that's a proper protection ward,' Nathan said nervously. 'Those are expensive.'

'Should I pay her back?' Cynthia asked, eyes wide.

'I'll do it.' Expertly crafted roving protection wards, ones which would warn you of danger and actually shield you if you were attacked, sold for easily five grand apiece. Unless Cynthia was secretly a millionaire, she wasn't going to be able to afford this one.

'I'll take her for dinner or something before she leaves,' Nathan said.

'She's leaving?'

'Back to Morocco—she's staying for my eighteenth and then flying back,' he replied, but his mind was still on the ward. Cynthia slid the bangle on, and it started pulsing with powerful magic.

'Ooh,' she whispered. 'Are you sure I can take this? It seems powerful.'

'It is,' Nathan said. 'Monica's already keyed it to you. Did you give her anything of yours?'

'She asked for a hair, but she said she just wanted to see if she could make a better anti-tracking ward.'

Nathan sighed. 'You know I said don't look vampires in the eyes? Rule number two: never give witches anything that's linked to your DNA. You're lucky Monica's just sneaky and made you a more powerful ward. A witch can do a lot with a single hair.' Like binding rituals.

Cynthia grimaced. 'I'll remember that. What does this ward do?'

Nathan gestured to the house. 'Shall we go inside?'

'Oh yeah.'

The house was empty. Cynthia let them in, explaining as she went that her mum worked from home to look after her sister, and that they had probably gone to the supermarket. 'I'm sure they'll be back soon. You want a drink?'

They settled in the kitchen with cokes, and Nathan tried to explain the difference between the bangle Monica had made and the wards he had made, without accidentally giving away that Monica had made something extremely fancy.

'So, protective wards — proper protective wards — can actually act as shields,' he said. 'That's these runes —' He indicated them. 'For shielding and defence. This one is anti-tracking, and this one is safety from harm. If someone touched you and meant you harm, the ward would burn them, or maybe push them back. Whatever it does, which depends on what magic Monica put in it, the goal is to give you a chance to run away and get help.'

'Oh wow,' Cynthia said. 'That seems fancy.'

The bangle had settled into the mix of elemental colours that made up Cynthia's innate magic. It pulsed steadily.

'Why don't you have one like this?' Cynthia asked.

'Because they're hard to make,' Nathan said. 'It's much easier for Monica to make those because she's a witch. For humans to make powerful wards like that would take at least three times as long, and you'd have to be a master ward crafter... and hunters don't like buying wards from witches.'

Cynthia parsed that, fingering the bangle.

'How much does this cost?'

Nathan grimaced. 'Um. Five grand?'

Cynthia looked horrified. 'I can't accept this!'

'Monica made it for you,' Nathan said. 'It's keyed to your essence—that's what she needed the hair for. She can't exactly give it to someone else.'

'I don't have five thousand pounds!' Cynthia eyed him, panicked.

'Don't worry,' Nathan said. 'I'll take care of it.'

'I can't ask you to pay that for me! Where are you going to get five grand?'

'There are other ways to pay back witches,' Nathan said. 'Favours, for example.'

'So I could owe Monica a favour?'

'No, I owe Monica a favour,' Nathan said. 'I originally asked her to make this. Cynthia, don't worry about it.'

'I don't need you to take care of me! I can pay my own way!'

'I'm not saying you can't!' Nathan groaned and buried his face in his hands. Girls were so difficult. 'I'll talk to Monica and ask her if she wants anything, and then you and I can figure out how to pay her back together,' he compromised.

Cynthia still had a stubborn set to her face. 'I suppose,' she said. 'But she made the ward for me, so I feel like I should pay her back.'

Nathan couldn't figure out how to express how much Cynthia should not want to be indebted to a witch, so he just said, 'Relax, I'm sure she's not expecting much.'

After that, they managed to settle down a little bit. Cynthia had lots of questions about wards and other magic, but Nathan couldn't answer most of them.

'I'm not a witch,' he said. 'Hunters don't do magic.'

'Warding feels like magic,' Cynthia argued.

'It's a very fine difference,' Nathan said. 'Spells are powered by the magic of the witch. Wards draw on magic in the world around us, but you don't have to use magic to make them.'

'It all feels magical to me,' Cynthia said. 'Hey, shall we go upstairs?'

'Uh, sure,' Nathan replied, and then it hit him that she'd just invited him to her bedroom, and suddenly he was panicking. He trailed Cynthia up the carpeted stairs and into the room at the end of the hall.

'It's kind of crappy,' she said. 'I mean, the landlord won't let us paint the walls, so it's just very plain.'

Was she nervous? Nathan was certainly nervous.

'Ah, you saw my room, remember?'

'Yeah, but you have all those ornaments. Where'd you get them?'

'My dad brings them for us sometimes when he travels abroad,' Nathan said. Cynthia switched on the lights, and he examined her room with interest. She had a couple of posters up. A little desk sat under the window, with what looked like French homework spread over it, and she had a single bed with a green cover. Her lacrosse gear sat in the corner, along with a tennis bag, and she had a small bookshelf that was filled to the brim with books.

'You play tennis?' Nathan asked.

'Yeah,' Cynthia said. 'I like sports. I swim as well.'

'Cool.'

Cynthia curled up on her bed like a cat, and Nathan looked at her desk because seeing her on the bed was awakening all sorts of inappropriate thoughts.

'French?' he asked.

'It's one of my A-Levels, but I think I suck at it,' Cynthia admitted. Nathan studied her neat, printed handwriting.

'Looks okay,' he said.

'Don't you do, like, maths and bio and physics?'

'No physics, I dropped physics,' Nathan said. His dad had been furious. 'I hated it. But I speak French. And a few other languages. It's part of hunter training.'

'A few other languages?' Cynthia asked incredulously.

'German, Spanish, Russian,' Nathan said, feeling very uncomfortable. This felt too much like boasting. 'And I'm learning Arabic.'

'Oh wow,' Cynthia said in a very small voice.

'We sometimes have to travel for work,' Nathan said. 'Are you okay?'

'It's just...' Cynthia said, her voice going faint, 'Uh, you know so much.'

'I'm still failing maths and econ,' Nathan said. 'I...' But he didn't know what to say. He'd put his foot in it, and he wasn't sure how.

'Why didn't you take French to A-Level, if you already speak it?'

'My dad wouldn't let me,' Nathan said. 'Hunters don't pick easy outs.' He shifted his weight uncomfortably.

'What's your dad like?' Cynthia blurted out.

Nathan shrugged. He pulled out the desk chair and sat on it, looking at the small collection of photos Cynthia had stuck to the wall because every time he looked at her, he started wondering what she'd look like without her top on. Did she have the same tan under her clothes? Did Adrian ever feel this awkward around women?

'My dad's, um... I guess he's kind of strict. He really loves his work, so he's always off on hunts. They say he's one of the best trackers on the force.' Nathan thought about his dad. Benjamin Delacroix was tall and sturdily built, still in perfect shape at the age of fifty. 'People say we look pretty similar, but I've always thought I take after my mum more.' His mother was slender and short, with blond hair. She was highly pragmatic, but she'd never been homely. She was also a hunter, and Nathan had seen her shoot ferals at fifty feet with a rifle without even batting an eyelash.

'My parents are quite hard, I think,' he said finally. 'I'm not sure hunter families are ever very close, or at least, there's not much time to do family stuff together.'

'That's a shame,' Cynthia said softly. 'You should get to have time with your family.'

'I have Anna. And Jess, when she's not being a brat.'

Cynthia shrugged. Nathan asked hesitantly, 'Cynthia? What's wrong?'

'It's just—it's stupid! You're probably going to laugh.'

'Why would I laugh?' Nathan asked, confused. Were all girls this hard to keep track of? Had they changed the topic somewhere without him realising?

'I keep thinking you're going to, like, get bored of me or something. I mean, Monica's a witch, and—'

'I would never date Monica!'

'—I know, but she's your friend, and Adrian's a vampire, and Lily, I don't know, but she must be something, and I'm just me, you know, I can turn into a cat, but it's not as useful a skill as you'd imagine, and I go to school and play a few sports, but I can't speak five languages and beat up a guy twice my size.'

'Why would you need to?' Nathan asked.

'I don't know! Why would you like me?'

'Uh,' said Nathan, embarrassed. 'Is that a trick question?'

'No!' Cynthia looked dangerously close to tears, so Nathan hastened to provide an answer.

'You're pretty, and you're good at sports, and you don't think I'm mad,' he said.

'You think I'm pretty?' Cynthia asked. 'Monica's pretty.'

'Monica scares me,' Nathan said frankly. 'But don't you dare tell her I said that—she'd be furious. I look at Monica and worry that next time I see her she's going to have starved herself dead.'

'She's not that skinny.'

'She's four inches taller than you and I think maybe she wears a smaller size than you,' Nathan said.

'That's the point!' Cynthia cried in frustration. 'Anyway, how do you know that?'

'Hunters are trained to be observant,' Nathan said. Realising that maybe he should keep future observations on clothes sizes to himself, he added, 'Anyway, I like you, not Monica, and that's not dependant on your clothes size. I like you because you look happy when you win at lacrosse, and you have this freckle on your nose that I always want to kiss, and, um—' He sounded like a lunatic. *Nathan, shut up.* 'And you laugh at my jokes,' he finished lamely. 'No one else thinks I'm funny.' Probably because all of his friends were older and, at least nominally, wiser than him.

'I think you're funny,' Cynthia said.

'Why would you want to date me?' Nathan asked. 'I'm failing maths and econ.'

Cynthia blushed and stuttered something.

'Huh?' Nathan asked.

'Kept seeing you at lacrosse matches and Jenny Byrnes kept going on about how hot you are.' She grimaced. 'And you're really nice to me.'

'Who's Jenny Byrnes?' Nathan asked. 'And can I send her flowers?'

Cynthia giggled. Then she got up and sat straddling Nathan's lap. He blinked at her. 'Um, hello.'

'Hi,' Cynthia said breathlessly. 'Kiss me?'

'Sure,' Nathan said. Cynthia tangled her fingers into his hair and then her lips were on his. Nathan wasn't quite sure where to put his hands and ended up cupping her neck. Then, on a whim, he pulled out her ponytail. Her hair was really soft. She swiped her tongue against his, and quite a bit of his blood took a detour south. She put her arms around him, and that pressed her body up against his in all sorts of ways.

A door slammed downstairs. 'Cynthia, are you home?'

Cynthia jumped back from him. Her skirt was askew, and he'd managed to mess up her hair. Her cheeks were flushed, and her lips were swollen. Nathan needed a cold shower. Shit.

'Upstairs, Mum!' she called back, sitting on the edge of the bed. 'Nathan's here!'

What felt like two milliseconds later, Ms Rymes appeared in the doorway.

'Hello, Nathan,' she said sternly. Nathan had the impression that she knew what they'd been up to and was maybe not best pleased. Damn. 'Cynthia, I don't think you're old enough to be on your own with boys.'

'I was expecting you to be home already, Mum,' Cynthia said patiently. 'Can Nathan stay for dinner?'

'He may.'

'Only if it's not a problem for you, Ms Rymes,' Nathan said.

She softened a little bit. 'It's not a problem, but I think you two should come downstairs.'

'Alright,' Cynthia said. 'I'm just going to change out of my uniform though.'

Ms Rymes nodded and absented herself. Cynthia picked up a stack of clothes, glanced at the door, and put them down again. She launched herself at Nathan and kissed him hard.

'Sorry,' she whispered. 'She's so overprotective.'

'I get it,' Nathan replied. 'Um, can I use your bathroom?'

'Sure! It's just next door.'

Nathan left Cynthia to change and went to splash water on his face. He was trying not to imagine Cynthia changing, but it wasn't really working. Cynthia's hair and skin were very soft, and she smelt clean, kind of like vanilla, and she was so very pretty. Had he given her long enough to change yet? He wet his face again, then went out into the hall.

Cynthia was waiting for him. 'Ready to face my mum?'

'Can't be worse than my folks.'

'Will they come for your birthday?' Cynthia asked as they

descended the stairs.

'I don't know,' Nathan said. He hadn't actually considered it. 'I'm not sure. We never discussed it.'

'Do they usually?'

'Sometimes,' Nathan said. 'They'll come for Jess's birthday, which is in November. But she's still at an age where she cries if they miss her birthday. I don't really mind, I suppose.'

'It's your eighteenth,' Cynthia protested.

'Is it your birthday?' asked Emma, who was sitting at the kitchen table and drinking coke.

'Next week,' Nathan told her. 'Tuesday.' He ruffled her hair, like he would have done to Jess when she was seven. 'Whatcha working on?'

'Maths,' Emma said, pouting. 'Maths is horrid.'

'I agree,' Nathan said cheerfully.

'See, you should have been smart and taken French,' Cynthia said. 'Mum, did you know, Nathan speaks five languages. *Five.*'

'Fluently?' asked Ms Rymes. 'When do you find the time for it?'

Cynthia glanced at him curiously. Truth be told, Nathan wasn't sure he was finding time for it all.

'I train afternoons after school,' he said. 'And Saturdays from seven-thirty until five.'

'Wow, it's like working a full-time job,' said Ms Rymes.

'I actually think once you graduate training it's less intense,' Nathan said. 'But I guess the logic is work hard now, reap the rewards later.' The reward being not dying in combat.

'Hmm, I suppose they also argue that you learn better when you're younger,' said Ms Rymes.

'Well, I started training when I was five,' Nathan said. 'Can I help with anything?'

It ended up being a fun, blissfully supernatural-free evening. Considering that they could turn into animals, the Rymes family were remarkably normal. At the end of the evening, before Nathan left, Cynthia tugged him upstairs again. Her mum was half asleep on the sofa, but Nathan couldn't help but feel like they were violating some kind of rule.

'I just want to do one thing, quickly,' she said. 'Seeing as you introduced me to Adrian, so I feel like, um.' She hesitated. They stood in her room, about five feet apart. 'Turn around and count to ten slowly?'

Confused, Nathan turned and counted up. 'One...two...three...' When he got to seven, he heard a soft thud, and then a cat was winding around his ankles.

'Ten,' Nathan said and turned around, but Cynthia was gone, leaving only a neat pile of clothes. Well, she wasn't gone. She was the cat. He crouched down and scratched it behind its ears, hearing it purr. It—she—brushed her nose against his hand and made a little meow sound. She had green eyes and short, soft fur.

'Hey,' Nathan whispered. The cat meowed its own greeting and flicked its tail. Then it jumped up on the bed and nosed its way under the covers, and before Nathan's eyes the lump grew and became human-sized. Cynthia poked her head out.

'Uh, will you go out in the hall so I can get dressed again?'

'Sure,' Nathan said and retreated hastily.

By the time she came out into the hall, he had managed to reassert some calm. 'You really can turn into a cat, then,' he said hoarsely.

'You're taking this pretty well,' Cynthia said.

'Eh, well, as long as you don't turn into a rabid monster and bite me on the full moon...'

'Promise you I won't.' Cynthia grinned.

Nathan said goodbye to Ms Rymes and Emma, then Cynthia followed him out the front door. She watched as he unlocked his bike.

'Thanks for coming over.'

'I had fun,' Nathan said. 'Hey, I'm probably doing something for my birthday next week, if you're interested.'

'Sure,' Cynthia said. 'Um, do you want something? A present, I mean. Is there anything you want?'

'You don't have to get me anything, but I'd like it if we could hang out.'

'Text me the details,' Cynthia said, then leaned up and kissed him. Nathan made a surprised noise and pulled her closer. His tongue tangled with hers and she wrapped her arms around his neck.

'Cynthia!' her mother called from inside.

'Your mum has terrible timing,' Nathan whispered against Cynthia's lips.

She giggled and pulled away. 'It's a sixth sense,' she said. 'She just knows when we're kissing or something. Maybe she's psychic.'

Nathan recalled all of the inappropriate thoughts he'd had about Cynthia recently. 'God, I hope not.'

Cynthia laughed and retreated to the doorstep. 'Have a good weekend!'

Nathan smiled to himself as he cycled off down the Headington Hill. For one evening, life was good.

There was a black Mercedes S-class parked in the driveway when Nathan got home, and that was all the warning he got. Heart racing in his chest, he locked his bike in the garden and let himself in the front door.

'Nathan, is that you?' Aunt Anna asked, appearing in the kitchen doorway. She looked worried. Then Dad stepped out of the lounge.

'Where have you been?' he demanded.

'Uh, I was out with a friend,' Nathan replied. 'Aunt Anna knew where I was. Hey, Dad. Is Mum here?'

Benjamin Delacroix glared down at him. 'What friend is this?'

'Cynthia Rymes.' If there was one rule Nathan adhered to with his father, it was always giving as little information as possible to get by.

'A girlfriend?'

'She's a girl, yes.'

'You know what I mean, Nathan.'

'A friend who is a girl.'

'So you're not dating.'

They'd been on one date. 'No,' Nathan said.

'Good,' said his father. 'You don't need any distractions right now.'

Nathan didn't twitch, but inwardly he was thinking, *oh, shit.*

CHAPTER ELEVEN

NATHAN'S FATHER ACCOMPANIED NATHAN to training the next day. Normally, when he was in town, Nathan got Saturday off training so he could spend one-on-one time with his father. Today, Benjamin Delacroix was waiting expectantly when Nathan came down the stairs, dressed in tracksuit trousers and a T-shirt.

'That's what you wear to training?'

'Grey's never told me I should wear anything else,' Nathan said.

'You don't wear your uniform?'

'No, I mean, not if we're doing combat training in the garage.'

'Hmm,' his father said, but he didn't elaborate.

Nathan felt uncomfortably scrutinised throughout breakfast, and the silence in the car was deafening when his father drove him to Grey's house.

They were around the corner from Grey's house before his father spoke.

'Grey is concerned that you've been distracted lately. This isn't because of that girl, is it?'

'Dad, can we forget about the girl? Please?' Nathan asked. 'I'm trying to remember my Arabic conjugations. I think Grey's going to quiz me on them this afternoon.'

'He's not,' Dad said certainly. Well, he would probably know. He set Nathan's training schedule. 'I've heard from your school, as well. Did you know you're failing maths and economics?'

'Yes, actually,' Nathan said sarcastically. 'I am aware.'

'I know that hunter training has to take precedence, but I don't want you failing your classes.'

'Yes, Dad.'

They pulled up in Grey's driveway, and Nathan's dad parked behind Grey's car.

'You probably shouldn't park their car in. Mrs Larson might have to go out later,' Nathan said.

'I can move the car,' his father replied.

Grey was waiting for them, and he immediately set Nathan to jogging up the street and back for a warm-up. It was a relief to get away from his father. Amazingly, his father had no magic, therefore no aura, and yet still he somehow seemed to fill up every room he entered. It was like he was followed around by his own personal ominous black cloud.

Nathan performed better in training than he had in a long time. Having his father there focused him. He was hyperaware of everything and made fewer mistakes, but having his father standing by and waiting for him to mess up was pretty nerve-wracking.

He was put through his paces in hand-to-hand, knife fighting, general fitness, and assorted other weapons. He was even asked to spar with a sword, which was his worst style. When was he ever going to need it? No one carried swords anymore these days. After lunch, he got tested in all of his languages, along with magi-science, general knowledge about the supernatural, tracking and espionage skills, and warding. By seven o'clock his head was spinning, and it was a miracle that he managed to answer the questions on warding correctly.

On the drive back, he got the first opportunity of the day to check his phone and discovered that Cynthia had sent him an essay.

> **Cynthia:** Hey
>
> **Cynthia:** I had fun last night
>
> **Cynthia:** I just wanted to say, I'm sorry for being a bit weird yesterday. I've been thinking about it, and you didn't deserve that. It's just, you're so talented at everything, and you don't even seem to realise it
>
> **Cynthia:** Bet you're even better than me at lacrosse and tennis
>
> **Cynthia:** Anyway, I'm just being stupid and girly. I know you have training, so I'll leave you to it :)
>
> **Cynthia:** Okay, I hope you're busy at training and not ignoring me
>
> **Cynthia:** Please don't be ignoring me
>
> **Cynthia:** I'll stop being annoying now
>
> **Nathan:** I'm so sorry, my dad pitched up unexpectedly and I've been busy all day

Cynthia: Hey, that's great!

Nathan had a sudden inkling that he had not explained his relationship with his dad very well yesterday.

Cynthia: Is he staying for your birthday?

Nathan considered that message very carefully, before replying.

Nathan: I'm not sure

Cynthia: I hope he does!

On Sunday morning, Nathan came down to find his father in the kitchen, bag packed and ready to go.

'Morning, Dad,' he said. Catching sight of Aunt Anna, he added, 'Good morning, Aunt Anna. Do you need help with breakfast?'

'I think your father is taking you out.'

Dad picked a café for breakfast, irrespective of Nathan's preferences, and he had soon elicited them a table. Nathan studied the people walking by outside and wondered if he was going to have enough time to make a moderate effort on his geo and econ homework this weekend.

'I came down here,' his father began gravely, 'Because Grey was concerned that you were having doubts about your own capabilities.'

Nathan looked at his father. Dad hadn't shaved since he'd arrived, and he was now starting to look a bit scruffy.

'To be honest, I'm a little bit confused as to what's going on here, son. You performed excellently yesterday in training. Based on that, I would happily recommend you straight into an advanced apprenticeship.'

'Really?' Nathan asked in surprise. His father had never actually expressed any kind of pride in his achievements before.

His father waved that comment away as though it was nothing. 'It's your head that's the problem, Nathan.'

Ouch.

'I'm not sure you want to be a hunter.'

'Of course I want to be a hunter, Dad,' Nathan said. 'I've never wanted anything else.'

'I don't know that I'm too sure,' his dad said. 'I think you're letting yourself be pulled in different directions, and you're losing discipline.' And then he said the damning words: 'I don't think you're ready.'

'I am ready!' Nathan protested. 'I've worked my butt off for this!'

'No,' said his father. 'I think you think you're ready, but moving on to an apprenticeship is no joke, Nathan. You'll be in the field—I know you've been in the field before, but this is different. You won't be observing. People will be depending on you to hold up your end of the team. You'll be pulling difficult hours, and I can't have you failing school because you're struggling to balance competing commitments. You need to get your marks up, and we'll revisit this in the new year. For now, I'm pulling you out of your initiation.'

An odd feeling filled Nathan—frustration, disappointment, anger... relief. He'd been so scared of making a decision, making the wrong decision, and now it had been taken out of his hands.

'That's not fair, Dad. This should be my decision.'

'I have to sign off on your training. I want you to take this as an opportunity to get your head back in the game, Nathan. I think initiations have been worrying you. Maybe you didn't even realise it. Without that looming over you, you'll have a chance to get your priorities straight.'

Nathan stared at the tablecloth and tried to figure out what the right answer was. What would demonstrate the right level of frustration at being robbed of the chance to initiate immediately, but the right level of subordination to his father, who was a senior agent?

'Yes, Dad,' he said finally, 'I understand.'

'Good, I'm glad we got that sorted out. So, do you have plans to celebrate your birthday with your friends? How is that friend of yours—what was his name, Matt—doing by the way? Did his parents sort out their drama?'

And Nathan ate his breakfast and gave stock answers and wondered what the hell he was going to do now.

For the next two days, Nathan was listless and demotivated. He felt robbed of purpose and wasn't quite sure what to do with himself. On his birthday, he avoided well-wishers, sequestering himself in the gym over lunch.

He was eighteen today. He should have been happy. His usual training had even been cancelled today—not because it was his birthday, but because Grey had a training day over at HQ. That had meant he was able to sleep in a bit longer, which meant he had dodged Jess's ongoing tantrum about how unfair it was that Dad had spent all his time with Nathan and barely spoken to her all weekend.

Nathan was on his third set of push-ups when Matt entered the school gym.

'There you are. Mate, you know it's lunch, right?'

'Mm-hmm.' Nathan continued to count. Seven-eight-nine-ten.

'Come on, it's your birthday, and we literally haven't spent any time together. What's got into you lately, anyway?'

Nathan stared at the ground. What had got into him? He didn't know, and that was the problem.

'Look, whatever it is, just come spend time with your friends and forget about it. Are we going out this weekend?'

'You're right.' Nathan stood up and grabbed his bag.

'I'm right?' Matt asked, looking confused.

'Yeah, you're right. I'm getting out of here.'

'What?' Matt asked. 'Wait, you can't just walk out of school! Aren't you failing econ? Mr Matthews will kill you!'

'So? If I'm going to fail econ, I can fail econ from home just as well as from here,' Nathan said. 'See you tomorrow, maybe.'

He headed for the bike shed. Matt chased after him.

'Have you gone insane? You never skive. You've skived, like, once in seven years!'

'This makes twice,' Nathan said, unlocking his bike.

'They'll catch you. You can't just walk out!'

'I'll see you tomorrow,' Nathan repeated. He swung his leg over his bike and cycled off of school grounds.

He texted Adrian from the traffic lights, before cycling up to Lily's house.

Lily lived with Damien in a house in Park Town which Nathan was sure had cost over a million pounds. It wasn't even a big house, but it made up for that by being old and fancy and having a snazzy address. Also, the inside looked straight out of an interior design catalogue for the 1800s.

If you needed proper sympathy and a serious ear to listen, well, Nathan probably had the wrong friends for that, but Lily would do in a pinch. She opened the door for him.

'I've been pulled from initiations,' Nathan said, standing on her doorstep in his sports kit and feeling a bit like a dog that had been shut out in the rain. This was as pathetic as it got.

'Oh no,' Lily said sympathetically. 'I see why you wanted to meet. Come in. Do you want tea?'

'Fuck tea,' Adrian declared. 'This calls for something stronger than tea.'

'I'm eighteen, anyway,' Nathan said. 'May as well celebrate the first day I can drink legally by getting smashed at two PM, right?'

Adrian helped himself to Damien's wine cabinet. Monica arrived about half a bottle in, took one look at Nathan's sorry expression, and threw his present down on the other sofa.

'Oh, Nathan,' she said, and hugged him.

'My dad decided to postpone my initiations to January,' Nathan mumbled into her cashmere jumper.

'My brother's an arse,' Adrian said. 'He's afraid you'll be a better hunter than him.'

'Why?' Monica asked, squishing herself onto the sofa with Nathan and Lily, her legs across Nathan's lap. 'I thought you were really good.'

'He said I performed excellently in all aspects of my training, but he isn't sure if I actually want to be a hunter,' Nathan said dully.

'Do you want to be a hunter?' Monica asked in her typical undiplomatic way.

'No clue.'

'So he's right?'

'It's not fair, though,' Lily said. 'The decision should be up to Nathan.'

'No, that's the thing,' Nathan said. 'Monica's right, Dad *is* right. He got it in one.'

'Nathan's problem is he has a conscience,' Adrian put in. 'Hunters aren't supposed to have a conscience.'

'I like you as you are,' Monica said. 'You don't complain when I put my feet on your lap. Pass the wine.' She stole Nathan's glass, topped it up, and downed half of it in one go. Nathan gave her a look. 'What?' she asked. 'Morocco's Muslim. No alcohol. Besides, I'm doing you a favour. You should pace yourself.'

Nathan let his head fall back against the sofa. The ceiling had little swirls in the paint. 'Can we order lunch?'

'Chinese takeaway?' Lily asked hopefully.

Over lunch, Nathan texted Cynthia telling her where he was and offering for her to join them. He doubted she would skive off school, but hopefully she'd come afterwards. Lily, in particular, was in favour of this plan.

'I can't believe I'm the only one who hasn't met her! You've been holding out on me.'

'I don't think you've missed much,' Adrian said. 'They're not technically dating—I'm not sure Nathan has figured out how to get past the holding hands stage of the relationship yet.'

'I have to managed to get past that!' Nathan said. 'And I'll have you know I like holding hands with Cynthia!' He regretted that second part immediately.

'So innocent,' Monica said in a baby voice.

'Have you managed to get her top off yet?' Adrian asked.

'We've been dating for a week,' Nathan groaned. 'She'll take her top off for me when she's good and ready to.'

'Have you managed to get her top button undone yet?' Adrian continued innocently.

Nathan slugged Adrian as hard as possible on the arm.

Cynthia joined them around five, dressed in sports clothes and with a tennis bag on her back.

'Wow, who lives here?' she asked, impressed.

'Lily,' Nathan replied, gesturing to the blond girl. Lily waved.

'I'm not dressed for a party,' Cynthia added, bestowing Lily with a nervous smile.

'This isn't a party,' Nathan said reassuringly. 'And we're definitely not going out.'

'We are going out,' said Monica. 'You just don't know it yet.'

'We are not going out,' Nathan repeated.

'What happened?' Cynthia asked softly, squeezing his wrist with her hands. 'Did you skip school?'

Nathan avoided her gaze, suddenly a little bit ashamed of his behaviour. 'Um, I got pulled from hunter initiations,' he said. 'Come meet Lily.'

Lily had the temperament of a socially awkward sixteen-year-old, so of course she and Cynthia got on like a house on fire. Within about ten minutes, Lily was plaiting Cynthia's hair. Cynthia gave Nathan a sheepish smile.

'Want wine?' Nathan held the bottle out to her.

'I, um, my mum will kill me,' she said.

'You can always stay over here,' Lily said.

'It's a school night,' Cynthia protested. 'My mum really will kill me.'

'In fairness,' said Adrian, 'This is probably the safest place in Oxford for you to be. We have a hunter, two vampires, and a witch all under the same roof.'

'All drunk.'

'Vampires can't get drunk.' Adrian toasted her.

'Oh, really?' Cynthia launched back into her never-ending questions about the supernatural. Monica put a glass of wine in her hand, and she drank it, and they soon discovered that shifters couldn't get drunk either.

'I mean, we heal pretty fast,' Cynthia said, 'And I never get sick. Oh, this sucks! Hey, though I guess I don't need to avoid alcohol at parties for fear of getting grounded anymore.'

'Your mum does grounding?' Nathan asked incredulously. 'That's a bit... old-fashioned.'

'Don't your parents?' Cynthia asked. 'Won't your dad be mad?'

'Dad went back to London on Sunday,' Nathan said.

'What? But it's your eighteenth! Why didn't he just stay the extra two days?'

'That's not his M.O.,' Nathan said.

'He's a shit father,' Adrian said.

'Adrian,' Nathan warned.

'No, Nate, he is,' Adrian said flatly. 'Alright, even our dad actually showed his face more than about once every three months. He sat in on my training so often that he was practically training me himself. Made me want to smack him, but at least he was there.'

'Dad's busy,' Nathan defended.

'Busy avoiding his kids!'

'Alright, you two,' Monica said. 'Have another drink.'

Damien arrived around six. Nathan, who was fairly buzzed by then, was the last to notice. Cynthia fell abruptly silent, and Nathan turned to see the man, in slacks and a blue button-down shirt with Oriel College cufflinks, watching them from the doorway.

'Lily Elizabeth, why are there underage people drinking in my living room?' His tone was deceptively mild.

'Technically only one underage person, and she can't get drunk,' Lily said cheerfully. She was definitely tipsy, which was an impressive effort on her part. 'Nate's eighteen today.'

'Ah. Should I be offering congratulations or commiserations?'

'Would we be drinking in daylight hours if we were celebrating?' Adrian asked.

'Possibly not,' Damien acquiesced. He raised an eyebrow at Nathan.

'Depends, I guess,' Nathan said. 'Do you think it's a good thing that there's going to be one fewer hunters qualifying this year?'

'In that case, you have my congratulations,' Damien said. 'You have just significantly reduced your chances of meeting the same fate as Adrian before you turn thirty.'

'That's not a huge comfort, frankly,' Nathan said, wondering where his crazy courage had come from. Clearly, alcohol made him fearless.

Damien smirked at that, and then turned his gaze on Cynthia. 'A friend of yours, I take it?'

Uh oh...

No one spoke, which led to a very guilty silence. Damien arched an eyebrow.

'I see you have all been keeping secrets,' he told the room at large. 'Very well, I shall not report your animal friend to the Council, though on your heads be it.'

'Thank you,' Nathan told him, relieved beyond measure. Cynthia spluttered a bit.

'I'm human,' she whispered.

'Not in the slightest,' Damien assured her.

'Take that as a compliment,' Lily said. 'Damien, this is Cynthia. Cynthia, Damien—my father.'

Cynthia looked between Lily and Damien with an impressed gaze. Damien turned to Nathan.

'Seeing as you have invaded my home for your celebration, I have a gift for you.'

'*You* have a present for *me*?' Nathan asked, gobsmacked.

'There's no need to be so surprised, Mr Delacroix. I am prone to occasional bouts of benevolence. I believe I may have exceeded my quota for this year already, but on the occasion of your coming of age, I suppose I can be persuaded to fit one more into my schedule.' Nathan stared at him. Damien smirked. 'I will return momentarily.' Then he was gone.

'What,' Nathan said, completely floored.

'He's joking,' Lily said. 'Don't worry.'

Nathan worried about everything Damien did. It was literally top of his worry list all the time.

'What?' he repeated numbly. 'Why's he got me a present?'

Lily shrugged. 'Why does Damien do anything?'

Damien returned with a bottle of forty-year-matured whiskey and a long, slender knife wrapped in leather.

'You can't give him that!' Adrian cried. 'That's mine!'

'It's useless to you,' Damien said. 'And I cannot get it to function either. The magic bound to it is… uniquely human.'

'Holy shit,' Monica whispered. Nathan accepted the knife with reverence, removing it from its sheath. The blade was made of an almost iridescent metal, and the handle had the Delacroix coat of arms on it: a shield with a gothic cross in the middle. Numerous names were inscribed on the blade. The most recent were *Jonathan Delacroix, Huxley Delacroix, Sebastian Delacroix, Adrian Delacroix.* Huxley had been Nathan's great grandfather. It had skipped his grandfather's generation and gone straight to Adrian's oldest brother. When Sebastian died, it had become Adrian's.

Nathan looked at Adrian, who had a very odd look on his face. He held the knife out to his uncle.

'No,' Adrian said. 'He's right, you should take it.'

'I'm not a hunter.'

'You don't have to be,' Adrian said. 'If you can wield the knife, it's yours. No one can take it from you.'

Nathan looked down at the blade.

'Uncle Jeff was always gutted it didn't pass to him next.'

'Jeff would have never managed to use it,' Adrian said sourly. 'He shirked all his classes.'

He stood up from the windowsill and strode over to Nathan. 'Do you know how to bind it to yourself?'

Nathan could guess—with blood; it was always blood—but he shook his head.

'Cut your palm and press the cut against the knife.'

Nathan took a deep breath. He balanced the knife in his right hand, and then sliced his left palm and pressed the bloody wound to the blade.

A burn started in his left hand and spread rapidly up his arm. It gathered in his chest, increasing until he felt like his heart was going to explode. His vision tunnelled. Then the sensation was gone, as fast as it had come. His palm was healed, not a drop of blood to be seen. A faint white line showed where he'd cut, but it looked like an old scar. Under the light, it was almost silver.

Nathan turned over the knife. It was also free of blood. Under Adrian's name, a new one had appeared.

Nathan Delacroix.

'I probably should have asked my dad before doing that,' Nathan said, feeling oddly numb.

'Fuck your dad,' Adrian said. 'It was my spirit knife; I get to pass it on. Chuck it here.'

Nathan tossed the knife to Adrian, who caught it by the hilt. Vampires were so irritatingly talented.

'Picture it in your hand.'

Nathan closed his eyes and imagined holding the knife. This was just like warding: pure self-belief. What had he told Cynthia? Blood, sweat, and tears. He gritted his teeth and focused, and felt his fingers close around the unyielding handle.

'It's yours,' Adrian declared. 'Same goes for changing the blade — you want wood, it'll turn into wood.'

'Instant stake,' Nathan said, and held it out threateningly towards Adrian, but he was joking. After a second, he slid the knife back into its sheath. Then he smiled. Suddenly, his birthday was looking up.

CHAPTER TWELVE

NATHAN ENDED UP SPENDING the night at Damien's, although Cynthia went home at nine. Lily insisted on doing a sleepover, because she had apparently never had one before, and so they all ended up on mattresses on her floor. Lily snored. Adrian's body lost all heat whilst he was unconscious. Nathan awoke with a mild headache when his alarm went at six AM.

'Switch it off!' Lily groaned, but Monica sat up and mumbled something.

'What?' Nathan asked as he scrambled through his bag to find his phone. He switched the alarm off and discovered that he had seventy thousand text messages from Aunt Anna.

'I said, I have to go home and pack.'

'I'll take you,' Nathan said.

He bade Lily and Adrian goodbye and cycled through early-morning Oxford with Monica on the back of his bike. The city was still asleep. Nathan had always found it kind of peaceful to be the only person out and about. He cycled past his place and dropped Monica at hers.

Monica stood on the doorstep, looking generally dishevelled.

'Nate,' she said seriously, 'You promise you'll keep yourself safe?'

'Don't I always?'

'Promise me,' she insisted.

'I promise,' Nathan said. 'Promise me you'll look after yourself?'

'I'll do my best,' Monica replied. Monica never promised anything if she couldn't keep the promise, and between the two of them, they both knew that she wasn't going to look after herself. Monica was terrible at looking after herself.

'Hug?' Nathan asked.

Monica jumped off the step and into his arms. She was so easy to lift and swing around, because she weighed a fraction of what she should. Nathan set her back on the step and inhaled the scent of her jasmine shampoo.

When Nathan pulled away, Monica said, 'Save the drama until after Christmas, yeah? I'll be back in town then.'

'Of course,' he said. 'What would we do without our handy witch and warding expert?'

Monica's eyes went wide. 'Wait here,' she said and darted into the house. She emerged a minute later, clutching another paper packet.

'Monica, again?' Nathan sighed. 'Too many wards give me a headache.'

'This one's special,' Monica said. 'This one will tell you if Cynthia's in danger.'

Nathan untwisted the paper bag and looked at the contents. It was just a plain leather keyring, with a tracking ward burnt into it.

'It's keyed to the bangle I made her,' Monica said.

'M... I can't pay you back for this,' Nathan said. He felt oddly touched by the gesture and found himself looking at his friend in a new light. Funny how Monica could drive him up the wall, but she just got him on a level that no one else did. What was he going to do without her?

'You don't have to,' Monica said. 'The Sahir... this is dangerous shit, Nate. You need to keep her safe.'

'I know,' Nathan said. Hunters may have the wrong of it about killing all vampires, but that didn't mean Nathan didn't believe in the ethos of fighting for the people. He was just willing to fight for more people than the traditional hunter. It was his duty to keep people safe if they couldn't do it themselves.

Monica nodded.

'I'm going to miss you,' Nathan blurted out.

'I'll miss you too,' Monica said, and for a second she seemed oddly vulnerable. Then she added, 'Don't worry, I promise to make fun of you every day on WhatsApp. It'll be like I'm right here.'

'I'll hold you to that,' Nathan said. He tugged her plaits, making her squeak, then told her, 'See ya, M.'

'See ya, Nate.'

Aunt Anna was already up, sitting in the kitchen and sipping tea, when Nathan tried to sneak in.

'I'm impressed,' she called when he tried to creep up the stairs. 'Wherever you were last night, it had anti-scrying wards. You've been doing your homework. Using hunter skills to bunk off and hide from us, very good.'

Shit.

Nathan redirected into the kitchen. Aunt Anna was at the table. Uncle Jeff was rinsing a pan at the sink. Uncle Jeff had the same strong jawline as Nathan's father, but that was where the similarities ended. Adrian, Sebastian, and Jeffrey had come from his grandfather's first marriage, and Benjamin, Matthew, Helen, and Lucy were all from the second marriage. They had the look of disapproval in common, though. Nathan flinched when it was directed at him.

'Sit,' Uncle Jeff said.

'Would you like a cup of tea?' Aunt Anna asked.

Was that a trick question?

'Yes, please, Aunt Anna.' Nathan crossed his fingers that he wasn't about to get hemlock in it.

Aunt Anna made tea and set it in front of him. Uncle Jeff kissed her goodbye and headed off to the office. Uncle Jeff worked for the Council; a nice stable job for the few hunters who ever made it to retirement age. The other options were training, admin, or research.

Nathan fiddled with his cup.

'This isn't poisoned, is it?'

'Tempting, but no,' said Aunt Anna. 'It's just tea. Where were you?'

'Out.'

'I got the Lefebvres to scry for you.' The Lefebvres were Monica's foster family. 'I was worried. You didn't answer your phone.'

'I'm fine.' Nathan hoped minimalistic answers would work on Aunt Anna like they did on his father, but he wasn't too optimistic. She had the look of a woman who wanted answers and wouldn't quit until she got them.

'Where were you?' she repeated.

'With friends.'

Aunt Anna sighed. 'Here's what I know happened. You left school at lunchtime yesterday, because they called me when you didn't pitch up to class in the afternoon. I told them you'd come home sick, so you're welcome.'

Nathan lifted his head in surprise.

She continued, 'I also know you met up with Monica, because she told the Lefebvres that was where she was going. And I hope you stayed with her the entire time, because I know you brought her home. Malcolm Lefebvre just texted me that you had dropped her off.'

Nathan winced. So much for subtlety.

'Here's what I think happened,' Aunt Anna said. 'I think you met up with Monica's friends, who are all older than you, and probably mostly of supernatural descent. I think you probably drank more than you should. I think you had the sense to stay in one place, and behind decent wards, but I think you might have been in the company of vampires.'

Because it was known that Monica hung out with vampires, it was therefore concluded that Nathan had done the same. He studied his tea, feeling vaguely sick.

'Would I be right so far?' Aunt Anna asked.

'Maybe,' Nathan said in a small voice.

'I ought to ground you for this,' Aunt Anna said, 'But I'm going to give you a chance. Nathan, please tell me what's going on. I've had worried calls from the school, and your dad was here—and we both know he never checks in on you. What's going on?'

Nathan continued to watch the steam rising off his tea.

'Look at me, please.'

He looked at his aunt. She was not related by blood, so she didn't share her features with anyone in the family. Even her own children, who were all out of the house by now, took after the Delacroix side more than the Taylor side. Anna had soft features, frizzy hair which had long since gone grey, and laughter lines around her eyes. She didn't have the hardness of the hunters, neither in body, nor in personality.

'It's okay to have doubts,' Aunt Anna said. 'We all have them.'

'I'm not having doubts,' Nathan replied defensively.

'Nathan, I'm sixty-one and I'm not a fool,' she said. 'I raised two children who both became hunters. Do you think they never doubted themselves? Do you think Jeff never doubted himself? Doubts and fears are part of being human. Talk to someone about them. Get them off your chest.'

'I've talked to loads of people,' Nathan said petulantly. 'No one's helped.'

'Talk to me,' Aunt Anna replied. 'You haven't talked to me yet.'

Nathan considered her offer. Anna was in the unique position in his family of having no allegiance to the hunters — or to anyone else, for that matter. It meant that she sort of lived between two worlds. She might understand.

'I'm not sure if I want to be a hunter,' Nathan admitted.

'I see,' Aunt Anna said. 'How long have you been worrying about this?'

'A while,' Nathan said. 'I saved a kid who was being chased down by witches,' he added. 'Turned out she was... supernatural, too. Hunters would have said, don't get involved, it's witch business. But...' He paused and tried to shape the words in his mind. 'I want to help people, not just humans, but all people. Anyone who needs help. I can't do that through the hunters. The hunters wouldn't want me to help... Monica, say.'

'Does Monica need help?' Aunt Anna asked.

'No more than usual,' Nathan said. He remembered how the Witch Council had looked down on her. 'I think she does, but she'd never ask for help.'

Aunt Anna sat back, sipping her tea and considering that. Nathan drank his own tea. This, he realised, was what he liked about Aunt Anna. Okay, she could be strict. Okay, she was probably going to punish him. But when you had a problem, she didn't just give stock answers. She actually thought about it.

'When has your father postponed your initiation to?' she asked after a moment.

'At least January.' Nathan felt the familiar pang of hurt.

'Okay,' Aunt Anna said. 'Here's what I think we're going to do. You need to explore what's the right path for you. You're eighteen now, you need to learn to make your own decisions. You also need time and space to do that, and I'm not sure you have either right now. I think if you wanted to, you could do initiations tomorrow, without any preparation.'

'Probably,' Nathan said. 'I mean, training-wise.'

'Yes,' Aunt Anna said. 'But you have until January. I'm going to have a word with your dad to see if we can't cut back on your training. You are perfectly capable of keeping yourself fit and trained in your free time. You don't have to go see old Larson every day. When you do go, maybe he can start teaching you a few different things. After all, not every hunter ends up doing the same track 'em and kill 'em routine. There are different options.'

'Sounds good,' Nathan agreed cautiously.

'And in the meantime, you and I are going to work together to explore a few different options, as well,' Aunt Anna said. 'So that when the time comes you can make an educated decision.'

'I'd like that,' Nathan said.

'Very good,' she said. 'We'll brainstorm when you get home from school, but off the top of your head, is there anything you'd like to start with?'

To his surprise, the answer came to him immediately. 'Warding,' he said. 'I want to learn how to craft protective wards.'

Aunt Anna tilted her head and regarded him. 'Not at all what I was expecting,' she said, 'But I don't see why not. It's an extremely valuable, highly sought-after skill.'

'Can you teach me?' Nathan asked.

'Oh, I can certainly teach you the theory. Whether you can do it in practice will depend on how badly you want to learn.' Aunt Anna smiled, and it was the smile of someone who had won. 'Never fear, you'll have plenty of time to learn, seeing as you're grounded for the next two weeks.'

Nathan's jaw dropped. 'What?'

'And you're lucky I'm not telling your father,' she added.

'Seriously?'

'Yes, Nathan, seriously. You'll go to school and to training, and otherwise you'll come straight home. You can keep your phone— heaven knows you're joined at the hip to it—but you're not going out with Matt, Cynthia, or anyone else.' She gave him a stern look. 'Skipping school is not on.'

Nathan groaned.

'And you know that,' Aunt Anna said. 'You've never done it before, which is why I'm going easy on you. But I don't want you to think that it's acceptable to skip out on school every time you're upset about something.'

'I'm not upset,' Nathan replied reflexively.

'Worried,' Aunt Anna said, and patted his shoulder. 'I forget, you boys never get upset. Now off you go and shower. You can't go to school dressed in yesterday's clothes.'

Nathan sighed and heaved himself up from the table, draining the rest of his tea. He put the cup in the dishwasher and headed for the door, pausing in the doorway.

'Aunt Anna?'

'Yes, Nathan?'

'Thanks for listening.' He darted away before she could say anything embarrassing.

CHAPTER THIRTEEN

OCTOBER SLIPPED AWAY SURPRISINGLY quickly. Aunt Anna had cleverly timed the grounding so that he was stuck at home for the half-term holidays, with nothing better to do than catch up on schoolwork. She'd also made good on her promise to get his training reduced. He now went two evenings a week—he'd picked Tuesdays and Thursdays—and Saturday mornings. It meant a lot more free time, but it also meant Nathan was doing the majority of his fitness, self-defence, and weapons training on his own.

Luckily, Aunt Anna had a plan for that, too. It turned out Jess needed practice fighting people who were bigger than her—which was pretty much everyone. Nathan went along to her daily self-defence classes and let her try and beat him up. This allowed Jess to purge her apparently endless frustrations, and he got to use the gym for free after.

It was an annoyingly elegant interim solution.

It was also just plain annoying because Jess had sharp elbows and got frustrated when she couldn't beat him, at which point she usually devolved into name-calling and crying.

They had a long way to go before they made a hunter out of his little sister. To be honest, Nathan was a bit glad for that. He couldn't imagine sending little Jessica, whose favourite colour was pink and who cried when Mufasa died in *The Lion King*, out to kill vampires.

On the second weekend of his grounding, Nathan succeeded in making a successful knock-back ward. He tested it on Jess, to Aunt Anna's disapproval. She stumbled back on the first punch, but on the second the ward failed, and she hit him in the solar plexus. It wasn't going to be stopping Adrian in his tracks any time soon.

'You'll get there,' Aunt Anna said. 'It's all about self-belief.'

'So's everything else in life,' Nathan grumbled, rubbing his abdomen. 'And I've only got a limited quota.'

'If that's the truth, then you might want to reconsider warding.'

'No thanks,' Nathan replied.

The day his grounding ended, Adrian texted him.

> **Adrian:** Monica asked me to keep an eye out for this Kseniya girl. She said you met her. What's the deal?
>
> **Nathan:** She grabbed me at TWL and seemed really strung out
>
> **Adrian:** Like drugs?
>
> **Nathan:** M said it was magic
>
> **Adrian:** Can we scope out TWL?
>
> **Nathan:** Sure, but you have to do something for me in return. I need a sparring partner. Jess is driving me crazy
>
> **Adrian:** Sure

That weekend was Halloween. Nathan's school had their dance on Friday, and Cynthia's was holding theirs on Saturday. Cynthia suggested they attend both, which Nathan hoped was because she had missed hanging out with him whilst he was grounded.

Friday night, they met by the whiskey shop on Turl Street. Adrian was already waiting when Nathan and Cynthia walked up from her bus stop.

'Really?' Adrian asked, looking at Cynthia.

'Come on, it's Halloween, no one's going to care,' Nathan said.

'You hope,' Adrian said. He hadn't dressed up, but Nathan had done the stereotypical hunter outfit—no one at school would have to know it was real—and Cynthia was looking cute as a black cat.

Adrian held out two leather wristbands. 'Courtesy of Monica.'

They had her witches' mark on them, a lightning bolt hitting a stone, and Nathan could feel the residual magic.

'What are they?' Cynthia asked.

'Put it on, I'll explain as we go up.' Nathan fastened his own around his wrist and felt it latch on. Cynthia made a noise under her breath. Nathan hoped they could get them off again. Monica would have thought of that, right?

Adrian wasn't wearing one, and it hit Nathan that he'd just given his to Cynthia.

They ducked through the false wall and ascended the stairs to the witching level.

'Wow,' Cynthia said.

'Magic,' Nathan told her. 'Don't take the wristband off—it's a witches' mark. Usually, they put them straight on your skin, but this is a temporary version. It means no witch except the one who owns the mark can touch you.'

'Touch me?' Cynthia asked in alarm.

'Channel you, take your magic, use you in a spell, sleep with you,' Adrian rattled off.

'Thanks, Adrian,' Nathan said when Cynthia turned white.

'Oh, any time,' Adrian replied flippantly.

Nathan took Cynthia's hand, and they entered the secret top floor of the Covered Market. Spooky electric music swelled out to greet them. It was only seven PM, but everyone was dressed up for Halloween and swaying drunkenly.

'I didn't even know this place existed!' Cynthia called.

'This is the witching level!' Nathan explained. 'I showed you the front entrance on our first date, remember?'

'Ooh, yeah,' she said, turning away in embarrassment at the reminder. 'Sorry about that, by the way.'

'No problem,' Nathan said. 'We're looking for a girl, probably about your height, very pale skin, blond hair, tattooed arms, Russian. Name: Kseniya Krovopuskova.'

'Why?'

Nathan looked at Adrian.

'Don't ask me,' Adrian said. 'Monica asked me to keep an eye out for her. I assumed you knew why.'

'I think Monica's worried,' Nathan said. 'And Monica never asks for help with anything, so...'

'So when she does you take it seriously,' Adrian said. 'Especially when she asks me, because Monica hates me.'

'You lot have strange logic,' Cynthia said, 'But okay. I'll help.'

Nathan had to get the drinks because the young woman who was bartending wouldn't speak to Adrian. As it was, she spent more time glaring in Adrian's direction than she did watching the drinks she was pouring. She was too distracted to notice that Cynthia looked way too young to be eighteen.

'Three Devil's Brews,' she said, slapping the drinks on the counter. 'Seven pounds twenty.'

Nathan handed her the cash. 'Can I ask a question?'

'Will it get your vampire friend out of here quicker?'

'Yes,' he lied.

'Ask.'

'I'm looking for a girl. She's a friend of a friend.'

'You think I know every idiot who passes through here?' the bartender demanded, looking irritated.

'You'd know her,' Nathan said. 'She's very pale. Russian. Lots of tattoos.'

'Don't know her,' the bartender said, but there was something mechanical about her answer, and she wouldn't look at Nathan's face.

'Okay, thanks anyway.' He took the drinks back to Adrian and Cynthia.

'Bartender just lied to my face about not knowing Kseniya,' he reported.

'I've asked three people—the ones who will speak to vampires,' Adrian said. 'Same.'

'Never thought I'd say this, but can't you compel anyone?' Nathan asked.

'Not witches,' Adrian said. 'They're immune. Find me a human, sure, but not if they have a witches' mark. You don't compel marked people, or you end up with vengeful witches coming after you.'

'*Great.*'

They gave up after an hour because everyone was starting to give Adrian a wide berth. Outside, Adrian vanished into the ether without saying goodbye. Nathan and Cynthia rode Nathan's bike down to Magdalen College School.

'I've always thought your school looked kind of fancy,' Cynthia said as Nathan locked his bike to the bike rack.

'Well, I hope we don't disappoint,' he said.

'We will,' she said. 'Headington's dead boring, and our theme this Halloween is lame.'

MCS didn't have a theme, and when they got in the gymnasium most of the guys were in street clothes and zombie masks. Matt and Poppy found them immediately. Matt was in some kind of heavy metal get-up, and Poppy was dressed as Cleopatra.

'Cool costume!' Matt called out, his words slurring just slightly. He reached for the knife strapped to Nathan's left arm, and Nathan batted him away.

'You're so drunk, you could cut yourself on a plastic knife,' he said.

'Hey!'

'Let's dance,' Poppy suggested. Nathan took Cynthia's hand and tugged her onto the dancefloor. Dancing lessons had not, unfortunately, been part of his hunter training, so he suspected that embarrassment was imminent. But his stomach was warm from Devil's Brews, so what the heck? May as well.

Cynthia wrapped her arms around him, and Nathan found he was less worried about his lack of dancing prowess when she was all pressed against him.

'Your knives aren't fake,' she whispered in his ear.

'Nope, but no one else needs to know that.'

'Are you ever not armed?'

'Nope,' Nathan repeated. And that was the sad truth. Once a hunter, always a hunter. 'Hunters are paranoid by nature.'

'Can you switch it off for five minutes?' Cynthia asked, her eyes flicking to his lips. Nathan suddenly felt rather warm.

'I can try.'

'Good.' Then she kissed him.

After that, the dance was rather enjoyable, not that they did much dancing. Cynthia's costume encompassed a surprisingly small amount of clothing, and she wasn't shy about letting Nathan explore. At length, she took his hand and mumbled, 'Let's go outside.'

Nathan led her out and they meandered down the side of the gymnasium. Cynthia leaned against the wall and pulled Nathan close. Nathan wondered what Adrian would do now. Probably take advantage. Nathan was scared of going too far, of not going far enough, of hurting her… Too many thoughts.

'Kiss me,' Cynthia said.

'You sure?' Nathan asked. It felt different, out here, alone.

'I'm sure,' Cynthia said. She took his hand and slid it between the wall and her back, down to the curve of her butt.

'Hmm,' Nathan murmured. 'Nice.' He caught her lips with his and kissed her, slowly, sliding his hand over her bum. His other hand tangled in her hair, which was loose today. Her butt was rather nice. It was hard to concentrate on more than one thing at the time, but luckily Cynthia didn't seem to find his slow kisses lacking. She explored his mouth and arched her body into his, pressing her breasts against his chest. Nathan was starting to get turned on, and he worried that she would feel that he was hard.

Cynthia had her fingers in Nathan's hair, and one hand was tracing over his chest, sliding under his black vest... Nathan couldn't have said what it was, but there was a shift in the air, and he acted on instinct. Shoving Cynthia away, he whirled around and pulled the spirit knife from the holster on his hip, right in time to block a blow from a guy who was twice his size with tattooed arms as thick as tree trunks.

Cynthia screamed, which was utterly unhelpful. Nathan glanced back at her, but she was fine.

'Look out!' she cried, and he jerked around again, ducking a blow that would probably have smashed his face. These guys meant business.

Adrian made fun of Nathan for not being the tallest guy around all the time, but it had a distinct advantage here: he was fast. He was much faster than the huge, burly thug he was fighting. He ducked and parried and managed to slash the knife hard across the guy's thighs. It met flesh and he was rewarded with a cry of pain. After that, the man was even slower. He was too sturdy for Nathan to trip, but Nathan managed to position himself in front of the wall then dodge at the last moment. The man's momentum carried him towards the wall, and Nathan helped him along, slamming his head against the bricks.

He went down.

There had been a second guy, but he was gone and so was Cynthia. Nathan dashed to the end of the alley and reached the road right behind them.

'Let her go!'

The man spun around, inches away from a van. He had a knife to Cynthia's neck.

'Drop your weapon,' he said. Nathan immediately lowered the knife.

'No!' Cynthia cried. 'Don't listen to him.'

'And all the rest,' he told Nathan. He had the sort of accent of someone who spoke many languages, whose true accent had become diluted. It was hard to say where he was from. He was tall and very strong, and his tattoos were familiar. Nathan was sure he'd seen them somewhere before, though he couldn't remember where. He observed all of this whilst he stripped two knives off his upper arms, removed another from his hip, and pulled out the one strapped to his back.

Moving slowly, he placed them all in a pile on the floor.

'Kick 'em over here,' said the man.

'No, no, no,' Cynthia said. Nathan wished there was something he could say to reassure her, but it seemed more sensible to just keep his mouth shut.

'Got any others?' the man asked. 'In your boots, for example?'

He did, but Nathan shook his head in what he hoped with a cooperative manner.

'Hmm, well, it's not gonna help you, anyway. Stand against the van, hands behind your back.'

A terse word in another language had the driver climbing out the van. It was idling; Nathan could feel it shuddering every time the engine turned over. They were ready to make a quick getaway. He closed his eyes and prayed—not for a miracle. Just for luck. The driver came over to him and grabbed his wrists. A cuff closed around one.

Spirit knife!

The knife materialised in Nathan's hand in the perfect position to be jabbed straight into the driver's liver. Nathan did that with macabre relish. He whipped around and hauled the knife out. The driver staggered and collapsed.

The other guy had managed to get Cynthia into the van, but the rear doors were still open. Hardly sparing a thought for what he was about to do, Nathan lunged at him. He caught the man by surprise and they both went down. They rolled, wrestling for the knife, but the other man must have cut himself on the blade and his blood made it hard for Nathan to keep his grip.

The other man ended up on top, and then he had a knife in his hands as well. It was dark, but Nathan felt the aura and recognised the weapon.

It was a Sihr knife.

Then the knife was in his stomach. Pain seared him. He dropped his spirit knife. The other man began to chant in his strange language. Nathan picked out words. Arabic, but it sounded wrong somehow. He felt himself weakening and struggled to pull away.

Knife.

Spirit knife.

He had to fight. He had to…

Nathan's vision was starting to tunnel. His fingers closed around something hard.

His arm moved slowly, like he was trying to swim through jelly.

The number one thing vampire hunters were taught was aim for the heart and don't miss. When in trouble, revert to habit. Always aim for the heart.

Nathan aimed for the heart. The man was kneeling over him, giving him enough room to manoeuvre. The spirit knife obeyed his will. It slid between the man's ribs like butter and pierced his heart. The man collapsed sideways, dead.

Nathan's strength began to return. For several seconds, he just lay there, stunned. First his vision came back, then his strength, then the pain. The knife was still in him, and it *hurt*.

He pulled it out, his fingers slippery with blood, and threw it away.

His legs were trapped. With some difficulty, Nathan managed to get out from under the dead man. He staggered to his feet, his vision fading in and out. There were two men on the floor. Cynthia's white face stared at him from the back of the van. Nathan stumbled towards her.

'Are you alright?' she choked. 'Oh my God, you're bleeding. Oh God.'

Nathan pulled his phone out of his pocket and unlocked it with shaky fingers. He'd cracked the screen, but it worked. *Thank fuck.* He held it out to her.

'Call Adrian,' he croaked.

Cynthia took the phone and fiddled with it. It rang, then Adrian's voice came over speaker.

'Nate, what's up?'

'MCS,' Nathan said. 'Need your help. Now.'

Perhaps it was a mark of their relationship, perhaps it was the desperation in Nathan's voice, but Adrian didn't ask any stupid questions. He didn't make any snarky comments.

'I'll be there in five minutes.'

'Good.' Nathan collapsed on the back of the van, trying to put pressure on his wound, and prayed no one found them before Adrian arrived.

He must have dozed—Cynthia obviously hadn't watched enough films to know not to let victims of knife wounds pass out—because he woke up when Adrian smacked him in the face.

'What the fuck?'

'Need a hospital,' Nathan muttered.

'You nutjob,' Adrian said. Then he shrugged his jacket off and bit his wrist.

Nathan hated drinking blood. He'd have rather had the hospital, even if it did mean Aunt Anna finding out what had happened.

He took Adrian's wrist and forced himself to swallow a mouthful of blood. After the second mouthful, Nathan was already healing. He felt the pain slipping away. The tunnel vision stayed.

'Yuck,' he said.

'Oh good, you're back,' Adrian said. 'What the fuck happened?'

'They snuck up on us. I got distracted with one guy, and the other tried to get Cynthia in the van.'

'How'd they sneak up on you?'

'Um,' Nathan said.

'Were you otherwise occupied?'

'We were snogging,' Nathan snapped. 'Is this important? Can you do something about the bodies?'

Thankfully, Adrian seemed to realise that they were outside a school, and anyone could catch them at any moment. Where was everyone, anyway? Probably drunk. He lugged the two bodies into the van. One guy was still alive, just about, which ended when Adrian snapped his neck. Efficient and brutal. Cynthia let out a sob. Great, they were about to have a panicking girl on their hands, too.

'Where's the third one?'

'Beside the gym.'

Adrian disappeared and reappeared carrying a guy twice his size over his shoulder. He dumped him in the back of the van, too.

'This one gets to live,' Adrian said. 'Damien needs practice on his interrogation techniques.'

Nathan collected his knives and decided that the scene was adequately clear. Hopefully, no one would notice the pool of blood on the tarmac before the rain washed it away.

Adrian drove the van up to Park Town. Nathan sat leaning against the window, feeling like he'd swum the English Channel. He was just that exhausted. Cynthia sat beside him, still as a statue, breathing very deliberately through her mouth. The van smelt of blood.

Damien was waiting for them in the doorway before Adrian even killed the engine of the van. Nathan opened the passenger door and practically fell out. To his immense surprise, Damien had the courtesy to catch him.

'Can I use your shower?' he asked stupidly.

'Can you stand up to use it?' Damien replied, amused.

Nathan assessed himself. 'Maybe,' he said.

'We have one live dark mage in the back of the van,' Adrian said. 'What should I do with him?'

Damien shrugged. 'I suggest putting him in a Council holding cell for the night. It is what Jeremiah would expect, and we may as well use the Council resources available to us. He can stew until morning.'

Adrian nodded.

'Cynthia, out,' he said, and Nathan realised she was still sitting in the van. She didn't move. Adrian reached in and hauled her out, setting her on the ground. He held her shoulders.

'Oi, Nathan wouldn't date someone who fainted at the first sign of violence,' he said. 'Get a grip.'

'Adrian!' Nathan said.

Cynthia shook herself.

'I'm okay,' she said in a small voice.

'Good,' Adrian said. 'Go inside. I'll be with you in about twenty minutes.'

He drove off. Damien supported Nathan inside.

'I believe Lily has got into the habit of keeping tea here for stray humans,' he said. 'Shall I check? Miss Rymes, there's a blanket in that cupboard. Please lay it on the sofa so Mr Delacroix can sit down.'

Cynthia laid out a blanket, then retreated to the far side of the room, watching the proceedings warily. Nathan spent the next few moments wondering when the hell Damien had managed to learn Cynthia's last name, and how, and deciding that sometimes it was best not to know these things. No doubt, Damien now knew everything about her, from the precise time she'd been born to the exact shade of her favourite colour. Damien was thorough like that.

The man in question pressed a cup of tea into Nathan's hands. He was dressed more casually than Nathan had ever seen before. Usually, Damien wore smart clothes. This evening, he was in soft tracksuit trousers and a plain white T-shirt. His feet were bare. He had probably been on his way to bed.

'Sorry,' Nathan muttered.

'What for?' Damien asked.

'For disturbing your evening.'

'No need to worry, Mr Delacroix. Lily is fond of you. She would be most disapproving if I were to turn you away in your time of need.'

Damien's logic: If you were Lily's friend, you were special. Fuck everyone else.

'Thank God for Lily,' Nathan replied.

'Indeed, Mr Delacroix.'

Okay, this was getting too weird.

'Only my teachers call me that,' Nathan said. 'You may as well use my first name. I use yours.'

'Nathan, then,' Damien replied, unbothered. Like he'd just needed an invitation to use Nathan's first name. Old vampires were so strange.

Nathan sipped his tea and began to feel vaguely human again. Tired, but human. He wasn't in shock, at least.

Adrian got back halfway through his second cup, which was good because he didn't want to find out if Damien would make him a third cup. Damien made his tea far too strong, and there was only so much earl grey Nathan could drink in one go.

'Here,' Adrian said, handing the Sihr knife over to Damien. 'For your perusal. We seem to be collecting them.'

Damien took the knife and, with the lack of personal regard of someone who could not die, sliced his own arm with it.

'Curious,' he said. 'It is designed to draw strength from the person it cuts. I suppose there's a ritual involved.'

'Chanting,' Nathan said. 'In Arabic.'

'Talk me through the events of this evening,' Damien said, so Nathan did, including both the salacious and the gory details this time. When he explained how he'd used the spirit knife, Adrian made an impressed sound.

'It'd be a waste if you didn't become a hunter,' Adrian said once he was done with his story. 'I mean you're eighteen and you just fought off three guys twice your size.'

'Humans are easy,' Nathan said. He looked at his hands. A cloying realisation had just hit him. 'I killed the one guy. I didn't even think about it. I just stabbed him in the heart.'

'Uh oh,' Adrian said. He got up and went to the drinks cabinet, pouring a tumbler of whiskey.

'Drink.' He shoved the tumbler into Nathan's hands.

'Is that a good idea?' Cynthia asked.

'Yes,' Adrian said grimly. 'Trust me, I've been here. Drink, Nate. Then I'm getting you in the shower and you're going to bed.'

'I concur,' Damien said. 'In the morning, we will investigate these Sahir. For now, I will open the guest rooms for you.'

'Just one,' Adrian said. 'Put Nate in my room.'

Damien nodded and left the room.

'Drink, Nate,' Adrian repeated. Nathan drank. The whiskey burned his throat. It was smoky, like Monica's magic. Adrian refilled the glass and had him drink again.

'That's enough,' he decided. 'Let's get you upstairs.'

Adrian took Nathan into the guest bathroom and helped him strip his clothes off.

'I can do it myself,' Nathan said, trying to bat his hands away.

'You sure?' Adrian asked. 'I don't want to come in here and find you trying to drown yourself in the shower.'

'I'm sure,' Nathan said, even though he wasn't. He wanted space. Adrian seemed to sense that.

'Don't lock the door,' he said. 'I'll bring you a towel.'

Nathan did manage to get himself undressed and under the shower. It took a while to heat up. Nathan stood under the cold spray, which got hotter and hotter until it burnt him. When he couldn't take it any longer, he turned the temperature down. It wasn't as though he could hurt himself. He had Adrian's blood in his system; he'd just heal. But he was so tired, and he couldn't get into bed until he'd got the blood off.

Compartmentalising his emotions was second nature. He put his worries and fears to the back of his mind and focused on the now. Wash the blood away. Wash his hair. Scrub himself down a second time, just in case. He had a new thin scar on his abdomen, which went to show that vampire blood wasn't a perfect remedy. Once Nathan deemed himself clean, he climbed out the shower and dried himself. Then he wrapped the towel around his hips and went in search of Adrian.

Cynthia was sitting in the hall, wearing Lily's silky pyjamas. She squeaked in surprise and scrambled to her feet.

'I wanted to make sure you were okay—I—oh God,' she blurted out.

'Sorry!'

'It's alright,' Nathan said. 'I'm just really tired. Will you... be okay?'

'Yeah,' Cynthia said. 'I called my mum and she's freaking out, but Adrian convinced her I was safe until morning. It is safe here, right?'

Nathan nodded. 'It's safe. There are all sorts of wards, and Damien would kill anyone who tried to break in, anyway.'

'Okay,' Cynthia said. 'I'll see you in the morning. I hope, well,' she paused and seemed to rethink what she'd wanted to say. 'Never mind. Nathan?'

Nathan grunted to show he was still listening.

'Thanks. I don't know what I'd have done without you.'

'You're welcome.'

Adrian's room was one of the guest rooms, though he seemed to have pretty much made it his own. Nathan wondered how close he and Damien really were, that they lived in the same house when Adrian was in town. Adrian was sitting on the bed, and he chucked Nathan a T-shirt and boxers.

'You okay?'

'Fine.' Nathan was too tired for modesty. He changed where he was and crawled into bed.

'Fucked up, insecure, neurotic, and emotional?' Adrian asked.

'That too.'

'I'm worried at how tired you are,' Adrian said.

'Worry tomorrow,' Nathan mumbled. Then he was asleep.

CHAPTER FOURTEEN

WHEN NATHAN WOKE UP, the room was lit by daylight. It was raining outside. Adrian was sprawled out on the bed beside him, fully dressed and playing with Nathan's phone.

'Anna texted you,' he said, tossing the phone onto Nathan's pillow. 'I sent her a reply telling her you were staying at Matt's place—he seemed like your closest friend, or maybe your only friend, based on your message history. And by the way, your passcode was pathetically easy to crack.'

'Dick.'

'Are you more alive today? I was kind of worried you were going to die in the night or something.'

Nathan took a moment to assess. No aches of any sort, but he did have a blinding headache.

'I'll live,' he said. 'Does Damien have food? I'm starving.'

Adrian snorted. 'Cathy Rymes is on her way over, and will be bringing human food,' he said. 'I reckon you have about fifteen minutes to make yourself presentable before she descends upon us.'

'Brilliant.' Nathan sighed.

Damien was a perfect gentleman and did not appear concerned about surrendering his kitchen. Cynthia went with her mother. Emma ended up with Nathan, somehow, because seven-year-olds were curious and had no sense of self-preservation. Nathan would know. That was how he'd met Adrian.

She perched herself on the sofa where Nathan had taken up residence. Damien had no paracetamol for his headache and trying to move around had revealed that he was still alarmingly weak. He felt like an invalid, and he hated it.

'Hi,' Emma said.

'Hey,' Nathan answered hoarsely.

'Did you really save Cynthia from the bad guys?'

'Apparently so,' Nathan said.

'That's cool.' Emma peered around and caught sight of Adrian, lounging on the other sofa.

'Are you two related?'

'Yes,' Adrian said without looking at her.

'Are you brothers?'

'No,' Nathan said. 'Adrian is my dad's brother.'

'He looks funny,' Emma said. 'The air around him is all dead.'

Auras were what happened when a person had magic. Full human meant no aura, so Nathan had none. Monica's was the smoky haziness of her magic, grey in colour — that, she had once confessed to him, was the irrevocable stain of having used dark magic. Her aura had apparently once been blue. Cynthia's family all had a mix of colours, possibly because shifters were more in tune with the elements.

Vampires didn't have magic, but they were magical. Magic kept them alive after death. As a result, their auras seemed to have a sort of anti-magic effect: the air around them went dead. It was like the vampire was a black hole, sucking in the energy around it. Nathan hated looking at it, so he had got into the habit of blocking the sight when he was around Adrian. This applied to all vampires except Lily and Damien, whose auras were the colour of red wine.

'I'm a vampire,' Adrian explained.

'No, you're not,' Emma replied.

'Pretty sure I am, actually. I died forty years ago, kid.'

'That's not possible,' Emma said. 'You don't look forty.'

'I just turned sixty-eight,' Adrian said. He tossed his phone on the coffee table and sat up. 'Why's it not possible?'

'It's day, and vampires burn in the daylight,' Emma said. 'I saw it on TV.'

What TV programmes was she watching?

'Not if we drink blood,' Adrian said. 'Sorry to disillusion you.'

At that moment, Damien entered the room. 'How are you feeling, Nathan?'

'Rough.'

'Freaking weird that my blood didn't heal you,' Adrian said.

'Don't swear,' Emma told him. Nathan burst out laughing, which made her look very put out, but Adrian getting scolded by a kid was just too funny.

'Are you hysterical?' Adrian asked. 'Can I hit you?'

'No!' Nathan snorted.

'I expect it's the nature of the magic in the knife,' Damien said. 'Although you could heal the physical wound, the actual harm was in the draining of his spirit, which is something vampire blood cannot touch.'

'That's problematic,' Adrian said. 'Will he get better?'

'The fact that he is still alive means he will make a full recovery, I'd expect,' Damien said. 'If he was going to die, he would have already done so.'

'Wow.' Nathan flopped back on his sofa. 'That's so reassuring.'

'You're welcome,' Damien said.

Cynthia and her mother brought the breakfast into the dining room a short while later. The moment Nathan entered, wearing Adrian's size-too-big clothes and feeling rather sorry for himself, he was engulfed in a huge mum-hug.

'Oh Nathan,' Ms Rymes sighed. 'Cynthia told me what happened. That's twice you've saved my girls. I don't know what we'd do without you.'

Nathan didn't get hugged particularly often. A bit bemused, he said into her hair, 'Cynthia'd probably find less trouble.'

'Oh dear,' she said, pulling back. 'You don't know my daughter very well, Nathan.' She patted him down, her eyes roving his face. 'Are you alright? Have you told your parents? Won't they be worried?'

'I doubt it,' Nathan said. 'I think Dad's in Taiwan, anyway, and I don't know what the time difference is.'

Ms Rymes looked rather alarmed. 'I thought you were injured.'

'Adrian fixed me up.' Nathan steeled his shoulders. 'It's okay. Hunters don't really worry about this stuff.'

That made her look even more concerned. Nathan considered how to dig himself out of this hole, but luckily Adrian—smirking like the jerk he was—came to Nathan's rescue.

'It's alright, Cathy,' he schmoozed. 'I'll look after Nathan.'

Ms Rymes gave him a rather dubious look.

'Adrian is Nathan's uncle,' Cynthia said helpfully.

'I see...'

'It's complicated,' Nathan said. 'Can we eat now? It smells

delicious.'

'Yes, sorry Nathan,' Ms Rymes said, hurrying him into a chair. 'You must be starving.'

Monica called halfway through breakfast. Adrian answered his phone, listened for about a minute, then put the phone in the middle of the table.

'You're on speaker,' he said.

'Oh good,' Monica said. 'Nathan Sebastian Delacroix, what part of 'don't get stabbed by the Sihr knife or you'll die' did you not understand?'

'Hi, Monica,' Nathan replied tiredly. 'I was a bit too busy with other things at the time to remember your advice.'

'You idiot!' Monica howled. 'You can't die, you stupid bloody idiot!' And then she burst into tears. Nathan gave Adrian a horrified look. Adrian looked dumbfounded. Monica never cried.

'Um, I'm not dead,' Nathan said tentatively. 'Still around for you to bully. Hoping it stays that way for a long time.'

'Shut up.' Monica sniffed. 'You're an arse. Next time I see you, I'm going to slap you.'

'You do that,' Nathan said. He'd promise pretty much anything if it made Monica stop crying. 'In the meantime, reckon you could clarify my chances of dying?'

'Let me ask Noura.' Monica must have put her phone down, because there was nothing except for white noise for a few minutes. 'Okay, Noura says that if the ritual wasn't completed you have a good chance of surviving. It depends on your soul's ability to fight off the black magic.'

'Oh joy,' Nathan said. 'How do I do that?'

'By being strong, I guess,' Monica said. 'Noura says the pure of soul usually prevail.'

Nathan felt like he'd swallowed a stone. 'How do you suppose purity of soul is measured?' he asked. 'Reckon the fact that I murdered the guy who tried to do me in is going to be, like, a black mark against me?'

'Er,' Monica began tentatively. 'I'm not sure... I think it's okay, I mean... it was self-defence, so I don't think that would affect it. I mean, when I—' Nathan coughed loudly, and she cut off. 'Um, yeah, I'm on speaker, so we won't go into my history with black magic, but I don't think self-defence damages the soul,' she finished. 'Anyway, magic doesn't tend to be that precise. Purity of soul could mean anything really. Purity of spirit, purity of mind, purity of body...'

Nathan managed to inhale a sip of coffee. He spluttered loudly. When he returned to the conversation, Monica asked, 'Nate, what are you going to do about this?'

'Not precisely sure, yet,' Nathan said. 'But I seem to be better at improvising than planning. Why?'

'I believe she wants to know whether we intend to tell the Council,' Damien said.

'Yeah, that,' Monica said.

'Shouldn't you have done that?' Adrian asked.

'I did tell the Witch Council they had a black mage in their territory, and they were very la-di-da about it,' Monica pointed out.

'Wasn't that a separate issue?' Nathan asked.

'Well, it shouldn't have mattered,' Monica said. 'They clearly didn't investigate Kseniya, or they'd have found the other mages, too. And whilst we're on the topic, how'd they find you and Cynthia? I know you gave her an anti-tracking amulet, and as we all know, your anti-tracking amulets are solid gold—'

'Monica,' Nathan said warningly, shooting an uneasy look at Damien. Damien raised an eyebrow.

'So it was you who provided my daughter with her amulet,' he said, unamused. 'Clearly hunter services are dependable these days.' His tone made it clear that those words were *not* intended as a compliment.

'An-y-way,' Monica enunciated, 'How'd they find you?'

'I think I know the answer to that one,' Adrian said grimly. 'They used good old-fashioned tracking methods.'

'Damn,' Nathan said.

'What?' Monica asked.

'We went from TWL to the dance,' Nathan said. 'We were looking for Kseniya, you know, the city's worst kept secret...'

'You took Cynthia into TWL?' Monica asked. '*You idiot!*'

Nathan winced. He definitely deserved that.

'Maybe not our brightest moment,' he said. 'They must have just followed us from there.'

'And Nate was too busy snogging to notice,' Adrian said. Nathan kicked him. 'Ouch, Nate!'

'Nate,' Monica said, 'Sometimes you really do miss the blindingly obvious.'

'I had noticed, thanks.'

'Maybe I should fly back,' Monica said. 'You lot clearly can't manage without me.'

'You don't have to fix everything,' Nathan hastened to reassure her. 'I'm sure we can handle it.'

Monica sniffled.

'Anyway,' Nathan added, 'We've got two dead Sahir and one in prison. How many of these guys are there? How likely is it that they're going to be back on their feet and trying to kill us again tomorrow?'

'I don't know,' Monica said thoughtfully. 'Hold on—Noura!' She vanished. Nathan caught Adrian's eye.

'Even if they crawl out of the woodwork,' Adrian said, 'You're not handling them.'

'Oh, don't,' Nathan said. 'What are you going to do? You can't stalk me and Lily at the same time.'

'I prefer the term 'providing remote protection'.'

'There's a very fine difference between that and stalking,' Nathan pointed out. 'If you pop up at my school, they'll try and arrest you for creeping.'

'I'm more subtle than that.' Adrian huffed.

Adrian actually made an excellent bodyguard, or at least, no one had ever managed to land a scratch on Lily—despite Damien's innumerable enemies. But Nathan had a much more personal issue with Adrian trailing him to keep him safe.

'If Dad found out, I'd be up the creek,' he said, helping himself to more coffee. 'And I'm already up the creek with Dad, so thanks, but no thanks.'

'So,' Monica said pointedly over the phone, 'Noura says that the Sahir are a renegade branch of the West Asian Magical Convention, which governs the practice of magic in that region. About a hundred years ago there was a big power struggle over whether it's acceptable to kill humans for magic. The Sahir were stronger, but the WACM enlisted the help of the Council and the Russkiy Shabash—which is a huge Russian coven, one of the biggest in the world—and the Sahir were forced to surrender. Most of them went to ground after that, so they have no idea how many exist and no way of finding out.'

'Well then,' Adrian said. 'We're screwed.'

'Language,' Cynthia said.

Something had just occurred to Nathan—something which he should have thought of earlier. 'Would Kseniya have been part of Russkiy Shabash?'

'Maybe,' Monica said. 'But she might have come from a smaller coven. I mean, even when I knew her, she practiced very, ah, non-mainstream magic.'

'By non-mainstream, we're referring to black magic,' Adrian deduced.

'Let's say it was in that sort of moral grey area that the Council turns a blind eye to, mostly,' Monica said. 'Why, Nate?'

'Because it just occurred to me that Kseniya had the same tattoos as the guy I... yeah,' Nathan said.

'Are you sure?' Monica asked.

'Pretty sure.'

'Be sure.' Monica sounded scared. 'When I knew Kseniya, she did bad stuff, but she wasn't murdering kids.'

'She did get kicked out of your coven,' Adrian said. 'Why?'

Silence.

'Monica?' Nathan asked delicately.

'I, uh, I've gotta go,' Monica said. 'Noura needs my help with a spell, and Jeremiah's gonna murder me when he sees my phone bill. Nate, don't get killed. I'll get back to you. Ciao.' She hung up.

Adrian picked up the phone and started at Nathan.

'So, Monica's hiding something.'

'Witches,' Nathan said. 'They're as bad as you vamps.'

'There's someone else we could ask,' Adrian said. 'If we think this is important.'

Nathan considered and discarded that idea in an instant. 'Monica would never forgive us if we went behind her back and spoke to Jeremiah.'

Adrian made a face but didn't disagree.

'Perhaps we could turn our attention to an aspect of the issue which we have so far neglected,' Damien said. They all turned to face him. He nodded to Cynthia. 'Why have the Sahir appeared in Oxford, under the noses of the Council?'

'I think they're being protected by the Witch Council,' Adrian said.

'I agree,' Nathan said. 'But why?'

'No idea, but the alternative is that the witches haven't noticed, and that would be literally mind-blowingly stupid.'

'On the other hand, that means they lied to us when Monica and I reported Kseniya,' Nathan said.

'You've been to the Witch Council?' Adrian asked jealously. Nathan ignored him.

'Why would they lie?' he asked.

'I presume they feared that whatever they told Monica would find its way back to the Vampire Council,' Damien said. 'No doubt, they wish to handle the problem by themselves. It's typical of the three sides of the triumvirate.'

That felt like another dead end. Nathan sipped his coffee and thought that they were kind of going around in circles with this. No one seemed to be doing anything, or if they were, it wasn't working. And no one was sharing information. Was this how hunters felt all the time?

'At least they followed us to my school, not Cynthia's,' he said thoughtfully.

'I think we should leave town for a bit,' Ms Rymes put in. 'At least until things die down.'

'Mum! No!' Cynthia said.

'I believe that would be unwise,' Damien said. 'Seeing as the Sahir are pursuing your children, you would be better off remaining here, where there are people who can protect you.'

'I'm no expert,' Ms Rymes said cuttingly, 'but whatever this Council is, they don't appear to have made much of an impact.'

That was unfortunately true. Nathan winced.

'Why are they even after you?' Adrian asked.

'We don't know,' said Cynthia, 'But it's not the first time they've caught up with us. We've had to move a few times.'

Her mother shifted guiltily. Nathan turned his gaze on her.

'You know,' he said certainly.

Ms Rymes chewed her lip. 'I was in contact with them when the girls were younger,' she admitted. 'After my husband died.'

'Mum?' Cynthia asked very quietly.

'It was a bad time,' Ms Rymes said. 'I was alone with two girls. I spoke to a specialist in... necromancy. I may have inadvertently put them on our trail then. Shifters have been pursued for various aims, particularly by witches, for centuries. It doesn't surprise me that they're trying to get us now.'

Nathan wasn't sure that was the full story, honestly. Adults never gave the full story on the first try. A glance at Adrian said he thought the same, but they mutually let it slide. Nathan felt like he was on an information overload, and his head was beginning to pound.

'I need paracetamol,' he told the group at large. 'And probably to go home before Aunt Anna figures out what happened.'

'We need to pop by the prison, too,' Adrian said casually.

'Can we do that after I sleep?' Nathan asked.

'I don't see why not,' Damien said. 'I shall liaise with Jeremiah. I'm sure the Council will relish the opportunity to play intimidation games for a few extra days.'

Adrian yawned, showing off a mouthful of fangs. 'Old vampires get bored so easily,' he said. 'Just tell them not to kill the prisoner before we can talk to him.'

CHAPTER FIFTEEN

THE VAMPIRE PRISON WAS accessed through a secret entrance in the old Oxford Castle. Nathan met Adrian at the base of the Mound, an artificial hill of a purpose Nathan had yet to determine. He had climbed it in the dead of night with Matt many a time to go drink beers illegally and laugh at how cool they were. How long ago that seemed now. How young they'd been.

As with everything in Oxford, if you knew the right thing to say, you could gain access to all sorts of secrets. The secret sessions in the Sheldonian. The secret entrance under Magdalen College.

'Permittitis intrare,' Adrian said to the middle-aged ticket clerk, and discretely showed her a plastic ID card with Damien's name on it.

'That'll be ten pounds each, or eight pounds with student ID.'

Adrian pretended to withdraw the cash.

'Here's your change,' she said, but she didn't give Adrian coins. She handed him a hammered-down token with a triskelion on either side. Adrian passed it to Nathan, who pocketed it. They each took a ticket, which said 'premium tour' on it.

The guy who checked their tickets pointed them off in the opposite direction to the other tourists. 'Premium tour starts down there; we'll be with you in a moment.'

Adrian led Nathan down the passage, and they descended a flight of steps into the extensive, draughty dungeons of the prison. A false wall, operated by another acne-ridden student worker, gave entrance to the inner sanctum of the vampire prison.

Nathan studied everything curiously, marking the differences to the Witch Council's inner sanctum. For one, there were no magical illusions. For another, the anti-witch wards screamed at him from every wall. *Wow.*

'I'm not going to encounter anyone from the Hunter Council here, right?' he asked nervously.

'Damien made sure that there wouldn't be any schedule conflicts,' Adrian replied as they stepped into an antechamber. A guide was waiting for them, a man dressed in a long grey robe. His hood was down, showing that he was young, with blond hair in braids and strange iridescent tattoos on his face. A druid.

'Don't stare,' Adrian said, which was totally redundant because Nathan couldn't look away. Druids were basically a myth. They'd been ancient mages, human mages. They had no innate magic but had learnt how to tap the magic of the earth and the elements. Some people said that the origins of hunter wards lay with the druids, but others said the druids had never existed.

'I don't mind.' The man's voice had an ethereal quality to it. Timeless. 'I imagine he has never seen one such as myself before. We died out many years ago.'

'You were a druid,' Nathan whispered.

'Before I was turned, yes,' the guide said. 'I am Aodhán. I will be your guide. Will you allow me to check that you bear no witches' mark?'

'I guess,' Nathan said.

He was asked to take his top off, and the druid studied his skin. 'You have been marked in the past,' he concluded. 'You should be wary, young hunter. If you allow a witch to mark you too often, eventually it will not come off.'

Nathan felt like he'd swallowed rocks.

'Monica wouldn't do that,' he said, less certainly than he'd have liked.

'Witches are as the serpent was to Eve,' the druid pronounced. 'Their slippery magic perverts their morals. There is no telling what they would or wouldn't do.'

Clearly there was no lost love there.

Nathan was allowed to put his shirt back on, which he did with some relief. Vampires couldn't feel cold like humans could, and it wasn't warm down in the dungeons.

'Jeremiah wishes to greet you personally,' Aodhán explained as he led them through the secret passages. 'Please keep your token on you, hunter. There are many vampires who patrol these tunnels, and some may find the allure of warm, fresh blood hard to resist.'

'Delightful,' Nathan replied.

At length, after Nathan was sure they'd been led in circles a few times to confuse them, the druid stopped in front of a wooden door and knocked.

'Enter.'

The druid opened the door and led them in. He bowed low. 'Adrian and Nathan Delacroix.'

'Thank you, Aodhán.'

Aodhán retreated, leaving Adrian and Nathan to face Jeremiah. Weirdly, Aodhán had to be at least a thousand years old — ancient, even for a vampire — and yet he bowed to Jeremiah, whom Nathan knew was only about six hundred years old. Clearly, age wasn't the only indicator of vampire hierarchy.

Jeremiah didn't strike a dangerous figure. He had olive-toned skin and neatly trimmed black hair. He was in his late thirties, with cool brown eyes, a short beard, and a stocky, sturdy build. He was dressed in beige chinos and a white button-down shirt. Nathan had never seen him from up close before, but he knew the man by reputation. Jeremiah led the Vampire Council. He was scrupulously fair and absolutely dedicated to the protection of the vampire race.

'Greetings, Adrian and Nathan Delacroix,' he said in smooth, lightly accented English. Nathan couldn't place the accent. 'I don't believe we've met before,' he added to Nathan, and held out a hand.

Nathan shook it, feeling slightly disbelieving. What did you say to old, powerful vampires? 'Hi.'

'Hello,' Jeremiah replied. 'Monica has mentioned you to me before. She thinks very highly of you, and I am told that she will wreak a vengeance most painful if you are to be harmed by a vampire in my territory.' He said the whole thing with a faint air of amusement, as though Monica was an unruly child, and he was humouring her threats.

'I... I would be very grateful if I wasn't harmed,' Nathan said. 'I seem to have enough trouble with witches, these days.'

'You have my assurance that the vampires will extend you the highest standards of hospitality,' Jeremiah said. 'Can I offer you a drink? We are waiting for Damien. I would excuse him for being late — he makes a habit of it. His way of chafing against authority.'

Adrian smirked at that, and even Nathan managed a smile. Damien chafing against authority like a preteen. Vampires could be hilarious, sometimes.

'I'm okay, thanks,' he said.

'Very good, then we shall wait.'

They all sat in an awkward, but brief silence. Five minutes later, Damien strode in. He didn't have to follow a guide.

'Let's get started,' he said.

Jeremiah nodded. Together, they walked even deeper into the rabbit warren of tunnels and descended another flight of stairs. Nathan would have missed the stairs if Jeremiah hadn't been leading them; they were well hidden. At the bottom, the walls were closer together, and everything seemed darker. The wards became even louder, and he rubbed at his temples.

'Forgive me,' Jeremiah said. 'Vampires are less sensitive to anti-magic wards. I did not consider that they would be a problem for you, Mr Delacroix.'

'It's fine,' Nathan said. 'I can tolerate it for a little while.'

'If it is required, I can find an amulet that will block their effect for you.'

'No, really,' Nathan repeated. 'It's fine. I don't need any favours.'

You never wanted to owe a favour to a vampire. It was an irritating fact of their extraordinarily long lives: they never forgot when you owed them a favour, just like they never forgot a grudge. Adrian had once hinted that Damien had turned him because of a grudge he'd held against a long-dead Delacroix ancestor. Nathan didn't want his hypothetical future grandchildren paying in blood because he hadn't been able to tolerate a few anti-magic wards.

'Your nephew has a most sensible attitude,' Jeremiah remarked to Adrian.

'It runs in the family.' Adrian's tone was totally devoid of respect. Nathan admired Adrian's ability to sass literally anyone. He had no sense of self-preservation whatsoever.

Finally, they entered a corridor with a row of cells down one side. Their black mage was the only prisoner in residence, and despite the wards Nathan felt his presence. It was like being in a room with a decaying corpse.

'I think you will have more trouble with this one than you anticipate,' Jeremiah said as they stopped in front of the second last cell.

'He has proven remarkable stoic.'

He certainly looked stoic. He sat on the floor, arms resting on his legs. It was cold, but he appeared unbothered. His tattoos seemed to writhe on his skin in the flickering torchlight. Now that Nathan could get a good look at him, he was about forty, with blond hair and a thick scar slashed across what was otherwise a fairly attractive face. A few days' worth of beard growth was gathered on his chin, but otherwise he was smooth skinned. Probably of northern European descent. He regarded them coolly, and his blue eyes finally fixed on Nathan.

'You're the boy who killed Hans.'

The familiar guilt roiled in Nathan's stomach. Hunters frowned on the killing of mortals, and witches, despite being supernatural, were also mortal. There was a special branch of the hunters who dealt with witches, but Nathan knew almost nothing about them.

Adrian shifted slightly in front of Nathan, an oddly protective gesture. 'You don't talk to him,' he said.

'You brought him here, vampire, which means I can speak to him as I wish.' The mage gave them a toothy grin. 'I rather speak to him. He is unusually talented for a boy. And he has borne the mark of a witch. I think he and I have much in common.'

'You have nothing in common,' Adrian replied. 'You're steeped in black magic.'

'Strange how you deplore me, yet you yourself have many marks against your soul,' said the black mage.

Adrian didn't flinch.

'We are not here to compare scores,' Damien said smoothly. 'I assure you, you will lose. In the interest of expediency, I suggest you answer our questions.'

'I have no information for you, vampire.'

'Perhaps I have not made myself clear.' Funny how Damien could make such a mild tone sound so threatening. 'You answering would be the expedient route. However, I have cleared my schedule for the whole afternoon, and I assure you that I have plenty of creative ways to extract the information I seek.'

'You may try.'

Nathan thought that challenging Damien was a foolish idea. When vampires had been alive as long as Damien had, they tended to get rather bored with life. They also had an awful lot of experience to draw on. Bored and creative was a dangerous mix when it came to torture.

Jeremiah handed Damien a key, before heading for the stairs.

'Do recall that someone has to clean up your mess,' he called as he walked off. 'The last person who had to clean up after you was traumatised and had to have their memory erased.'

'I shall endeavour to improve on my previous performance,' Damien replied in what was probably as close to a flippant tone as the man ever got. Nathan shuddered.

'Will the boy watch as you torture me?' the mage asked with amusement. 'You induct your hunters young these days.'

'You think I can't take it?' Nathan asked boldly, irritated that the mage had singled him out as the weak link.

'You will not,' the mage said certainly.

'We're not inducting him,' Adrian said, coming to Nathan's rescue as usual. Nathan felt another surge of irritation. 'He can come and go as he pleases. And if he pleases to watch you suffer, well, that's his due. Your friend nearly killed him.'

'He doesn't seem like such a vengeful soul,' said the mage.

Nathan took out one of his knives, playing with it in what he hoped was a casual way. 'How can you tell?'

The mage laughed. 'Ahh, you are trained by hunters, but you act more in the fashion of the original hunterkind. It is written in your aura, the mark of the *druidēs*. They upheld peace and balance, not vengeance.'

What?

'Humans don't have auras.'

'Perhaps not to your eyes, but to those trained to see it, it is there,' the mage replied.

Nathan glanced at Adrian, who looked as dumbfounded as he felt.

'Don't listen to him,' Adrian said. 'He's just trying to distract us.'

'Why would I?' the mage asked. 'I have no interest in postponing my torture. The Sahir are trained to be unbreakable.'

'Seeing as you are so confident,' said Damien, 'Let us begin.'

He unlocked the cell door without a care for the prisoner trying to run away. Why would he be bothered? No human could run faster than a vampire. Adrian entered the cell and Damien locked the door behind him again. Nathan felt his stomach turning in anticipation.

Did he really want to see his uncle torturing someone? Half of him said yes, because maybe then he could go back to hating vampires.

Whatever the answer was, he steeled his shoulders.

'Question number one,' Adrian began in an affable tone. He had a knife in his hand suddenly, and Nathan hadn't seen where it came from. 'What do the Sahir want in Oxford?'

'The Sahir are strong. The Sahir are all-powerful.'

'Wrong answer,' Adrian said mildly. Then he backhanded the mage. The resounding clap of flesh on flesh only met Nathan's ears several moments after his eyes had processed what had happened. The mage's whole body flew sideways, and a red mark bloomed instantly on his skin. He righted himself, smirking.

'The Sahir are strong,' he repeated. 'The Sahir are all-powerful.'

Adrian twirled the knife.

'I wonder how all-powerful this Sahir will feel when he's missing a few fingers?'

'The Sahir are strong. The Sahir are all-powerful.'

'Trust me,' Adrian said without a hint of impatience. 'I heard you. What do you want with the shapeshifters?'

'The Sahir are strong. The Sahir are all-powerful,' the mage repeated. It was becoming his mantra. Nathan had been trained in basic techniques for resisting interrogation. Repeating the same words over and over had been part of the training.

Adrian didn't seem concerned. He raised the knife and then, too quick for Nathan's eyes to register, there was a line down the mage's arm. It cut through two of the tattooed cuffs around his biceps.

'Who is giving you your orders?' Adrian asked.

'The Sahir are strong. The Sahir are all-powerful.'

Then Adrian punched the man. His head flew back and slammed against the wall, and it was the first time that he showed any sign of weakness. It took him several moments to right himself. His mouth was bloody, and he spat a mixture of blood and saliva onto the floor.

'You will break my body before you break my mind,' he promised.

'I'd hardly count that as a loss,' Adrian said. 'Nate here's quite adept at knocking out your mates. We can always pick up someone else.' He launched the next question immediately. 'Where is the headquarters of your operations?'

'More will come, stronger will come,' the mage said. 'The boy will die. His death will be on your conscience.'

'I don't have a conscience,' Adrian said agreeably. 'Ask Nate, he's constantly complaining about it.' The knife flashed. Blood welled up from the man's forehead and cheek, obscuring one of his eyes. Nathan's stomach turned.

'Why is the Witch Council protecting you?' he asked.

'The Sahir are strong. The Sahir are—'

'All-powerful, yes, yes, we got that,' Adrian replied, sounding bored. 'If they're so all-powerful, why haven't they come for you yet? I'd have thought the all-powerful Sahir could get one guy out of prison.'

The mage spat blood again. He didn't wipe his face. 'The Sahir are too complex for your simple mind to comprehend.'

'Ah,' Adrian drawled. 'Is that your way of saying they're not coming for you? They've left you to die.'

'No one is greater than the whole,' the mage said.

'Well, you're certainly not.' Adrian hit him again. Nathan's stomach turned again.

'Why do you want the shifters?' Adrian repeated his earlier question.

'The Sahir are strong. The Sahir are all-powerful.'

Adrian crouched down right in front of the mage. His voice, when he spoke, was soft but penetrating. Nathan thought you could cut glass with that tone.

'I see you haven't quite grasped how this is going to work yet,' he said in a powerful approximation of Damien's easy manner. He played the knife over the man's neck. 'That's okay,' he murmured. 'I have time.'

The knife barely flicked, and Nathan's brain seemed to shut down for precious seconds. When it came back, he registered blood, so much blood, and then the wound, raw flesh. Adrian had literally sliced a chunk out of the man's arm.

'The Sahir are strong,' the mage repeated in a hoarse voice. As if he'd been screaming, except he hadn't. 'The Sahir are all-powerful.'

Nathan couldn't take it anymore. He backed away. Damien heard him and turned to look. Nathan forced himself to meet the man's eyes.

Damien nodded to him, as though granting permission. Nathan retreated, desperate to get out of hearing distance before he regurgitated the contents of his stomach. He didn't want the mage to know he'd been right.

Nathan was the weakest link.

Adrian found him outside, at least an hour later. Aodhán had shown Nathan the way out and provided him with a bottle of Lucozade. He was sat on the railing going up to the Mound, his legs dangling over the side.

Adrian leaned beside him, picking blood out from under his nails.

'It's okay, you know.'

'It's not okay,' Nathan replied.

'It is okay,' Adrian disagreed. 'Hunters kill because it's necessary, not because they enjoy it. Not wanting to watch someone being tortured does not make you weak.'

'What about feeling guilty because I killed a man who tried to kill me?' Nathan asked.

'That makes you human, Nate.'

Nathan kicked his foot against the fence support and felt it bounce off. Again. Again.

'Cynthia's not talking to me,' he said at length. 'What if she's scared of me, now?'

'Then she's an idiot,' Adrian said. 'You saved her life.'

'She's human,' Nathan pointed out. 'Humans are scared of people like us. Because we are capable of killing.'

'People like us?' Adrian asked.

'You know what I mean.'

'I think you just put you and me in the same box,' Adrian said. 'Nate, I think your logic is flawed. You're worried you'll become me, but the truth is, we've never been the same. The only thing we have in common is that we were both equally talented. But I was arrogant. I went for initiations immediately. I pursued bigger and bigger prey. I got reckless. You're not like me. And the truth is, you probably never will be.'

Nathan stared unseeingly at the ground below him. Finally, he pushed himself off the fence to land on the flagstone floor.

'It wouldn't be terrible,' he said, 'Being like you. You're strong.'

'Thanks to circumstances,' Adrian said. 'I think you're doing okay. Don't be so hard on yourself.'

'I can't let it lie,' Nathan said. 'The hunters might not protect the right people.'

Adrian reached over and ruffled his hair. 'You'll work it out.'

Nathan ducked away from him sheepishly. He wasn't sure he liked Adrian complimenting him. It felt off. His own father didn't seem to believe in him, but Adrian—the vampire—did.

'I can't believe you played the vampires off against the witches like that,' Adrian said. 'That was smart. And *brave.*'

'What, the hospitality comment?' Nathan asked. 'I didn't even mean it the way it came out.'

Adrian shook his head. 'You are rubbish at taking credit for your own abilities, kid.'

CHAPTER SIXTEEN

NATHAN RAN HIS TOWEL over his forehead once more and stretched his shoulders. The gym was almost empty. It had been a good session, the first really good one he'd had since his injury.

'You're back on form,' Adrian remarked.

'Finally.' Nathan shoved his towel in his bag. 'That knife really took it out of me.'

'Never again,' Adrian vowed.

Nathan frowned. 'Had any luck with the mage?'

'Not yet. I know Damien was down there today.' Adrian looked grim. 'Never met someone who Damien couldn't crack.'

Nathan shifted. 'Maybe we need to find another way.' *A better way,* he wanted to say.

Adrian's gaze was dark. 'Leave it to us. You don't need to worry about it.'

'But I do.' His phone buzzed. Nathan pulled it out and saw the time. 'I have to go, it's almost dinner time.'

'Want a lift?'

'No thanks, I've got my bike.'

Adrian nodded. They picked up their bags and meandered out. As they went, Nathan idly checked his messages. Monica was being awfully chatty; her way of dealing with her worry.

Nathan: I met a druid

Nathan: He hates witches

Monica: Holy shit, like an actual druid

Monica: They died out like a thousand years ago

Monica: Course they hate us, they never could do real magic

Adrian laughed when Nathan relayed the conversation.

'Aodhán is something else. He creeps me out.'

Nathan shrugged. 'Most old vampires creep me out.'

'Yeah… but you're food.'

It shouldn't have been funny, but they both laughed. Nathan hit Adrian on the arm. They reached his bike and he unlocked it.

'See you soon?'

'Text me,' Adrian replied.

'Sure.'

A week into November, it was starting to get cold. Nathan cycled briskly through town, dodging the traffic, and soon pulled up at home. The sweat turned cold on his back when he saw his Dad's car.

Oh fuck.

He locked his bike and reached for his phone, but before he could ring Adrian, the front door opened.

'Nathan, is that you?' Aunt Anna called. 'You're late—your parents are here.'

'Why?' Nathan stepped into the light from the front door, trying not to give away his panic. His hands were sweating. 'I thought they weren't coming until Jess's birthday.'

'It was unexpected. Come in, they can explain it to you.'

Nathan trailed his aunt into the kitchen, running over a thousand different reasons why his parents might be here. He was unable to shake the feeling that they'd somehow found out about his friendship with Adrian. That would be the worst.

'And where have you been?' His father was sat at the head of the table, in full uniform, looking painfully imposing.

'Training,' Nathan said. His father frowned.

'Training?' he asked. 'You didn't have training today. It's Sunday.'

'I train on my own, now,' Nathan reminded him. 'Sundays are a good day to train. The gym's pretty empty.'

'What about homework?' his father asked.

'What about it?' Nathan asked. 'I did it yesterday.' Except bio, but no need to tell Dad that.

Aunt Anna set a plate of food in front of him. Nathan tucked in hungrily. 'What are you doing here?' he asked between bites. 'How long are you staying?'

'Nathan,' Aunt Anna chided, 'at least say hello to your mother.'

'Hi, Mum.'

Nathan's mother had long blond hair which she always wore in a strict ponytail, and she was sturdily built. She could probably pick

Nathan up. He wasn't sure about his odds in a fight against her, not that he wanted to fight his mum, anyway. Would she ground him if he won? Would she be proud? Nathan's mother had never expressed any kind of affection towards her children, that he could remember. She had never been the sort of mother to kiss scrapes and bruises better or read bedtime stories. Aunt Anna had done that.

'Hello, Nathan,' she replied. 'How's school?'

'Fine, thanks.' Nathan turned expectantly to his dad.

'We've been called here by the Council,' Dad said. 'They need us to look into a few things. It might keep us in town for the next few weeks.'

'Oh,' said Nathan. His stomach was making a concerted effort to tie itself into knots. 'What's the business?'

'Classified.'

'Come on!' Nathan scowled at his plate. 'Everything's always classified.'

'I can't discuss Council business with non-Council members, Nathan.'

That was what Dad always said. Nathan gritted his teeth in irritation. Nothing ever changed.

When his parents were both there, they always became forcefully involved in everything, and conversely, everything in Nathan's life got ten times harder.

Mum drove him to school the next morning, but Nathan couldn't think of a word to say to her. He checked his phone instead and found that Cynthia had messaged him.

>**Cynthia:** My mum is driving me CRAZY
>
>**Cynthia:** Ughhhh
>
>**Nathan:** Anything I can do?
>
>**Cynthia:** Can I come over tonight? Just for a bit?

Nathan hesitated with his fingers over the keyboard.

>**Nathan:** Sure, but my parents are here
>
>**Cynthia:** O.O cool. Will they mind?
>
>**Nathan:** Maybe? But come. We can always go out to the pub
>
>**Cynthia:** Thanks!

'Can I have a friend over tonight?' he asked.

'You'd better ask Anna,' Mum said. 'It's her house.'

'She usually doesn't mind.'

'And that means you don't need to do her the courtesy of asking?'

Nathan huffed. 'Fine, I'll text her.'

Aunt Anna was fine with it, of course, but the more Nathan thought about it, the more stressed out he got.

'Matt, have your parents met Poppy?' he asked during a spontaneous bout of nerves at lunch.

'Maybe?' Matt asked. 'I think Mum did, for like five seconds on her way to work one day. She was pretty cool with it. Why? You thinking of introducing Cynthia to Anna and Jeff?'

'No, to my folks.'

Matt had never met Nathan's parents, but he'd certainly heard tales. His eyes went wide.

'Um, you sure, mate? That seems serious.'

Nathan shrugged. 'I like her.'

'Wow, how'd that happen?' Matt asked, bemused.

'Not sure,' Nathan said. 'It just did.' He thought about it for a moment. 'I guess it just makes sense.'

'Lucky,' Matt muttered. 'Nothing about Poppy makes sense.'

Dad picked him up from school. When Nathan climbed in the car, his father held up a hand for silence. A voice was emanating from his phone, which was mounted on the dashboard.

'...know Jeremiah's hiding something.'

'We'll crack it,' Dad said. 'Anyway, Patrick, I've got to go. I'm picking my son up from school.'

'That's alright. I'll ask June to pull those photos for you and leave them on your desk.'

'Bye,' Dad said. He hung up and turned to Nathan. 'How was school?'

'Fine, same as always.' Nathan buckled his seatbelt. 'Who was that? Patrick Longhorn?'

Patrick Longhorn was the head of the Hunter Council, Uncle Jeff's boss.

'It was,' Dad said reluctantly.

'Was it about the case?'

'Nathan, that's enough.'

'Come on, Dad.' Nathan scuffed his feet against the footwell. 'You never tell me anything.'

'If every hunter broke the rules for their children, we would have no discipline whatsoever.'

They drove in silence for a while. Nathan stared out the window. Oxford had turned cold and grey; it was raining. Even the thought that Cynthia was coming over later didn't lift his low mood.

'Anna said you're having a friend over,' Dad said suddenly.

Uh oh. 'I am.'

'Who is this friend?'

'Her name is Cynthia Rymes. She goes to Headington school.'

'Is this the girl we spoke about the last time I was here?' Dad slowed the car to turn onto their street.

'Yeah.'

'I thought you said you weren't involved with her.'

'I wasn't last time you were here.'

Dad sighed. 'Nathan, you're meant to be sorting your priorities out, not muddling them with some girl.'

'She's not some girl!' Nathan scowled. 'All hunters have lives outside of hunting. Why am I not allowed to?'

'That's not what I'm saying. You need to learn to only take on what you can manage.'

'I don't decide what I take on! You're the one who pushed all this stupid training on me that I'm probably never going to need!'

'That's enough, Nathan.' Dad turned into the driveway a bit more forcefully than necessary and braked sharply. The moment he cut the engine, Nathan jumped out and stomped inside.

'Nathan?' Aunt Anna called.

'Not now, I have homework!'

But although that was true, he didn't get much done. When Cynthia texted him that she was on her way over, he pulled on a hoodie and jogged down to the bus stop to meet her.

'I am so glad to see you.' Nathan kissed her firmly. When Cynthia pulled away, her cheeks were red.

'What was that for?'

'My parents are so...' Nathan shook his head. 'You'll see.'

'Are you sure they don't mind?' Cynthia slid her hand into his. 'I really don't want to intrude.'

'They hate everything I do.' Nathan swallowed his anger. Cynthia was looking more and more worried. 'Look, don't worry. I'm sure they'll be nice to you.' He tugged her in the direction of his house.

'What did they come for?' Cynthia asked.

'Council business. They've been asked to look in on something. It happens occasionally.'

'How long are they here for?'

'However long it takes.' Nathan squeezed her fingers. 'It's okay, I guess. They're not staying with us, but they'll be in and out at random times. And they like to get involved in everything.'

'And you're not used to that. I get it.' Cynthia laced their fingers together. 'You could always come to mine sometimes. Deal with my mum, instead of yours.'

'What's up with her, then?' Nathan asked.

'She wants to leave town.' Cynthia sighed gustily. 'Like we didn't just get here. And find a nice place to live. And make friends. It's just — this is what we always do. It's not fair.'

'We'll figure it out,' Nathan promised. *I hope.*

They reached his house a short while later. Everyone else was already in the kitchen. Nathan and Cynthia joined them, Cynthia looking distinctly uncomfortable.

'So, this is the girl?' Dad asked.

Cynthia steeled her shoulders.

'Hello, Mr Delacroix,' she said. 'Nathan's told me all about you.'

Dad looked at her, weighing her with his eyes. Cynthia stared right back at him.

'Interesting,' Dad said. 'Usually he tries to pretend he doesn't have parents.'

'Really?' Cynthia asked. 'I get the feeling he wishes his parents were more involved in his life.'

Oh no.

'He's right here,' Nathan said before they could get any further into their battle of wills. 'Dad, this is Cynthia Rymes. Cynthia, my parents — Benjamin and Kathleen.'

'Pleased to meet you,' Cynthia said haughtily, as though she had proven some kind of point against them.

'Well, at least she doesn't back down from a fight,' Dad said.

Cynthia made a face. She didn't come from a family where not backing down from a fight was a trait to be admired.

Nathan gave her a sheepish grin and gestured to a chair.

'Have a seat,' he said and slid in beside her.

They served themselves and began eating, accompanied by an

awkward silence. At length, Aunt Anna broke it.

'Cynthia... what does your mother do?'

'Um, she's a digital assistant. She does PA work for people online.'

'Sounds useful,' Mum said.

'I guess. It's flexible.' Under the table, Nathan caught Cynthia's hand and squeezed it.

'Nathan said you might be in town for a while,' Cynthia continued tentatively.

Dad frowned in Nathan's direction.

'Nathan, you know you shouldn't be talking about these things,' Mum chided.

'What was I supposed to do, not tell people you were here?'

'A few weeks,' Dad said, cutting across them. 'We've business for the Council. It's not the sort of thing to discuss over dinner, though.'

Silence fell again. Cynthia was frowning. Nathan cast about for something to say to reassure her, but nothing came to mind. In the end, Dad broke the silence.

'I saw Jason this afternoon,' he said. Jason was Nathan's cousin, Anna and Jeff's son.

'Yes, he said he was in town,' Jeff said. 'He's hoping to transfer to the local division.'

'He's getting married in April,' Aunt Anna said proudly.

'To the Gainer girl?' Mum asked. 'What was her name—Ella?'

'Elladora,' said Aunt Anna. 'That's the one. She's affiliated with the southwest division, so Jason's hoping to transfer either here or Bristol.'

'To be honest, we need the labour here,' Uncle Jeff said. 'The Council runs us ragged. Did you hear about the murders last year? A journalist and a professor. Wiped under the carpet of compulsion, of course. The vamps call it 'taking care of the secrecy statute'.' He glared at his plate as though his peas were personally responsible for vampire corruption.

'It's a sin,' Dad agreed. 'Running the Council out of such a small city. We've tried a dozen and one times to get them to move to London. Or, hell, Brussels, Frankfurt, anywhere with a decent population where they could blend in. There's just too much risk of discovery here.'

'And of course,' Uncle Jeff said, 'The civilians find out, and the vampires take it as a carte blanche to hunt.'

Nathan sat very quietly, chewing his food.

'What's the new replacement like?' Dad asked. 'That—Christian?

He was always a problem. Savaged a few hunters for doing their jobs.'

'He got what was coming to him,' said Uncle Jeff. 'Hope the new guy does, too. Although they say it was a human who got Christian— but no one can prove it, thank God, last thing we need is the Vampire Council coming down on the hunters for breaching the treaty.'

'An untrained human?' Mum asked. 'That's unheard of.'

'Must have had some training,' Uncle Jeff said. 'But then, it would have to be one of ours who did the training, and that would be treaty breach, as well.'

'It's a bad situation all round,' Dad said.

'Isn't it always, with vampires?' Mum asked. She looked at Nathan and Cynthia. 'I hope that's a lesson to you two,' she added. 'Don't you go getting involved with vampires. It never ends well.'

'Yes, Mum,' Nathan mumbled.

'Are they all that bad?' Cynthia asked.

'Yes,' Uncle Jeff said firmly. 'Don't trust them for a second. The moment you turn your back, they'll sink their fangs into your neck.'

Nathan glanced at Cynthia. She met his eyes, confused. He caught her hand under the table and squeezed it, trying to convey that he didn't believe what his parents believed.

Some vampires were different. They had to be.

Nathan walked Cynthia to the bus stop again after dinner.

'Sorry,' he said. 'That probably wasn't the relaxing evening you were hoping for.'

'Are your parents always like that?' Cynthia asked nervously.

'More or less.' Nathan scuffed his toe against the floor. 'They care,' he said finally. 'They just don't show it very well.'

'You're not like them at all.' Then Cynthia smiled. 'I like your aunt.'

'Aunt Anna's great.' Nathan grinned. 'But don't get on her bad side. She can be brutal, too.'

Cynthia laughed.

Once he'd seen her onto the bus, Nathan dragged his feet back to the house. Predictably, Dad was waiting for him, stern look firmly in place.

'We need to talk.'

Nothing good ever followed those words, in Nathan's opinion. Grimacing, he joined the adults in the lounge.

'I know what it looks like, Dad, but—'

'You are lucky Anna thought to warn us that your girlfriend wasn't human,' Dad snapped. 'Nathan, *what are you thinking*?'

Oh shit.

'It's not like—she's not a vampire,' Nathan said. 'I'm friends with Monica. Come on, Cynthia's one of the most normal people I know!'

'We are hunters. Doesn't that mean anything to you?'

Nathan felt his temper flaring up again. 'Well, I'm not. Thanks to you.'

'So that's an excuse to go kissing a shapeshifter? Don't be ridiculous. We have *values*, Nathan!'

'Maybe our values are wrong!'

His father stared at him. Nathan watched the emotions play over his face. Confusion, anger, sadness, more anger.

'You bring supernaturals into the house, you spend time kissing and holding hands with them.' His father shook his head. 'I can't help but feel this is my fault.'

'What?' Nathan asked, confused at the change in tack.

'If I had been more present when you were growing up, you wouldn't have entertained so many doubts. If I had been firmer with you when I caught you spending time with Adrian—'

'Dad, can't you let the thing with Adrian go? I was seven and I didn't know he was a vampire!'

'I know,' said Nathan's father. 'I can't help but feel that I've failed you.'

'You haven't failed me,' Nathan said. 'Maybe I just want to... explore different options.'

'What other options are there?' his father asked. 'You're a hunter. We are hunters. What could possibly be more important than keeping humanity safe?'

Looking his father in the eye, Nathan was afraid. He was terrified. He steeled his shoulders. 'It's not protecting humanity that's the problem, Dad,' he said. 'It's the way we do it.'

The room exploded. Everyone was talking at once, Nathan caught snatches of anger from almost everyone. Only Aunt Anna was calm. She crossed her arms.

'This is completely unreasonable,' Dad snarled.

'Don't call your son unreasonable,' Aunt Anna replied. She got right up in Dad's face, even though she was more than half a foot shorter than him, and glared Nathan's father down like he was an errant teenager. 'He's eighteen. This is natural.'

'This is not the way we work! He wants to protect this—this creature—for what? Because she's his girlfriend? Because he'd rather hold her hand and kiss her than protect humans from vampires?'

'It's not because she's my girlfriend,' Nathan said clearly. His heart raced in his chest. Everyone turned to look at him.

'It's not because she's my girlfriend,' he repeated. 'It's because this is the right thing to do.'

'Nathan!' Mum hissed, but Nathan was finished. He jumped up and headed for the door.

'We're not done here,' Dad called.

'I'm done,' Nathan replied, heading for the stairs.

CHAPTER SEVENTEEN

NATHAN CLOSED THE FRONT door gingerly, shivering in the brisk wind which had come up. Silently, he crept around the side of the house and let himself into the garage.

It wasn't that excursions to the garage needed to be kept secret; it was that his parents were still around, and that after their argument four days ago, they were sticking their noses into his business more than ever.

The garage was cold. Nathan flicked on the lights and the electric heater and settled himself at Uncle Jeff's workbench. His latest amulet was still where he'd left it, almost complete. He only had one rune left to add, and then it would be finished and ready for testing.

Not one of them had worked yet, but seeing as hunting was becoming an increasingly distant career option, Nathan was determined not to give up on warding.

Flicking on the lighter, he lit the seven candles arranged around the workspace and carefully checked the chalk circle which Aunt Anna had helped him design. It channelled magic from the environment and the elements into the amulet, which Nathan placed in the centre of the circle. Seven runes, each on their own little tablet, made up his protective sequence. Of those, he'd finished six. Now, clearing the others from his workspace, Nathan set into carving the seventh. This one was *brindaz*, to burn. Aunt Anna thought he might have better luck with fire amulets.

Once the rune was carved, Nathan sanded the wood and set the tablet in the middle of the circle. Picking up a piece of chalk, he closed the front edge of the circle, and then he focused his energy.

There wasn't really a formula for this part. All Nathan had to do was concentrate on his intention and soak the tablet in a mixture designed to allow it to absorb magic. Simple in theory; in practice, he was soon sweating, and his mind kept wandering.

Would it work?

Probably not.

Was this really worth the amount of time he was putting into it?

What would Dad think of this hobby?

Was the amulet starting to glow? Please let it be starting to glow.

SLAM!

Nathan's focus shattered as the house door fell shut. That was Dad; he couldn't seem to come and go quietly. Voices filtered down to him a moment later.

'...seems to get more complicated by the day,' Dad complained.

'Antonius was hinting that he thinks it's one of us,' Uncle Jeff replied.

Nathan froze, hardly daring to breathe.

'I certainly hope not,' Dad said. 'That'll be a mess.'

'If it gets back to the witches...'

'Dark magic is dark magic,' Dad said. 'The kill was probably justified.'

'If every one of our hunters went off on their own whenever they saw a dark mage, half the witches in town would be dead and we'd have anarchy on our hands,' Uncle Jeff complained. 'The treaty only works because we all keep our people in line.'

'I know. What's their evidence?'

'Looks like it was done with a spirit knife.'

A chill ran down Nathan's spine. Outside, his father made a noise of surprise. 'A spirit knife? Haven't run across one of those in a few years.'

'Almost unheard of these days.'

'Can't even think what would have happened to ours.'

'Adrian had it.' Uncle Jeff's tone was grim. They'd stopped moving only metres from where Nathan sat. A car door opened.

'Can't have been him,' Dad said. 'Lore says they can only be wielded by marked hunters.'

'That's what I've heard.'

'So we're looking for, what? Old family. Head of a family, if they've got the spirit knife.'

'Maybe. I'm not sure how many families even hold to those traditions, anymore.'

Both men were silent for a moment, contemplating.

'Can they be sure?' Dad asked.

'No, never sure. Especially with the bodies being mishandled. But you know vampires. They're not going to miss a chance to pin an Abuse of Power charge on us.'

'Messy,' Dad said. 'We might have to pull in more resources. Well, we'll discuss it tomorrow. Nine o'clock?'

'See you then.'

The car door slammed, and the engine started. A moment later, the front door shut as well, and Dad's car pulled away. Nathan sat where he was, not moving, staring at the faintly glowing amulet.

Oh shit. Oh *shit*.

After a few moments, he forced himself to snap out of it. This was bad. This was epically bad. He fumbled his phone out of his pocket.

Nathan: Bad news, we need to meet NOW

Adrian: Crap. Where?

Nathan: Do you know how to get onto the Mound from the back? Without paying?

Adrian: I'm a vampire. I do not pay

Nathan: Meet me on top.

Adrian was already waiting when Nathan scrambled up the muddy bank. The first thing he did was pass Nathan a bottle of Jack Daniels.

'I thought we might need a bit of liquid courage.'

'We might.' Nathan sagged onto the bench and opened the bottle, taking a swig from it. It tasted foul without any mixers, but it burnt, and he was screwed, and alcohol did not judge.

'Spit it out then.'

'Dad's onto us.' Nathan relayed the conversation he'd just overheard. When he finished, Adrian was silent for a moment.

'Shit,' he said finally. 'Jeremiah's not let anything on; I've been working with him.'

'Jeff mentioned Antonius. He's the new Vamp Council member, right?'

'Christian's replacement.' They both stared pensively off into the darkness. After a moment, Adrian added, 'It was self-defence. The law is definitely on your side.'

'Think that's going to fly with Dad? I didn't report it.'

'Can you report it now?'

They exchanged grimaces.

'Dad won't like it,' Nathan said. 'And I'm not sure it will help.'

'Jeremiah will advocate for you, probably. He doesn't want dark witches around town either.' Adrian paused and held his hand out. Nathan passed him the bottle. He drank long and hard. Vampires healed too fast to get drunk, which meant they had to drink too fast to heal. Or something. 'I've been hearing whispers.'

'More bad news?'

'The witches don't seem to be too pleased either; there were two dead witches, but I can't find out more. They won't tell us anything.'

'Dead Sahir?' Nathan asked, alarmed.

'Civilians.'

'Do you think it has something to do with the Sahir?'

'Hard to say. They blame the vampires. But if we have evil witches in town and people are dying, I'm not inclined to go looking for a different culprit.'

'Occam's razor.'

'Precisely.'

Nathan took the bottle back and cradled it in his hands. 'Do you... think I'm doing the right thing?' he asked finally, swigging from the bottle.

'Not sure anyone's asked me that in a long time,' Adrian replied, accepting the bottle back and taking another pull. 'I'm not exactly considered the local expert on moral behaviour.'

'I looked in my dad's eyes and told him I didn't want to be a hunter if it meant killing people who didn't deserve it,' Nathan said. 'I mean, I didn't say those words, but as good as.'

'So? He deserves to finally hear that you feel differently to him.'

'You never told me that being accepted by the spirit knife made me the head of the family,' Nathan mused.

'I never told you anything about it,' Adrian said. 'For example, that any wound inflicted on another family member, you will feel double. Or that the punishment for attempting to claim it and not being worthy would be a curse. Every Delacroix who isn't worthy and tries to claim the knife is destined to die young in battle.'

'Is that true?' Nathan asked, helping himself to more whiskey. 'Or an old wives' tale?'

'Who the fuck knows?' Adrian asked. 'Sebastian's name was on it, and he died at twenty-five. It skipped my father, and he lived for-freaking-ever. And he was the arsehole who told me if he ever saw me again, he'd kill me.'

Nathan passed the bottle back over. Adrian needed it more.

'If I ever initiate,' Nathan said, 'Which is seeming increasingly unlikely, when I have to thank the people who helped train me, I'm going to have to mention you.'

'Dare you,' said Adrian. 'I'd pay good money to see the look on your father's face.'

'I thought vampires never pay.'

'I might make an exception,' Adrian replied. 'It'd be... the ultimate revenge, for him to realise that he raised you to hate me, and I beat him.'

'Is that what this is?' Nathan asked. 'Is that why you approached me?'

'Nah,' Adrian said thoughtfully. 'You look like Sebastian.'

'Really?' Nathan asked. 'I don't think I've ever even seen a photo of him.'

'My dad hid them all,' Adrian replied. 'Seb was... the prodigal son, you know? None of us ever came close, he was brilliant. No. I was brilliant. He was perfect. And he — excelled. I mean — I never came close to beating him... And then, suddenly, he was dead. Dad was never the same.' Adrian stared at the sky. 'You look the same as him, you did back then, and I guess I just... wanted to know you.'

'Am I like him now?' Nathan asked.

'Nah, we were an arrogant generation, thought nothing could touch us. You'd have hated Seb, he was a snob,' Adrian replied.

Adrian's phone rang, then. He handed the whiskey back to Nathan. 'I have to take this, it's Lily. I'll be right back, okay?'

Nathan nodded. Adrian jogged off a little way down the Mound, and then he was out of sight. The streetlights didn't reach up here to illuminate him, and Adrian's aura didn't glow.

One moment Nathan was alone, and the next he wasn't. He didn't see or feel it happen. He blinked, and a figure was there. A robed figure. He used his phone as a torch and saw blond braids and iridescent tattoos.

'Aodhán,' Nathan said. He put the bottle down and stood up.

'Good evening, Nathan Delacroix,' said Aodhán. 'My apologies for intruding upon your evening.'

'Good thing you did it now,' Nathan said. 'I don't plan on being sober for too much longer.'

Aodhán smiled with that same faintly patronising humour that most old vampires had.

'I should warn you, you are not the first youth to think of drinking up here. In fact, it is such a prevalent habit that we have a number of young vampires who enjoy lying in wait to feed on easy prey,' he said. 'Perhaps it is not wise for one such as you to linger in such proximity to our inner sanctum. It might be considered... temptation to breach the Council treaty.'

'Is that why you're here?' Nathan asked.

'I only feed on particular victims,' said Aodhán. 'You do not fulfil the criteria.'

That was enough information to last Nathan a lifetime. 'Cool,' he said. 'Wish I hadn't asked, really.'

Aodhán chuckled. 'Fear not, young hunter,' he said. 'I merely wish to talk.'

He reached for Nathan. Nathan froze, but Aodhán only touched the protective amulet around his neck. It was the one he'd been working on earlier. He'd strung the tablets from a twisted leather cord.

'You pick oak,' Aodhán said. 'Not a typical wood for amulets. It signifies wisdom, power, survival. Why were you drawn to this wood?'

'I don't know,' Nathan said honestly. His brain was shorting out with the vampire's hand so close to his chest.

'Did you know that the oak tree was the symbol of the druids?' Aodhán asked.

'No.'

'We were the people of the oak. Druids had a complex reputation, but at the heart of it we sought wisdom, inner strength, and communed with the elements to maintain balance,' Aodhán said. 'For a time, your people and mine were one. Eventually, the hunters separated themselves. They believed there could be no balance with the supernatural and dedicated themselves to its extermination.'

'That's... quite a leap.'

'Indeed, it was also quite a betrayal,' Aodhán said, 'to take teachings of balance and turn them to murder.'

'Yeah... I can see that,' Nathan said.

'Should you ever have any interest,' Aodhán said, 'there is much I could show you. The world is not so narrow a place as the hunters believe, and magic is in everything, if only you understand how to draw it out.'

'I…' Nathan breathed.

'Think on it.' Aodhán dropped the amulet and drew back.

'Oi, Nate, Lily wants to know if we want to meet her at New College!' Adrian called.

'Sure!' Nathan shouted back. He blinked.

Aodhán was gone.

CHAPTER EIGHTEEN

NATHAN WAS SURPRISED AND relieved to find himself alone in the house the next day. Mum, Dad, and Jeff were at the Council, even though it was Saturday, and Aunt Anna and Jess were out. Nathan took the opportunity to invite Cynthia over.

'Sorry we haven't seen much of each other lately,' he said as Cynthia kicked her shoes off in the hall. 'Feels like Mum and Dad are everywhere.'

'It's alright.' Cynthia shrugged her coat off. 'Things haven't been much better back home.'

'I get it,' Nathan said. 'Come on, Aunt Anna made lunch for us to reheat.'

After lunch, they found themselves in Nathan's room doing homework. Well, Cynthia was doing homework. Nathan was fiddling with her hair and occasionally helping.

'S'ennuyer?' she asked.

'To be bored of something. Come on, that's not hard.'

'Shut up and conjugate it, then.'

Nathan rolled onto his back. 'Je m'ennuie. Tu t'ennuies. Il/elle s'ennuie. Nous nous ennuyons. Vous vous ennuyez. Ils/elles s'ennuient. And in a sentence, conjuguer les verbes françaises m'ennuie.'

'That's mean,' Cynthia said, knocking him on the arm with her book.

The doorbell rang.

'I better get that.' Nathan padded downstairs, pulling open the door. On the doorstep was a figure in a hooded burgundy robe, with a purple aura. A Witch Council guide. They were almost never seen outside of the Council inner sanctums; at least, not in official uniform.

'Woah!' Nathan backed up a step, drawing a knife.

'Nathan Delacroix, I mean you no harm,' the guide said. It was a man.

'Yeah, take your hood down and tell me that to my face.'

'It is not the way of Council guides to reveal themselves frivolously,' the guide said. 'Nathan Delacroix, you have been summoned before the Witch Council.'

'What? Why? What would they need me for?'

'You are permitted safe passage to the inner sanctum. They merely wish to speak.'

'What about?' Nathan asked.

'That is not for me to reveal. The elders will explain.'

Holy crap, he was being summoned by the witch elders. *This is bad.*

'I'm going to need some kind of guarantee,' Nathan said.

'Time is of the essence. What guarantee would you like?' the guide asked.

Nathan thought fast. 'I want my friend to come, too, also with safe passage.'

The guide went still for a moment. His aura dimmed and brightened again.

'I am permitted to make this bargain. Fetch your friend.'

'I'll be right back.' Nathan shut the door in the guide's face. Cynthia was waiting on the stairs.

'What's going on?' she asked.

'No freaking clue, but I hope you don't mind visiting the Witch Council.'

'Oh, wow.'

Nathan wrote a note for his aunt, and they left. The guide was still waiting on the doorstep. Behind him on the street was a black Audi sedan. The driver was utterly silent as he opened the doors for them.

On the trip over to Magdalen Bridge, Nathan called Adrian to explain the situation.

'What would the Witch Council need you for?' Adrian asked.

'No idea, I was hoping you might know.'

'No effing clue,' Adrian said. 'Please keep your eyes sharp. I can't protect you in there.' Vampires were not permitted in the inner sanctum of the Witch Council.

'I know,' Nathan said.

The driver dropped them and their guide at the punt rental place, which looked rather gloomy now that winter had arrived. There was no need to prove themselves to the whiskery old man; he recognised the guide and waved them through. Before they could get on a punt, the guide stopped them.

'The Elder has asked me to provide a mark to give you and your friend safe passage. Or you may wear the mark of another witch, should you have one in mind.'

It wasn't sensible to wear the mark of a witch you didn't know. 'I do, actually,' Nathan said. He looked at Cynthia. 'Have you got Monica's wristband?'

'Yes.' Cynthia pulled it out of her bag.

'Will that do?' Nathan asked.

'Yes,' the guide said. Cynthia put the wristband on. Nathan stayed as he was.

'Won't you wear a mark?' the guide asked.

'No,' Nathan said. He could always put it on later, but he wanted to see what happened.

'On your head be it.' The guide handed them each the Council token. 'This will grant you entry to the wards.'

The guide steered the punt, and Nathan held Cynthia's hand. In summer, this might have been romantic. Today, Nathan felt like he'd swallowed rocks. The wards seemed particularly hostile.

Cynthia oohed softly as they entered the tunnel.

'Where are we?'

'This is witchspace,' the guide said. 'We are nowhere that corresponds to the human world.'

'Technically, though,' Nathan said, 'We're under Magdalen College.'

'Don't ruin the mystique,' Cynthia said.

In the main hall, there was one elder and a small army of aides. Nathan counted seven. This must be big business.

'Pay your respects to Elder Nettle,' the guide instructed. A different elder, then, although Nathan couldn't really tell the difference. This one's robe was grey.

Nathan knelt, tugging Cynthia down beside him.

'Nathan Delacroix, be welcome,' said the elder. He had a very gravelly voice, but he wasn't as discernibly ancient as Elder Rowan had been.

'Elder Nettle,' Nathan said. 'To what do I owe the pleasure?'

'A small matter,' said Elder Nettle. 'Easily resolved, I hope.'

'The hunters have no quarrel with the witches that I'm aware of,' Nathan said cautiously. 'And I would not be able to answer for them.' This was easier when Monica was here to do the talking.

'The druid vampire guide has brought to our attention that we owe you a boon,' said Elder Nettle.

'You do?' Nathan asked. *Aodhán had done what?*

'You were injured by one of our own. This is in violation of our treaty with hunterkind. Therefore, we will grant you a boon, as an apology.'

Nathan considered that for a moment. The witches shifted impatiently.

'May I confer with my colleagues?'

'Our guide will accompany you to a room from which you may use your mobile phone,' Elder Nettle said. The guide headed for the door, and Nathan obligingly followed him. Cynthia fell into step beside him.

'What's going on?' she whispered.

Nathan had no idea, but there was no way he was admitting that. 'I want to get advice from Monica,' he said instead. 'Supernaturals are tricky, and I don't want to say the wrong thing.'

'Wise,' the guide remarked, proving that—as Nathan had expected—he was listening in.

They were led into an antechamber, and Nathan dialled Monica. Aunt Anna was going to kill him when she saw his phone bill this month.

Monica was incredulous. 'Are you joking?' she demanded once Nathan had explained the situation.

'I wish I was,' Nathan said. 'What do I do?'

'Will they let you postpone the boon?'

'I don't think so.' Nathan shot a cautious look at the guide. His face was still hidden, but he somehow managed to convey impatience. 'Yeah, probably not.'

'Shit.' Monica was silent for a moment. 'What do you need?'

'Dunno. Immunity from the dark mages? For them to leave Cynthia alone?'

'I wouldn't aim too high,' Monica warned. 'This is like… a ritual. The witches are saying, *oops, we fucked up and let someone stab you, and we really don't want you to report us, so please take a little present in exchange for your silence.* You need to ask for something that says, *I'm really not happy, and you're going to have to try harder in future, but for now I'll play your game.'*

'I'm never going to be a politician.'

'Can I make a suggestion?' Monica asked.

'Go ahead.'

'We need information, and the prisoner isn't talking. That means we need access to someone who will talk, and a way to force them to talk.'

'Uh... this is starting to sound like one of those ethical grey areas.'

'It is,' Monica said. 'You have to name someone by name, and we only know one black mage in town by name.'

'Kseniya.'

'Yeah,' Monica said.

'So I ask for her, and then what?'

'She becomes yours. You can mark her.'

'WHAT?' Nathan asked, aghast.

'Nate, it's okay, just roll with it,' Monica said.

'It's okay?' Nathan hissed. 'Monica, people aren't birthday presents! You can't just give them away!'

'It's not what you're thinking, not like binding a slave,' Monica said. 'It's more of a kind of guardianship. Look, this might be a good thing, Nathan. You could help her.'

'You're so sure she needs help.'

Monica was silent for a long moment. 'If it were me,' she said finally, 'and I was the one involved in some shit magic...'

Nathan swallowed. 'I wouldn't leave you to fuck things up, I swear.'

'I don't know if Kseniya has anyone to help her,' Monica said. 'She grabbed you, at TWL that time. I don't think that's a coincidence, Nate. I think she knew you could help.'

Nathan wanted to say, *I'm just eighteen and I have no idea what I'm doing.*

But he couldn't say that. If it were Monica, he would do whatever he could to help her.

'Fine. Tell me what to say.'

Monica coached him. Witches loved loopholes and messing this up could go badly. 'You have to say it exactly right,' Monica instructed.

'Don't get anything wrong, or they'll try to wriggle out of it.'

'I know.'

'It's time,' the guide said. 'The elders grow impatient.'

'Alright, got to go,' Nathan said.

'Good luck!' Monica replied. Nathan had a feeling he was going to need it.

The guide led them back to the main chamber.

'Have you made your decision?' Elder Nettle inquired.

Nathan took a deep breath. This was it.

'As my boon, I would like you to transfer guardianship of the witch and marked black mage, Kseniya Krovopuskova, to me in my capacity as a hunter and guardian of the balance between the supernatural and human worlds.' His heart was pounding as he finished speaking. He stared at the elder and tried to show no fear. *This is what I want, this is what I want...*

The aides were all shuffling in dissatisfaction. Nathan's request had unsettled them. *Good.*

'We will confer,' said Elder Nettle. He stood and exited the room, surprisingly fast for someone so old. Everyone in the room seemed to relax a bit. The air cleared of some of the tension. After about five minutes, two aides looked startled and hurried out the room. A few minutes later, Elder Nettle returned.

'Your boon has been granted.' He looked to a doorway. The two aides appeared, leading Kseniya between them. She looked even worse than she had before; basically skin and bones, her clothes hanging off her body. Her hair had been cut at some point. It hung misshapenly around her head, chopped sharply at the top of her neck. When the aides stopped, she stumbled. Nathan darted forwards and caught her. She was light as a feather, and she clung to him.

Even if Nathan hated this idea, it was probably a good one. For humanitarian reasons, if nothing else.

'Kseniya Kovopuskov has been transferred to your guardianship, hunterkind,' said Elder Nettle. 'You must mark her in the presence of our Council, before you may remove her from the premises.'

Nathan stared at the elder in panic. Mark her? He wasn't a witch. How the fuck did he do that? Thinking fast, he said, 'Cynthia, can you support her?'

Cynthia took Kseniya's weight. Nathan pulled the oak ward, the same one Aodhán had admired, from around his neck. It probably wasn't hugely effective in defending, but the important thing was that it was a token of his own abilities. He handed Kseniya the amulet. She stared at him with wide eyes.

'Go on,' Nathan murmured, using the same voice you'd use to soothe a scared animal. With shaking hands, she dropped the leather cord around her neck.

'Will that do?' Nathan asked the elder.

'If it must,' Elder Nettle said. Maybe he was trying to sound bored, but he actually seemed frustrated. Nathan got the feeling he'd just interfered with their plans in a big way. If only he could figure out what the plan was, and how he'd ruined it.

'Now leave,' the elder added. The guide stepped forwards. Nathan slung an arm around Kseniya. He ended up taking most of her weight. They made an oddly shaped beast, stumbling down the stairs, and she practically fell into the punt, but Nathan wanted them out of there ASAP. Kseniya didn't have any protection from the Witch Council.

'What have you done?' Cynthia asked once they were back on dry land and had returned their tokens.

I don't know, Nathan thought. 'Hopefully the right thing.'

'She doesn't look too good,' Cynthia said worriedly.

'Yeah.' Nathan pulled his coat off and shucked his jumper, handing it over to Kseniya. It probably needed washing, but it would be warmer than what Kseniya was wearing.

'They fetched her awfully quickly,' Cynthia said. 'You think she was a prisoner?'

'Maybe,' Nathan said. He took out his phone and called Monica.

'Did it work?' she greeted.

'It worked,' Nathan confirmed. 'Kseniya's with us.'

'Already?'

'She was on the premises.' Nathan frowned. 'She's not looking too good. I think we need to take her to the hospital.'

There was a long pause.

'Yeah,' Monica said. 'Okay. Do you know who the doctor is at the JR who works with supernaturals?'

'Doctor Govender?'

'Right. Ask for him. I'm going to check for flights.'

'You're coming back? Don't do that,' Nathan protested.

'Someone's going to have to look after Kseniya. You guys need the help. Nate—I heard from Adrian. *Adrian!* That your dad was here and investigating the Sahir. Not cool.'

Nathan winced. 'I didn't want to worry you.'

'Consider me worried.' Monica didn't sound worried. She sounded furious. 'I'll try to get hold of Jeremiah now, see how soon I can fly back.'

Nathan's stomach churned with worry. 'Are you sure?'

'Yes.'

'Okay, then. I'm going to call Adrian. See if he can give us a lift to the hospital.'

'Do that. I'll see you soon.'

'Yeah, see you.'

Monica hung up. Nathan scowled at the phone.

'Alright?' Cynthia asked.

'Monica wants to fly home. She always does this.' Nathan groaned in frustration. 'She always tries to solve everyone else's problems.'

'Sounds like someone else I know.' Cynthia jerked her chin towards Kseniya, who was sitting on a low wall, shivering. 'We need to get her out of the cold.'

'Yeah. Let me call Adrian.'

Adrian was as frantic as Monica had been. 'Are you alright?' he demanded. 'I don't need to kill any witches, do I?'

'Fine, and no,' Nathan said. 'But I do need a lift.'

'Where are you?'

'Magdalen Bridge. We have Kseniya with us.'

'What?'

'I'll explain later,' Nathan said. 'How quickly can you get here?'

Adrian had no regard for traffic laws, so he pulled up in his Volkswagen Golf in double-time.

'Can you take us to the JR?' Nathan asked.

'I'm okay,' Kseniya whispered. Nathan glanced back at her. She was huddled up like a frightened animal.

'You need to go to a hospital,' Nathan said.

'I'm okay, please,' she begged. 'No hospitals.'

'Yeah, I agree with Nate,' Adrian said drily. 'And lucky me, I'm driving.'

He didn't pull off yet, though. Nathan gave Kseniya a pleading look. 'Just let them make sure you're okay,' he said. 'We'll keep you safe.'

Kseniya fingered the amulet around her neck. 'You made this?' she whispered.

'Yeah,' Nathan said. 'I won't let anything happen to you, I promise.'

Kseniya nibbled on her lip nervously and finally nodded. Adrian pulled the car off the pavement.

'How the fuck did this happen?' he asked.

'I got a boon from the witches because that guy stabbed me,' Nathan said as Adrian did a hair-raising U-turn, making the tyres squeal. 'Seriously, I'm surprised you have tyres left, Adrian.'

They made quick progress to the hospital, and with some persuasion, elicited Doctor Govender's presence. Kseniya was whisked away into a hospital room, and Nathan, Cynthia, and Adrian settled outside to wait.

'Monica wants to fly back,' Nathan told Adrian.

'Figures,' Adrian said. 'I'll bet she's been planning it since Halloween.'

'I wish she wouldn't. The internship was important to her.'

Adrian just shrugged. 'It's Monica. Anyway, Jeremiah can sort something out for her.'

Nathan turned away in dissatisfaction. A moment later, the doctor came out of the room and headed off. A nurse followed him out and beckoned to Nathan. He stood up to join her.

'Are any of you related to Kseniya?' asked the nurse.

'No, we're… friends,' he replied awkwardly.

'We need to know what happened to her,' the nurse said. 'So that we can figure out the best treatment.'

Nathan mulled that over for several moments.

'I'm not exactly sure,' he said finally, trying to stick as close to the truth as possible. 'I hadn't seen her in a while, but she called me for help today.'

The nurse looked unhappy. 'She's over sixteen, right?'

Nathan honestly had no idea. 'Yes.' He shrugged.

'I can't discuss her treatment with you, but she seems quite unwilling to talk to the doctor. Is there any way you could…?' The nurse frowned.

'Let me speak to her,' Nathan suggested, even though he had no idea what he'd actually say.

He steeled himself and headed into the hospital room. There were two beds, separated by a screen. A middle-aged lady was sleeping on the other. Kseniya looked very small and young, lying in her bed and covered by a thin blanket. Nathan felt an odd surge of protectiveness.

'Hi.' He edged over to the bed. Kseniya watched him, wary like a wild animal. She brought a hand up and clutched at the amulet, so tight her knuckles went white.

'It's okay.' There weren't any chairs, so Nathan sat on the edge of the bed. 'How're you feeling?'

Kseniya's eyes darted to the nurse and back to Nathan. She nodded hesitantly.

'Okay?' Nathan asked, not understanding. Hesitantly, he switched to Russian. 'Ty v poryadke?'

'Da,' Kseniya mumbled. It was pretty obviously a lie.

'Okay,' Nathan said again. 'Well, Doctor Govender is one of us, so you can trust him. Hopefully we can sort you out and then you can come home with us, alright?'

Kseniya nodded. With shaky fingers, she took the amulet off and held it out. Nathan frowned.

'You can keep that.'

'You don't need it?' Kseniya croaked. 'You're not... protected without it.'

'I don't think it works,' Nathan told her gently, mindful of the nurse who was fluttering about the other patient. 'It was just an experiment to see if I could make it.'

Kseniya stared at him in confusion. She looked down at the amulet, strung between her slender fingers.

'Keep it please,' Nathan said. 'I can make another one.'

Kseniya put the amulet back around her neck, pressing it to her chest.

'I will talk to the doctor,' she mumbled. 'If you think it's okay.'

'Yeah,' Nathan said. He hesitated briefly, then grabbed her hand and squeezed it. 'I'm just outside if you need anything.'

He left the room as the doctor entered again and collapsed onto the plastic chair beside Cynthia.

'Hey, Cynthia, you can see magic, right?'

'Yes,' Cynthia said, watching as nurses and patients bustled by.

'You know that.'

'The amulet I gave Kseniya... what do you see when you look at it?' Nathan asked.

'It glows white and gold,' Cynthia replied, furrowing her brow. 'Like all your other wards. Why?'

Nathan fiddled with a loose thread on his jeans. He'd worn old, ripped jeans in front of the Witch Council—his father would die of embarrassment if he ever found out.

'No reason,' he muttered, but his mind was racing. The amulet had never worked well for him, and it had never really looked very magical. Magic was sixty percent belief. Kseniya and Cynthia had no reason not to believe that the amulet worked, so they thought it did. Was it really that simple? Were his protective amulets failing because he didn't believe in them?

Hunters weren't brought up to believe in things they couldn't see. It was why they usually only made basic amulets. Complicated magic required leaps of faith: faith in yourself, in the person performing the magic, and in the magic itself. Hunters were too busy killing to worry about faith.

Cynthia reached over and caught his hand in hers. 'Hey, you'll figure it out.'

'I hope so.'

Nathan could do with a bit of faith in his life.

CHAPTER NINETEEN

THE DOORBELL RANG AT eight-thirty on Monday evening. Mum and Dad had just headed to their hotel, and Aunt Anna was helping Jess with her homework. Nathan opened the door and was immediately pulled into a hug.

'Monica!' He wriggled his way free. 'You're back.'

'What were you thinking?' Monica promptly burst into tears. Nathan stared at her in alarm, then beckoned her into the house. She shook her head.

'Get your stuff,' she said between sobs. 'Come over to mine.'

'Sure.'

Five minutes later, they were on their way. Monica had mostly mastered the tears, but every so often she'd hide her face behind a hand and sniffle loudly.

'I really didn't mean to worry you,' Nathan said lamely. 'I didn't want you to fly back early.'

'It's fine—I hated Morocco anyway.' Monica wiped her eyes, to no avail. 'I just... you're such an idiot. I can't believe you got stabbed. You could have died!' Her voice went up into a wail at the end.

'That's generally the intention behind stabbing someone.'

'Nathan!' Monica smacked him on the arm. 'It's not funny!'

'Ouch! Alright, alright, I'm sorry. I really didn't want you to worry. It's not like I meant to get stabbed.'

Monica looked distinctly unimpressed.

'When did you get back?' Nathan tried.

'This morning. I've unpacked, and I picked up supplies.'

'Supplies?'

'For protective wards.'

'Oh.'

Monica let them into her house, and through the kitchen into the garage. Much like Nathan's garage, Monica's had been converted into a workshop. The air was pungent with a mixture of incense, smoke, and magic. Candle stubs littered every surface, and the shelves were packed with a range of tools and materials.

'Are you running a business out of here?' Nathan joked.

'Maybe I should. Might help keep you alive.'

'Har-har. Want tea?'

'Sure.'

Whilst Monica set up, Nathan ducked back into the little kitchen and made them tea. Once he was done, he settled on a padded bench against one wall, watching Monica, who was grinding herbs in a mortar and pestle.

'Have you seen Kseniya yet?'

'Yeah, I went there before I came to fetch you.' Monica's hair hid her face as she spoke.

'And?'

'Better. She wasn't too pleased to see me.'

Nathan blew on his tea and took a sip. 'Wonder why?'

For several moments, Monica feigned intense focus on her herbs. Finally, she said, 'We parted on awkward terms. It's nothing—we'll get over it.'

'If you say so.'

'I do.'

Nathan considered that for a few seconds. Monica would come clean eventually. She usually did. He decided to let it slide. 'Any word on when she'll be discharged?'

'In a day or two. They had the drip out. They've just been watching her to make sure she doesn't get refeeding syndrome. I'm going to bring her here when she's out.'

'Is that safe?' Nathan asked.

'As safe as any other option.' Monica shrugged and set her mortar and pestle aside. From a drawer, she took two thin wooden bangles, one smaller than the other.

'Think they'll wear these?' she asked.

'Who?'

'Cynthia's mum and her sister.'

'I guess.'

Monica set about transferring her rune sequences onto the bangles.

Nathan drank his tea slowly.

'What are you going to do next?'

'I've been thinking about that.' Nathan studied the design on his cup. 'I think I should have another chat with Cynthia's mum.'

'You think so?' Monica looked up, suddenly interested. 'You think she knows something?'

'I don't buy what she told us before. The Sahir could go after any target they wanted—they're a big organisation. And they have no reason to just chase one family around the globe. It's too... neat.'

'They always struck me as opportunistic, I mean, they grabbed Emma from school, and they got you because they saw you and Cynthia at TWL.' Monica frowned. 'I wonder how they got Kseniya?'

'They definitely seem opportunistic to me,' Nathan said. 'And it's not as though they seem to be snatching shapeshifters left, right, and centre, or we'd have heard of it. So...'

'What's the missing link?'

'Exactly.'

Monica studied her bangle critically, twisting it so the runes caught the light. 'How will you get her to talk?'

'By asking nicely?'

'You think that will work?'

'Can't hurt to try.' Nathan shrugged. 'If not, I don't know. If we force her hand, she'll take the family and run. She's already giving Cynthia a hard time.'

'Has to be rough, not being able to settle anywhere, being afraid all the time.'

'Yeah, but why?'

They both fell silent, considering that. No matter how Nathan looked at it, he was missing a piece of the puzzle.

'When can you finish the wards by?' he asked.

'Give me a day or two, why?'

'I'm meant to be getting dinner at Cynthia's place sometime this week. Maybe if I take those as a peace offering...'

Monica studied the bangle thoughtfully. 'Yeah,' she said slowly, 'that could work. If I...' She frowned. 'Nate, check in that cupboard if there are any keyrings.'

Nathan pulled open one of the many cupboards at the back of the garage.

'Third shelf,' Monica added. 'There should be a box.'

'Got it.' He pulled it out and passed it over to her. Monica checked the contents.

'Perfect,' she said. 'Give me a few days, and I can whip you up something really good.'

It didn't take long for Monica to come through on her promise. On Friday, Nathan met Cynthia at the bus stop on the High Street and passed over the wrapped paper package.

'Wards for your mum and sister,' he said. 'Courtesy of Monica.'

'Thanks.' Cynthia untwisted the paper enough to catch a glimpse. 'Huh, cute. Monica's pretty artistic.'

'If they're in trouble, they can snap the bangles in half. I have the key.' Nathan showed her his keyrings. 'They'll heat up.'

'Neat!'

'Hopefully it'll be enough to get your mum to relax a bit.'

'I hope so.' Cynthia scowled. 'She's driving me up the wall. I'm sure she's hiding something, too. She dances around the topic... and she won't look me in the eye.'

Nathan grimaced. 'In my experience, adults always keep secrets.'

'I wish they wouldn't.'

'Me too.'

Nathan steered Cynthia down Cornmarket. 'Where are we meeting the others?' she asked.

'Duke of Cambridge. It's a bar. I guess Adrian's planning on compelling the bartender not to ID you.'

'Oh.'

'It's not far.' Nathan caught her hand. 'Let's talk about something fun.'

'It's almost Christmas,' Cynthia said. 'I love Christmas.'

'I can't wait for the holidays.' Nathan grinned.

A short walk later, they arrived. The Duke of Cambridge was a student bar up in Jericho, which tended towards dark, elegant décor. Adrian and Monica were already waiting. Adrian went up to buy the first round and persuade the bartender not to ID Cynthia.

'That's creepy,' Cynthia whispered.

'It's downright unethical. And by the way, it's also very bad for people,' Nathan said pointedly as Adrian came back to the table with their drinks.

Adrian rolled his eyes. 'Convenient, though.'

Nathan made a face.

'Cheers,' Monica said, and they clinked their glasses together. Nathan hoped the topic of vampire mind control would be forgotten, but of course it wasn't his lucky night.

'Can all vampires do it?' Cynthia asked after she'd taken a sip of her drink.

'Most of us,' Adrian said. 'Except Damien and Lily.'

'How does it work?'

'By imposing your will on humans,' Adrian said. 'Hypnotism, basically.'

'Only humans, though,' Nathan added. 'Doesn't work on witches.'

'Nathan's touchy because he's the only human in the group,' Adrian teased.

Nathan bristled. 'That's not true—'

Adrian smirked. 'Afraid, nephew?'

'Do you suppose it works on me?' Cynthia asked, cutting off Nathan's angry response. They all looked at her.

'No idea,' Monica said. 'You're a supernatural. It might not.'

Cynthia was the most normal, human person in the group, if you excused the fact that she could turn into an animal at will. Nathan felt his stomach twist at the idea of Cynthia being compelled.

'We could test it,' Adrian said casually.

'No,' Nathan replied immediately.

'Oi, I'm not going to make her do anything crazy. I don't even need to make her do anything. I'll know if the compulsion is taking hold.'

'No!'

'What does it feel like?' Cynthia asked. She looked at Nathan when she said that.

'I've never been compelled,' he had to admit.

'Really? What are you scared of, then?'

Nathan tensed. The comment stung. He took a drink from his mojito then put it down again—maybe a bit too hard, as some of the liquid slopped out the glass onto the table. Nathan stared at it dispassionately.

'I mean,' Cynthia pressed, 'what if—'

'I'm not going to compel Nathan,' Adrian said, and when Nathan looked up Adrian was watching him with something like pity in his gaze. It leant the lie to his next words: 'There's nothing I need from him, anyway.'

'Oh, good,' Nathan said, sarcasm barely concealing his fury. 'I doubt it would take, anyway.'

Adrian made a 'pfft' sound between his teeth. Knocking back the rest of his drink, he said, 'Next round's on Monica.'

'Drink a little slower, some of us actually have to pay,' Monica said. Adrian rolled his eyes.

'Whilst we wait for you to drink at the pace of a dead snail,' he said, 'rehash for me what Nathan's new pet witch said when you saw her.'

'Don't call her that,' Nathan said.

'You marked her,' Adrian said. 'I mean, I can't believe the Witch Council went for this whole thing.'

'It's weird,' Monica said, swirling the straw in her drink. 'I mean, witches can be weird, but this goes beyond the norm.'

'Something's off,' Nathan agreed. 'They're hiding something. You should have seen how mad they were when I asked them to free Kseniya.'

'So, she's crucial?' Adrian asked.

'If she is, she doesn't know it,' Monica said.

Nathan took another sip of his drink. 'Something feels off. I just can't figure out what.'

'This is nothing like last year,' Adrian said. 'We knew the Vampire Council was offing people, we just had to catch them at it.'

'Yeah,' Nathan muttered. 'Nothing makes sense.'

Thinking about things that didn't make sense, he reached into his pocket and pulled out a paper package. 'M, help me in an experiment?'

Monica took the package and unwrapped it deftly. 'What...' But she trailed off as she pulled out Nathan's latest protective ward.

'Is this yours?' Monica asked in awe.

'Yeah,' Nathan said. 'It's the same as the one I gave to Kseniya—'

Monica deftly draped the amulet around her neck and grinned at him. 'You've improved.'

'It doesn't work! Neither does the one I gave to Kseniya.'

'Looks pretty functional to me,' Adrian said.

'What's wrong with it?' Monica asked. 'I can feel it.' She pulled a tiny knife out of her pocket and nicked her finger, dripping blood onto the amulet. It began pulsing with a purple-grey aura.

'See, it works,' Monica said.

'Yes, but…' Nathan frowned, trying to put his frustration into words. 'Not for me.'

'Ah,' Monica said. To Nathan's considerable frustration, she gave Adrian a knowing glance.

'Kid, you're not very good at protecting yourself,' Adrian said mildly.

'I'm plenty good at it!'

'In a fight, sure,' Adrian said, but he didn't elaborate on what he meant by that. Nathan raked his fingers through his hair.

'You're not making sense.'

'You'll understand eventually,' Adrian said. 'Take it as a compliment. You're clearly very good at looking after strays.'

'I'm not a *stray*,' Monica said, offended.

'Course not.'

Monica huffed and downed her drink. 'What are your orders?'

Monica had barely stood up to go to the bar when she stiffened abruptly and slammed her hand to her side where her witches' mark was. She lurched slightly, as though drunk.

'M, what's up?' Nathan asked.

'It's witch stuff,' Monica said. She flicked her gaze all around, then started to the door. Nathan, who was closest to the edge of the booth, jumped up after her.

'Stay here,' he told Cynthia. 'I'll be right back.' He ran after Monica. She was out on the street, looking this way and that. Nathan grabbed her arm.

'What's going on?'

'I don't know,' Monica whispered. 'I felt something…'

'Focus,' Nathan said. 'Close your eyes, see if you can pick up what it was.'

Monica squeezed her eyes shut. She chanted softly under her breath, and Nathan found himself surrounded by her aura, blanketed in it. Then her eyes snapped open.

'Black magic,' she said.

'Seriously?' Nathan asked. 'Here?'

'Close,' Monica said. 'Nate, I know black magic. I've done black magic.' She grabbed his wrist, skin on skin. 'Do you mind?'

Nathan shook his head and forced himself to relax.

Being channelled by a witch was the weirdest sensation. It was like she pulled something out of him, and her magic flooded in to fill the void. Nathan felt like smoke, disconnected and dispersed. He took a deep breath and smelt the scent of Monica's magic, like a hazy room filled with candles and a big bed and the sensual touch of a lover. Monica's magic was very seductive.

Monica chanted for longer this time, before she finally opened her eyes. 'It's gone,' she said, 'but I know where it was.'

Adrian and Cynthia stepped out of DoC. Nathan could have kicked himself for leaving Cynthia alone with Adrian.

'What's going on?' Adrian tossed their coats to them.

'This way.' Monica let go of Nathan's wrists. Cynthia was staring at him oddly.

Monica led the way. Nathan fell into step beside his girlfriend and caught her hand. 'Monica was just channelling me,' he whispered. 'Borrowing magical strength.'

'I'm not jealous,' Cynthia whispered back. 'I just find all this so weird.'

'Me too,' Nathan admitted.

They followed Monica into Jericho, which was a residential area heading out towards North Oxford, all poky streets lined with lots of cars and small terraced houses. Monica walked down the middle of the road and turned into a street that was identical to the one before and the one after. As soon as she did, Nathan felt it.

Something came flying out of the darkness at them. Nathan grabbed the girls and dragged them to the ground. The magic dispersed above them, but not before Nathan had got a good handle on its feeling.

Sticky, cloying, stinky black magic. The same as the Sihr knife.

'Defendo ex malo!' Monica shouted. The air shimmered around them, but no further attacks came.

'Drop the shield,' Adrian said after about two minutes.

Monica lowered it, sagging against Nathan. Shield magic was brutal on the energy, which was why witches liked wards. Better to keep evil away than to have to defend against it. Adrian vanished from sight, moving too fast for the human eye to track. After a moment, he was back.

'They're gone.'

'I know,' Monica said. 'That was just a defence system. We triggered a ward when we entered the street.'

Adrian's face was uncharacteristically grim.

'What is it?' Nathan asked tiredly.

'They left something behind,' Adrian said, 'But I don't suggest you look unless you've got a strong stomach.'

Monica staggered to her feet. 'I'll look,' she said.

Nathan supported Monica down the road. Cynthia jogged after them and caught them at the scene of the crime.

It was... Nathan's eyes darted around, taking in everything, comprehending nothing. He caught the smell of the magic, and it smelt like nothing Monica had ever done. This was evil. This was the stench of decay. This was what ferals smelt like before hunters killed them.

It wasn't even a body, really, what was left. It looked like the body had been dehydrated until it shrunk down to the size of a prepubescent child, and then burnt. The corpse was completely blackened and oddly boneless. It didn't look like a body.

Cynthia had to go and throw up in the bushes. Monica, still leaning on Nathan, was shaking.

Adrian came up behind them, speaking into his phone. '...near the Harcourt Arms, you can't miss it. ...Thanks.' He hung up. 'Damien's on his way over. He'll take this to the Council.'

'Good,' Nathan muttered, relieved that they were passing this on to someone more capable.

Monica staggered suddenly, as though all the strength had drained out of her legs. Nathan grabbed her automatically, pulling her close. She clung to him.

'Nate, this was... this was...'

'I know, M,' Nathan mumbled. 'I know.'

This was what happened if the Sahir got you with their creepy draining rituals.

This was what they'd tried to do to Nathan.

Suddenly, regurgitating the contents of his stomach looked like quite an appealing option.

CHAPTER TWENTY

NATHAN WAS STILL REELING from discovering the body when Kseniya was discharged on Sunday. Nathan, Monica, and Adrian agreed to meet in Starbucks, on neutral territory, hoping that Kseniya would be more relaxed in a public place.

The coffee shop was full to the brim with early Christmas shoppers when Nathan arrived. He bought himself a latte, before ascending the stairs, scanning the crowd anxiously. How likely was it that there was a vampire or witch amongst this crowd? What if someone overheard them? He soothed his own fears with what he'd learnt in hunter training: the best place for a private conversation was somewhere crowded. It was much harder to pick out individual voices. Don't stand out, and no one will notice you. The guiltier you looked, the more likely people would think you were up to something.

Monica and Kseniya were sitting at a table in the corner. Nathan slid into an empty chair. 'Hey.'

'Hi,' Monica said. Kseniya just stared at Nathan.

'Hello, Kseniya,' Nathan tried.

'Hello,' Kseniya whispered back. She wrapped her hands around her coffee and continued to watch him.

'Adrian just texted me, he's on his way,' Nathan said. 'How are things at home? Are you settling in alright?' The last question was directed to Kseniya, who didn't reply.

'Fine,' Monica said. 'She has the guestroom, and I lent her some clothes, but this is really just a temporary solution.'

'I know,' Nathan said. 'Let's focus on one problem at a time, though.'

'Sahir first,' Monica said. 'Seeing as that's the potentially fatal problem.'

Adrian arrived at that moment, pulling up a chair and ruffling

Nathan's hair as he sat. 'Hey, kids.'

'Oi, you're the one with the mental age of a ten-year-old,' Monica said.

'Hey, I've been upgraded!' Adrian grinned. 'Last time, I was only five.'

Monica rolled her eyes. She dropped a ward in the middle of the table and tapped it rhythmically. Nathan felt the magic flare to life. With every tap, it expanded a little bit. Monica stopped when it surrounded them.

'Privacy ward,' she said. 'We've got about fifteen minutes to talk in private.'

'Great.' Adrian turned to Kseniya, who suddenly looked worried.

'This isn't an interrogation,' Nathan said hurriedly. 'If there's anything you're not comfortable telling us, you just say so, okay?'

Kseniya continued to stare at him.

Nathan sighed. 'Okay, we want to know about the Sahir,' he said. 'Who are they, why are they here?'

Kseniya curled her legs under herself and pulled the sleeves of Monica's jumper over her hands. 'I'm not sure who they are,' she said at length. 'I was sent to them by my family... six years ago.'

'How old were you?' Nathan asked.

'Seventeen.'

That made her twenty-three now. Nathan would never have guessed.

'Why were you sent to them?' Adrian asked.

'My parents died,' Kseniya said matter-of-factly. 'I could not go to my other family, I was not allowed join their coven, so they sent me to another. It was a... transaction.'

Nathan felt cold all of a sudden.

'You mean they paid money for you to join the Sahir?' he asked.

'Yes.'

Oh hell. Nathan had no words for that. He glanced at Monica, and she looked how he felt: absolutely horrified. After several moments, he cleared his throat.

'You don't have to go back to them, now,' he said. 'We'll work out something else.'

Kseniya frowned and wrapped her hand around the amulet again. She'd imprinted it, and her magic was grey, shot through with pure silver. Nathan had never seen anything like it.

'I think you do not understand the Sahir,' Kseniya said finally. 'They are not forgiving.'

'Yeah, I had noticed that, funny enough,' Nathan said darkly. He reflexively pressed a hand against his abdomen, tracing the scar there. He could just feel the raised skin through his jumper.

'You have faced them,' Kseniya said. 'But you live still.'

'Just about,' Nathan agreed uneasily.

'I think you must be very skilled,' Kseniya said. 'This is unusual. The Sahir train their warriors very hard.'

'Maybe I'm just lucky,' Nathan said. 'Can you tell us what they want?'

'They want power,' Kseniya said. 'The most powerful victims are the half-humans, the shifters, weres, witches. Mortal supernaturals. These are the people they kill.'

'That's who they're after,' Adrian drawled. 'It's not a statement of purpose. They aren't just killing for the sake of it. Why do they need their power?'

'I...' Kseniya clenched her fist around the amulet, turning her knuckles white. 'I don't understand.'

'What's their higher purpose?' Monica asked gently. She frowned at Adrian, who glared back at her. Nathan understood Adrian's impatience; he wanted answers, too. But Kseniya seemed so fragile, and they'd get nothing at all if she fell apart.

Understanding dawned on Kseniya's face. 'That's... they want...' She struggled for a moment, then looked hopefully at Nathan. 'Zakonnost.'

'Legitimacy,' Nathan translated. Kseniya looked relieved, and she abruptly launched into a tirade in Russian. It was more words in one go than Nathan had heard from her in total since they'd first met. After a few seconds, he waved his hands at her to get her attention. 'Slowly,' he said. 'I'm not that good at Russian.'

Kseniya repeated what she'd said, and Nathan translated for Monica, who was the only one who didn't understand. 'The Sahir take in mostly outcasts, but there's a... core group... who are... loyalists? Also, some who joined voluntarily, but others are like Kseniya. They collect witches who have been excommunicated from their own covens and give them the chance to practice magic again.'

'So they want coven status,' Monica surmised. 'They're here to try and get the buy-in of the Witch Council.'

'Yes,' Kseniya said. 'They want... make deal with the Council.'

'Fuck,' Adrian said.

'Have they succeeded?' Monica asked.

'I don't know,' Kseniya mumbled. 'This is for Sahir leaders to know.'

'Damn,' Nathan muttered.

'If they did make a deal, what would it be?' Adrian asked.

'They'll be asking for coven status,' Monica said. 'That means they can regulate themselves, they're official. People can join their coven. They can have an influence on who gets elected to the Council, what laws are passed.'

'That would be epically bad,' Nathan said.

'What would they give the Council in return, though?' Adrian asked. 'What could they possibly promise? Death magic is illegal under Council law, meaning the Witch Council can't legitimise them. What can the Sahir offer that would get them to overlook that law?'

'The vampires and hunters would never allow it,' Nathan said, and then suddenly everything came clear. 'Unless—'

'Unless they're not asking, they're threatening,' Adrian said. 'Forcing the Witch Council. Can they do that?' he asked Monica.

'The Witch Council is incredibly powerful,' Monica said. 'I'd find it highly unlikely.'

Adrian frowned, but Nathan's mind was racing ahead. 'If the Witch Council can't be threatened and they can't legitimise the Sahir without the buy-in from the Hunter and Vampire Councils,' he said slowly, 'Then it's not the Witch Council they need to threaten, is it?'

Adrian frowned. 'You think they'd go after the other Councils?'

'Maybe,' Nathan said.

'Shit,' Adrian said. He pulled his phone out and started texting. Monica turned to Kseniya.

'Something has been bothering me. Why did you approach Nathan, that first time in TWL? Was that just a coincidence?'

Nathan looked back at Kseniya. Her cheeks had gone pink with embarrassment.

'This is not the first time I am seeing him,' she said.

'Huh?' Nathan asked.

'You rescued little girl,' Kseniya said. 'I was there.' She touched a spot on her arm. 'I have... nevidimost.'

'Invisibility,' Adrian filled in when Nathan drew a blank.

'Yes, I can be invisible. For short time only.' Kseniya nodded firmly. 'I run away at the same time as the child. I see you helping her.'

'And you thought I'd help you, too,' Nathan guessed.

'Yes,' Kseniya said. 'You are kind. Not like other hunters. And I remembered Monica.'

Monica grimaced.

'It's okay,' Kseniya told her. 'You are forgiven.'

'For what?' Adrian asked. Monica shook her head hurriedly.

'Never you mind.' Monica turned to Kseniya. 'For now, you'll stay with me, okay? We'll deal with the Sahir first, and then we can sort out what you're going to do.'

Kseniya wrapped her arms around herself. Her gaze flicked to Nathan, and he had the impression that she was asking for permission. But to do what? Nathan nodded at her, and that must have been the right response. Kseniya turned back to Monica.

'Thank you,' she murmured sincerely.

Adrian looked up from his phone. 'I have to go speak to Damien,' he said. 'Nate, you fancy a trip to the prison?'

'I guess.' Nathan downed the last of his coffee and grabbed his jacket. 'You good from here?' he asked Monica.

'Sure. Let me know what you find out?'

'Won't Jeremiah tell you?' Adrian asked.

Monica scowled. 'Get lost, you.'

Nathan and Adrian headed out. It was a short walk over to the prison, which was good, because early December had brought drizzle and a frosty chill to the air. Inside the prison was similarly cold. Damien met them immediately at the foot of the stairs and led them towards the cells.

'The Council believe that this death may be the latest in a string of disappearances,' he said as they walked. 'Which would mean that we have at least two other bodies that are unaccounted for.'

Adrian swore under his breath. 'Why was this kept quiet?'

'In all likelihood, for the same reason that the witches have been keeping quiet about their business,' Damien said mildly. 'They wished to deal with it on their own. Jeremiah has agreed to put it before the

Hunter Council. Perhaps they can force the hands of the witches.' His gaze settled on Nathan. 'I rather fear the time has come and passed for the Councils to get involved in this matter.'

'You don't say,' Nathan muttered.

'What's that bring the death toll to?' Adrian asked. 'Three witches, two vampires?'

'I believe so,' Damien said. 'Jeremiah has asked us to have a word with our black mage once more, before he convenes with the hunters. What did you find out from Kseniya Krovopuskova?'

Adrian recapped their conversation briefly.

'It's more or less what Jeremiah and I had already surmised,' Damien said. 'But if there's a threat to the vampires, they certainly haven't come forward with it.'

'Maybe they have another in with the Witch Council?' Nathan asked.

'Maybe. Nevertheless, we will alert the hunters. We should be on our guard, especially as the Witch Council appear to have knowingly concealed the presence of the Sahir in Oxford.'

'For how long, I wonder?' Adrian asked.

'A good question.' Damien made a motion for silence as he led them down the stairs and into hearing distance of their prisoner. 'Good afternoon,' he said courteously. 'It seems we have much to discuss.'

'You're welcome to tell me all you know, vampire,' the mage said smugly. 'It's not as though I can tell anyone.'

'I saw an interesting thing, recently,' Adrian said conversationally. 'Strange, really. Never seen anything like it. And I've seen a lot, you know. Comes with the territory.'

'Is that so?'

Adrian held up the Sihr knife. 'Seems to be a result of using these. I was thinking we might test it. How do you suppose we get it to work?' He shot a glance at Damien. 'Reckon we could test it on this guy, I mean, it's not as though we need him anymore. We have Kseniya.'

'The lowlife won't be able to give you the information you seek,' the mage said.

'You'd be surprised.' Adrian stepped closer to the bars. 'I've learnt a thing or two. One of them is, be careful how you treat the people who work for you. You never know when they turn on you—and they always know more than you think they do.'

Damien shifted slightly, shadows from the torches playing over his face. Nathan flicked a glance between him and Adrian. There was a story there. He was sure of it.

'Perhaps a simple test,' Damien said. 'I'm sure Ms Krovopuskova can assist us in discovering the correct methodology.'

'Come closer, vampire, and I'll show you how it works,' the mage mocked.

'I think not,' Damien said, perfectly politely. 'I am quite attached to my ongoing existence.'

'Shame. With you as a victim, I would be unstoppable.'

'Is that so?' Adrian asked. 'I didn't think vampires made good victims.'

'Not all of them.' The mage's gaze was calculating. 'But this one will. You're not like the others.'

'You're mistaken,' Damien said coolly. 'I am very much like the others. I will enjoy the taste of your blood as much as any other.'

'Perhaps more. Isn't that so?'

'I am capable of being civilised,' Damien said. 'With the right incentive. Come, I don't believe we've anything else to gain from being here.' He turned and strode away. Nathan and Adrian exchanged confused glances before following him.

Why had Damien cut things short? That was weird.

They ascended the stairs in silence. Damien took them on the most direct route through the maze-like passages, eventually stopping outside a sturdy door.

'This is where I leave you. Adrian, please show Nathan out, then meet me back here.'

Adrian nodded sharply. 'Let's go.'

They headed for the stairs. Abruptly, Adrian grabbed Nathan's arm, bundling him into an antechamber.

'What—'

Adrian slammed a hand over Nathan's mouth. 'Shh!'

A few moments later, Nathan heard what Adrian had picked up: footsteps and voices echoing down the passageway.

'...not too optimistic. As always, the Vampire Council seem to delight in leading us around by the noses.'

'I assure you, you have our fullest cooperation,' Jeremiah replied.

Nathan met Adrian's gaze; seeing his own panic echoed back at him. Who was Jeremiah speaking to? A moment later, it got worse.

'It's taken long enough, hasn't it?' a familiar voice said. A chill ran down Nathan's spine. That was his father! 'This is at least the fourth request we've made.'

'Initially, we thought we had the investigation handled,' Jeremiah replied smoothly. 'I apologise that that wasn't the case. But the Vampire Council has nothing to hide. We want to figure this out as much as you do.'

'Let us hope that's the case,' the first voice said heavily. Nathan edged to the door, peering through the crack as the men passed: Dad, Jeremiah, Uncle Jeff, and another man. It was Patrick Longhorn, the head of the Hunter Council. Nathan had only met him once or twice, and he'd never had much of a favourable impression. Longhorn looked more like a politician than a hunter, in his well-pressed suits, with his perfectly combed hair.

He was young for a Council head, but despite that no one dared disrespect him. His reputation was fearsome.

'Most assuredly,' Jeremiah said.

'Good,' Longhorn said. 'It will take our combined resources to solve this mess.'

'Have you any idea what could have caused this?' Dad asked. 'I presume you're familiar with the photos by now.'

'It's out of our remit,' Uncle Jeff said. 'Nothing in the hunter records.'

'Nor ours,' Jeremiah said. 'We have, however, succeeded in isolating a weapon. Damien was supposed to be speaking to the prisoner to understand how it works, but the mage has proven harder to crack than we previously thought.'

'A weapon?' Longhorn asked, his voice fading out of hearing. 'I thought this had to be spellwork…'

For at least a minute after their footsteps disappeared, Nathan and Adrian stood frozen in the gloom. Finally, Adrian shook himself.

'Let's get you out of here.'

They headed upstairs in silence. Nathan was panicking over the thought that they might run into more hunters, but it was getting towards closing time, and everything was deserted. Outside, Adrian sighed in relief.

'That was too close.'

'I know.' Nathan felt sick to the stomach.

CHAPTER TWENTY-ONE

'WHAT IS THIS THING Monica wants to do?' Cynthia asked as they walked over to Monica's house the next weekend, overnight bags in tow. Nathan's clinked audibly from the wine Monica had requested.

'Some witch thing,' Nathan said. 'I'm not exactly sure, but she thought it would be nice to get away for a day or two.'

To say she'd thought it might have been an understatement. She'd actually called Nathan up in a complete huff on Wednesday and more or less ordered him to get permission to go away that weekend.

'We all need a break,' she had informed him. 'And I have an idea. Group bonding.'

Nathan relayed that now, and Cynthia laughed.

'Group bonding? Sounds fun.'

'Witchy group bonding,' Nathan replied. 'It's probably not going to be, uh, holding hands and telling scary stories by torchlight.'

'Is that hunter group bonding? Shifters usually go running in the woods.'

Nathan grinned down at her. 'That sounds fun, actually.'

The temperature had dropped below freezing, and they were both bundled up in thick coats. Cynthia wore a matching red scarf, hat, and gloves with snowflakes on them. She'd been embarrassed. Nathan thought she looked adorable.

'I don't think hunters do group bonding,' Nathan said after a few moments.

'Are there any other hunters your age around here?'

'A few. I used to train with some of them occasionally, but Dad thought they were holding me back, so he switched me to one-on-one training.'

'Intense.' Cynthia rubbed her hands together. 'So what does witchy group bonding mean?'

'Haven't a clue.' Nathan shrugged. 'But Monica was fretting about animal sacrifices, and we're definitely getting out of the city for the night, so… yeah…'

'You're really selling it,' Cynthia said, rolling her eyes.

'Just be prepared,' Nathan told her. 'You can always hide your eyes against my chest when Monica does the killing bit.'

'Hmm,' Cynthia mused. 'That idea has merit.'

'It does,' Nathan said.

'Do you think we could sneak off and get some kissing done?' Cynthia asked. 'We never seem to find time for it, in between all the supernatural drama.'

'I think that's an excellent idea,' Nathan agreed. 'We could do that instead of going away.'

Cynthia pretended to consider it. 'Monica would kill us.'

'Probably.' They had reached Monica's house. Nathan rang the doorbell, and a moment later the door swung open.

'There you are! I was beginning to think I needed to send out a search party.'

'Okay, we're not that late.' Nathan pushed past Monica into the hallway. 'Mum and Dad were roleplaying the Spanish Inquisition. It's freezing, isn't it? We better be going somewhere warm.'

'Definitely not,' Monica replied cheerfully. 'We're leaving as soon as Lily and Adrian get here.'

Kseniya was waiting for them, bundled up in a thousand layers of warm clothes. Nathan was starting to get used to the way she stared at him whenever he was in the room. She seemed to be waiting for something, but he didn't know what it was, so she was going to be waiting for a long time.

'Hi, Kseniya,' he said.

'Hello, Nathan,' she whispered.

'Where are we going?' Cynthia asked Monica curiously. Monica had a huge bag waiting to go, and she was trying to stuff even more into it.

'Oh, you'll see,' Monica said distractedly. 'It's a long drive, though, so I hope you have a book or something.'

'There's enough space for six people, right?' Nathan asked. Thinking, he added, 'And we're not going to have trouble with inviting people in?'

'The cottage belongs to Jeremiah, so no,' Monica said. 'No trouble there.'

Nathan didn't know what sort of places Jeremiah kept for private use. He kept expecting old vampires to live in castles, but he'd been thoroughly disappointed so far; there wasn't a single castle amongst Damien's offering. Maybe Jeremiah would even the score. A guy could hope.

A car hooted outside. Nathan pulled the door open and saw Lily's sleek grey Porsche and Adrian's battered Volkswagen parked on the road.

'They're here.'

'Great, let's go,' Monica said.

They all piled into the cars. Nathan and Cynthia ended up riding with Adrian.

'Do you know where we're going?' Nathan asked Adrian once they'd pulled off. 'Did Monica give you the address?'

'Yep,' Adrian said.

'And…?'

'Suffolk.'

'What?' Nathan asked. 'Are you joking?'

'You think I'd joke about a four-hour drive?' Adrian rolled his eyes. 'Text her and ask. She was being all secretive.'

Nathan pulled his phone out. Adrian fiddled with the radio, tuning it to some old-timey song.

Nathan: Seriously? Suffolk?

Monica: Oh come on it's not that bad

Monica: The other options were Lake District or Scotland

Monica: At least we can do Suffolk in an overnight trip

Nathan: What does Jeremiah even need with a cottage in Suffolk?

Monica: Sometimes it's better not to know

They drove mostly in silence. Nathan found himself once again worrying about his father's investigation. He felt trapped, like every second his father was drawing closer to finding out the truth. Worse, he didn't feel like he could talk to anyone about it. Monica had Kseniya to worry about, and Cynthia couldn't help anyway. There was only Adrian, but even he was looking tired and stressed out. The thoughts chased themselves in never-ending circles around his brain.

What if? What next?

Cynthia, for her part, put her head against the window and went straight to sleep. She looked tired, too. Nathan thought getting out of town would probably be good for all of them.

After Stanstead, they pulled off the M11 and into a service station.

'I thought vampires didn't get tired,' Nathan teased.

'Lily pulled off,' Adrian said, nodding to the Porsche.

'Nice of them to text,' Nathan said sarcastically. 'Keep us updated.'

Adrian shrugged. He pulled up beside the Porsche and rolled his window down. Nathan shivered as the cold air drifted in.

'Petrol,' Monica called across from the other car. 'Also, let's get coffee.'

'Is there a Costa's?' Cynthia asked sleepily from the backseat. 'They do this mulled apple drink…'

'I'll get it for you,' Nathan volunteered, clambering out the car. The others shouted out their drinks orders, and he headed inside.

'We're like an hour and a half out,' Monica said when he came back with coffees and teas for everyone. 'Thanks,' she added, accepting her tea.

'We should get going,' Nathan said.

They were all cold, so no one argued against piling back into the cars. As they pulled out, Adrian checked every which way.

'I doubt I was followed,' Nathan told him. 'My parents definitely have better things to be doing.'

'I know,' Adrian said. 'Paranoia's getting to me, too, I guess.'

Some hours later, they reached Suffolk. The cottage was across the River Alde from Orford. They were right up on the coast, a short walk from the stony beach. Nathan's castle couldn't have been further off from the grey stone cottage, which stood on open land with not a single tree to break the persistent wind.

England always seemed to have a harsh, rugged beauty in the winter. When Nathan finally unfolded himself from Adrian's car, he couldn't help but admire the desolate grey-brown landscape. They were probably the only people crazy enough to come out here in the middle of winter.

Lily pulled up beside them and the girls piled out of the car.

'It's freezing,' Monica said, pulling her wool poncho tighter around her.

'You could wear a proper coat,' Nathan pointed out.

'Tch, men, no care for fashion,' Monica replied. 'Come on, let's get inside.'

Inside was also cold: both the heating and electricity were off. Nathan drew the short straw and ended up hunting for the fuse box and connecting the gas. Adrian drew the even shorter straw and got to build a fire.

'Vampires hate fire,' he grumbled.

'I'll light it,' Monica replied. 'But you're bringing the logs in. You're the strongest here.'

'All I'm good for is free labour.' Adrian skulked out the house again. Nathan located the gas cylinders and took one out to hook up to the mains outside. He'd just twisted the valve open when Adrian appeared silently beside him.

'You're worrying about something again,' he said. 'I could tell in the car.'

'It's nothing. Just worried that someone's going to let something slip.'

'Self-defence, Nate. You're in the clear. You know that.'

Nathan shrugged. 'Does Dad know that?'

'Well—'

The back door opened, cutting them off.

'Are you two gossiping Gerties coming in?' Monica asked.

'Who even says *gossiping Gerties* anymore?' Nathan asked. 'What are you, sixty?'

'Oi, punk,' Adrian said.

'Just get inside. It's freezing,' Monica huffed. 'Nate, is the gas on?'

'It's on.' Nathan climbed up the step and through the door.

The inside of the cottage had modern décor, but it was sparsely furnished. The walls had been taken out downstairs so that there were only two rooms: the kitchen and a large open-plan living room. Upstairs there were three bedrooms and one bathroom. It wasn't bad, for an overnight stay.

Nathan helped Adrian build the fire, and Monica lit it with her handy magic.

'Portable fire,' she said, sprinkling a liquid over the logs. 'Accendo!' Flames flared up and quickly settled into a merrily burning fire.

'Neat,' Cynthia said.

Monica and Lily vanished into town for an hour and came back with ample supplies, including a live chicken which Monica put in the garage and refused to answer questions about. She then whipped up lunch and mulled wine, plus an assortment of food for later.

When it started getting dark, they dressed in their warmest clothes and hit up the beach to collect driftwood. Adrian and Nathan built a bonfire, which Monica lit with her magical fire-starter.

Monica went from one of them to the next. When she reached Nathan, she pressed a lump of wood into his hand. He turned it over and, by the light of the fire, saw a rune engraved into it.

Sceoldan. Protect, shield.

'We'll all make an offering,' she explained.

'Monica…' Nathan turned the piece of wood over in his hands. Monica had smoothed the edges down, but she hadn't shaped it. Rough around the edges, but somehow still beautiful. Just like Monica. 'Why this rune?'

'It's perfect for you, Nate.' Monica closed his hands around the piece of wood. 'You could make your own, quickly, but… please use this one? For me?'

'Of course,' Nathan said. Monica beamed at him and went to find Cynthia. Nathan studied the rune, wondering what runes she'd used for the others.

Cynthia wandered over to him a moment later. She was turning her rune tablet over in her fingers.

'It's sort of beautiful, don't you think?' she asked. 'The fire, the beach, no one else around…'

'Wild,' Nathan said quietly, 'natural. It's beautiful.' He looked at Cynthia. Her face was lit by the fire, and Nathan could have been describing her. The fire reflected in her eyes. Her hair hung messily around her face, and her nose was red from the cold. She'd unbuttoned her jacket now that she was closer to the fire, and underneath she had ripped jeans and a purple T-shirt. She was beautiful. Nathan leaned in and kissed her gently.

When they parted, Cynthia smiled at him. 'What was that for?'

'You're really pretty.' The words felt lame and insufficient out of his mouth, but they made Cynthia's smile grow.

She held out her rune tablet. 'What does this mean? Monica said I should ask you.'

Nathan studied it. '*Wilþijaz* and *gaistaz*. Wild spirit.'

'Because I'm a shapeshifter?'

'Yep,' Nathan replied.

'What's yours?'

'*Sceoldan*. Protect or shield,' Nathan said, running his fingers over the piece of wood again.

'It suits you.'

'Thanks, I think.' Nathan took her hand in his and squeezed it gently. Cynthia squeezed back.

Monica called them all closer to the fire.

'Alright, it's time,' she said. 'I'm just going to run and get the chicken and then we can start. Ah... you don't have to say anything when you make your offering, but if you want to, you can. So think about that?' She jogged off.

'Like what?' Lily asked her, but Monica was already gone.

'When you make offering you can also say thanks for successes of last year,' Kseniya explained quietly. 'And ask for favours for next year.'

'Oh.' Lily screwed her nose up in thought.

Nathan held his hands out to the fire to warm them whilst he thought. Everything that came to mind was too embarrassing. The others would probably poke fun at him if he said something sappy.

Then again, why not? Adrian made fun of him all the time, and he was doing this for Monica... Nathan stared into the fire and made up his mind.

Monica came back with the chicken. It lay limp in her arms. Had she killed it? Monica caught his questioning glance and said, 'I put it to sleep. Can I borrow one of your knives?'

Nathan took one from a holster at his hip and handed it to her. 'Pretty sure the hunters would frown on this.'

'Fuck 'em,' Monica said. 'This is harmless. It's not even magic, really.'

She laid the chicken out on a large stone and crouched beside it. 'Everyone who's squeamish, look away for this part.'

Monica slit the chicken's throat and caught the blood in one of her bowls. She dipped a finger into it and whispered a chant in what Nathan thought was some kind of old Germanic language as she drew lines onto her face: from her forehead down to the tip of her nose, and then three lines across each cheek. It looked like war paint. Then she did the same to Kseniya.

'Okay.' Monica put the bowl aside and straightened up. 'I'll go first.' She took a deep breath and stared into the fire. 'This last year... sucked. First the shit with Damien and the Council, and then nearly losing Nathan... Yeah. This year's been pretty crappy. But... what doesn't kill you makes you stronger, right? So, thanks. Thanks for my friends surviving intact. Thanks for the Lefebvres being understanding, and not kicking me out, and weathering my crazy. Thanks for me having good friends.' Monica smiled. 'I don't want anything for next year... but I'd like it if everyone else could be happy.' She cast her rune tablet into the fire. It crackled merrily. Monica seemed to sag in on herself, and she took several deep breaths before turning to Kseniya. 'Your turn.'

Kseniya stepped up to the fire and mumbled in Russian. Out of respect, Nathan tried not to listen in. She was asking for strength, to be able to make the right decisions. Nathan focused on Cynthia beside him, instead.

They went around the circle. Lily was next, and she spoke at length about how grateful she was to have Damien and her friends. Adrian didn't say anything at all. Then it was Nathan's turn.

'Whatever happens next year... I just want to be able to keep my friends safe,' Nathan said. Then he chucked his rune tablet into the fire. The flames seemed to flare higher for a few seconds, before dying down again. Nathan glanced at Monica and found her smiling at him.

Cynthia stared into the fire for several long seconds, then dropped her rune tablet in. 'Just let my family be safe, please,' she whispered.

Monica held both hands out to the fire and chanted in the same Germanic language for several moments. The flames rose up and up, until they were taller than Nathan, and then died down to nothing in an instant.

'It's done,' Monica said.

'What now?' Adrian asked.

'Now we have wine and I cook the chicken.' Monica grinned.

'Seriously?' Lily asked, sounding ill.

'Seriously.'

They headed back up to the cottage. Kseniya lagged behind as they walked over the stony beach. After a moment of watching her, Nathan patted Cynthia's arm. 'I'll catch up with you in a moment, okay?'

Cynthia nodded. Nathan dropped back to fall into step with Kseniya.

'You alright?'

'I'm okay,' Kseniya said. 'I am… grateful to be included.'

'You're welcome,' Nathan said. Kseniya glanced at him and ended up stumbling a bit on the uneven stones. Nathan took her arm gently.

'Careful.'

'Thank you,' Kseniya said.

They walked in silence for a moment, as Nathan tried to think how he wanted to frame his question.

'Is everything alright with you?' he asked finally. 'I mean, is there anything you need? I know things have probably been kind of tough. You can let me know if there's any way we can help you.'

They reached level ground, stepping on the dirt path that led up towards the cottage. Nathan used his phone to light the ground so they could avoid the muddy patches. Kseniya was silent.

'Kseniya?' Nathan prodded after a few moments.

'What do you want from me?' Kseniya demanded. The sudden heat in her voice took Nathan by surprise. Why was she angry?

'I don't want anything,' he said. 'What do you mean?'

'Why you not ask me to do anything?' she asked. 'Why you give me this?' She tugged on the amulet around her neck. 'Why you take me away from Witch Council? Why you are helping me?'

Nathan's mind went blank. 'Uh… I wanted to help you?' Thinking about it, he added, 'That's the answer. I mean, I'm not expecting anything from you. Monica asked me to help you, so I did. And the amulet, yeah, it's just a token, really. I'm not even rightly sure it works. I just needed something to get the Witch Council off our backs.'

'That's it?'

'That's it,' Nathan replied. 'I don't want anything.'

The others were way ahead by now, invisible in the darkness. A wind had come up, whipping around them. Nathan zipped up his jacket.

'You don't want anything from me?' Kseniya asked. 'The Sahir made me do things. I can do many spells.'

'I don't need you to do anything for me,' Nathan said. 'I don't *want* you to do anything for me.'

'I was not expecting you to come back for me,' Kseniya said. 'Witch Council found me, they track me, and the Sahir thought I was a traitor. Why did you help me?'

'Why shouldn't I?' Nathan asked. 'Look, Kseniya, I just want you to be okay. Alright? I'm not expecting anything in return. We—my friends and I—we're just trying to help.'

Kseniya was silent. She started walking again, and Nathan went back to lighting the path. At length, she said, 'The amulet is working fine, I think.'

'Monica thinks so, too.'

'You are more powerful than Sahir,' Kseniya said.

'I can't do magic,' Nathan said. 'I'm just human.'

'Humans have power, too,' Kseniya said. 'Sahir kill humans, too.'

'Okay,' Nathan said slowly. The conversation had just taken a nosedive. 'I'm not going to let them kill anyone else if I can help it.'

'I think you are good,' Kseniya said softly. 'You are kind, Nathan Delacroix.'

'Thanks, I guess,' Nathan said. 'I hope it will be enough.'

'The Sahir do not know kindness,' Kseniya said. 'It is their greatest enemy.'

That made Nathan smile. 'I'll remember that,' he said. 'Come on, let's join the others before they drink all the mulled wine.'

'Okay.' Kseniya nodded, and Nathan thought that maybe she was smiling a bit. They both hurried to catch up to the rest of the group. Nathan slid his hand into Cynthia's as they stepped through the front door of the cottage. She glanced at him.

'Alright?'

'Great,' Nathan said and kissed her on the cheek.

CHAPTER TWENTY-TWO

AS NATHAN WAS LEAVING school on Friday, his phone vibrated.

Dad: Have you finished school yet?

Nathan: Yeah

Dad: Please come to the Hunter HQ

Nathan: Now?

Dad: Now

Nathan felt as though he had lead in his stomach on the cycle over. What could his father want?

The Hunter Council office building was a dull sixties structure behind the Westgate Centre, Oxford's old shopping mall. Nathan didn't need a token to get in there; the receptionist recognised him and buzzed him through the front door.

'Hi, Nathan,' she said. 'Head on up.'

'Thanks, June.'

His father was sharing his uncle's office, so they were both there, pouring over a photo at the desk. Uncle Jeff had his tie off and Dad's jacket was thrown over the back of his chair.

Nathan knocked on the door, and they looked up.

'Dad, you wanted to see me?'

'Come in, Nathan. Shut the door.' Dad sounded oddly shaken. Nathan did as he was told.

'Is everything alright?'

'Sit.' Dad gestured to a chair in front of the desk.

Nathan sat. His dad studied him. Nathan's school uniform was rumpled, and he felt oddly self-conscious. He was usually in hunter uniform when he came to the office.

His dad began laying photos out on the desk, and Nathan knew the writing was on the wall.

An unmarked van. Two bodies.

More photos of the bodies.

'I saw the Vampire Council last week,' his dad opened. 'I've been struggling for a while to get all the pieces together. So many things I just couldn't figure out.'

Another picture, close-ups of the wounds.

'An overly helpful guide just so happened to mention that the prisoner was brought in by one of Damien von Klichtzner's men and that Damien had led the interrogation. All too happy to share the gory details, I assure you. Which of Damien's men? Oh, it was that ex-hunter, Adrian Delacroix. Was in an awful hurry, too. Family emergency. Funny that, wouldn't have thought he was still in contact with his family.'

Nathan's heart sank like a stone.

'Dad,' he started, then stopped. What could he say?

'Let me do the talking,' said his father. 'That was when I started to understand, but there were still some things that didn't make sense to me. Adrian had a spirit knife. He couldn't wield it. Okay, we have a hunter who can. How did the other body's neck get snapped? How is Damien involved? More questions. I did a bit of digging.'

More photos, three of them. Dad had saved the most damning for last. These were recent images: Adrian and Nathan chatting together. Nathan getting out of Adrian's car. Adrian, Nathan, and Monica hanging out together. Someone must have followed Nathan.

His dad had had him followed. Betrayal burned in Nathan's chest.

'Tell me what happened on the night of October thirtieth,' his father said. 'Here's what I know: you had a Halloween party at school. You left home a bit before seven and cycled into town. The party should have ended at eleven. Eleven-thirty, you weren't home. Anna texted you, and you replied that you were sleeping at Matt's place. You came home the next morning, acting like you were hungover. Then you were sick for about three or four days.' Nathan quailed under his father's gaze. 'Explain.'

'Dad, please—'

His dad held up a hand. 'Just explain, Nathan.'

Nathan sighed.

'I met Cynthia at the bus stop on the High Street,' he said. 'Around five to seven. We walked to Turl Street and met Adrian at the entrance to the witching level.' He wanted his dad to interrupt, or something, but he didn't. 'Monica had asked us to look for Kseniya, a witch friend she was worried was in trouble. We stayed there about an hour. Then Adrian left and Cynthia and I went to the school. We hung out with Matt. I think we were inside for an hour, maybe an hour and a half, so… nine-thirty. Nine-thirty, we went outside. We were making out. Two guys snuck up on us.'

Nathan paused. For what, he didn't know. His father nodded.

'I follow so far,' he said. 'Continue.'

'I fought the one guy and managed to knock him out, but I lost sight of the other. He got hold of Cynthia and dragged her to the road. I caught up with them by the van.' For a moment, Nathan felt like he was losing it. Facts, he had to stick to the facts. A deep breath, and he spoke again. 'He had a knife to Cynthia's neck and told me to drop my weapons. I did. He told me to lean against the van. The driver got out and tried to cuff my wrists. I summoned the knife and stabbed him.'

Dad nodded once. Nathan couldn't read his expression.

'I threw myself at the other guy and we both fell. He managed to roll on top and pin me. He had a knife, a Sihr knife—I have one at home, I can show you—'

Dad looked alarmed. 'In the house? How?'

'I've had it since September,' Nathan replied. 'When I saved Cynthia's sister from the Sahir. The knife works by… it drains the strength of the person it cuts, through a ritual. The mage stabbed me here.' He touched his abdomen. 'He was chanting… I…' *Was dying.* 'I managed to get the spirit knife back in my hand. I stabbed him in the heart. When he died, the ritual ended, and I could move again. I called Adrian. He snapped the other man's neck. He dealt with the bodies.'

'Where did you go?'

'To Damien's house. That's where Adrian stays when he's in town.'

'Why?' Uncle Jeff demanded. 'You could have called Anna. Me.'

Nathan shrugged. 'Adrian always comes when I call.' But it was more than that. Adrian was a friend, almost a brother. Adrian was proud of him. Adrian didn't care if he became a hunter.

Adrian wanted him to be happy.

'Nathan,' his father started, then he stopped. He shook his head. 'You should have called me.'

'What was I supposed to say to you? Hi Dad, sorry we haven't spoken since before my birthday—which you couldn't be bothered to stay for, by the way—and I know you're in Taiwan and it's probably four AM, but I just killed a guy by accident, and I don't know what to do? Also, I might be dying, not really sure, jury's still out, guess we'll see in a few days.' Nathan stared at his father. 'Yeah, I don't think so.'

'Was I in Taiwan?' Dad asked.

'Yes!' Nathan snapped. 'You were in Taiwan. And you know what? Adrian was here. Right there. No questions asked. Adrian helped me out. Adrian was the one who took me home and got me a drink. Adrian was the one who put me to bed. Adrian was the one who helped me get my head on straight because I killed a guy.'

'Adrian should have stayed the hell away from you,' his father said. 'And he knew that.'

'Yeah? Well I'm glad he didn't!'

'Nathan—'

'Would you have flown back if I had called you? Would you have come here?'

His father was silent.

Uncle Jeff held up a hand.

'Two questions,' he said. Nathan glared at his father but nodded tersely. 'One, how long have you had the spirit knife? Two, you never mentioned how you went from bleeding out to fine and healthy.'

'Adrian gave me the knife on my eighteenth birthday,' Nathan said, with a pointed look at his father. 'And he gave me his blood to heal me. I was bleeding out.' He pulled his shirt up and showed them the scar. When he lowered his shirt, Nathan looked at his dad. He had gone completely white in the face, but his shock wasn't as satisfying as Nathan wanted it to be.

'What role does Damien play in this?' Uncle Jeff asked.

'Damien helps whoever his daughter tells him to help,' Nathan said.

'Which includes you?' Dad asked, his voice hoarse.

'Which includes me,' Nathan confirmed.

'Unbelievable,' Dad said grimly. 'Is there anything else we should know?'

'I think we've covered it,' Nathan said. 'Although if you just mean things that you would know if you called me more than once every month, then there's plenty.'

'Your melodramatics are uncalled for,' his father snapped.

'Ben, don't,' said Uncle Jeff. 'If you shout at him, he's going to walk straight out of here and call Adrian.'

Nathan crossed his arms over his chest.

'This is unthinkable,' his dad said. 'Everything our family stands for—'

'Killing vampires,' Nathan said. 'We don't have much else going on in the way of family values.'

His father stared at him. He looked down at the desk, the photos. Evidence that Nathan had killed someone.

'Why?' he asked finally. 'Why would you get close to Adrian? You know what he is.'

'Adrian's always been good to me.'

'How would you know? He could have erased your memory a thousand times over,' Dad pointed out.

'I could have killed him,' Nathan said. 'We train together. Accidents could have happened. He trusts me. I...' Could he say it aloud? As much as it scared him, it was the truth. Was he a fool for denying it this whole time?

'You trust him,' said his father.

'Yes,' Nathan said quietly.

'You don't know anything about him,' Dad said.

Nathan turned that over in his head. He thought of Adrian, who loved seventies rock and leather jackets, and would kill for good Chinese food. Adrian, who could crack a joke over literally anything. Adrian who, despite being hopelessly immature, still always knew what Nathan was worrying about before he'd figured it out himself. 'I know he misses his family. I know he'd do anything for his friends.'

'Nathan, he's a vampire,' Uncle Jeff said.

'You're saying that because you don't want to admit there's anything left of the man he was,' Nathan replied. 'Your brother.'

'Whoever he was before, that person is lost. He lost his soul during the change. Just because he looks like Adrian Delacroix doesn't mean Adrian Delacroix still exists.'

'I never knew him before,' Nathan said. 'But there's someone there now, and I trust that person. I don't care what came before.'

'He's killed people, innocent people,' Dad said. 'We have the evidence.'

'We've all killed people, Dad,' Nathan said.

'You will never be a hunter,' his father said. 'Not with an attitude like this.'

'That's okay, Dad,' Nathan said shakily. 'I have other options.'

Maybe his father would have asked what those were, but a buzzing distracted all of them—Nathan's phone was ringing. He pulled it out of his pocket.

Adrian.

Speak of the devil.

Dad must have seen something in his face. Before Nathan could answer the call, Dad had rounded the desk and snatched the phone.

'Dad!' Nathan protested. He was ignored. His father answered the phone.

'You have some nerve, calling my son.' Then he went silent, his face contorting oddly. Nathan's heart was pounding in his chest. *Shit... shit... shit...*

His father lowered the phone and looked at Nathan, confused and angry. Dad didn't like being confused. It made him angry when he didn't know what was going on.

'Why does the Vampire Council want to see you?'

CHAPTER TWENTY-THREE

NATHAN WOULD HAVE LIKED to go to the castle on his own. He would have liked to grill Adrian for information, too, but as it was, he was lucky to have got his phone back. Dad had been in favour of confiscating it.

Nathan saying, 'That's not going to stop Adrian from finding me,' had probably not helped his case, either.

Adrian was sitting in his usual spot, on the railing at the entrance to the Mound. He jumped down when Nathan, Dad, and Uncle Jeff walked up. The older two hunters regarded him in stony silence. If Nathan had had to choose a place for a family standoff, he would have picked literally anywhere else.

'This is going to be priceless.' Adrian smirked.

'Don't make it worse,' Nathan begged quietly. Adrian studied his face for a moment, then nodded.

'Let's go see what the old man wants.' He sauntered towards the castle entrance, already pulling out Damien's ID.

'Permittitis intrare.'

'I only have two booked for the premium tour,' said the cashier.

'There's been a change of plan.' That was certainly one way of summarising the Delacroix family drama. Adrian handed over a credit card. The woman frowned, but handed the card back, along with four premium tickets.

No tokens. In the past, Nathan had been given a token at the ticket office. Why was this time different? He glanced at Adrian, and Adrian met his gaze. The vampire looked uneasy.

'Do you know what this is about?' Nathan asked softly.

Adrian held Nathan's ticket out to him, shaking his head. Nathan swallowed and took his ticket. The rules had changed, and that was never a good thing.

When they got to the first chamber of the inner sanctum, Jeremiah was waiting for them. Today's outfit was a grey suit over a white shirt, no tie. His hands were clasped in front of him, and he looked quite affable.

'Ah, Mr Delacroix,' he said, speaking only to Nathan. 'Thank you for coming on short notice. Am I to presume from your entourage that the hunters are finally aware of your involvement in this case?'

There was a hint of a smile on his face—he was teasing. Nathan was getting good at ignoring teasing.

'Hi, Jeremiah,' he said. His father gave him a horrified look at the informal greeting. 'What's going on?'

'All in due time,' said Jeremiah. 'We will be joined by Monica. She should arrive shortly.'

How was it that Jeremiah always seemed to know where Monica was?

Jeremiah continued, 'Whilst we wait, I must confess to some curiosity, Mr Delacroix. It would appear that you are quite popular amongst my territory. I hear Aodhán even picked a quarrel with the Witch Council on your behalf.'

'…I'm sorry?' Nathan asked. 'Is that what this is about?'

Monica jogged into the room. Uncharacteristically, she was dressed all in black, and her hair was in a ponytail. Nathan couldn't remember the last time he'd seen her look so… functional.

'We need to work on that summoning thing,' Monica told Jeremiah. 'It gives me a headache.'

'You were supposed to refine the mechanism,' Jeremiah said.

'I haven't had time,' Monica snapped. 'Do you have the amulet? I'm not going below without it.'

Jeremiah raised an eyebrow at her rude tone and held out an amulet. It was more complex than any Nathan had seen before: no fewer than five wooden medallions were held together with braided cord, all covered in runes which Nathan didn't recognise.

Monica draped it around her neck with a sigh of relief.

'Thank you,' she said in a gentler tone, almost apologetic. Jeremiah nodded. He reached into his pocket and withdrew another object, flicking it into the air towards Nathan. It glinted silver beneath the light. Nathan caught it automatically and opened his hand to look. It was the Council token.

So he wasn't going unprotected into the lion's den, after all.

'I believe you already know the ropes,' Jeremiah said, stepping towards the door.

'Why is my son entitled to protection from the Vampire Council when I am not?' Nathan's father demanded. Nathan winced.

Jeremiah turned back, still with a mild expression. There was no sign of irritation on his face, but he somehow still managed to convey frustration. Had Nathan really got that good at reading the finer details of vampiric moods?

'I am not in the habit of breaching the trust of my people,' Jeremiah said. 'Nor permitting them to be assaulted in my inner sanctum.'

Nathan looked at the token in his hands, and then up at his father. They should have expected this. Uncle Jeff had Council diplomatic protection thanks to the badge on his uniform, but Dad—as a field hunter—did not. Somehow, Nathan had become more adept at navigating the political landscape of the Council than his father.

It didn't matter.

'Here, Dad.' Nathan passed the token to his father. He took it, staring at Nathan.

'...Nathan?'

'I don't need it,' Nathan said with confidence he didn't feel. 'After all—' He shot a smile at Monica. '—If I'm harmed, Monica's going to—what was it?—wreak a vengeance most unpleasant.'

'Painful,' Jeremiah corrected.

Monica went scarlet and let out a squeak. 'You told him about that?'

Jeremiah raised an eyebrow at her. Monica went even redder and looked away.

'To business,' Jeremiah said.

It made Nathan uneasy to be walking the halls of the vampire inner sanctum without protection. It wasn't as though the token would have actually stopped a hungry vampire. It was just... yeah, it was all in his head. Amazing. The ritual of receiving the token had always made him feel safe.

I can protect myself, though.

Still, it seemed as though there was an abnormally large number of vampires strolling the halls that evening.

At length, after being led in circles for a while, they entered the receiving room which Jeremiah had used the last time. Damien was waiting for them, of course, lounging arrogantly in his chair. When he saw their party, his eyebrows rose.

'I see we have the full force of the Delacroix hunters today,' he drawled. 'Let us hope they do not disappoint.'

'Let us not goad our compatriots from the Hunter Council,' Jeremiah said mildly. 'They are, after all, supposed to be our allies.'

Damien's answering smile was faintly patronising.

'Can we hurry this up, please?' Monica asked.

'As you will.' Damien glanced at Jeremiah. 'You called this meeting.'

'The Witch Council have discovered that we have the mage in custody and demanded his extradition to their Council,' Jeremiah explained. 'An unfortunate consequence of having involved the hunters in our affairs, I'm afraid.' His tone held just a hint of disdain by the end. 'The main reason why we prefer to handle our business in private.'

'This is about more than just the vampires, now,' Uncle Jeff said, his tone studiously polite. 'There are dead witches and humans, too.'

'Indeed, as we have been made aware,' Jeremiah replied. 'And I have already assured you of our cooperation. Nevertheless, we will not make quarrel with the witches over one prisoner, so after today we will return him to them.'

'And we get one last crack at him?' Adrian asked. 'What's the point? The guy would rather bite his own tongue out than tell us anything.'

'He asked to speak to your nephew,' Jeremiah said evenly. 'However, I shall not prevent you from using the time as you see fit.' He held out the cell key to Damien. 'Damien can lead you downstairs.'

Damien looked pretty dissatisfied at being ordered around, but he stood and took the key. 'Perhaps I shall lose a few of them along the way.'

Jeremiah smiled indulgently and gestured them out of the room. Nathan had to grin at the interplay. Who knew ancient vampires could behave like petulant children?

They soon reached the secret entrance to the dungeons. Damien descended in the front. Nathan's father brought up the rear. Nathan could see how edgy he looked, and he'd noticed his father wouldn't turn his back to Adrian. If Dad thought Adrian was the most dangerous person here, then he had a serious problem.

A vampire guard languished at the bottom of the stairs. He eyed their party coming down, and when he saw Nathan, he smiled ferally. His eyes began to glow.

Nathan turned away, watching the man from the corner of his eyes.

'Matthaeus, enough,' said Damien, without turning around. The guard looked disappointed and slunk off down another corridor.

When they reached the row of prison cells, Monica was breathing erratically, clutching the amulet so hard that it had to be digging into her skin. Of course, there were anti-magic wards down here that were specifically designed to keep witches out. Despite that, the prisoner looked unbothered. It was a stark contrast. He studied each of them, and his eyes lingered on Nathan for far too long. A smirk curled around his lips.

'Visitors,' he mocked in a hoarse voice. 'I suppose you would like to make one last attempt to make me answer your questions before I am freed.'

'Nah,' Adrian said cheerfully. 'Pretty sure you don't know anything useful, actually. This is something else.'

Damien unlocked the cell door and glanced at Monica, who sighed.

'For fuck's sake,' she muttered under her breath, but she stepped towards the cell anyway.

'Monica?' Nathan asked.

'I have to put a tracking spell on him.' Monica made a face.

'Will your magic work here, witchling?' the mage asked. 'Do your vampire masters routinely force you to practice magic in the face of their oppressive wards?'

'I have no master,' Monica said. 'And I'm protected from the wards, thanks.' She entered the cell and began to chant. After a moment, she cast her hands forwards and a sort of net fell over the mage. It glowed silvery for a moment, then faded into his skin. The mage examined his hands.

'Fascinating,' he said. 'So, you are the witch who marked the boy.'

Uh oh. Nathan grabbed Monica and dragged her out the cell again.

'And here I thought hunters were firm believers in 'thou shalt not suffer a witch to live'.'

'Clearly you don't know us very well,' Nathan snapped. Damien locked the cell door behind them.

'Now, tell us what you wished to say that was so very important,'

Damien said. Dad was watching Nathan with a very disappointed look. Nathan chose to focus on Monica, instead. She was swaying a bit on her feet. He put an arm around her shoulders, and she gave him a grateful look and leaned into him.

'I asked to speak to the boy alone,' the mage said.

'No,' several people said at once.

'Not on your life,' Adrian added.

'I am prepared to die,' the mage replied. 'The question is, are you, Adrian Delacroix?'

'Technically, I'm already dead. Some would argue that my soul has departed. There's not much further to fall.'

'There is always further to fall.' The mage laughed mockingly.

'Well, I could be in your position,' Adrian said airily. 'Seeing as I'm not, though—you can talk to all of us.'

'I talk to the boy alone, or no one at all.' The mage crossed his arms. 'It's no skin off my back.'

'It's fine,' Nathan said. 'I can handle it.'

That earned him a few incredulous looks.

'Nate, no,' Adrian protested.

'I won't let him get to me,' Nathan said. 'Just wait upstairs for me, let's get this over with. Better to have some information than none, right?'

No one could argue with that, although Adrian looked prepared to try. Monica said, 'I'm going upstairs,' and took off, and that seemed to decide the rest of them. They withdrew, grumbling all the while, leaving Nathan alone with the prisoner.

He stepped closer to the bars of the cell.

'Tell me,' he said.

'You wished to know how our ritual functioned,' the mage said easily.

'And you're just going to tell me?' Nathan asked.

'I am not one to pass up a potential recruit. You have no magic of your own, but you are undeniably powerful,' the mage told him. 'You could be an asset to our cause. Loyalty is highly prized among the Sahir.'

'I will never be one of you,' Nathan said.

'The touch of darkness, once it takes root, is not so easily resisted,' the mage said. 'The witch marked you, but you have marked her, too, have you not? She wears your mark openly. She teeters on the brink between light and dark, and if she falls, you will go with her.'

'Monica's a good person,' Nathan said. 'And she'd never drag me down. I'd help her. I wouldn't let her fall.'

'Perhaps,' the mage said, 'but you walk a tightrope, and it will only take one act to tip you both over the edge.'

And the mage wanted to be that act.

'I don't want to know,' Nathan said firmly.

'It is really quite simple.'

'No.' Nathan turned and began walking away. 'You can rot for all I care.'

'You must want to draw their strength into you!' the mage shouted after him. 'Pull it to you and it will come. The knife is the vessel. The activation words are—'

Nathan tried to close his ears, tried not to listen. Why were these corridors so long? Why did sounds travel so far?

'—Ana uwsikum biqutik, falaykun li, de hayatuk tqwwy…'

He clamped his hands over his ears and ran, trying to drown the words out.

He would not use it. He would never.

Nathan climbed the stairs and let himself out of the dungeon. The rest of his group was waiting in stony silence. Adrian detached himself from the wall he was leaning against.

'Thought I was gonna have to come rescue you.'

'How long were you going to give me?'

Adrian checked his phone. 'You had two more minutes.'

'I can take care of myself.' Nathan scowled.

'Course you can.' Adrian glanced at Damien. 'I'll walk them out.'

Damien nodded sharply and disappeared off in the opposite direction.

'Where'd Monica go?' Nathan asked as they fell into step with Adrian.

'Fuck if I know, she never tells me anything,' Adrian replied. 'I think the wards made her sick.'

'They give me a headache,' Nathan muttered. He didn't blame Monica at all.

'Poor, frail human,' Adrian mocked. Nathan punched him in the arm. 'Poor, frail, violent human.'

'Tease me a bit more, I'm pretty sure I have a stake with your name on it.'

'You wouldn't have the guts,' Adrian said. 'What'd your pet dark mage want?'

'More mockery.' Nathan shrugged, trying to act casual. No way was he admitting that he had the key to a dark ritual in his head. Dad would go ballistic. 'More fucking around. More trying to get me to lose my cool. I get it. I'm the weak link, right?'

'If he thinks that, he's a crying fool.'

'No, he's right,' Nathan replied bitterly.

'You've pulled your weight more than any of us, Nate,' Adrian said as they finally reached the upper level. 'Don't let the guy get in your head. He's scared of you.'

'I doubt it.'

As always, it was a relief to emerge outside. The effect of the wards ebbed. It was fully dark, and the Christmas lights were on. People were hanging about outside the bars and restaurants in the shopping area alongside the castle. It was hard to believe there was a secret vampire prison beneath their feet.

Adrian paused in the courtyard, glancing between Nathan, his father, and Uncle Jeff. 'Nate, you going to be alright?'

'Sure.' Nathan shrugged. 'When am I not?'

'If you need a place to crash for a few days—'

'You have some nerve,' Dad said, his temper finally fraying. 'I think it's about time you got the hell away from my son.'

'Nathan's eighteen. He can decide for himself what he wants to do,' Adrian said.

'Adrian, don't,' Nathan said uncomfortably. Adrian gave him a searching look, but Nathan couldn't quite meet his gaze. What was going to happen now? Dad was undoubtedly going to be absolutely furious; the trip to the prison had only postponed the fallout. Nathan was well and truly screwed. But he had no one to blame for it except himself.

'I think it's time we go,' Dad said.

Adrian ignored them. He managed to meet Nathan's eye, and there was a question in his gaze. *We good?*

'It's alright,' Nathan said weakly. There were so many things he wanted to say, but with his Dad breathing down his neck, he struggled to find the words. Adrian nodded and turned back to the castle. Dad was already heading for the road; Nathan made to follow, but he hesitated after two steps.

The courtyard had gone eerily quiet.

A prickle ran up his spine.

'GET DOWN!' Nathan threw himself to the ground.

A flare of aggressive magic passed overhead, catching Uncle Jeff in his arm. He staggered against the wall. Nathan smelt rot, decay, death, and then they were surrounded.

He clambered to his feet, thinking, *spirit knife!* He felt the unyielding handle, the weight comforting in his hand. Four men. More than he'd faced before.

Someone was chanting. One of the mages sent a blast of magic at Nathan, and he stumbled out the way. Suddenly he was in front of one of the other mages. A knife flashed in the air. Nathan knew he had to move, but he felt paralysed.

A body slammed into him from the side, and he was on the ground. His vision was blocked—Adrian was on top of him—and then his uncle's body went limp, and he rolled to the side.

'Fuck.' Adrian coughed, and there was blood on his lips. He'd taken the blow that was meant for Nathan.

Nathan sprang up, gripped the spirit knife, and sank it into the mage's neck.

'DESIST!'

Nathan took two steps back, watching as the mage fell to the ground, clutching his throat. Jeremiah appeared in their midst, and his mere presence brought the fight to a halt. His expression was black with rage.

'What is the meaning of this?' he asked, and his voice was soft, but the anger was unmistakable. 'The Vampire Council will not condone attacks on those under our protection—on our territory, no less.'

One of the mages stepped forwards. 'The Belladonna has ordered us here.'

'The Belladonna holds no jurisdiction here. This is my territory, and these are my men.'

'Jeremias Akropolites makes claim to hunters?' the mage asked. 'The witches were not aware of this.'

'How remiss of me,' Jeremiah said in a tone that was threatening mostly for its lack of emotion. That was the voice of a man who could kill without compunction. 'I must have forgotten to inform them.'

Nathan was looking straight into Jeremiah's face. He saw the man's expression flicker. He didn't see Jeremiah move, but then the mage's head was in Jeremiah's hand, and his body was on the floor. Blood splattered over Nathan, Jeremiah, it wet the flagstone floor. Nathan was shaking, full-body trembles. He fought to control them.

'Leave,' Jeremiah ordered. 'Inform the Belladonna that further encroachment into the Vampire Council's territory will be met without compromise.'

It was over. The remaining two mages retreated hastily. Jeremiah announced, 'I will find someone to clean this mess up,' and then he, too, was gone.

Holy fuck.

Nathan crouched beside Adrian again, his heart racing with fear. Adrian managed to grapple himself upwards. His face was twisted with pain.

'Adrian—I—you—' Nathan said in panic.

'I'll heal.' Adrian's voice was strained. 'I'm immortal.'

Nathan didn't know what to say. He'd seen his father injured on training hunts before... but... there had never been this much blood.

Adrian managed to work his phone out of his pocket, but his fingers were shaking, and he dropped it.

'Fuck it.' He sank the fingers of one hand into his other wrist, drawing blood. Nathan started in horror. Adrian's aura flickered with something close to magic, the same red as Damien's aura.

Then it was gone. Adrian shut his eyes and sighed.

'Damien will come,' he told the world at large. 'Thank God I'm still useful to someone, right?'

That seemed... awfully sad. Not that there was someone who cared enough to help Adrian. Just that he was useful to someone. Nathan knelt beside him, wanting to reassure him but unsure what to do or say. Just sitting there didn't feel like enough.

'Nathan, let's go,' his father barked.

'No,' Nathan said stubbornly. 'I'm staying here.' Adrian seemed to be healing, but not fast enough. No way was Nathan was leaving him to get picked off.

'Kid, you should go,' Adrian coughed. 'Unless you're planning on volunteering yourself as a source of blood.'

Nathan reeled backwards instinctively and hurt flashed over the vampire's face. Then Adrian schooled his expression, his eyes sliding away.

'I'm staying,' Nathan repeated weakly. Adrian's shoulders shook; his face was pained. Nathan hated feeling helpless.

Damien arrived a moment later, with the same eeriness of other old vampires: Nathan blinked and then he was there. He didn't waste a moment of time, hauling Adrian indelicately to his feet. Adrian staggered drunkenly as Damien began guiding him towards the castle. Nathan followed and was opening the door even before Damien asked him to.

He watched them enter but stayed in the doorway like a coward.

'Damien.'

The ancient vampire half-turned back.

'Is there anything I can...' Nathan started hesitantly.

'Unless you would like to donate blood, Nathan, I suggest you absent yourself.' Damien guided Adrian towards the dungeons. Chastised, Nathan remained where he was, watching them until they were out of sight.

He had never felt more useless.

CHAPTER TWENTY-FOUR

UNCLE JEFF'S ARM WAS broken. Nathan's pride was in tatters. Overall, though, they could have come off a lot worse.

Aunt Anna met them at the hospital with Cynthia in tow. The moment Cynthia saw Nathan, she threw herself at him.

'When we heard what happened—oh my God—are you okay?' She sobbed into his chest.

'I'm fine,' Nathan mumbled. 'I'm okay. We're all okay.'

Aunt Anna hugged him next. 'You're giving me grey hairs,' she said.

'Why is this my fault?'

Aunt Anna pulled back and examined him from top to bottom. 'Have you looked in a mirror recently?'

'Um, no?'

'You're covered in blood.' She nudged him towards the bathroom. 'You look like you've been in a car accident.'

Nathan found the toilets and peered in the mirror. Car accident victim wasn't far off the mark. Somewhere along the line, he'd gotten his blazer and trousers splattered with blood, especially his right arm. It was on his face, too. He wet a tissue and tried to rub away the blood, but that made him look worse. Finally, he just took his blazer off and wet the sleeve, using it to wipe his face and neck.

'Better?' he asked Cynthia when he came out.

'Well, you look less like a zombie.' She hesitated. 'Um, zombies aren't a thing, right?'

'Do you want the honest answer or the nice answer?'

'They're a thing?'

'Necromancers can raise zombies, but they decay very quickly,' Nathan said. 'And they're kind of useless, not really the monstrous creatures from films.'

'Oh, phew.'

They sat in the hall. Cynthia tentatively put her head on Nathan's shoulder. He stayed very still, not wanting to disturb her. Cynthia felt like the one bastion of calmness in the rough seas of Nathan's life. Everything else was fucked to high hell—he didn't want to scare her off, too.

'Will you tell me what happened?' she asked at length.

'Dad knows about Halloween and there was another attack,' Nathan said shortly. 'Can we discuss it later? I'm just...'

'Tired?' Cynthia asked.

'Yeah.'

'Me too,' she mumbled.

They sat like that until Dad and Uncle Jeff came back and they could leave. Nathan climbed into Aunt Anna's car before Dad could trap him into an awkward, angry ride home in his car.

'You know, we should practically reserve rooms at this hospital,' Aunt Anna said. 'I swear we're here every few months.'

'It's a risk of the job,' Uncle Jeff said shortly. 'Let's get home.'

Home was the last place Nathan wanted to be right now. He clung to his phone for the whole drive, hoping that someone would text him an update, but no one did. The entire car ride was spent in tense silence. It was the most uncomfortable trip of his life.

Mum and Jess were waiting at home. Mum took one look at their grim group and said, 'Kitchen.'

'Can I change?' Nathan asked.

'No. Go sit.'

He sat in the kitchen with the rest of the family, and Aunt Anna made tea. Tea was incongruous with the atmosphere, a tiny bit of niceness amidst the most unpleasant day of Nathan's life. Dad relayed the entire story in a monotone that managed to convey exquisitely clearly how angry he was.

At the end, Mum asked, 'Do you have anything to say for yourself, Nathan?'

'No,' Nathan said. 'Can I go change now?'

'Nathan!' his mother snapped.

'I'm covered in blood,' Nathan pointed out. Adrian's blood, amongst others. 'I need a shower.'

'How long have you been having *clandestine meetings* with Adrian?'

his mother asked.

Nathan had to think about that for a moment. 'About two years? Yeah, that sounds about right.'

'Unbelievable.' Dad managed to turn the word into about fifteen syllables.

'Were you planning on telling us about this?' Mum asked.

'Of course not,' Nathan replied. 'What do you think I am, stupid?'

'After everything we've done for you—' Dad blurted out, but he cut himself off at a look from Mum.

'Has he ever come in the house?' Aunt Anna asked.

'No, never. I wouldn't put Jess in danger like that.'

'Hey!' Jess cried.

'Oh, you're worried about Jess?' Dad asked. 'No concern for the rest of the family, but never mind, you kept your sister safe?'

'Hardly,' Nathan said angrily. He took a big gulp of tea and promptly scalded his mouth. 'If Adrian wanted at Jess, he'd have got at her when she was at school, wouldn't he? And last I checked, the rest of you are perfectly capable of looking after yourselves.'

'Don't you take that tone,' his mother said immediately. Nathan just shrugged, too tired to care. He just wanted to shower and sleep. And hopefully not dream of Jeremiah beheading a man. Or Adrian getting stabbed. Too much had happened today.

'Tell me how you managed to get Jeremiah's protection,' Uncle Jeff said suddenly.

'I don't know.' Nathan pinched the bridge of his nose, but it didn't help his budding headache. 'Why do old vampires do anything? They're incomprehensible.'

'You don't know? You didn't offer him anything?' Uncle Jeff asked.

'Of course not,' Nathan said. 'I'm not stupid, alright?'

Dad muttered something which sounded suspiciously like, 'Could have fooled me,' and Nathan snapped.

'Adrian,' he told the table at large, 'Is the reason I'm still alive today. None of you even noticed what was going on, and it's your fucking jobs. I'm done. I'm just done.' He stood up. 'I need a shower, and then I'm going to go and find out if my friends are alright. You lot can just… talk amongst yourselves, or whatever. It's all you ever seem to do.'

He dumped his half-finished tea in the sink and marched out the room.

'Nathan!' his mother shouted after him. 'Don't you dare walk out! Nathan!'

Nathan ignored her.

It was a relief to shower. He scrubbed himself over and over again, imagining that he was scrubbing his brain of the image of Jeremiah holding the severed head. If only he could scrub his brain of that. At least he could finally get the taste of blood out of his mouth. After he'd showered, he pulled on one of Adrian's hoodies—he couldn't remember how it had ended up in his cupboard, but it was darned comfortable—and tracksuit trousers, and went to his room.

Cynthia was curled up on his bed.

'Your parents are nuts.'

'No, I get it,' Nathan said tiredly. 'They told me to stay away from Adrian. I didn't. He's a vampire. It goes against everything we stand for.'

'Adrian's alright,' Cynthia said. 'I mean, he's a bit messed up, but you can tell he likes you.'

Nathan sagged on the end of his bed. 'You don't think I'm an idiot?'

'You're doing your best,' Cynthia said. 'I don't think you're any more of an idiot than the rest of us. I'd be terrified if I faced half of what you face, and your parents expect you to do it as a job!'

'Not anymore. I'm pretty sure that ship has sailed.'

'Then it has,' Cynthia replied. 'You're capable. Bet plenty of other people will want you on their side.'

She meant it as a comfort, but Nathan found it pretty hollow. He crawled up his bed until he was lying beside her and nuzzled his face into her neck.

'You alright?' Cynthia asked softly.

'Yeah, sure,' Nathan mumbled. 'I'm fine. It's Adrian that got stabbed.'

'He'll be okay, though, won't he?'

'Sure, he's immortal,' Nathan said, but he wouldn't believe it until he saw it. 'I'm gonna take a nap, okay? Will you stay?'

'Won't your parents be mad if they find us in bed together?' Cynthia asked warily.

'Why? We're fully clothed, and I don't know where they'd get off caring, anyway,' Nathan replied, 'seeing as the only time they care about anything is when they find out I've been hanging out with vampires.'

'I'm sure they care. They're just rubbish at showing it.'

'Yeah.' Nathan stifled a yawn and buried his face in her hair. It smelt of soap.

Then he was asleep.

Nathan dreamt that Adrian was dead. He'd risen again as a zombie, all grey flesh which had rotted away to expose his shiny white bones. He was dressed in a white T-shirt and his leather jacket. Somehow, that stood out.

Zombie Adrian staggered around and practically fell on Nathan.

'You did this to me,' he said. 'It's your fault I'm dead. You could have saved me!'

'No!' Nathan cried. 'You said you'd be fine! I didn't know! I didn't know!'

'You knew! You could have saved me! You're a coward!'

'I'm not! I'm sorry!' Nathan said desperately. 'I'm sorry, Adrian!'

'You don't deserve to live!'

'I'm sorry.' Nathan sobbed. 'Please, I'm sorry, I'll do anything!'

'Nathan?' Someone was shaking him and whispering his name. 'Nathan? Your phone is ringing.'

Nathan managed to grapple himself back to wakefulness. He was in his bed. It was still dark. The ancient radio-alarm on his bedside table said it was only ten PM—he'd slept through dinner.

He picked his phone up. It was Monica.

'Hey,' he croaked.

'Nate? Fuck, are you okay?'

'What?' Nathan sat up and tried to coax his brain into motion. 'Yeah, why wouldn't I be?'

'I've texted you, like, fifteen times. Adrian too. Where are you?' Monica sounded worried. It occurred to Nathan that he'd had her in tears more times in the last few months than in all the years he'd known her before. Well, shit. Now he felt like a bad friend.

'I'm at home. I was asleep.'

'You're alright!' Monica sighed. 'You prat, I wish you'd just text me updates, or something.'

'I was waiting for you to text me,' Nathan said, frustration welling up. 'I didn't know if you were busy, or what the fuck was going on.'

Monica was silent for a long moment, long enough that Nathan regretted losing his cool. He took a deep breath. 'M—'

'Are you okay?' she interrupted him. 'Is your dad mad?'

'That doesn't matter,' Nathan lied. 'Is Adrian okay?'

'Course he's okay—he's more worried about you. You two are idiots, you know that?' She was silent for a second. 'We cleaned up the mess, but I'm freaking exhausted. I'm heading home, but you could... meet me at my place?'

Nathan weighed that for a second. His parents were unlikely to allow it. Go anyway? Yay or nay? Realistically, could they get any madder? What was mad squared? Apocalyptic fury? Had they already reached that level?

'Sure,' he said. 'Text me when you get home?'

'Will do.'

They hung up. Nathan laid back down, staring at his ceiling. There was a spot above his bed where he and Matt had managed to destroy the plaster. They'd been playing indoor football on a rainy day. Not one of his better ideas.

'You feeling better?' Cynthia asked.

'Less like death warmed over,' Nathan said. 'Monica wants to speak to me at her place. You can come if you want, but, um, I get it if you don't want to get in trouble.'

'Your aunt said to tell you your dinner is in the fridge,' Cynthia said, putting her head on his shoulder. 'Would you mind if I went to bed?'

There was a slightly frustrated note in her voice, as well. The whole situation was wearing on all of them, and Nathan didn't know how to fix it. Could this be fixed? Every decision just seemed to make it worse. An odd feeling lingered between them, some unspoken tension that Nathan couldn't name.

'I don't mind,' he said as gently as he could. 'It would be good for me to speak to Monica on my own—I think she's upset.' It would be good for Nathan, too.

'Thanks,' Cynthia said.

'Have you had dinner?' he asked.

'Yeah.'

'Alright.' Nathan kissed her chastely. 'Goodnight.'

'Night.' Cynthia slipped out. Nathan grabbed his phone and padded downstairs. Aunt Anna was sitting in the kitchen, alone. The house felt deserted, but it was probably just because everyone else was in bed.

'Nathan,' Aunt Anna said softly. She searched him over with her eyes, looking for what, Nathan didn't know.

'Hi, Aunt Anna,' Nathan said. He abruptly remembered his tirade from earlier and felt kind of embarrassed. 'Um, did Mum and Dad go back to the hotel?'

'Yes.' Aunt Anna slid him a sheet of lined paper. 'For you.'

Nathan unfolded it. His Mum's neat, utilitarian print was scrawled across the page. *Dear Nathan, please consider yourself grounded until further notice. We will discuss how to proceed tomorrow. Love, Mum*

Why bother adding the 'love' part, Nathan wondered cynically. It wasn't as though she'd ever said it out loud. Maybe she was just trying to soften the blow.

'Have you read this?' he asked his aunt.

'No need, I discussed it with your parents.' She closed the lid of her laptop and set it aside.

'And?'

'Do you want to talk?' Aunt Anna asked. 'Or are you just spoiling for a fight?'

'I haven't been spoiling for a fight,' Nathan said. 'I'm honestly just… tired.' He fetched his dinner plate from the fridge, but it seemed like too much effort to heat it up, so he just started eating it cold. Aunt Anna was silent whilst he ate. Nathan glanced at her a few times. She wasn't looking at him; she just stared at her hands, which were folded on the table.

Finally, when Nathan was almost finished, she said, 'I knew Adrian before he was turned. Jeff and I were dating at the time. Adrian was always… Jeff looked up to him, you know? He was very compelling, even then. Charismatic… manipulative.'

'Adrian isn't manipulating me—' Nathan started immediately. Aunt Anna raised a hand to stop him.

'I'm trying to give a balanced view,' she said. 'Hunters, by nature, are not very forgiving. Adrian became what they hated the most. Before he was turned, he was the older brother they all looked up to.'

'So? It's not as though he chose to become a vampire,' Nathan pointed out.

'He chose to live, Nathan,' Aunt Anna said gently. 'And I dare say there are some, Jeffrey included, who feel that there was another choice.'

A cold sort of horror was growing in Nathan. He swallowed hard. 'You mean… kill himself? Or… let them kill him?'

'Yes,' Aunt Anna said.

'That's horrible,' Nathan said. He tried to imagine it and found that he couldn't. When had Adrian become integral to his life? The thought of his uncle or his father killing Adrian made him shudder.

'It's the hunter ethos, which Adrian himself also once ascribed to,' Aunt Anna reminded him. 'If you initiate, you also have to uphold that, Nathan. You are agreeing to never allow yourself to be turned. If it does come to that, it's expected that you will take your own life.'

Nathan stared at his empty plate. He was glad he'd finished eating, because he was pretty sure this conversation would have killed his appetite.

'What if I don't think that's right?'

'Would you want to be a vampire?'

'No, but I wouldn't want Adrian to be dead either,' Nathan said. 'Honestly, I'm closer to him than my dad. Or Uncle Jeff.'

'I know,' Aunt Anna said. 'I see that now. And I think that's a failing of ours—not of yours. But do you see why you need to stay away from him?'

Her words made Nathan angry. No. No, he didn't see. He bit his tongue hard, letting the pain ground him. 'Yes,' he lied.

'Good,' Aunt Anna said. 'I suggest you think about that and tell your parents tomorrow. Maybe they'll go easier on you.'

'Yes, Aunt Anna,' Nathan replied. 'Thanks for the chat. I'm going to bed now.'

'Okay.' Aunt Anna smiled at him. 'Are you alright? I know today has been difficult for you.'

'I'm alright, just tired.' Nathan put his plate in the dishwasher and added, 'Goodnight.'

'Goodnight.'

Nathan headed upstairs and shut his bedroom door. He lay in bed, listening to Aunt Anna shuffling around downstairs, closing up the house for the night. He felt her testing the wards, something which she did at least once a week. They buzzed in the back of his consciousness, reminding him they were there. Then he heard her ascend the stairs. She checked each room, first Jess's, then his, lastly the guestroom where

Cynthia was sleeping. Then she closed herself into the master bedroom.

His aunt and uncle were deep sleepers. Nathan had never snuck out before. He'd never had to. Now, he silently dressed again. He found a ward he'd worked on a while back, for silent movement, and slid it into his pocket. Barefoot, he padded downstairs and let himself out the house.

Nathan held his breath as he shut and relocked the door. The lights in the master bedroom stayed off. He was in the clear. He sat on the step and pulled his trainers on, then set off at a jog for Monica's house.

Monica opened the door for him in her pyjamas. She put a finger to her lips and whispered, 'Everyone's asleep. Let's go to my room.'

Nathan followed her up the stairs. Monica's room was very bohemian. She collected dreamcatchers, which she hung from hooks above her bed. The curtains were gauzy and didn't block the streetlight which filtered in through the window. She had a double bed with blue sheets, and her cupboard was open, showing a haphazard mass of clothing. On her desk, her laptop was shoved into the corner to make way for her collection of wards.

Nathan kicked his shoes off and slouched onto her bed. Monica locked her door.

'How bad is it?' she asked.

'On a scale from mildly awful to end-of-the-freaking-world, we're pretty much at nuclear apocalypse,' Nathan said glumly.

'Oh, Nate.' Monica sighed, collapsing onto the bed beside him. 'What will you do? I'd offer you to stay here, but I'm pretty sure Malcolm will kick me out if I try to house anymore strays.'

'S'alright,' Nathan said. 'I have to go home. I have school and homework, and training…' He trailed off at the last one. 'Maybe not training. They might decide to pull me out altogether.'

'Fuck them,' Monica said. 'It's their loss.'

'Thanks,' Nathan said, even though it didn't make him feel better in the slightest. 'Anyway, they know everything now, so hopefully that means it's their problem now, right?'

'Define everything,' Monica said.

'About Halloween. About me and Adrian. About the Sahir. Everything. Hell, they even know I'm friends with Lily.'

'All that in one day? You had a busy day.'

'It's not even over yet,' Nathan said glumly. 'It can still get worse.'

'Don't say that.' Monica prodded his side. 'Look on the bright side—maybe the Hunter Council will take over this whole mess. At least now they know what they're up against.'

'Yeah…' But remembering the attack, Nathan also remembered how outclassed they'd been. And something else.

'Do I owe Jeremiah for protecting us?' he asked worriedly.

'Probably not,' Monica said. 'He was protecting the reputation of the Vampire Council. Probably better not to bring it up, though, or you'll give him an opportunity to spin it that you owe him.'

'So not the answer I was hoping for,' Nathan told her.

'I live to serve,' Monica said ironically.

They lapsed into silence. Nathan studied the pattern on Monica's socks. They were yellow with little black and red birds. Cute.

'Monica,' Nathan asked at length, 'Have you ever let a vampire drink your blood?'

'For sure,' Monica said, not sounding particularly surprised by the intimate question. 'Adrian did, for one. But vampires don't really love witch blood. He said it tastes kind of acrid. It's the magic.'

'Oh,' Nathan replied.

'Jeremiah has, too,' she added.

'I don't want to know how that situation came about,' Nathan said hastily.

'No.' Monica pulled her legs up to her chest. 'Why were you asking?'

'Because…' Nathan hesitated. 'Because Adrian saved my life, and it nearly cost him his,' he said. 'And I just… couldn't. I couldn't give him my blood, even though it would have helped.'

'I don't think he expected you to,' Monica said. 'Anyway, Damien helped him.'

'I feel like I should have, though,' Nathan said. He grasped around for words to explain how he felt. 'I—I don't—I mean—he said Damien found him useful,' he finally blurted out. 'There's no one who would save him because they want to, because they like him. And I wanted to, but I was just a fucking coward.'

'Lily would,' Monica said. 'Lily loves Adrian, platonically. Anyway, it wasn't the time or the place, was it?'

'I can't think of a better time or place than when he's just saved my life.'

'In front of your dad? He'd have killed you on the spot.'

That hadn't occurred to Nathan at the time, nor afterwards, but now he thought about it and grimaced. Hunters believed that humans who had been bitten were tainted. Three bites and you could be turned. It was the first step on the path. He'd have been shunned for life.

'Yeah,' Nathan said, leaning his head against the wall. 'For sure.' But he felt dissatisfied with that answer, for reasons he couldn't exactly pinpoint. It felt like a cop-out.

'Can we sleep?' Monica asked. 'I was weaving high-level illusions all evening, and I'm beyond exhausted.'

Nathan glanced at her. She had dark rings under her eyes, although honestly Monica usually hid her fatigue under a layer of makeup, so for all he knew this was normal. Probably not, though. He remembered Cynthia. They were all just tired.

'Are you okay?' he asked softly.

'Fine, just need to sleep,' Monica said shortly.

'M, really—'

'I'm fine,' she cut him off.

Nathan had overstayed his welcome. He pulled Monica into a hug and whispered, 'I'll head home. See you when my parents finally release me from the grounding of the century?'

Monica clung to him for a second, before she took a deep breath and pulled away. 'Good luck,' she said. 'I'll let you out.'

Outside, Nathan waved once and set off home. Halfway there, he stopped and sat on a convenient stretch of wall. He pulled his phone out. From tomorrow, he was probably going to be grounded, without phone or internet, or pretty much anything else. Maybe his parents would come up with some equally terrible punishment. Maybe he could make nice and act contrite, but his parents weren't stupid. They wouldn't let him off the hook too easily.

He ought to take advantage of this last moment of freedom.

Nathan dialled Adrian and put the phone to his ear. It rang what seemed like a thousand times, before finally connecting.

'Nate, do you have any idea what time it is?' Adrian asked. He sounded like he'd been sleeping.

'Sorry,' Nathan replied. 'I just wanted to…' *Make sure you were okay.* 'Check in.'

'Oh,' Adrian said. 'Sure. I hope Benny's not too mad.'

'For real?' Nathan asked. 'What do you think?'

'How long are you grounded for?'

'Unclear,' Nathan replied. 'We haven't discussed it yet. They've gone back to the hotel for the night.'

'Shit,' Adrian said. 'Wish I could talk sense into them, but I'm guessing that'll make it worse.'

'Much, *much* worse.'

'I wanted to ask you earlier; how much do they know?' Adrian inquired.

'Everything,' Nathan said. 'It's all in the open now.'

'Did you tell them I approached you?'

'Does it matter?' Nathan asked. 'I could have walked away at any moment. I brought this on myself.'

Adrian was silent, and it was a silence filled with self-recriminations. Nathan could empathise. He was beating himself up, too.

'Maybe I should talk to Benny—or Jeff. He was always pretty level-headed. Or Anna?'

'No!' Nathan said immediately. 'No, Adrian, don't get more involved. There's no point. They're stuck in their own beliefs and… I'm just not compatible with that.'

'You're dumping the hunters, then?' Adrian asked.

'Maybe,' Nathan said. 'I haven't decided yet.' Just saying it out loud scared him. Hunting had been the one goal, the one purpose of his life for as long as he could remember. Even having his initiation postponed had been a blip in the system. He'd always known what he was working towards, and now that was just… gone.

'You'll be okay,' Adrian said confidently. 'Hunting's not the be-all and end-all.'

'I hope so,' Nathan mumbled.

'Will you let me know what your father says?' Adrian asked. 'How long I have to lay low for?'

They were winding down, and Nathan still hadn't said what he wanted to say.

'Um, sure,' he said hastily. 'I doubt it'll be forever. Dad has to go back to London eventually. Look, Adrian—I just wanted to say—'

'Nate, it's okay.'

'You don't know what I'm going to say!'

'Bet I do,' Adrian replied with his usual irritating confidence.

'What do you think I'm going to say, then?'

'I'll bet it starts with thank you,' Adrian said. 'Nate, you don't have to thank me.'

'But I want to thank you!' Nathan said heatedly. 'You saved my life.'

'I did what I would always do,' Adrian said, sounding utterly unruffled. 'You don't have to thank me for it.'

Nathan scowled and kicked a pebble at the base of the wall. It skittered into the road. 'I totally froze up. I have no idea what came over me.'

'A lot of people do that in their first fight after killing someone,' Adrian said. 'You recovered. It's okay.'

'You saved me, and I couldn't even do anything in return,' Nathan insisted. He couldn't have said why it pissed him off so much. It was like he didn't want Adrian to let him off the hook.

'Nathan, it's okay,' Adrian repeated. 'We're family. You don't owe me anything.'

Being released from the debt didn't help Nathan's confused feelings in the slightest. 'I should have let you drink my blood.'

'No.' Adrian's tone was so firm that Nathan actually jumped in surprise. 'Nathan, no. I know I've teased you about that before—maybe I shouldn't have. I would never ask that of you.'

'But—' Nathan started pathetically. He almost said, *I thought you wanted to*, but then he thought the better of it. 'You needed it.'

'I needed blood, it didn't have to be yours,' Adrian said. 'The Vampire Council keeps willing donors on hand. It wasn't as though I would have died from blood loss.'

'I couldn't do anything to help.'

'It was enough that you stayed,' Adrian replied. 'It meant a lot to me.'

'But...' Nathan was running out of arguments.

'Go to bed, Nate,' Adrian said. 'Stop torturing yourself. You did fine. You did better than fine. Tomorrow's going to be hard enough, without adding a lack of sleep to the mix.'

'Fine.' Nathan sighed. 'Thanks, anyway. For chatting, I mean.'

'You're welcome.'

They rang off and Nathan shoved his phone into his pocket. Reluctantly, he stood up and began walking back towards his house.

His prison for the foreseeable future. He dragged his feet, kicking a loose stone along. He'd fucked everything up. Worse, he'd known this would happen, but he'd gone ahead with it anyway. Kept hanging out with Adrian. Got close to Adrian. A vampire.

A cloud drifted in front of the moon as he reached his street, casting everything into darkness. Their streetlight was still out. Seriously, couldn't the county council fix anything? Humans were as bad as vampires. Nathan snorted at the thought.

He caught the tail end of a whisper and jerked around abruptly. He could have sworn he'd heard someone speaking. Chanting. Had the air gone unusually still? Nathan's breath fogged in front of him, and he suddenly felt bone-weary. Why now? Why did everything happen to him?

There was a flicker of white, but it vanished before he could identify it. More whispering. It could have been a voice, but it could have just been the breeze rustling through the trees.

Whatever it is, it can wait, Nathan thought. It was probably nothing. There was no movement in the shadows. Not even the neighbour's dog. He strained his eyes, suddenly struggling to keep them open.

'Fuck it,' he whispered and turned back towards his house. It had probably just been his imagination. He was overtired, overstressed. Worrying about tomorrow. He staggered towards the house.

It was a miracle he managed to get himself inside and up to his room without waking anyone up. He was just so freaking tired. Nathan collapsed, still fully clothed, on his bed and slept.

CHAPTER TWENTY-FIVE

BEEP-BEEP-BEEP.

Nathan's thoughts were sluggish and hazy. It took several moments for him to force his eyes open, and even longer to process what was going on.

He was in a hospital room.

What the hell?

He was hooked up to a heart rate monitor. His whole body felt heavy, fighting him as he tried to sit up. It was cold — the blankets were pathetically thin. Someone had dragged a plastic chair into the room and was fast asleep in it, wrapped in another blanket. It took him a moment to realise it was his mother.

'Mum?' he croaked. His mother jerked awake.

'Nathan?' she said. 'Nathan, oh my God!'

'What happened?' His throat was dry, and he was starving.

His mother was wide-eyed and pale. Nathan had never seen her look this panicked before. Not ever.

'You — we couldn't wake you,' Mum whispered. 'Your heart rate was low. You were dead to the world. We didn't know what to do.'

'W — what? I don't understand.' He swallowed and added, 'Can I get some water?'

'Yes, of course.' His mother jumped up and dashed out the room. She was back a minute later with a doctor in tow. Nathan barely had a moment to take stock of himself.

The doctor passed him a glass of water. 'Thanks,' Nathan said hoarsely. It was Doctor Govender again.

'Nathan,' he said with a smile once Nathan had downed the water. 'I'm glad to see you awake. Do you know who might have cursed you?'

'What? Why would anyone have cursed me?'

'You were in a cursed sleep,' Doctor Govender said. 'I'm glad you came out of it on your own. Let's say the fairy tales aren't completely accurate about cursed sleeps. They tend to be nasty to break.'

'But—' Nathan's head was spinning. 'No one cursed me.'

'No one gave you anything, you didn't touch anything that felt unusual, no one performed a spell around you?' he asked.

'Not recently,' Nathan said.

'Unless you count your Sahir mages,' Mum said.

'I'm pretty sure they were trying to kill me, not put me to sleep,' Nathan said. 'Were Dad and Uncle Jeff affected?'

'No, only you,' his mum replied. 'What about...' Her voice grew oddly tentative. 'Your friend, Monica?'

'Monica wouldn't curse me,' Nathan said immediately. He strained to remember what had happened. He'd spoken to Monica, phoned Adrian, then gone home to bed. He had the presence of mind not to mention his illicit excursion. 'Besides, the last time I saw her was before that thing with the mages, and she was too busy fighting off the wards in the Vampire Council to do any cursing.'

Speaking of, he should call Monica. Maybe she could figure out what had happened.

'Is my phone here?' he asked. 'What time is it, by the way?'

'Your phone's at home,' said his mother. 'I can ask Anna to bring it for you.'

'Can't I just go home?' Nathan asked.

'Not until I've done a few tests,' the doctor said.

'I feel fine.'

'Nathan,' Mum said quietly, 'it's Monday night. You've been asleep three days.'

Nathan's jaw dropped. 'What?'

'I'm afraid so,' Doctor Govender said. 'Now, if you'd just lay back, I'll see about those tests. We need to make sure the curse has run its course.'

Nathan lay down, his mind racing. What the hell? What the actual hell?

'Mum,' he managed to say. 'I think I need to speak to Monica.'

It was a mark of how worried his mother was that she didn't immediately deny his request.

Nathan wouldn't have thought it after sleeping for three whole days, but he was exhausted. He barely managed to get a plate of food in himself before he was asleep again. He awoke an indeterminate period of time later, aware of the fact that there were people talking in his room.

'...Couldn't not bring her, whatever you say, Kathleen, they're close friends.' Aunt Anna.

'...Might be the one at fault...' Mum.

'I DIDN'T CURSE NATHAN! What do you want me to do, take a vow of truthfulness?' The last one was Monica. She sounded angry and hurt. Nathan opened his eyes and sat up.

'Monica?'

'Nathan!'

There was a blur of red and then Monica was wrapped around him. She hit him on the arm and began sobbing into his hoodie.

'Hey, Monica,' Nathan croaked. 'I'm alright.'

'You're a fucking arsehole,' Monica said. 'I spend more energy worrying about you than anyone else!'

'What a waste of energy.' Nathan couldn't help but grin. He'd made Monica cry again. This had to be some kind of record.

'You're going to kill me before I hit twenty-five!' Monica pulled back and wiped her eyes on her sleeve. Today, she had no makeup on, and her dark circles were very prominent, like bruises on her pale skin.

'I'm sorry,' Nathan said hesitantly.

'You better be,' Monica huffed. She dropped his phone into his lap. 'I charged it for you.'

'Thanks.' Nathan powered up the screen. It was Tuesday, seven-thirty AM, and he had thirty-three missed calls and messages. Holy shit.

'What happened?' Monica demanded.

'I don't know,' Nathan said. 'My memory is blank. I went to sleep and apparently didn't wake up.'

'There was no warning?'

'No. Can you tell what happened?'

'I can reverse-engineer what spell was used on you,' Monica said.

'That won't put me to sleep again, will it?' Nathan asked in alarm.

'No.'

'Do it, then.'

'Nathan!' Aunt Anna protested.

'I trust Monica,' Nathan said. 'Can you do it now?'

Monica nodded determinedly, shrugging her backpack off her shoulders. 'I brought supplies,' she said. She pulled out a bowl and a tiny knife. 'Cut your finger.'

'Blood, always blood.' Nathan sighed in exasperation, but he did as he was told and let a few drops of blood trickle into the bowl. Monica poured a small vial of pearlescent liquid over the blood, and immediately smoke began to rise from the bowl.

'This should tell us what magic was used on you recently,' she said. 'I'm hoping the last spell will be the curse.' She had Nathan hold the bowl out to her, and then she began chanting rapidly, the same few words over and over in what Nathan thought might be Ancient Greek. It took several repeats before finally the wispy smoke dispersed around them and an eerie whisper filled the room. It wasn't English. The sounds ran together, elegant and smooth, but hard to distinguish individual words.

'What language is that?' Monica asked.

'Russian,' Nathan said.

'Well, that settles it. I don't speak Russian, so I couldn't have performed the spell,' Monica said.

Nathan had a sinking feeling in his stomach. 'But we know a witch who does speak Russian,' he said quietly, catching Monica's eye. 'A witch who could have snuck up on me, thanks to her invisibility rune...'

'Oh, fuck,' Monica whispered. 'Kseniya. Fuck.'

'She must have caught me on my way home,' Nathan said glumly. 'Shit.'

'You were with one of us from the end of school on Friday until you went to bed,' said Aunt Anna suspiciously. '...Nathan?'

'No,' he muttered sheepishly. 'I snuck over to see Monica—I knew you were going to ground me!' he added hastily. 'I just wanted to make sure everyone was okay!'

'Unbelievable,' his mother said.

'He was only with me for like twenty minutes,' Monica said.

'And then five minutes on the phone with Adrian,' Nathan said. 'After I left. Then I went home. That's when she got me. Damn. I was too tired to realise anything was off.'

'Do rules not mean anything to you anymore?' Aunt Anna asked.

'I'm eighteen!' Nathan protested. 'It wasn't a school night. I just wanted to make sure my friends were okay.'

'You live in my house, you follow my rules,' Aunt Anna said. 'If I say you're grounded, you are *grounded*.'

Nathan glared at her.

'Give me your phone.'

'No,' he said.

'Nathan.'

'No,' Nathan repeated. 'I need it. And I need to leave now and find out why Kseniya cursed me. Is she at your place?' he asked Monica. Monica nodded, looking pale and determined. 'She has to answer me if I ask, doesn't she?'

Monica touched the oak amulet around her neck. 'Yes,' she said.

'Right,' Nathan said decisively. 'Let's go.' He threw his legs over the edge of the bed and began detaching his heart rate monitor and IV.

'You haven't been discharged,' Aunt Anna said.

'I'm fine,' Nathan replied. 'And I'm going. Excuse me,' he added, grabbing the attention of a nurse who had just poked her head in. 'I'd like my discharge papers. And can you direct me to the bathroom, please?'

'I'll get the doctor,' the nurse said, hurrying away.

'Nathan, you've been asleep for three days,' Aunt Anna said. 'They're not going to just let you walk out of the hospital.'

Nathan gave her a pitying look. 'Pretty sure they are, actually,' he said.

Fifteen minutes later, he'd been discharged and had changed into fresh clothes. They piled into Aunt Anna's car. She muttered under her breath about teenage boys the whole way, but she did drive them home.

'We are going to be having a long chat about your behaviour,' she warned Nathan as they made their way up the Abingdon Road. 'I'm sure your parents will want to add their five cents as well.'

'Sure,' Nathan said. 'But later. Drop me at Monica's place, please.'

'Your behaviour is appalling,' his mum said.

'Please,' Nathan repeated. 'This is important.'

'What makes you think you can get this girl to talk?' Aunt Anna asked.

'Uh…' Nathan had thought he had no more secrets to tell, but it suddenly occurred to him that he hadn't told anyone about his dealings with the Witch Council. 'So, there was this time I got summoned by the Witch Council?'

'You *what*?' Mum asked incredulously.

'Please don't freak out... they offered me a boon because the Vampire Council kicked up a fuss that I'd been attacked by a witch on their turf. I asked them to free Kseniya, but to do that I had to kind of... take guardianship of her... which doesn't make sense to me, either,' Nathan finished. 'Because I'm not a witch, so I can't mark people. But they accepted it, and she did, so I think she's obliged to answer my questions...'

Aunt Anna pulled the car over outside Monica's house. Before Nathan could reach for the door, she jammed on the child lock. Then she turned to face him.

'I'm going to ask once,' she said. 'Is there anything else we don't know?'

'Um.' Nathan glanced at Monica, who shrugged.

'Kseniya might be involved with the Sahir?' she suggested.

'Yeah, that,' Nathan said. 'I can't think of anything else offhand.' The last few days had been pretty confusing. He didn't really have a handle on who knew what anymore.

'Do you even understand what it means to have guardianship over a witch?' asked Aunt Anna.

'I have a sketchy understanding,' Nathan replied. 'Please can we do this later?'

Aunt Anna frowned. She seemed to be weighing the situation, and Nathan fixed a sincere look on his face.

'I won't bail. I'll go to Monica's and then come straight home,' he said.

'Fine,' Aunt Anna said. 'I'm going to take a leap of faith *this once*. But only because you've proven that you will just sneak out again, and I don't want you doing anything stupid. You will keep me updated of all of your movements, and if you're not home in an hour you better have the world's best excuse prepared, understood?'

'Thank you, Aunt Anna!'

She released the child lock with a deep sigh. Monica and Nathan scrambled out of the car and jogged up to her house. Monica let them in.

'Is that you, Monica?' called a deep voice.

'Yeah, it's me.'

A man stepped out of the kitchen, tall and slender with coffee-coloured skin and a shaved head. He was about in his late forties.

'Oh, hello Nathan,' he said. 'I thought you were in hospital.'

'I'm better now,' Nathan said brightly. 'Hi, Malcolm. Don't worry, I won't impose for long.'

'No problem,' Malcolm replied. 'But don't you have school?'

'I think I'm going to be a bit late,' Nathan said wryly.

Monica was already halfway up the stairs. 'Oi, come on,' she called. Nathan waved to Malcolm Lefebvre and hurried upstairs after his friend. Monica knocked once on the guestroom door and threw it open, and Nathan was not surprised in the slightest to find it empty. There wasn't a trace that Kseniya had even been there. The bed was neatly made. There were no personal items lying around. Kseniya hadn't had anything, to begin with. She'd been borrowing Monica's things.

'Fuck,' Monica said eloquently.

'Was she here when you left this morning?' Nathan asked.

'No clue. I assumed she was, but I didn't check.' Monica looked frustrated. Nathan laid a hand on her arm.

'It's alright, M,' he said. 'We'll solve this.' He didn't know where this well of serenity was coming from, but he'd somehow already known Kseniya would be gone, and the same way, he somehow knew that getting angry at themselves wasn't going to help. They'd tried that already, and it hadn't worked.

Maybe getting three days' sleep really had helped him get his head on straight.

'I can scry for her,' Monica said. She pushed past Nathan and hurried into her room. Nathan chased after her.

'Monica, Monica, calm down,' he said. 'Take a breath. We'll call Adrian. He might know something.' Monica ignored him, grabbing a bowl and laying candles out on her desk. Her hands were shaking, and she kept knocking things over. She tried to strike a match and snapped it clean in half.

'Fuck!'

Nathan grabbed the matches and put them on the desk. 'Monica, sit.' He steered her to the bed and stood in front of her, taking her hands in his. 'It's okay.'

'No, you don't understand!' Monica wailed. 'This is my fault!'

'It's not your fault, Monica. You couldn't have known she was a spy.'

'Not that.' Monica sniffed loudly. 'It's my fault she fell in with the Sahir in the first place. If I hadn't—' The rest of her sentence vanished in a torrent of tears. Nathan stared at her in alarm.

'Monica,' he said soothingly, 'Monica, it's okay. Shh. It's okay.'

'It's not,' Monica sobbed. 'This was never supposed to happen!'

Nathan shifted to sit beside her and put his arm around her shoulders, pulling her against his chest. It was an awkward position. Monica clung to him, and he rubbed her back. It took her a few minutes to collect herself. Once Nathan thought she was calm, he said, 'Monica, Kseniya did this herself. You can't take responsibility for her actions.'

'When we were fifteen,' Monica mumbled, not moving her face away from his chest, 'she was… my first, I guess.'

'First?' And then it clicked. Nathan tried to avoid talking about sex with Monica, because she made no effort to hide that she'd slept around a lot, and she loved to tease Nathan about how inexperienced he was. 'Really?'

Monica nodded.

'I was with her before… before my parents died. She was, I dunno, exotic. Hot. Exciting. My parents hated it, we argued so much. Then they were dead, and I was… lost. Kseniya knew a spell, old magic, Russian magic. Banned by the Council.'

'To avenge your parents?' Nathan asked. Witches could place curses—Kseniya's sleeping curse didn't even come close to the full spectrum of vengeful magics that a witch could cast.

'No,' Monica muttered, 'to bring them back.'

'Oh, shit.'

'Necromancy is super dangerous,' Monica said. 'Pretty impossible, as well, zombies are like the closest you can get. Kseniya's spell, though… it could have worked. If we'd done it. Probably a good thing we didn't… spells like that often rebound on the caster. A soul for a soul…'

'You'd have died to bring your parents back?' Nathan asked in horror. He felt as though a hand had reached into his chest and was squeezing his heart. He couldn't imagine a world without Monica.

'Maybe.' Monica's gaze was distant. 'We got caught. The coven elders figured out what we were up to. We were both chucked out the coven. Death magics are forbidden, zero tolerance. Jeremiah brought me here—vampires can use distraught fifteen-year-old witches with no moral compass. Kseniya's parents took her away. I don't know where. She was forbidden contact with me.'

'That's why you wanted to help her, now,' Nathan said, putting the pieces together in his head.

'Yes. I don't know how she ended up getting involved with the Sahir... but helping me... that was the first step.'

'That's a pretty big leap,' Nathan said. 'It's been seven years since then. Anything could have happened during that time.'

'Nate, you don't understand what it means to be excommunicated as a witch. No other coven will take you,' Monica insisted. 'I should never have involved her in my drama—it's what I do, drag everyone down with me. I'm doing it to you, too. It's just the same.'

'Stop,' Nathan said firmly. 'For one, trust me, I do know what it means to be excommunicated. Hunters have the exact same traditions. For another, you have never dragged me down. I'm capable of making my own decisions, Monica. So is Kseniya. You can't take responsibility for other people like that. We're free agents.'

'Free agents who got involved in my shit.'

'I'm pretty sure this one is my shit,' Nathan said. 'Anyway, I'm not giving up now. We'll find Kseniya and get her out of there. Maybe this is a mistake. Maybe they threatened her. We can still help her.'

Monica sniffled and pulled away from him. 'You think?'

'Sure. No one's beyond help, right?'

Monica smiled, and Nathan had an inkling that they were no longer talking about Kseniya here. Well, he'd help Monica too. After this crisis was resolved.

He got up. 'What do you need to scry her?'

'Something personal.'

'Did she leave anything?'

'She didn't need to.' Monica went to her desk and opened a drawer, pulling out a Ziplock bag. 'I have cuttings of everyone's hair, just in case.'

'Mine, too?' Nathan asked in alarm. Monica nodded. 'Wow, paranoid much?'

'I don't like the idea that you could be in trouble, and I couldn't find you,' Monica said defensively.

'Fine.' Nathan sighed. 'Do your thing.'

Nathan sat on the bed whilst Monica set up the scrying circle. The circle itself was painted onto her floor in white paint, hidden beneath the rug. The runes were witch runes, not the sort that hunters used. They might have been Greek. Monica filled one bowl with water and sprinkled a few white-blond hairs into another, setting each of them in the circle. She lit one candle and drizzled wax onto the floor, using it to stick four candles at each of the four compass points around the circle.

Then Monica knelt in front of the circle and began to chant. This was the part that took time. Nathan laid his head back against the wall and shut his eyes. He was still tired. After a second, he opened them again. He didn't have time to go to sleep now. He glanced around for something to distract himself, and his eyes lit on something suspicious.

Hidden amidst the feathers of Monica's collection of dreamcatchers was a little hunk of wood with a word carved into it. Not a rune, this was in Cyrillic: слух. Hearing. The writing glistened greenish-grey to his magical sight. He reached up and plucked it down.

'I can't get anything clear.' Monica sat back on her heels. 'Wherever she is, the anti-scrying wards are phenomenal.'

'I can think of a few places.'

'Yeah, the Witch Council inner sanctum, for one,' Monica said. 'What's that?' She gestured to Nathan's hand.

'Oh.' Nathan showed her the ward. 'I'm guessing Kseniya left it, to keep an eye on us.'

Monica's eyes lit up. 'It's her magic? Fantastic, give it here.'

Nathan tossed it to her and watched detachedly as Monica got rid of the water and set up a new spell. His phone buzzed in his pocket, and he pulled it out. It was Aunt Anna.

'Hi,' he said. 'I'm just on my way back. Kseniya bailed and Monica's trying to do a spell to track her.'

'Never mind that,' said Aunt Anna. She sounded... terrified. Nathan's heart clenched. 'You need to come home right now.'

'What happened?'

'Cathy Rymes just called,' Aunt Anna said. 'Cynthia's missing.'

CHAPTER TWENTY-SIX

'NATHAN!' AUNT ANNA SHOUTED as Nathan dashed past her to his room. 'I've told Ms Rymes we'll—'

'Be there in a sec!'

He dashed into his room. It was an unholy mess, clothes all over the floor. His keys were on his bedside, where he usually left them, and he saw instantly that Cynthia's tracking ward had triggered. Unable to get Nathan's attention—because he didn't have it on him—it had eventually burnt out. Now, it smouldered a bit, and when he picked the keys up, he discovered a burnt patch in the shape of the leather keyring on his bedside table.

Monica had followed Nathan in. He showed her the keyring. 'Fuck.'

'Give here,' she said. 'I can use that to track her.'

Aunt Anna and Mum were waiting downstairs.

'Nathan,' Mum started immediately. 'I know this is a blow, but—'

'Don't start, Mum!'

'I don't think you should go rushing off.'

'This has nothing to do with her being my girlfriend,' Nathan said. 'She's my friend and she's in trouble, and even if I didn't have a lick of hunter training, I still wouldn't leave her to rot.'

'I know, but—'

'Can I get on with helping her, then?'

Mum was silent for a moment, her lips twisting. Finally, she said, 'I'm coming with you.'

'I don't need a babysitter!'

'Nathan, calm down,' Aunt Anna said firmly, 'we're all trying to help.'

Nathan glared at them impatiently. Couldn't they see there was no time to waste?

'Rushing off doesn't help anyone,' Mum said, 'you know that. Take a deep breath, think about what your next steps are.'

'We need to get something of Cynthia's, to scry her with,' Monica said.

'I told Cathy you'd call her when you got home,' Aunt Anna said.

Nathan forced himself to take a deep breath.

'Okay,' he said. 'Okay.' He pulled his phone out. 'Will you drive me up there?' he asked his aunt.

'I'll take you,' Mum said. Nathan was about to protest, but she stopped him. 'I know we've had our differences, your father too, but we're not going to leave you to fight your battles alone, Nathan. You're our son.'

Nathan stared at her, feeling rather touched. 'That's... I mean... Mum...' He scrambled for words and finally settled on, 'Thanks. It means a lot.'

Mum clapped him on the shoulder and turned to Monica. 'You need to set up a scrying circle?'

'On the kitchen table,' Aunt Anna said. 'I'll get candles.'

She and Monica vanished down the hall. Nathan called Cynthia's home number, and a moment later, her mother picked up.

'Hello? Cynthia?'

'Hi, Ms Rymes. It's Nathan.'

'Oh God, oh God. I heard what happened—thank goodness you're okay—first you and now Cynthia—'

'It's okay,' Nathan said firmly. 'Please calm down. I need you to tell me what happened.'

Ms Rymes made a show of taking deep breaths. 'I got a call from the school about forty minutes ago. Cynthia never turned up for her first class.'

'Go on.'

'I've driven up and down the road, looking for her. I tried calling her phone, but I found it on the ground, smashed. Her bag was thrown into the hedge. Oh God, they've got her, I know they have, please tell me that bracelet you gave her will work and you can track her—'

'Monica's working on it now.' Nathan tried to pitch his voice to be comforting, but it was hard when panic was threatening to close up his throat. 'I've got Mum and Aunt Anna helping me. We'll find her.'

'Please—I—God, this is my fault. She asked me and I lied to her! I should have told her—'

'It's okay, Ms Rymes. This isn't your fault.'

'It is,' Ms Rymes wailed. 'You don't understand!'

Nathan took a steadying breath. He could hear voices from the kitchen, and he wanted desperately to go and see what was happening. Mum watched him worriedly. He forced himself to focus. One problem at a time.

'This is on the Sahir, not you,' he said.

'That's just it,' Ms Rymes sobbed. 'I lied, to Cynthia, to you. I should have come clean, but I just couldn't. I was too ashamed. If I'd told her, she would have understood the danger, she might have come away with me by now...'

'I don't understand.'

'Cynthia's father... he's one of them.'

It was like a rug had been pulled out from under Nathan's feet. For a moment, he was robbed of words.

'One of... the Sahir?'

'I met him when I was nineteen, I didn't realise, I swear. I ran as soon as I found out, and I don't know how he knew about Cynthia, but he's never stopped following us since—'

Well, fuck.

'Okay,' Nathan said, scrambling for an intelligent answer. 'Okay, thank you for telling me, but—' *That doesn't help me.* He bit his tongue. 'Okay. Monica is scrying for Cynthia. I'll let you know as soon as we have news. You need to make sure you and Emma are safe. Can they—how well protected is your house?'

'I... not very. I don't know anything about wards. That was always witch business.'

'Alright. Maybe the best thing would be for us to come up there—'

'Nate?' Monica called.

He lowered the phone. 'Coming!' Returning to Ms Rymes, he asked, 'Can I call you back?'

'Of course, of course.' She paused to take a deep breath. 'Please find her.'

'I will.'

'Thank you.'

'Speak to you soon. Bye.' Nathan hung up and hurried into the kitchen. Monica and Aunt Anna were hunched over the table, peering into a bowl of water. It took Nathan several moments to understand what he was seeing: Cynthia's protective bangle was lying amidst all manner of junk on a riverbed, no longer attached to its wearer.

'They threw it in the river?'

'Off Magdalen Bridge, looks like,' Monica confirmed.

'Fuck!' Nathan slammed his fist into the wall. Cynthia had been in trouble, and he'd been too busy sleeping to help her!

Pain lanced up his arm, numbing his fury.

'Nathan!' Aunt Anna snapped.

'I'm fine.' Nathan shook his hand out. It hurt and his knuckles were scraped, but otherwise there was no damage. He couldn't even punch walls properly.

'Getting in a temper won't help,' Mum said.

'I'm not in a temper,' Nathan said. 'I just need to think clearly. Let me call—' He stopped himself before he said 'Adrian'. The last thing he needed now was a row with Mum over his vampire uncle. He caught Monica's eye and she nodded.

Nathan left the room and pulled his phone out. He called Adrian, but the call went through to voicemail. So did the next two tries. Nathan left a message.

'Hi, it's Nate. They've taken Cynthia. Monica's trying to scry her, but no luck yet. Call me when you get this.'

Then he called Lily. The phone rang and rang. Nathan was beginning to despair when she finally picked up.

'Hi, Nate. Sorry I made you wait. I had to sneak out of my lecture.'

'Sorry to interrupt,' Nathan said. 'I'm trying to get hold of Adrian, but he's not picking up.'

'Oh,' Lily said, and that one word contained a depth of information that Nathan couldn't quite grasp for a second. Delicately, she continued, 'Nathan, I haven't heard from Adrian. He went to visit you in hospital, but he never came back.'

Adrian had come to visit him in hospital? Touching, but not helpful right now. Nathan pushed those thoughts away.

'When was that?'

'Saturday afternoon,' Lily said. 'I was… I've been worried. Did you see him? Are you alright?'

'I'm fine,' Nathan said. 'I was under a sleeping curse. I didn't see Adrian—I didn't even know he was there.'

'Oh,' Lily said again. 'If you hear from him, will you call me?'

'Yeah. I'm sorry to disturb you.'

'That's okay, I'm glad you're alright,' Lily said.

'Bye.' Nathan hung up. His heart was beating frantically in his chest, and he forced himself to take a deep breath as he went back to the kitchen.

'Mum, did Adrian ever come by the hospital whilst I was there?' Despite his best efforts, the words came out like an accusation. Mum looked up sharply.

'No, I never saw him. Unless he came at night, when your father was there.'

Dad had been at the hospital? Nathan pushed that revelation away as well. He could think about it later. 'Saturday afternoon.'

'I was there all of Saturday from when we took you in until about seven PM,' Mum said. 'I never saw him.'

'Nate?' Monica asked worriedly.

'I called Lily,' Nathan told her. 'Adrian's been missing since Saturday.'

'Shit,' Monica said. 'That's bad.'

'Yes,' Nathan said. It was all that needed to be said. Adrian was missing. Cynthia was missing. Someone, somehow, had known where all of them would be and was steadily splitting up their group. Divide and conquer. Nathan immediately resolved not to let Monica out of his sight.

His phone buzzed.

'It's Dad. What would he want?' Nathan asked in confusion. He put the phone to his ear and said cautiously, 'Hi, Dad.'

'Nathan,' Dad said sternly. 'Where are you? Longhorn's asking for you. I'm coming to pick you up.'

'What? Why?'

'I have no idea,' Dad said. 'But please, for the love of God, just be respectful. I can't take any more trouble from you this century.'

Ouch.

'Fine, I'm at home,' Nathan snapped. 'Want me to change into a suit and tie, too?'

'Whatever you're wearing will be fine,' Dad said, matching Nathan's angry tone. 'Just be ready when I get there. I'll be fifteen minutes.' He hung up.

'What is it?' Monica asked.

'I've been summoned by the Hunter Council,' Nathan said. 'Dad's picking me up.'

'Damn,' Monica said. 'Is that bad?'

'I doubt it's anything good,' Nathan said. 'Probably more trouble over Adrian, right?' He glanced at Mum, but worryingly she looked as confused as he felt. *Great.*

Nathan dressed in his hunter uniform and was strapping the last of his knives in place when he heard the car pulling up outside. He took the stairs two at a time and stopped in the kitchen.

'I'll try and make it as quick as I can.'

'Okay,' Monica said. 'We're going to drive up to Cynthia's place.'

'Thanks.'

Dad entered the kitchen. 'Are you ready?' He looked Nathan up and down, and Nathan must have passed muster, because he looked grimly satisfied.

'What's going on, Ben?' Mum asked.

'No idea. Longhorn requested him,' Dad said. 'Let's just hope this isn't more trouble for our family. The last thing we need is Nathan's teenage rebellion dragging us all down.'

Nathan flinched. Monica laid a hand on his arm.

'Good luck,' she whispered.

'You, too,' Nathan replied. Then he followed his father outside and climbed into the car.

Dad said nothing as he pulled away from the house. Nathan considered asking him questions, but one look at his father said that Benjamin Delacroix was not in the mood for talking. He drove out of their street, but instead of turning left towards the Hunter Council office, he turned right. A nasty suspicion started up in Nathan's chest.

Fuck...

They pulled onto the A34. 'Dad, where are we going?' Nathan asked.

'The prison.'

'What?' Nathan said. 'Dad, no! I can't leave town right now. You have to take me back.'

'Longhorn wants to see you at the prison.'

'You don't understand! I don't have time for this—Cynthia's in danger!'

'Hunter business takes precedence,' Dad snapped. 'This is your problem—you go running around after witches and shapeshifters. You're a hunter first. You need to learn to put the hunters ahead of your personal drama.'

'Being a hunter is not more important to me than Cynthia's life,' Nathan snarled.

'I don't care about your little animal girlfriend,' Dad said. 'Belt it, Nathan.'

Nathan glared at his father, but his father just ignored him as he accelerated down the dual carriageway. Nathan pulled his phone out and sent a frantic text to Monica.

Nathan: Dad's taking me to the fucking prison

Monica: The what?

Nathan: Hunter facility halfway to London. Won't turn back. What do I do?

Monica: SHIT

Monica: Won't he listen to reason?

Nathan: Of course not

Monica: Your dad's such a shithead

Monica: Calling Jeremiah

There was a long wait before she sent another message. Nathan's heart was in his mouth. Finally, as they hit the M40, his phone buzzed again.

Monica: Jeremiah has agreed to help, but you're going to owe him big time

Monica: Sorry Nate, was the best I could do

Nathan: I don't care if he wants my firstborn right now

Monica: Got it. Aodhán is going to back me up

Nathan sighed in relief. He didn't know a damn thing about Aodhán, but Aodhán worked for Jeremiah, and Nathan was probably going to pay for Jeremiah's help in blood, so he better damn well deliver. One thing you could count on with Jeremiah was that he had a sense of honour a mile wide. He'd come through.

They rode in stony silence for the remainder of the trip. After what seemed like forever, they reached the gates of Wedley Manor. Dad rolled the window down and handed their IDs over without a word.

'You're not on the list,' said the security guard.

'This visit is sanctioned by Agent Longhorn,' Dad said.

The security guard paged through the papers on his clipboard. 'Ah, got you.' He handed their IDs back. 'You can use the staff parking lot.'

'Thank you,' Dad said. The gates slid open, and they drove inside.

Aside from the grounds being muddier and the trees having lost their leaves, the prison still looked the same. They entered via a side entrance, using Dad's ID to unlock the doors. Dad walked swiftly, and Nathan had to work to keep up. He still felt tired and drained, and he struggled up the two flights of stairs to Longhorn's office.

His father paused in the top of the stairwell, his hand on the door handle. 'Nate,' he started gruffly.

'Don't fuck up?' Nathan guessed, unable to keep a bit of bitterness out of his tone.

'Language,' his father scolded. 'But, yes, that's the essence. I know you probably don't think so, but the reputation of the family depends on all members toeing the line. Longhorn isn't just the head of the Hunter Council. He's also my boss. Your behaviour here will reflect on me.'

'I know that, Dad,' Nathan said tiredly. 'I never set out to embarrass you or anything.'

His dad stared at him for a long moment. '…I know, but I also know that things don't always work out the way we want them to, and sometimes it takes a lot of hard work to atone for that.' He squared his shoulders. 'And that hard work starts now, understood?'

There were so many things Nathan wanted to say to that, but now wasn't the time. 'Fine, I'm ready.'

'Good.' Dad led the way to the office at the end of the hall. He knocked firmly.

'Come in.'

They entered a spartanly furnished office. The furniture hadn't been updated in several decades. Old school filing cabinets lined one wall.

'Ah, Benjamin, Nathan, thank you for coming,' said Agent Longhorn, standing up from behind the desk. He was wearing a navy suit that looked like it cost the same as Nathan's annual school fees. Longhorn's dark hair was combed and gelled to perfection. This was not a man who got his hands dirty. Was this really the man who led an elite fighting squad against the supernatural? Had this man ever actually been in the field, got blood on his hands, been injured, seen comrades die? Or did he send other people out to do that for him?

Nathan pushed his ruminations away and shook Longhorn's hand.

'Have a seat,' Longhorn said, gesturing to the sofa. 'Can I offer you any tea or coffee?'

'Coffee, please,' Dad said.

Nathan would have liked to say 'no', so they could hurry this along, but he muttered, 'Me too.'

Longhorn poked his head out the door for a moment, before returning.

'Stella will bring our drinks up,' he said as he sat in an armchair. He steepled his hands under his chin and regarded Nathan.

'Thank you for coming on short notice, Nathan. I hope you don't mind; I know it's a school day, but I'm sure you'll agree that hunter business take precedence. Especially considering… recent events.'

Okay, what the hell was going on?

'Of course.' Nathan had to fight not to show his impatience. How long had it been since Cynthia had gone missing? Had Monica found anything yet? He wished Longhorn would hurry up.

'How are you doing?' Longhorn asked. 'Forgive me for prying—I'm only going on what I've heard from your father and uncle—but you appear to have been struggling a little with balancing our lifestyle.'

Brilliant. Nathan darted a glance at his father, who managed to look both worried and stern at the same time. He gave Nathan a very pointed look.

'It's been a bit rocky,' Nathan replied uneasily, 'but I think I'm back on track now.'

'Any news on when you'll go for initiations?' Longhorn asked. 'I must confess, I have a vested interest in encouraging young trainees to go for initiations. We seem to be perpetually understaffed.' He chuckled. The wrongness struck Nathan again. Understaffed? Was that really what he wanted to call it? As though they were down a few nurses on an A&E nightshift? They needed people to initiate in order to fill the places of hunters who had died in service. That was no joking matter.

Nathan flicked his gaze to his father, but Dad's face was like stone, giving nothing away.

'I… I wouldn't want to go into the field before I'm ready,' Nathan managed. His head felt heavy and slow. 'That would be a risk to the rest of my team… as well as myself.'

'A very sensible attitude,' Longhorn said. Someone knocked on the door and he called, 'Come in!'

A woman in uniform stepped in. Nathan thought she was maybe ten years older than he was, and she had a couple of stripes on her jacket, but not nearly as many as his father had earned. She was a field hunter, then.

She brought a tray over to the table, passing a mug to each of them. 'Anything else I can get you, Sir?'

'No thank you, Stella.' Longhorn waited until the woman was out of the office again, and the door had shut behind her, then he turned to Nathan. 'I'll jump right in, then. Your father tells me that you have managed to acquire unusual connections with the Vampire Council.'

What?

Nathan glanced at his father, confused.

'I had to report our visit to the prison,' his father said. 'Standard protocol, Nathan.'

'Oh, okay.'

'Could you elaborate on how this came about?' Longhorn requested.

Nathan fiddled with the handle of his coffee cup. Something felt off, but he couldn't have said whether it was a genuine feeling or just paranoia born of tiredness. Longhorn was scrutinising him closely, making Nathan feel rather uncomfortable.

'I have a friend who's a witch,' Nathan said hesitantly. He glanced at his father, who nodded grimly. 'She's the... ward of Jeremiah.' He caught the flash of disappointment on Longhorn's face and stopped.

'It's not because of your uncle, then?' Longhorn sounded almost eager. 'I understood that he was... in the employ of Damien.'

'Well, yes,' Nathan said, 'but Damien's not on the Council. And Monica, my witch friend, is the one who asked Jeremiah to... protect me?' Was that the right word? 'Well, she petitioned on my behalf, anyway,' he added. 'Although I hadn't met Jeremiah at that point. It was Adrian who got me into the prison, these last few times.'

'Fascinating,' Longhorn drawled. Nathan didn't really see what was so fascinating. 'You know, Nathan, we've been trying to get hunters into the prison on business pretty much since the inception of the Council, and yet in at least ninety percent of cases they refuse. You've been there... twice?'

'Three times,' Nathan corrected.

'Three times in the last few weeks,' Longhorn said. 'All unsanctioned visits, and yet you've never been turned away. How did you do it?'

'I'm really not sure, to be honest,' Nathan said. He was starting to get a little frustrated. Did he really have to come all the way here to have this conversation? They were going *nowhere*.

'You didn't make a deal with them?' Longhorn asked.

'No,' Nathan said irritably, 'I know better than to make deals with vampires.'

His father made a noise under his breath. Nathan hastily reined in his temper. 'Sorry, I'd really love to explain it to you, but I think maybe I just have good friends.' He picked up his cup of coffee and took a big sip.

'Of course,' Longhorn said. 'I'm not implying that you would make deals with vampires. I'm simply... trying to understand how this situation came about, and whether we can take advantage of it for the good of the Hunter Council. After all, I think the present situation has demonstrated that we are nowhere near where we need to be in terms of communication.'

'Right.' Nathan sipped his coffee again and tried to think of a way to close this discussion so he could get back to Oxford. 'Well, I supposed I could write down everything I remember of the interactions so that you could see if there's anything I missed?'

'That would be good going forwards,' Longhorn said. 'As for Damien—you are familiar with him, right?'

Damn, Longhorn wouldn't take a hint.

'I suppose,' Nathan said. 'We've met a few times, although I know his daughter better.'

'Ah yes. How would you assess her threat level?'

'Who, Lily?' Nathan asked incredulously. 'Uh, I don't think she's a threat. Why?'

'But Damien would go to quite some lengths to protect her, right?'

Nathan glanced at his father, but he looked baffled by the turn the conversation had taken, too.

'Uh, probably,' Nathan said. 'It's hard for me to say. I really don't know Damien that well.' He shifted uncomfortably. 'I don't understand how this is... relevant to the Council?' It felt more like he was being interrogated about his friends.

'This is invaluable information,' Longhorn said. 'We've never been able to gain an insider perspective into the Vampire Council before.'

'Damien's not on the Council, though.'

'Yes, yes, but we suspect he will be soon, and it's better to be forewarned,' Longhorn said.

'Damien's not really a politician. I doubt he'd want the Council position.'

'Nathan, I hope you'll forgive me for disagreeing,' Longhorn said. 'In my experience, all vampires want to expand their power base. I doubt Damien has any other reason for putting up with working for the Council.'

Nathan frowned. Longhorn looked straight at him, and he hastily covered the expression, but he wasn't fast enough.

'You seem distracted,' Longhorn said.

Crap!

Nathan glanced at his father, who looked displeased. No help there. Thinking fast, he said, 'I'm sorry. It's the Sahir—we think they might be behind the disappearance of one of my friends. I understand that this is important, though. Better communication between the Councils could lead to situations like the one with the Sahir being avoided entirely in future.'

Nathan tensed, certain he'd just put his foot in it. Longhorn nodded benevolently.

'Of course, I understand that would be quite worrying for you.' He smiled affably. 'Benjamin, you should have told me—I'd have postponed this meeting!'

'Hunter business comes first,' Dad replied.

'Ah, but even we didn't think that when we were eighteen,' Longhorn said cheerfully. 'Well, Nathan, finish your coffee and I'll let you get off. I'm sure you must be quite worried about your uncle.'

Nathan froze, his cup halfway to his mouth. *Come again?*

'Wait, what?' Nathan asked. 'I never mentioned Adrian—it's Cynthia who's missing—how did you know Adrian was missing?'

Suddenly, the pieces fell into place.

'Of course,' Nathan continued grimly. 'You have him.' He looked at his father, who looked horrified. 'Did you know about this too?'

'No!' Dad said indignantly. 'What is the meaning of this? Adrian's continued existence is the business of the Delacroix family alone. He's not in violation of Council law.'

That was probably a lie. Nathan was pretty sure Adrian had violated the laws a number of times. Not that that was important right now. He put his coffee cup down and rounded on Longhorn.

'Where is he?'

'Nathan, don't you think you're jumping to conclusions here?' Longhorn asked in a reasonable tone.

'No,' Nathan said. 'Not really. Because there's no way you could have known Adrian was missing unless you orchestrated it. I only found out this morning, and I doubt Damien told you.' He scowled and added, 'And now that I think about it, it's a little too coincidental that you wanted me here right now. Almost as though something important was happening in Oxford and you didn't want me finding out... and telling the Vampire Council, right?'

It was a leap of logic, but looking into Longhorn's face, Nathan knew he was right. Longhorn's expression was grim.

'Where is he?' Nathan asked. 'Is he being held here?' This was the only facility he knew of that could hold a vampire.

Several emotions ran across Longhorn's face in quick succession, before he finally said, 'I was hoping you wouldn't find out. Your uncle was found in violation of Council law, and we took him into custody on Saturday.'

'What law did he break?'

'He attacked a pedestrian in the city—luckily Damien was there and could control him and compel passers-by, or we would have had a serious security breach on our hands.'

'Damien can't compel people,' Nathan said quietly.

'Every vampire can compel people, Nathan,' Longhorn said in a patronising tone.

'Every vampire except Damien,' Nathan said with conviction. 'And Lily. It's a shame, really, because I'm guessing that if you got that wrong, the whole rest of the story was false, too.'

'Nathan, are you sure?' Dad asked.

'Positive,' Nathan said. 'But if you don't believe me, I can call Lily for you. She'll corroborate.'

Dad was silent for a long moment. Nathan held his breath. If there was one moment in his life that he really needed his dad on his side, this was it.

'No,' Dad said finally, 'That won't be necessary.' He turned to Longhorn. 'Is Adrian being held here? I think we should hear the story for ourselves.'

Longhorn gritted his teeth but nodded sharply. 'It doesn't matter. I can take you to him, but you won't be able to free him from this facility, and even if you did, he's been here close to three days. By now, the human blood has left his system. He won't be able to leave during daylight hours without burning to death.'

Nathan felt sick to his stomach. He glanced at his father and was gratified to see that he didn't look any happier. Maybe Dad did hate Adrian, but that didn't mean he wanted his brother to suffer.

Longhorn stood and collected his jacket from his desk chair. 'Shall we?'

'Please,' Dad said.

They descended the stairs in an uncomfortable silence. Nathan's tiredness had vanished, and his thoughts raced as he tried to fit the pieces together.

Longhorn had taken Adrian at the same time that Nathan had been put under a sleeping curse. Now Cynthia was missing. As soon as Nathan had woken up, Longhorn had lured him out of town with an excuse he had known Nathan's father would fall for. There was no way that this was a coincidence. Something was going down in Oxford, and Longhorn had helped get two of them out of the way. Cynthia being kidnapped meant it had something to do with the Sahir, which meant...

Longhorn was working with the Sahir.

Holy fuck.

They reached the first subterranean level, and Longhorn led them through the corridors. The wards seemed to bother Nathan even more than they had last time. It was like an itch beneath his skin, an ache in his brain. Had he just forgotten how bad it was last time? Or were they affecting him worse? Was he just more sensitive because he'd spent so much time crafting wards lately?

Nathan guessed where Longhorn was leading them long before they got there. It was the prison cell where the almost-lucid feral had been held. Of course.

The corridor leading to the cell was as claustrophobic as it had been before. Their rapid footsteps echoed off the walls, making it seem as though their group was much bigger. They stopped in front of the warded doors, but Longhorn made no movement to open either of them. Instead, he turned to Nathan, but Nathan beat him to speaking.

'You're working with the Sahir,' he said. 'How long?'

Longhorn seemed to be considering denying the accusation, but he finally said, 'The Sahir have been in the city for a little over seven months now.'

'That long?' Nathan asked, shocked. That meant... they hadn't arrived pursuing Cynthia and her family... which meant the attacks on Cynthia had been opportunistic.

'Yes, that long.' For the first time, Longhorn's affable façade cracked, and his voice took on a mocking tone. 'They have eliminated a number of high-profile targets of ours, without the Hunter Council having to get their hands dirty. Of course, it's unsavoury to collaborate with witches, but in the long run this will help us achieve our goals.'

Nathan honestly couldn't care less about his justification. 'You're the reason the Vampire Council didn't know about the other bodies,' he said.

'How do you know about that?' Dad asked, but Nathan didn't have time to explain now.

'You've been sweeping things under the carpet,' he told Longhorn. 'Ironic, that's exactly what everyone accuses the vampires of doing.' He turned to his father. 'We have to warn the others.'

'Yes,' Dad agreed to Nathan's surprise, but before he could pull his phone out, Longhorn held up a hand.

'There's no mobile phone reception down here.'

'Then we'll go upstairs,' Nathan told him, already calculating in his mind whether he could get past Longhorn without resorting to physical force.

'I'm afraid you misunderstand me,' Longhorn said. 'You won't be going upstairs. Even now, there's a team of hunters on standby to prevent you from leaving the basement, and even if you did manage to get out of here, your car has been put out of commission. You will not be leaving the premises.'

Dad bristled at that. 'You can't keep us here. We're not criminals.'

'That's where you're wrong, Benjamin,' Longhorn replied, still in the same easy-going tone. 'I can keep you here, and I will keep you here.' He turned to Nathan. 'I didn't understand when they insisted I remove you from the city. What can you do, as an uninitiated hunter?

But now I see. So many people willing to fight for you. It's a mystery to me how you've managed it, an eighteen-year-old boy who's failing maths.'

'If you think I'm planning on just sitting tight here whilst you threaten my friends, you have another thing coming.'

'I don't doubt that you'll try, Nathan.' Longhorn had the temerity to look genuinely apologetic. 'But I'm afraid I can't have you running back to Oxford until the Sahir have finished up. It's too risky. That's why you're going to have to go in with your uncle.'

CHAPTER TWENTY-SEVEN

NATHAN'S JAW PRACTICALLY HIT the floor in shock.

'You want to put my son in a cell with a rabid vampire?' Dad demanded.

'I'm sorry, Ben,' Longhorn said. 'I didn't want to involve you or him, but this is the way it has to be. It's for the good of the organisation.'

'It's okay, Dad,' Nathan said, but his voice wasn't as steady as he'd have liked. 'I trust Adrian.'

'This is madness!' Dad snarled. 'This isn't how the hunters operate. Nathan's just a boy—Adrian will kill him.'

'I sincerely hope not,' Longhorn said. 'After all, Nathan is a promising young hunter, if a little... misguided. I will, of course, allow him to go in armed, just in case.'

This had to be some kind of joke. Nathan stared at Longhorn in disbelief, wondering if the guy could hear the words coming out of his own mouth.

'You can't do this!' Dad said.

Nathan felt a momentary stab of pity for his father, the man who had always valued rules and discipline above all else. His father had always had absolute trust in the hunter ethos. Despite having been in the field for thirty years, Benjamin Delacroix was not prepared to handle being betrayed by his comrades.

Adrian would have seen this coming.

Nathan took a deep breath. 'Fine, let's get this over with.'

'Nathan—no!' Dad said.

'You're not going to put up a fight?' Longhorn asked.

'Is there any point?' Nathan replied. Turning to his father, he said, 'It's alright, Dad, I know what needs to be done.'

His father frowned, and Nathan could practically see the gears turning in his mind.

'I'll watch from next door,' Dad said. 'I won't—I won't leave you alone.'

'It's alright, Dad,' Nathan repeated. 'I should just give you this— just in case.' He unstrapped the spirit knife from his hip and held it out to his father. 'Wouldn't want it to fall back into Adrian's hands, right?'

His father looked at the knife, and then back at Nathan. For a moment, Nathan just looked into his father's eyes. Then his father nodded sharply and took the knife, sliding it into his jacket.

'We had our differences,' he said, 'but I never wanted this.'

'I know,' Nathan said. He turned to Longhorn. 'I'm ready.'

'How noble,' Longhorn said. He had an odd look on his face, like he couldn't decide whether he respected Nathan or pitied him. Nathan found he didn't want either. He went to the vaulted door and Longhorn scanned his access card, tapping in the code. Then he pulled out a hefty-looking key and unlocked the door. He swung it open, gun out and trained on Adrian.

Nathan entered the cell and the door shut behind him. The wards instantly came into force. Hundreds of anti-vampire and anti-magic wards pressed in on him.

Adrian was huddled in the centre of the room, his shoulders hunched as though the wards were a physical pressure. He was shackled at the wrists, ankles, and neck, and his skin was charred where the silver touched it. His shirt was ripped and stained with blood. Nathan had never seen him looking more pitiful. Then he looked up.

'Nathan?' Adrian said hoarsely. His eyes were hazy and red, and Nathan had a definitive realisation that he had never been in more danger from his uncle than he was at this very moment. Three days without blood weren't enough time to starve a vampire... unless you injured them to the point where they exhausted their energy and needed to feed in order to heal. Or tortured them for three days straight.

Or both.

'Fuck,' Adrian croaked, 'Nate, you cannot be here.'

'Actually, I'm pretty sure I'm right where I need to be,' Nathan said. Adrian shuddered.

'I don't... want to hurt you,' he mumbled, his words slurring around his fangs. Nathan avoided his eyes. Starving vampires weren't in complete control of their faculties. He didn't want Adrian to compel him. This needed to be Nathan's decision.

'If I gave you my blood,' he said, 'would you be safe to go out in sunlight?'

'Nate, no! I could... I'm not... I might not—control it...'

'I trust you,' Nathan said. 'Besides, you think I can't stop you? I've kicked your arse before.'

Adrian laughed and immediately began coughing like mad. There was blood on his lips. Internal injuries. *Shit.*

Nathan cautiously stepped closer. Adrian clenched his fists, rattling the chains.

'Don't... don't, please...'

'Adrian, you once said sorry that you had hung around me and blurred the lines,' Nathan said. 'And I wanted to say for a while now... I'm not sorry.' He turned his head away and held out his arm. 'You can drink my blood. Just... don't do that thing where you make it feel good. I don't want that.'

'Fucking crazy kid,' Adrian said, and then his hands were on Nathan's arm. He didn't hesitate for a single second. Nathan stared at the wall, translating the runes for the wards in his head as Adrian sank his fangs into Nathan's wrist. It didn't hurt a lot, more like having blood drawn, but exaggerated. Vampires could inject a venom from their fangs, kind of like snakes, which encouraged the release of endorphins in their victims—in other words, making them feel really good about dying. Adrian, true to Nathan's request, didn't do that. Nothing masked the pain or the strange drawing feeling of having blood removed.

All of the wards were the same. Nathan thought about science instead. The average man had about six litres of blood. You could pass out from blood loss if you lost forty percent of that, or two point four litres. The average human stomach could fit between two and four litres. Scientifically speaking, it was perfectly possible for a vampire to drain a human to the point of passing out, but unlikely that they would actually drain your body dry like on TV...

Okay, that wasn't helping either.

He went back to counting the wards until he felt himself grow a bit dizzy. Then he mustered the firmest voice he could manage. 'Adrian, enough.'

Adrian ignored him.

Nathan turned his head towards Adrian. Yanking his wrist away was a bad idea. He grabbed a handful of Adrian's hair and tugged his head back. 'Off, or we start playing with knives.'

Adrian retracted his fangs and backed off. Nathan let him. For a moment, the two of them just stared at each other. Adrian had blood smeared over his mouth. His eyes glowed red, then the glow faded, and he was staring at Nathan through the same brown eyes Nathan saw in the mirror every day. He hung his head.

'Fuck, Nate,' he said.

'We can worry about your ethical quandary later,' Nathan said. 'Time to get out of here.' He pressed his wrist against his leg to stem the bleeding. It wasn't too bad, considering.

'Tell me you have a plan for these?' Adrian asked, deliberately rattling his chains. 'And the door. And the facility full of trained hunters.'

'It's a work in progress.' Nathan looked around, trying to locate the concealed cameras.

'Okay, well you should know, I reckon Longhorn's the traitor. So don't count on too much support out there.'

'I had figured that out, thanks,' Nathan said. 'Given that he just put me in a cell with a rabid vampire.'

'Oi, less of the rabid.'

Nathan had to grin. Bantering with Adrian was familiar ground. Was it weird that he found it reassuring? Of course, Adrian would probably crack a joke on his deathbed, but it still lessened the tension a bit.

'I think Longhorn's working with the Witch Council,' he confessed. 'And the Sahir have Cynthia.'

'Brilliant.' Adrian snorted. 'I vanish for a few days, and everything goes to hell.'

'Tell me about it,' Nathan said. 'What would they do without the Delacroix dream team?' He looked into one of the cameras. 'This is just a diversion to get us out of town.'

'At least they know who their real enemies are.'

'Yep,' Nathan agreed. 'But lucky for us there's a few things that Longhorn doesn't know.' He fixed his eyes on the camera and hoped his father was watching from the next room.

Nathan focused on the spirit knife and imagined it forming into the key he'd seen in Longhorn's hands a few minutes earlier. In front of the cameras, he mimed reaching into his pocket and hoped that his father got the message.

It seemed to take forever before finally the cell door swung open. His father was holding the knife-turned-key.

'Longhorn's gone back upstairs,' he said, holding the key out to Nathan. 'I really hope you know what you're doing, Nathan.'

'Not a clue.' Grinning, Nathan took the key and allowed it to shift shape in his fingers. It took a few tries, but in short order, he had managed to unlock the shackles.

'Thank fuck.' Adrian rubbed at his wrists. Nathan's blood was clearly doing the trick; before his eyes, the blackened flesh of Adrian's wrists began to heal. 'Thank you.'

'Thank me later,' Nathan said. 'If Longhorn wanted you and me out of town, that means the real target isn't Cynthia.'

'Damien,' Adrian said certainly. 'It's always Damien.'

Nathan remembered the numerous times people had complained about Damien's sudden rise in power. 'Yeah, you're probably right. They're worried Damien is going to try for a position on the Council.'

Adrian snorted. 'They don't know Damien very well. He despises politics.'

'I know that, you know that,' Nathan said. 'Does anyone listen to us? Of course not.'

'Let's go,' Adrian said decisively. 'I can call him from the road. You got a spare knife?'

Nathan passed one over. Adrian gripped it and grinned. 'I'll try not to savage too many hunters on the way out.'

They both headed for the hallway. Nathan's father blocked the door, stopping them.

'Nathan, are you sure about this?'

'I'm sure,' Nathan replied.

'You're siding with him—' He jerked his head towards Adrian. '— Over our people.'

'Our people are working with black mages to wipe out political targets,' Nathan said. 'That violates the hunter code. If that's what it means to be a hunter, Dad, then I'll never be a hunter. That's one thing we can agree on.' He stared his father in the eyes. 'I need to get back to Oxford. Now. People are in danger.'

Dad was silent for a long moment before finally he nodded. 'There might be an easier way out,' he said. 'There's a back way, and Longhorn won't expect us to use it.'

Something about the way he said that told Nathan there was a good reason why they might not want to use it. His father's tone was just... too grim.

'Okay, let's go.'

Dad led them down to the third subterranean level. His hunter ID got them through the door, and then the wards were pressing in on them even worse than before. Adrian made a pained noise.

'Who designed the wards here?'

'They're even worse than the Vampire Council,' Nathan agreed. He was pretty sure they were affecting him worse than in the past.

'I think it was the du Tilleul family,' Dad said. 'They specialise in wardcrafting. Nathan, I'm surprised you feel the wards so strongly.'

'Me too.' Nathan tried his best to push away the sensation of fingernails digging into his skin and voices clamouring for his attention. He needed to be alert in case they passed anyone.

The main hallway was deserted. Their footsteps echoed off the stone walls.

'How long has this place been here?' Nathan asked his father.

'Centuries. The Wedleys were a were-hunting family. After the Purge, they abandoned Britain to pursue their prey and conferred the manor into the hands of the Hunter Council. It was repurposed to hold vampires instead.'

The Purge was something the hunters took credit for, but everyone knew they'd only been one of the reasons it happened. Many weres had left Britain for the USA in the mid-1600s; partly because the hunters were a real threat in Britain, but partly because what animal wouldn't be attracted by the promise of unlimited forests and open land to roam on?

Adrian looked as disgusted as Nathan felt. 'This place is practically one giant torture chamber.'

'I hardly think the vampires have the moral high ground in this case,' Dad pointed out.

'All three Councils are as bad as each other,' Nathan said. 'And humans are just as capable of being monsters—fuck!' Adrian staggered into his side, and they both crashed into the wall. Nathan's ears were ringing. He righted them both and slung an arm around Adrian's shoulders. Dad had covered a specific ward on the wall, which was what was making Nathan's ears ring.

'We triggered the security system. We should hurry.'

'Adrian?' Nathan asked.

Adrian drew himself up and took a deep breath. 'I'm fine. Let's go.'

The security system was silent, which was almost more eerie than if an alarm had gone off. Doors began opening up and down the hall. They sprinted down the hallway and Dad jammed his card against a keypad, stabbing the keys. The door slid open.

'Halt!' someone shouted behind them. Adrian spun around, too fast for Nathan to see, and then two hunters were collapsed against the wall. A third lunged at Nathan, who jabbed his fist into the taller man's solar plexus, then took him down by kneeing him in the nuts.

Nathan dived through the door. Adrian appeared beside him, licking blood from his fingernails. Dad hauled the door shut again and slammed a lever down.

'Security override,' he said. 'They might put the building into lockdown, we need to be out before then.'

They ran down another hallway, through a door, and emerged without warning into the gymnasium-sized hall containing at least half a dozen feral vampires. High above, Nathan could see scientists observing through a window.

'Fuck!' Adrian ground to a halt. The ferals turned to face them as one.

'That door,' Dad said, pointing. Then he pulled out a gun and shot two of the ferals straight in the hearts.

Ferals didn't die cleanly like vampires would. It was something to do with the decay process. Instead of turning to dust, they exploded.

Blood and rotten flesh went everywhere, and the other ferals went from insane to rabid in an instant. A few of them lunged towards Nathan's group, whilst another began tearing at itself. Nathan's dad shot that one, too.

Nathan felt a brief flash of panic, but ruthlessly pushed it away. Freaking out would have to wait until later. He summoned the spirit knife and slashed an approaching feral across the chest. The knife made a wet squelching noise. The feral kept coming, and then Adrian was there, and it had no head. Nathan drove the knife into the feral's chest, a single thought turning it from metal to wood.

That finished the job. He felt the pulse of whatever magic held a vampire's body together after death. There was a moment, the moment when their hearts were pierced with wood, where that magic gave out. It exploded outwards, and then Nathan was covered in stinking rotten flesh.

No time to think about that. Dad had dispatched another feral, but another was right behind him. Nathan took two steps and drove his knife into that one's heart, too.

Adrian beheaded two more, which Dad finished off. You had to stab ferals in the heart to be sure. Tearing the heads off was the method with the lowest guarantee of success—sometimes the bodies kept coming, like zombies.

The whole thing lasted maybe five minutes, and then the three of them were surrounded by a mess of blood and guts.

'This way!' Dad shouted. He already had the door open on the far side of the hall. They hurtled down another corridor, and the part of Nathan's brain that wasn't dedicated to trying not vomit recognised that they had to be heading away from the building. Several other corridors branched off from this one.

'What is this?'

'This is the way we bring prisoners in!' Dad called. 'Mind the wards!'

A moment later, they ran into another magical null area. Adrian staggered. Nathan grabbed his arm and dragged him onwards, and then they were racing up a narrow staircase, up, up, up, and they came out in another magic null room. It was completely windowless, but somehow Nathan knew they were above ground again.

Dad scanned his card, but it beeped uselessly.

'Never mind that.' Adrian punched the door.

'It's reinforced—' Dad started, but Adrian ignored him and punched it again. The metal began to buckle. Two swift kicks and the door had bent completely out of shape. Adrian pushed it back, the metal grinding loudly, and then there was enough space for the three of them to squeeze through.

'We need to update our security,' Dad remarked as they piled out into a large wooden building. One of the manor's outhouses, Nathan guessed. Huge double doors were closed in front of them, but Dad ignored them and ran over to the other side of the building, where a few prison transport vans were parked.

'Not a particularly comfortable ride, but they'll do.'

Nathan climbed in and Dad turned on the ignition. Adrian threw the barn doors open and dived for the passenger side, pulling the van door shut at the same time as hunters came flying into the barn. Dad floored the accelerator and drove straight for the doors, forcing the hunters to jump out the way. Then they were out in the sunlight and heading for the gates.

Nathan took several deep breaths to calm himself.

'Ugh, I thought being covered in blood was bad, but this is worse.'

'If you don't like the smell, you're going to have to find a different career, kid.' Adrian smirked.

'He will not,' Dad declared. They both looked at him in surprise. 'Nathan can hold his own with hunters twice his age. He will not be finding a different career.'

'Wow,' Nathan said. Thankfully they reached the gate at that moment, and he didn't have to come up with anything more eloquent to say.

Dad rolled the window down as the security guard came over. The light to one side of the gate was red. Nathan held his breath. They *had* to get through this gate to get back to Oxford.

'Picking up a potential patient,' Dad said tersely. 'Longhorn's orders.'

'Longhorn never mentioned any intakes today.' The security guard eyed Dad suspiciously.

'Unexpected change of plans,' Dad said. 'We're in a hurry. Longhorn was supposed to tell you.'

'Longhorn left half an hour ago,' the guard replied. Nathan glanced at Adrian in a panic. Adrian gestured for them to swap places, and Nathan managed to do an awkward shuffle to get onto Adrian's other side.

'We're on a tight schedule,' Dad said. 'I'll have to send you the papers later.' He leaned back, and Adrian managed to catch the guard's eyes. The man went a bit slack-jawed, and then he turned and flagged his colleague. The light by the gate began flashing as the gates slowly slid open. Nathan's heart was in his mouth.

'Thank you,' Dad said tightly.

'I'll need to check your ID,' the guard said. Adrian caught his eye again, and then he tensed suddenly.

'Fuck—'

The guard whirled around, staggering. He'd broken the compulsion.

'Stop! Close the gate! They're not allowed out—'

Quick as a flash, Adrian reached over Dad and out the window, grabbing the guy's collar and slamming his head against the van door. He sagged to the ground.

'GO!' Adrian yelled. Dad floored it, and they shot through the gate, metal scraping metal on both sides.

As soon as they were out of sight of the gates, Dad rolled up the window.

'That went well,' Adrian remarked.

'Are you joking?' Nathan asked. 'Seriously, is there anything you won't joke about?'

'What do you want me to say? That was a monumental fucking disaster and we're all screwed? At least we're out. Nate, lend me your phone.'

In addition to the cracked screen, Nathan's phone now sported a smear of an indeterminate substance. He wiped it uselessly on his equally dirty jacket and passed it over.

'Kid, you really gotta get a new phone.'

'Considering how many times I've gotten pummelled in the last few months, I'd probably just smash the new one, too.'

Adrian sniggered. He punched in a number and put the phone to his ear.

'Damien,' he said after a moment. Pause. Then: 'Wow, thanks for the concern.'

Nathan leaned his head against the window as Adrian summarised the situation in a few short sentences: 'Hunter Council is working with witches against you, don't trust anyone. Nathan broke me out of the hunter prison. We're on our way back to town.'

Adrian listened for a minute, and Nathan dearly wished he had enhanced hearing so that he could find out what Damien thought. Finally, Adrian said, 'I'll let you know as soon as we arrive.' Then he hung up.

'Nate, do you know what today is?'

'Tuesday fifteenth?'

'It's the day of the Council monthly meeting,' Adrian said grimly. 'It starts at eleven-thirty.'

Nathan glanced at the dashboard. Eleven-fifteen. 'Crap.'

'Damien's not the only target,' Adrian said. 'They're after the entire Vampire Council.'

'Crap,' Nathan repeated.

CHAPTER TWENTY-EIGHT

BEING TRAPPED IN A small van with his father and his uncle was quite possibly the most awkward thing Nathan had ever done in his entire life. If he had been asked to imagine how awful it would be, his brain would probably have rebelled. There were no words to describe how badly he wanted out of that van.

As they approached the turnoff to Oxford, Nathan called Monica. The phone rang a single time before connecting.

'What the fuck? I called you like fifteen times!'

'Hi, Monica,' Nathan said, 'I'm still alive. How are you doing?'

'Are you joking?'

'Nope. The head of the Hunter Council is colluding with the Sahir.'

'Well, fuck.'

'Maybe you should tell me what's happening on your end,' Nathan said. The adrenaline had worn off, and he felt exhausted again.

'Do you want the good news or the bad news?'

Nathan pressed his forehead against the window. 'Bad.'

'We didn't get up to the Rymes place in time. Cathy panicked and rushed out, and now the Sahir have her too.'

'Crap.' Nathan groaned. Adults, honestly. 'Emma?'

'Your Aunt pulled some strings and fetched her from school. She's safe.'

'Good. Great.'

'Now you.'

'Right, well Adrian is with me. Dad's driving us back to Oxford. We're about to turn off the M40. Where should we meet you?'

He heard indistinct conversation from the other end, before Monica said, 'I managed to get a lock on someone. Remember the mage I put the tracker on? He's finally left the Witch Council inner sanctum. We're watching him through a scrying bowl.'

'It's probably a trap,' Nathan said.

'I know, but it's the best lead we have.'

Nathan sighed. 'Okay, where are you now?'

'Headington. I'm about to head out and meet Aodhán so we can follow this guy.' Monica said.

'Fine, text me when you have more details.' Nathan checked the road signs. 'I think we're at least twenty minutes out still.'

'We'll wait for you,' Monica said. 'Nate... you know what today is, right?'

'The Council meeting,' Nathan said, 'I know. But I can only solve one problem at a time.'

'Alright, I'll keep you updated.'

They were approaching Oxford when Dad started in a strained voice, 'Adrian... I just wanted to say...'

'Save it, Ben,' Adrian said coolly. 'I don't need your condemnation or your forgiveness. I wonder what you would have done if it had been you. I wonder whether you would have made a different choice.'

Dad winced at those words.

'There's no way of knowing, though,' Adrian said.

'You should have died.'

'If I weren't here, Nathan might be dead now, too,' Adrian said. 'Of course, there's no way of knowing that, either. But it's a possibility.'

'I want what's best for my son,' Dad said.

'Funny enough, that's what I want too,' Adrian replied. 'It might be the only thing we agree on.'

Dad was silent for a long time. Nathan leant his head on the window and dozed. He was so tired. His phone buzzed.

Monica: Meet you at Westgate parking lot

Nathan relayed the message to his father, who grunted an agreement. They were about five minutes out when Dad said, 'A truce. I will work with you until the Sahir have been removed from the city... for Nathan's sake.'

'Fine,' Adrian said.

They pulled into a space on the top floor of the parking lot behind the Westgate Centre and piled out. It was a relief to get fresh air after the stench that had filled the van.

Nathan looked around the grungy structure. Cars were scattered about, but it wasn't too busy in the middle of a workday. The next building over was the Westgate shopping mall. It was partially closed and scheduled to be demolished and redeveloped in the summer.

'What the hell would the Sahir want in here?'

'Hell if I know,' Adrian said. 'There's Monica.'

Sure enough, Monica jogged out of the stairwell, accompanied by Nathan's mother and Aodhán. They made an odd group. When Monica reached them, she wrinkled her nose.

'Okay, I was going to hug you, but... no.'

'I forgive you,' Nathan said. 'I wouldn't hug me either.'

'Just... why?' Monica asked.

'It's a long story,' Adrian said.

Nathan's mum did hug him, which was thoroughly embarrassing, but at least she shared the embarrassment around by hugging his dad, too. She eyed Adrian warily.

'Ben, why is he here?'

'We're working with him for now.' Dad sighed. 'The hunters need to clean house. We can worry about Nathan's misdemeanours later.'

Mum took that in her stride with her usual pragmatism. 'Alright, where do we start?'

Everyone turned to look at Monica.

'They're below the parking lot,' she explained.

'What the hell?' Adrian asked. 'There isn't a basement level.'

'That's what the tracking spell says,' Monica said. 'That's all I know.'

'It is possible they have gained access to the friary beneath this site,' Aodhán said suddenly.

'A friary?' Dad asked. 'What would the witches want with that?'

'The friary would have no relevance whatsoever,' Aodhán said, 'Except in so much as they will shortly be excavating the ruins. However, the friary was built on an old druid site. This would be of great interest to them as a power source. It was commonly used for human sacrifice.'

He led them over to one of the outer walls of the parking lot, and they looked down on what had once been a public parking lot below them and was now an excavation site.

'Oh, brilliant,' Monica groaned.

'Just our luck,' Nathan said. 'Okay, how do we get there?'

Aodhán spread his hands in his version of a shrug. 'The site was long believed lost, which is why Jeremiah chose not to share knowledge of it with anyone.'

'Better and better,' Adrian said. 'You suppose Jeremiah knows how to get there?'

'Likely, but we cannot reach him,' Aodhán said. 'The Council meeting has begun; he will not be able to contact us until it concludes.'

Nathan had walked through the Westgate Centre a thousand times in his life and could vouch for the fact that it was about as unmagical as they came. So much for his second sight. But thinking that, an idea occurred to him.

'Monica, where exactly are they?'

'Roughly beneath where we are right now, why?'

'Because that has to be where the entrance is,' he said. 'And I'm guessing that someone told them how to get in there, one of the Council members, probably a witch. So that would mean we're looking for a high-level illusion which is hiding the entrance.'

'Like the Witch Council,' Monica said. 'Brilliant. Nate, give me your hands.'

Nathan reached his hands out. Monica made a face. 'What is that?'

'We had a run-in with feral vampires,' Nathan said. 'You probably don't want to know.'

'Yuck. The things I do for you.' She screwed her eyes shut and clamped her hands around his wrists to channel him. Nathan felt her magic rising within him. She chanted rapidly, and he felt the spell spread out, only for it to hit a wall.

'It's here,' Monica said in confusion, 'But something's blocking it.'

'You could try the druid words of power,' Aodhán said. 'It is likely that the illusion is using the site itself as a power source.'

Monica frowned and began mumbling in yet another language, but they were still being blocked.

'We should go downstairs,' Nathan said. 'Get as close as we can.'

'There is another thing we can try,' Aodhán said. 'The druids cannot be barred from their own sacred sites; the magic would recognise them.'

'You mean you could find it?' Adrian asked.

'I am no longer a druid,' Aodhán said. 'One cannot be both vampire and human. However, any human can, in theory, tap into the powers. Your nephew happens to have a particular aptitude.'

'Do I?' Nathan asked.

'He means these.' Monica dangled her oak-ward in his face. 'Come on, whatever we're doing, we're not doing it up here.'

They descended what felt like a million stairs. Downstairs, the car park was fuller, and they got several weird looks from shoppers. An old woman getting out of her car peered suspiciously at them. 'Move along!' Monica snapped. The woman muttered something rude under her breath and hurried off.

'Right,' Monica said, turning to Aodhán, 'do your stuff.'

'It is not I who must perform.' Aodhán turned to Nathan. 'Normally this would take years to learn, but I shall endeavour to condense it into five minutes. The druid beliefs were based on the principle that there is a physical energy running through every living thing on the planet. This is the magic of life, and it is based on the four elements. Yours is earth, yes?'

Nathan nodded.

'You will find it easiest to tap into the energy of the earth, plants, and trees,' Aodhán said. 'I suggest closing your eyes. You must sense the streams of energy and find the points where they connect to your own energy.'

That was frustratingly vague. Nathan sagged against the wall. 'You know, you'd think I'd be less tired after sleeping for *three days*.' He sighed. 'I don't suppose you could give me a bit more of a hint of what I'm looking for?'

Aodhán pointed to Monica's amulet. 'The same energy that runs through this.'

Nathan frowned and studied the amulet. Beneath Monica's magical signature was the energy of the ward itself. After a few seconds he found it. It glinted gold, the same colour as all protective amulets.

Nathan closed his eyes and tried to clear his mind. Immediately, he opened them again.

'Okay, it's kind of nerve-wracking that everyone's staring at me. Can you guys talk amongst yourselves, or something?'

Monica let out a huff, then grabbed Nathan's parents by the arms. 'If you let me channel you, I can try my spell again.'

Dad looked disgruntled, but Mum nodded reluctantly. They moved off, and Nathan shut his eyes again. He took a deep breath and tried to centre himself. It was the same technique which Grey had taught him years ago, when he'd been learning to block his magical sight, except that this time he was trying to see more, not less.

He opened his eyes, but nothing had changed.

'It's not working.'

'If you can produce functioning wards, you can do this,' Aodhán said matter-of-factly. 'It is merely a matter of self-belief.'

'If that's the case, we could be here a while,' Adrian said.

'Oh, fuck you.' Nathan turned away, shutting his eyes and taking another deep breath. Anger was good. Anger focused him and made him determined. He would crack this. He had to. Cynthia's life depended on him figuring this out.

An idea occurred to Nathan. He vaulted over the low wall separating the parking lot from outside and marched over to the nearest tree. Pressing his fingers to the bark, he focused on the feeling. It was rough, it was alive. It had energy, somewhere. Nathan just had to find it. He had to feel the energy, to see it.

He had to *believe*.

He opened his eyes once more, and there it was. Reddish-gold lines running through everything. The tree was powerful; its energy filled it up. The grass beneath his feet was not thriving. Tiny trickles of energy ran between the stems. Nathan looked at his own hands and was surprised by the energy he saw there. He hadn't realised how... alive he looked.

He turned back to Adrian and Aodhán.

'I see it.'

'Good,' Aodhán said. 'Now you must find the spot where that magic is flowing to. Witch magic is perverse; it draws magic out of living things. Follow the flow and you will find the magic.'

Nathan wasn't really interested in the ethics of witch magic versus druid magic. He clambered back into the parking lot and studied the air around him. It was easier here. In a man-made structure, almost everything was dead. Only the people and the ground had energy. The red-gold streams in the ground were all flowing to a point: the stairwell.

Nathan walked over there, waving his parents and Monica over. 'It's in here.'

Adrian threw the door open, and sure enough, all of the energy was streaming to one point, forming a wall which blocked off the empty space beside the flight of stairs up to the first floor. There was no staircase going down because there was no basement level, or so Nathan had thought.

Nathan stepped through the wall, and there the staircase was. Unlike the utilitarian concrete of the rest of the building, this one was hewn from rough stone. Nathan descended it and heard the others following him.

'Holy fuck,' Adrian said, 'you actually found it.'

Nathan smirked to himself. 'It's all about self-belief, Adrian.'

'Oh, shut up, you brat.'

The stairs went about two storeys down into the ground, before they levelled out into a hallway that was lined with flickering torches. By unspoken agreement, Nathan led the way. The hallway extended for about fifty metres and ended in a cast iron double door, which was covered in strange symbols.

'Anyone know what it says?' Adrian asked.

'This is not druid work,' Aodhán said, running a hand over the metalwork. 'It is too modern.'

'I don't recognise the runes.' Monica glanced at Nathan. 'Nate?'

'Me either,' Nathan replied. 'But based on our present luck... it probably says, 'beware all who enter here, thou shalt be cursed for all eternity'.'

'That's no joking matter,' Dad said sternly, but Monica and Adrian were both sniggering. That was a win. Monica almost never laughed at Nathan's jokes.

'It's the only way in,' Nathan said. 'And opening these doors is not going to be subtle, so...'

'Battle time,' Adrian said with an almost feral grin. 'Perfect.' He threw open the doors. Metal grated against stone, but it was no match for the strength of a vampire. Beyond the doors was a large chamber. It was at least ten metres long, and the centrepiece was the stump and roots of an absolutely enormous tree. An oak tree, Nathan knew without asking. He could see the energy in the room, and it all converged on that tree stump. The stump was *ancient*. Nathan could feel it in his bones.

A familiar voice screamed, 'NATHAN!' and his concentration wavered, his energy-vision vanishing.

Cynthia was against the wall to his right, along with her mother and several other people, including Kseniya. They were chained together with silver shackles. That was becoming a rather unpleasant theme today. There were six people in total, which struck Nathan as odd because magic didn't like sixes—

Until he looked into the middle of the room again and made out the seventh person, who was dangling from an ankle above the tree stump. The man's neck had been slashed and blood was dripping from it, drip-drip-drip onto the tree stump.

'This is heresy,' Aodhán whispered. 'The druids sacrificed criminals, not innocent citizens.'

There was no time to worry about that, though, because Cynthia's cry had attracted the attention of the Sahir. There were maybe fifteen Sahir in the room, and seven of them fanned out and began chanting.

'They're making a shield,' Monica warned.

'Can you break it?' Nathan asked.

'On my own? There's seven of them!'

Hunters were taught the bare bones of how shielding magic worked: it was very energy-intensive, and the best shields were maintained by multiple people at the same time.

'Take one of them out before the shield goes up,' Mum called. Dad shot one of the mages. Nathan really wished he had a gun right now. The Sahir mage collapsed to the ground, but another immediately stepped up to take his place, the chant barely faltering. Dad shot two more before he had to reload. Adrian flew in to take out another, but he hit a barrier and collapsed back on the ground.

The seven mages stood at regular intervals, their hands held out before them, silent spectres. Their shield was up.

'How do we break it?' Nathan asked Monica.

'Distract them? Kill one of them? I don't know!' She was panicking. Nathan grabbed her arm.

'Monica, you need to calm down.' She clung to him. Behind the line of shield-mages, the others were moving, removing the dead body from above the tree stump. Nathan could only imagine that was bad.

'I—' Monica choked out.

'Go upstairs,' Adrian said, without looking at her.

'No!'

'Monica, go. If you freak out, you're going to distract Nathan and he'll get himself killed.'

'Oh, thanks,' Nathan said sarcastically. Monica took several deep breaths, then she hugged Nathan hard and pulled off the amulet around her neck, draping it over Nathan's head. She darted out the underground hall.

Nathan didn't have a moment to feel relieved.

'Take the next sacrifice!' one of the mages commanded. The leader, maybe? He was wearing a long black robe decorated with silver embroidery. Two other Sahir, one of them female, both wearing all black, jumped to carry out his command. They marched to the line of prisoners, and for a second all Nathan could focus on was the look of terror on Cynthia's face.

But she wasn't the next in line. Kseniya was.

They hauled her up and unlocked her shackles. Kseniya struggled weakly.

'NO!' she howled. 'You promised! NO! I did as you were asking!' In her desperation, she switched to Russian, alternating between cursing at them and begging for her life. She fought like a cat, wild and ineffective, scratching and kicking. The Sahir were much stronger than her. The man picked her up and marched her to the tree stump.

'Shit,' Nathan whispered. 'Fuck, what do we do?'

Dad tried to fire through the shield, and the bullet ricocheted wildly into one of the walls.

'Watch out!' Adrian said. 'You'll hit us.'

Helpless, they watched as the Sahir wrestled Kseniya onto the tree stump.

'Hold her down!' the leader said, raising a machete. He slashed it downwards. Nathan couldn't look away.

They had failed.

All hell broke loose.

The moment the machete should have contacted with Kseniya's neck, the amulet she was wearing went *berserk*.

Flames poured out of it. The mage leader's robes caught on fire immediately. He screamed. Two other mages began chanting, trying to put out the flames, but they spread too fast, and all three of them ended up burning. No one was paying attention to Kseniya. She staggered upwards, grabbed the discarded machete, and sliced open the neck of one of the mages holding the shield.

The shield collapsed with a tangible burst of magic. Smoke poured out from behind it.

Nathan lunged in, taking out another mage before he could gather his senses. They had to move quickly. The tree stump had caught fire, the dead body was burning, and there were flames everywhere. The woman had had the shackle key. He cast around for her, but he couldn't see through the smoke.

'Fuck, Nate!' Adrian shouted.

'Go!' Nathan cried. 'You and Aodhán! Get out of here!'

Fire was far more deadly to vampires than humans. It would kill Adrian ten times quicker than it would Nathan.

Nathan didn't stop to see if Adrian was still there. He ran to the prisoners.

'Nathan!' Cynthia sobbed. 'You came.'

'I'm sorry,' Nathan said. 'We were almost too late. Let me see the shackles.'

But it was no use—they were chained to the wall as well. Cynthia's wrists were raw and blistering where the silver touched them.

'I'm going to get you out of here,' Nathan said. He looked around. His parents were fighting on the other side of the room. Kseniya had vanished. Nathan blinked and then Aodhán was beside him.

'I believe I might be of assistance.'

'What are you doing?' Nathan asked. 'The fire—you'll burn—'

Aodhán ignored him. He grabbed the point where the chain met the wall with both hands and, with a strength Nathan had never seen before, yanked it clean out of the wall. A hunk of stone came away with it and clattered to the floor.

Nathan grabbed Cynthia and her mother and hauled them to their feet. The other prisoners were a bit slower. He pulled them all up.

'Go! Get out of here!' he said. 'GO!' The last shout was to Aodhán, who sped out of the room. Nathan looked around, trying to catch sight of his parents through the smoke.

'NATHAN!'

Dad appeared beside him and grabbed his arm. 'Come on!'

They staggered out the door and down the hall, keeping low to try and avoid the smoke. Tears streamed down Nathan's face. Finally, they emerged at the top of the stairs and stumbled outside, choking and coughing. Everyone had made it out. Nathan collapsed against the wall, weary with relief.

'Nate!' Monica darted over to him, crouching in front of him. He was on the floor. When had he sat down? Nathan fought for breath, struggling against a wave of dizziness. After a few moments, he managed to reply.

'I'm okay.'

'Are you joking?'

'Nah, I'm not Adrian.' Nathan grinned weakly.

'Clearly not,' Adrian said, appearing behind Monica. 'I'm not stupid enough to rush *into* a burning room.'

'Haha,' Nathan muttered. He held out a hand and let Adrian haul him to his feet. His vision wavered, but he managed to stay upright. 'Okay, we're good.'

'You're going to end up in hospital again,' Monica said. 'And you were just discharged today.'

'Poor Doctor Govender,' Nathan grinned. 'He'll probably retire in protest.'

His eye caught something. Kseniya was lingering a few metres away, watching them. By her body language, she was about to bolt at any moment. Nathan pulled away from his friends and jogged towards her, and she immediately took a step back.

'Wait,' Nathan said, stopping and holding his hands up defensively. 'I'm not going to hurt you.'

'I have no choice,' Kseniya said. 'Please!' She touched the amulet around her neck. There were tears in her eyes and her face was smeared with soot and blood.

'It's okay,' Nathan said, 'just tell me what happened.'

'They threaten me,' Kseniya said. 'They say if I bring them your friend then they won't kill me. But then they want to sacrifice me anyway.'

Nathan sighed. Should have seen that coming.

'It's alright,' he said. 'I think you helped us in the end.'

'Is not me,' Kseniya said. 'Your amulet saved me.'

Nathan stared at the amulet, glinting innocuously around Kseniya's neck. 'Are you sure?'

'You still don't believe?' Kseniya asked incredulously. She swore at him in Russian, sounding like a spitting cat, and Nathan had to laugh. Maybe he was hysterical or something, but it was either laugh or cry, and Nathan wasn't planning on crying. The fight wasn't over yet.

'Come on,' he said, ushering her back over to Monica. Monica pursed her lips at him.

'Really?' she asked.

'She's as much a victim as we are,' Nathan said. 'And we might need her on our side.'

Monica sighed. Nathan left them to their less-than-happy reunion and went over to Cynthia. Aodhán had snapped the rest of the shackles open. Maybe vampires became more resistant to silver as they got older? Or maybe Aodhán just healed that fast. He certainly couldn't have been held in the hunter prison. He'd probably have been able to break himself free easily.

Cynthia threw her arms around Nathan's neck, sobbing loudly. 'I was so scared! Thank you, thank you, thank you!'

'You're okay,' Nathan said, patting her back awkwardly. 'Um, Cynthia, I'm sort of… covered in sludge. You might not want to hug me right now…'

Cynthia sniffled into his neck.

'Yeah.' She pulled back, squaring her shoulders, and smiled weakly. 'You kind of stink, too.'

'Romance at its finest,' Nathan joked, and was rewarded when her smile grew a little stronger. She'd be okay. He hoped.

Dad came over to join them, hanging up his phone. 'Jason is getting a few trusted members of the Hunter Council to investigate. He'll quarantine the area until the fire's out so they can make sure we haven't damaged the foundations of the building.'

'Great,' Nathan said.

'We'll wait here until they get here, and then you need to go home and rest. You look ready to drop dead.'

'I'm fine,' Nathan lied, standing up straighter. 'I'll be fine. Adrian?'

Adrian came over. Now that the fight was over, he was watching Nathan's father warily again.

'We need to make sure we've actually foiled their plans,' Nathan said. 'Is there any way of contacting the Council?'

'Not if they're in the meeting,' Adrian said.

'They were doing some kind of channelling ritual on steroids,' Monica said. 'I saw the circle when we first entered. They were using the sacrifices to power something. Or someone.'

'But we cut it off,' Adrian said.

'There is still one sacrifice,' Kseniya said quietly. 'Maybe enough.'

'Do you know what they were trying to power?' Nathan asked.

Kseniya frowned. 'They never told me. But I overheard a word, Belladonna. It's a plant, yes?'

'Oh no,' Monica said. Kseniya looked confused.

'The Belladonna is the head of the Witch Council,' Adrian explained. He looked at Nathan. 'You guessed the Sahir were working with the Witch Council as well.'

'Yeah,' Nathan said glumly. A picture was coming together in his head, and he did not like it.

'Okay—' Adrian started, and then he froze. His lips formed the words 'oh shit'. 'Nate, I need to borrow your phone.'

Nathan handed it over. Adrian put the call through. It rang and rang, before going to voicemail.

'Fuck.' Adrian hung up. 'Damien's summoning me. We need to go.'

CHAPTER TWENTY-NINE

NATHAN HAD NEVER CROSSED town as quickly as he did that day. Adrian and Aodhán ran ahead, and by the time Nathan reached the building, the two vampires had deftly dispatched two of the Sahir who were guarding the entrances.

Nathan jumped right in and managed to catch one of the mages by surprise. Where the normal Council guards were, he had no idea. This coup was very well planned.

'Behind you!' Cynthia yelled. He whipped around and managed to block a blow. This lot were better fighters. Of course, they'd kept their main fighting force here. A staggering blow caught the side of his head, and he stumbled.

'Mortuus iacebat!' a voice said, and then a foul magic brushed over Nathan without affecting him. As one, his two opponents collapsed to the ground. Nathan blinked, trying to clear his vision, and looked at his saviour.

It was a man, dressed in the black robes of the Sahir. He was about the same age as Nathan's father, with blond hair and a square face, and he looked Nathan right in the eye.

'You cannot enter the building.' He had an American accent. Somehow, the crispness of his accent struck Nathan. It was completely incongruous with everything that had happened today.

'Try and stop me.'

'I will not.' He looked past Nathan, to Cynthia. She stepped up beside him, jutting her chin out stubbornly.

'Why did you help us?'

The man's shoulders sagged a bit. He raked a finger through his long hair.

'It's too long a story for now,' he said. Turning to Nathan, he added, 'Keep her safe.'

He vanished from sight — by now Nathan could recognise the use of an invisibility ward.

'Was that —?' Cynthia asked. 'Mum told me —'

'Your dad?' Nathan finished. 'Today's been a pretty weird day, so why the hell not?'

They rejoined the others, who had dispatched all of the Sahir guards and were studying the doors.

'The doors are barred with magic,' Monica explained. 'I think they can only be opened from the inside.'

They all exchanged worried glances.

'What about the windows?' Cynthia asked. Everyone turned to look at her.

'Small, small windows,' Adrian said.

'Not for me.'

It hit Nathan what she was suggesting. 'No!' he said. 'That's dangerous.'

'I want to help,' Cynthia said. She glanced around and zeroed in on a pigeon that was wittering around by the fence. 'That will do.'

Her aura had been a replica of her cat. Before his eyes, it shifted to the pigeon. It was a pretty awesome sight.

'Can you unlock the windows by magic?' she asked Monica.

'I don't think they open,' Mum said, studying the nearest one.

'That's okay,' Monica said. 'Kseniya, let me channel you. I can make the glass permeable.'

Kseniya held out a hand, which Monica grasped. She mumbled under her breath and tapped the glass. It rippled like water.

'Go,' she told Cynthia.

Cynthia took a deep breath and closed her eyes. Everyone watched her as she began to shrink. Her body seemed to contort oddly, and a burst of magic sent prickles over Nathan's skin. Then her clothes fell to the ground and a bird fluttered up from the pile of fabric. It took her a few seconds to figure out how flying worked, and then she shot towards the window.

The glass rippled as she passed through it. Ms Rymes made a noise of fright. Nathan's mum reached over and touched her shoulder. 'She'll be alright.'

'She's only sixteen!' Ms Rymes blurted out. 'She shouldn't be involved in this.'

The door in front of them unlocked with an audible click.

'Let's go,' Adrian said. He exchanged a look with Nathan, who nodded and pushed the door open.

The door led into the dark walkway that ran behind the tiered seating of the Sheldonian Theatre. As Nathan entered, a pigeon drifted down and landed on his shoulder.

'How long can she stay like that?' Monica whispered. The pigeon pecked at Nathan's ear.

'I don't know,' he mumbled, wishing he'd thought to ask Cynthia these questions before they had to use her powers in an emergency situation.

They walked down the hallway and entered the main theatre. There were seats for the nine Council members arranged in a circle. The Council aides were arranged on the tiered benches. Everything was eerily quiet. Nathan could feel the magic in the air, hostile and dangerous. In the middle of the circle was a pile of vampire dust.

Nathan took in the scene, trying to figure out what was going on. Two of the Vampire Council members were locked in a glaring match with the witches. They were Ayotunde, an aristocratic woman of Nigerian descent, and an unfamiliar man whom Nathan assumed was Antonius. He had long brown hair held back in a queue and the broad, strong build of a warrior. Only Jeremiah looked relaxed. He lounged in his seat, seeming amused and perhaps a little bored by the proceedings.

The witches regarded the vampires, their robes obscuring their features entirely, radiating an aura of smugness. For the first time, Nathan saw the Belladonna in person, and he knew — without knowing how he knew — that she was both the youngest and the most powerful of the three. Her robe was pure black, not dissimilar to that of the Sahir.

The hunters were sat with their backs to Nathan and his cohort, so he couldn't make out anything of their faces, but he was relieved to see that Uncle Jeff looked whole and unharmed.

'You dare threaten us?' Ayotunde demanded.

'This is no threat,' the Belladonna said smoothly. 'It is an ultimatum. The vampires have held too much power in this city for too long. The hunters feel the same. It is time for you to pass on the baton.' Her voice sent a shiver down Nathan's spine.

'You have some nerve,' Ayotunde said furiously.

'This can be done peacefully, or it can be done violently,' the

Belladonna said. 'But it will be done.'

'Ayotunde, enough,' Jeremiah said. 'It seems we have uninvited guests.' He looked straight at Nathan, a smile playing about his lips.

The tension in the room seemed to break, and everyone turned to see the intruders.

'What is the meaning of this?' Elder Nettle demanded.

For a moment, no one moved. They'd got this far but there was no plan for what happened next. Nathan managed to catch Aodhán's eye, and the druid vampire nodded slightly.

'I'd like to speak,' Nathan said, marching in front of the group. He caught sight of Longhorn's face—the man had gone satisfyingly pale. Nathan focused on that pale, fearful face and let it remind him of why he was doing this crazy, *crazy* thing. Interrupting the Council? Jeremiah had probably beheaded people for lesser sins. 'We have uncovered a plot against the Council.'

Several aides gasped. Ayotunde stood up abruptly. She was wearing a flowing red dress, which swirled dramatically about her body.

'Preposterous,' she said. 'Hunters, this child belongs to your ranks. Control him.'

'Wait,' Jeremiah said. He didn't seem at all surprised to see Nathan. 'He is accompanied by two of mine. I will hear him out.'

Several people grumbled, but no one actually voiced an argument. Jeremiah turned to Nathan. 'This is not news to us,' he said. 'The witches wish for the vampires to step aside from the Council. They have already laid down their terms.'

Nathan took a deep breath.

'Patrick Longhorn is supporting them,' he said.

Longhorn lurched to his feet. 'Lies!' he shouted. 'The boy is trying to discredit me. Benjamin, control your son.'

Dad stepped forwards and laid a hand on Nathan's shoulder. 'You should have asked me that before you left my son to die.'

'I have evidence,' Nathan said. He spoke only to Jeremiah. Fuck the rest of them. Jeremiah would listen. 'Longhorn told me this morning. My father was there. He can corroborate. The Hunter Council have been covering up the presence of the Sahir in the city for over six months, in return for them eliminating political targets. Just now —'

His next words were drowned out by a wave of protests. The

hunters were all denying it at once. Ayotunde and Antonius seemed to be trying to out-shout each other. All they ended up achieving was a whole lot of noise.

'SILENCE!' Jeremiah yelled, getting to his feet. Everyone fell quiet. In the blink of an eye, Damien had left the front row of benches to stand beside Jeremiah.

'So,' Jeremiah said evenly, 'we have been betrayed on both sides.'

'You'll take the word of an uninitiated hunter over us?' Longhorn demanded. 'Look at the company he keeps. Disgraced witches and turned hunters.'

'Amongst that company is one of my men,' Jeremiah said. 'A spy, if you will. Aodhán, would you like to weigh in on the discussion?'

A fucking spy. Hah! Of course, Jeremiah had sent Aodhán to spy on them. Nathan had to choke back a laugh at that.

Aodhán stepped forwards.

'We come from an old druid site near the castle,' he said. 'The witches have preserved the site and have been using it to conduct vile rituals of dark magic. We interrupted one, the nature of which was to channel power to the Belladonna.'

'Dark magic is forbidden in the city.' Jeremiah turned to the Belladonna. 'What have you to say in your defence?'

'This is a farce,' Elder Rowan spat. 'The Belladonna upholds the law to the highest levels.'

'She's one of them,' Nathan said. He said it quietly, but the room had fallen silent, and everyone in the circle heard him. Well, it was out there now. He repeated, 'She's one of them.'

'You *dare*?' demanded Elder Nettle. 'A teenaged boy accuses the Belladonna, the highest authority in the city, of performing black magic?'

'If she's not,' Nathan replied, 'then she can lift the sleeves of her robe and prove she's not marked.'

Silence reigned. Finally, Jeremiah turned to the Belladonna. 'Let it be done, then we can lay the accusation to rest.'

The Belladonna didn't move, didn't speak. The silence lasted so long that finally Elder Nettle got restless and turned to his leader. 'What is the meaning of this? Surely you are not so modest that you will not set their minds at ease?'

'She cannot,' Aodhán said quietly, but certainly. 'Mr Delacroix is right. She is herself a member of the Sahir. Their leader, I suspect.'

Jeremiah moved, quick as a flash, and then the Belladonna's robe had been torn away at the sleeves, baring her arms. Sure enough, they were covered with the same distinctive tattoos that all the Sahir had.

'The markings are the same,' Adrian said.

'You have no proof,' the Belladonna snarled.

'Oh, but we do,' Adrian said. He looked at Kseniya. 'We have a member of the Sahir right here for proof.'

Kseniya looked terrified. Nathan reached out a hand to her. She took it hesitantly, and he laced their fingers together. 'It's okay. I won't let them hurt you.'

Kseniya nodded, and Nathan gently nudged her sleeves up, showing off her arms. The marks were identical.

'You testify that these are the markings of the Sahir?' Jeremiah asked.

'They give us tattoos so they can share magic of all members,' Kseniya said. 'Also for other things, like… invisibility.'

'Then it is proven,' Jeremiah said. 'The Belladonna is conducting forbidden magics in the city. She must be expelled from the Council.'

The two other witch elders turned to their leader. 'Is this true?' Elder Nettle demanded.

'You believe others over your own Lady?' the Belladonna asked. Her voice seemed twisted, anger making her sound inhuman.

'The evidence is incontrovertible,' Elder Rowan said. 'You are unfit to rule.'

Elder Rowan fired off a spell, but the Belladonna brushed the magic away as though it were nothing. Her laugh was like nails on a blackboard. It sent a shiver down Nathan's spine.

'You think your petty spells can harm me?' she asked. 'Even if the ritual went incomplete, I have been tapping the power of the druid site for years. I am protected beyond measure, and I will complete my mission. The vampires must concede power to the witches or die.'

She whipped out a knife from under her robe, one of the jagged knives belonging to the Sahir. It caught the light and seemed to glow like someone had switched on a blacklight, a sort of purplish-blue colour which was thoroughly unpleasant. Nathan's eyes hurt when he looked directly at it.

Elder Nettle began to chant, offensive magic gathering at his fingers and flying towards the Belladonna, but she slashed the knife downwards. It absorbed the magic first, and then it sliced Elder Nettle's flesh. He collapsed instantly to the ground in a dead faint. At least, Nathan hoped he'd fainted, but he didn't have any time to think about it. The Belladonna turned on the Vampire Council.

Ayotunde raised her head in defiance. 'You will not be able to kill us as easily as you think.' She moved in a blur. Nathan could hardly follow the movement, but somehow the Belladonna knew where Ayotunde would be. She swept the knife in an arc and the woman went flying across the room. She hit the first row of benches and collapsed to the floor. Her body didn't dissolve into dust, but she didn't get up either.

Nathan had objectively known vampires could be knocked unconscious, but it took a hell of a lot. Usually, they healed too fast.

The Belladonna began to move across the room. Slowly, step by step, she advanced towards the vampires. Nathan felt magic pressing down on him from all sides.

'I have sealed the doors.' She cackled. 'There is nowhere to run.'

Beside Nathan, Kseniya fell to her knees, making a choked noise. Elder Rowan went down next, her papery hands clutching at her chest. Monica staggered towards Nathan but fell short.

'Monica!' Nathan shouted, running to her. He crouched beside her. 'What's happening?'

'She's—draining—the—magic—out—of—the—room,' Monica choked out, straining to pronounce every word. 'And—us.'

'What can I do?' Monica stared up at him, and Nathan knew what had to be done. He looked up at the Belladonna, in time to see Antonius lunge at her. Antonius was a warrior. Nathan knew nothing about him, but you could see it in the way he held his body, in the way he approached the Belladonna. He lived—and died—by the same principles that the hunters did. He had probably trained every year of his life, and every year since his death, too.

He landed several blows that should have killed a mortal woman instantly, but they all seemed to bounce off the Belladonna. She slashed twice with the knife, and the second blow caught him. He crumpled, unconscious.

Nathan was on his feet without really thinking about it. The spirit knife formed in his hand, and then he threw it. Throwing knives had never been his favourite discipline, but he was suddenly grateful to Grey for insisting he learn. The Belladonna whipped around, parrying with deadly accuracy. The spirit knife clattered to the floor.

'That was foolish,' she said. 'Now you are unarmed.'

'Oh, you really don't understand hunters very well, do you?' Nathan asked. He held his hand out and the spirit knife reformed in it, like a reliable old friend.

'How?' the Belladonna demanded. 'The knife should have lost its magic.'

'Some magics are just uniquely human,' Nathan said. 'Whilst we're on the subject, do you want to know what else humans are good at?'

'Being bait?'

'I was going to say self-belief.' Nathan lunged at her. She brought her knife down, but it never came near him. The ward Monica had returned to him earlier flared with power. It ate ambient magic, and it had been fed by Monica's magic for weeks now. Monica, who was Nathan's best friend. Monica, whom Nathan would kill and die for. He was pretty sure she'd do the same.

He believed.

The Belladonna's robe caught fire. The flames licked rapidly over her body. She screamed.

'NO!'

In two steps, Damien was behind her. He stuck his hand through her ribcage with a crack that made Nathan shudder and tore her heart clean out of her chest.

The Belladonna collapsed, dead in an instant.

'We are also very good at distracting people,' Nathan joked, feeling a bit numb. Too much blood and gore in one day. He looked at Damien, and the vampire nodded back at him with respect in his gaze.

It was over.

Nathan went straight to Monica. She had managed to get herself upright again, and she threw herself into Nathan's arms. In the background, he registered that Longhorn was kicking up a tremendous fuss as Dad and Uncle Jeff arrested him — could they even do that, arrest their boss? — but most of his attention was focused on Monica sobbing into his chest.

'I thought she was going to kill you!'

'Your magic protected me,' Nathan said. 'Don't worry, I had faith.'

'Oh, of all moments for you to start believing in yourself!' Monica snapped, hitting him on the arm.

Nathan laughed, holding her close. 'I'm okay,' he said. 'We're all okay.'

Slowly, gradually, Monica relaxed. 'We did it.' She sighed into Nathan's shoulder.

'Yeah,' Nathan said, 'we did it.'

On the way out, the pigeon fluttered off his shoulder and into one of the side corridors. Nathan followed Cynthia, and courteously averted his eyes as she twisted and morphed and reformed into a human being. 'Here,' he muttered, shrugging his jacket off and shoving it at her.

'Thanks.' Cynthia took it. 'You can turn around now.'

Nathan's jacket was irredeemably filthy, and not nearly long enough. It fell halfway down Cynthia's thighs, and the rest of her was bare. If Nathan wasn't so tired, his imagination would have been running wild.

Cynthia stepped forwards and pressed her lips to his.

'You are amazing,' she whispered against his mouth.

'So are you,' Nathan replied.

'Nah, you're amazinger.' Cynthia pressed her body against his, kissing him again. Nathan put his hands on her hips, but he didn't dare do anything, because he was too aware that she had nothing on beneath the jacket.

'Later,' Cynthia murmured in his ear. She took his hand and slid it around to her bum. 'Maybe we can have fun.'

'Later,' Nathan agreed, smiling.

'After showering,' Cynthia said, wrinkling her nose. 'And having a nap.'

'Sounds like a plan.'

'Great.' Cynthia pecked him on the lips once more. 'Let's go find the others.'

They stepped outside into the weak winter sunlight.

EPILOGUE

MUM AND DAD STAYED for Christmas, but a few days before New Year, Nathan came home to find they'd packed their things together in the hall. His parents were sitting at the table with Aunt Anna, drinking tea.

'Hi,' Nathan said.

'Oh, Nathan,' Mum said. 'We were just waiting for you.'

'Me?' Nathan asked.

'Will you go to lunch with us?' Dad asked.

'Sure, I guess.'

They all piled into Dad's car and drove into the city centre. 'Where would you like to eat?' Mum asked.

'I guess we could get pizza?' Nathan suggested.

'Pizza it is,' Dad agreed. They went to Pizza Express. Nathan's mind raced as they walked. Things had been quiet for the last two and a half weeks. Christmas had been surprisingly pleasant; Mum and Dad were being peculiarly accommodating. It was almost unsettling. Nathan kept expecting the next thing to go wrong. Was he in trouble now?

They ordered their pizza. Once the waitress had departed, Mum said, 'She couldn't look away from you, Nathan.'

'Really? Eh, Cynthia's prettier.'

'Oh, I told you he'd break hearts one day.' Dad chuckled, taking Nathan by surprise. He was in an oddly good mood.

'Uh, what's going on?' Nathan asked cautiously. 'You guys are being... awfully understanding.'

'We've been talking,' Mum said. Normally that sentence would fill Nathan with dread, but today his mother had a smile on her face.

'Talking? About what?'

'The future,' Dad said.

'The events of the last few months,' Mum added.

'We were wrong,' Dad started.

It was a huge admission for a man who had believed in the absolute infallibility of the hunter ethos. Nathan wanted to smile, but he kept his face neutral, not wanting his father to take it back.

'You're not the typical hunter,' Mum said, 'but that's okay. You are your own person… and you're successful as you are.'

'Yes,' Dad said, 'I've never seen anyone get the Vampire Council on board that way… Jeff battles every day to get them to toe the line, but they listen to you. So…'

'So,' Mum took up when Dad ran out of words, 'We're going to… well, you can keep doing things the way you've been doing them. We'll support you for initiations—when you want to do them, if you want to do them—and we'll… support your… friendship with Adrian.' Every word pained her, but her voice rang with sincerity, and Nathan's smile had never been bigger.

'For real?' he asked.

'As long as you don't abuse that trust,' Dad said sternly. 'No more secrets. No more lies. You tell us what you're getting up to… you listen to our concerns as well.'

'This is a two-way street,' Mum said. 'We'll listen to you, as well. If you can argue your case… we'll try to trust that you know what you're doing.'

'Okay,' Nathan said. 'I'd like that. Thanks.'

Both of his parents seemed to sag in relief. Being profound had never been Nathan's forte, but he gave it a shot anyway. 'Guys, um, thanks. For supporting me when everything went down with the Sahir. I know it was… rough between us. And… I'm sorry I lied to you about, well, everything.' Nathan made a face. He felt like an idiot. 'I appreciated your support, and I appreciate this, too.'

'You're welcome,' Mum said.

There was an awkward pause, during which all of them tried to figure out where to go next. They weren't, Nathan reflected, the sort of family who shared their emotions freely. This was probably as deep as it was ever going to get… but Nathan was okay with that. After a moment, Dad changed the subject.

'Have you thought when you would like to go for initiations?' he asked.

'I'd like to finish school,' Nathan said. 'I'm finally actually passing all my subjects, which is kinda refreshing, to be honest. After that... hopefully by then I'll be sure,' he added. 'I am fairly sure, now, but I think it depends on who takes over from Longhorn.'

'They'll be holding elections in March,' Dad said. 'We're hoping to finish the inquest by then. I'm sure there will be more arrests to come, but we've scaled the mountain now.'

Several of the old, fiercely loyal hunter families had insisted on Dad running the inquiry into Longhorn's activities. There'd been a backlash within the ranks against people like Longhorn, new blood in the hunter organisation, who might be bringing in dangerous new ideas. Even Nathan could see the risk. The moment you started collaborating with the supernatural, where did you draw the line? He understood his parents' perspective, the reason why they'd been so angry with him for doing the same thing. Nathan had only been working with the vampires and witches for the good of everyone, but once you became friends with them, you started excusing their behaviour. Too many hunters stepping into that moral grey area was definitely dangerous for the organisation.

The biggest benefit out of it was that his family had seen an improvement in their reputation. Enough of one, at least, that his parents were willing to relax their stance on Nathan fraternising with the enemy.

'Well, we'll know soon,' Nathan said, 'but I still want to get my A-Levels first.'

'That seems wise,' Mum said. 'You're a terrible multitasker.'

'He gets it from you,' Dad joked.

'Oh, really?' Mum said threateningly. 'Do you really want to debate that?'

They all chuckled.

'Can we give you a lift back home?' Dad asked once they'd finished eating.

'No, thanks,' Nathan said boldly. No more hiding, no more secrets. His parents had said they were going to accept his way of doing things... no time like the present to put that to the test. 'I've been meaning to head over to the Vampire Council. I need to speak to Jeremiah about whether Kseniya can stay in town.'

Dad frowned. 'That's good of you,' he said slowly. 'Mind you don't promise Jeremiah anything, though.'

'I know that, Dad.'

Mum and Dad walked him all the way to the castle. At the doors, Mum hugged him.

'Keep safe.'

'And keep us updated,' Dad added.

'We'll be back in town in about three weeks,' Mum said. 'I think we're going to be working out of the prison for a while. From what your dad has said, we've quite a bit of cleaning up to do there, too.'

'I bet.' Nathan grimaced. He held out a hand, which Dad shook firmly.

'Good luck, son.'

'Thanks, Dad. You too.'

Mum and Dad watched him through the doors. Nathan turned back once to wave and grin at them, before telling the receptionist, 'Hi. Permittitis intrare?'

'Ah, welcome,' she said. 'I've been asked to pass this on to you.' She handed Nathan a brown envelope. 'It's your season ticket.'

Nathan opened the envelope and found a plastic ID card. *Nathan Delacroix, Hunter Council Liaison.* It had a photo of him, even though he wasn't aware that anyone from the Vampire Council had ever photographed him. Vampires, honestly.

'Thank you,' he said, trying not to sound as blindsided as he felt. Even Adrian didn't have a Vampire Council ID. He used Damien's.

The cashier printed a premium tour ticket and handed it over. 'Tour starts in five minutes.'

'Thanks.'

A robed guide brought Nathan to Jeremiah's office. A big wooden desk filled most of the room, and the walls were obscured by bookshelves. This trip hadn't been planned, but Jeremiah didn't look surprised.

'Ah, Mr Delacroix,' he said, 'I had been expecting to see you.'

'Nathan,' Nathan corrected.

'Very well.' Jeremiah nodded. 'What can I help you with, Nathan?'

Nathan had been considering this conversation for a while. The first thing he did was take out the Sihr knife, still in the box Monica had made for it.

'I thought you might want this.' He opened the box and handed the knife to Jeremiah. 'I figured you'd be the best choice to get it destroyed?'

'That would be wise,' Jeremiah agreed, taking the knife and laying it delicately on a side table. He clasped his hands beneath his chin and regarded Nathan.

'I would like to know how my debts stand,' Nathan said nervously. Being indebted to a vampire was not a comfortable situation to be in, but Jeremiah had sent help when they'd needed it, and not acknowledging that debt wouldn't make it go away.

'Monica has already expressed a willingness to pay off your debts on your behalf,' Jeremiah said.

'No,' Nathan replied firmly. 'I don't want Monica to do that. I can take responsibility for my own debts.'

'Very well,' Jeremiah said neutrally.

'And whilst we're on the topic,' Nathan added, 'I'd like to petition on behalf of Kseniya. Like Monica, she doesn't have a coven to stay in. The witches want her to leave the city.' They'd sent three missives already. 'She doesn't have anywhere else to go.'

'You want me to take her in as I did Monica?' Jeremiah asked. 'Monica's parents called in a debt long owed to their family, that I would care for their daughter.'

'I just want her to be allowed to stay until she's healthy and can arrange her own affairs. I have guardianship over her. She'd be my responsibility.'

Jeremiah considered that. 'I can liaise with the witches. What would you be willing to offer me in return?'

'Don't I already owe you a million unclaimed favours?' Nathan asked. 'Maybe you should tell me what you want.'

Jeremiah smiled, the smile of the cat which had the mouse in its sights. Nathan had the distinct feeling he'd just walked into some kind of trap.

'It seems to me,' Jeremiah said, 'that the Council is an inefficient, antiquated beast which struggles to withstand the demands of the citizens it is responsible for. None of the three branches of the triumvirate wish to work together. We seem to be missing a crucial part... someone who is independent of all three Councils, or perhaps loyal to all three Councils, who could act as a go-between.'

Nathan stared at Jeremiah, his mind racing. 'You want me to be a...

liaison?' he asked at last, wondering if he was misunderstanding.

'Indeed.'

'That's it?' Nathan asked. 'For how long? What's the catch?'

'You seem to be under the impression that I am given to taking advantage of my people, Nathan,' Jeremiah said. 'This is not the case. We would draw up a contract. It would be mutually advantageous. The main drawback is that I could not allow you to become a marked hunter during the period of your employment, not unless it were agreed upon that your employment to the Council would supersede your hunter responsibilities.'

Nathan's heart was beating a frantic, excited rhythm in his chest. 'Would that really wipe my debts clean?'

'You are not as indebted as you seem to believe. You helped rid the city of the threat of the Sahir. We consider that to be a not insignificant favour to the Council.'

Wow.

'I want to see the contract first,' Nathan said. 'Before I agree. And I want to know that Kseniya will be able to stay for as long as she needs.'

'You will have that,' Jeremiah said. 'I will contact you shortly. I know that modern humans are quite attached to their mobile phones. If it would be acceptable, you could give me your number.'

An ancient vampire on speed dial? Nathan had to suppress a smirk. 'Sure.'

Aodhán walked him out. Unlike the other guides, who all kept their hoods up, he always wore his down, showing off his tattoos. Lost in thought, Nathan toyed with the ward amulet around his neck. He needed to return it to Monica. An idea blossomed in his mind.

'Do you have time for a quick chat, Aodhán?'

'Of course, Mr Delacroix.'

Another vampire he was going to have to train not to be so damn formal. Nathan smiled to himself.

They entered a small antechamber and Nathan shut the door behind them.

'How can I help you?' Aodhán asked.

Nathan leant against the wall beside the door and considered for a moment how to frame his request. 'A couple of months ago,' he started, 'remember, you spoke to me on the Mound? You said there were… things you could teach me.'

'I recall.'

'I take it that's things like… like seeing energy, like I did that day when we found the druid site?'

'That is only one small part of druidic practices,' Aodhán explained. 'Druids believe in the interconnectivity of all life on the planet. Once you have learnt to see that energy, you can progress to accessing it, persuading it to your will.'

'I thought that you disapproved of that,' Nathan said.

'I disapprove of the practices of witches,' Aodhán explained. 'They drain the energy out of living things and twist it to their own ends. Druids ask the earth to help us, and it delivers as it sees fit. We never take the energy, at least not without giving back in equal amounts.'

Nathan wasn't sure he understood the difference, but he was fairly hopeful that he could figure it out.

'If your offer was still on the table… I think I'd like to learn,' he said hesitantly.

Aodhán smiled. 'Very well. We will work out a schedule. But in return you must assist me with a task.'

'That seems fair,' Nathan agreed cautiously.

'I would like you to purge the evil from the druids' sacrificial site,' Aodhán said. 'I expect that the night of the spring equinox will be the right moment. This will also give me enough time to teach you how.'

'It's not going to involve any human sacrifice, right?' Nathan said.

'Contrary to what you appear to believe, druid magic is rooted in life, not in death,' Aodhán said, his tone a mixture of patronising and amused. 'I will not ask you to kill.'

'I had to make sure,' Nathan said. 'Will you call me?'

Aodhán made a face. It made him look about ten years younger. How old had he been when he was turned? Nathan would have placed him at thirty-five, maybe thirty at the youngest, but when he wrinkled his nose like that, he could have passed for only a couple of years older than Nathan.

'I will contact you,' Aodhán said, 'shortly. I must first arrange my own schedule.'

No phones, then. Nathan nodded. 'I look forward to hearing from you.'

'Will you find your own way out from here?'

'Yes, thanks,' Nathan said. 'No need for you to lead me in circles every time.'

Aodhán nodded. 'Good day to you, Nathan Delacroix.' He vanished from one second to the next.

'Bye,' Nathan said to the empty room.

Nathan had one last task for the day. After leaving the Vampire Council, he took the bus up to Headington and walked to the Rymes residence. Cynthia opened the door for him. Instead of stepping back to let Nathan in, she wrapped her arms around him and kissed him.

'Hey,' Nathan said when they separated for air, 'you sure know how to stoke a guy's ego.'

Cynthia beamed. 'I was looking forward to seeing you. Come in.'

Nathan kicked his shoes off and followed her through to the kitchen. 'So, I think I'm going to be working for the Council next year,' he said. 'Oh, hi Ms Rymes.' Cathy Rymes was at the stove. 'Mmm, spaghetti?'

'Hello, Nathan of the bottomless stomach,' Ms Rymes said. 'I'm making extra. Will you stay for dinner?'

'I'd love to.' Nathan ruffled Emma's hair in greeting, making her squeal, and took a seat at the table. Cynthia sat beside him.

'Working for the Council?' she asked. 'So you're not going to initiate as a hunter?'

'I might,' Nathan said. 'But Jeremiah offered me a job and it seems like a good opportunity. Besides, I'm pretty attached to Oxford. If I initiated as a hunter, they'd probably move me to London. That's where most of the new hunters end up.'

'Well,' Cynthia said, 'what a coincidence. As it so happens, we have news too.'

'Go on.'

Cynthia glanced at her mother. Ms Rymes nodded.

'We've decided to stay in Oxford for the time being,' Cynthia said. 'I mean, we're registered with the Council now, and the vampires have been… pretty okay with it, and we have friends here, so… we're going to stay, at least until I'm done with school.'

'That's great!'

'Mm-hmm.' Cynthia reached over and laced her fingers with his. 'We should celebrate.'

Nathan grinned. 'We should. You know, we've been dating since September, but we still haven't gone on a proper date?'

'We should rectify that,' Cynthia agreed. She leaned in.

'We should,' Nathan repeated, but he was quite distracted. Cynthia's lips were close to his, then they were on his, and her tongue was in his mouth, and then she'd crawled onto his lap.

'EW! Mum, Cynthia's *kissing* Nathan!' Emma cried.

Cynthia and Nathan separated. Cynthia was giggling wildly.

'You two!' Ms Rymes groaned. 'Not in the kitchen.'

'You're the one who won't let me have him in my room, Mum,' Cynthia said.

'Oh, for the love of—' Ms Rymes flicked her oven mitts at them. 'Out! Off you go! But the door stays open, you hear me, Cynthia? Don't make me come up and check on you!'

'Thanks, Mum!'

Cynthia grabbed Nathan's hand and dragged him out of the kitchen. They ascended the stairs, both laughing.

Nathan grinned to himself as Cynthia pushed her door half closed. Life was looking up.

Cynthia crawled onto her bed and smiled at him. 'Come on. Let's celebrate.'

02-OCT-2016

'ALL ABOARD?' KURT CALLED out in his best English. 'Please stay seated and keep your seatbelts fastened. It will be a twenty-minute drive to the hotel.'

He manoeuvred the bus out of the usual queue of traffic around Berlin-Hauptbahnhof and headed for Invalidenstraße. Another day, another busload of tourists. Screaming kids, people standing up in the middle of the motorway, empty crisp packets, and orange juice spills. Just another day in his life.

He tapped the mic to check it was working. 'Shortly up ahead, we will be crossing the point where the Berlin Wall used to separate East and West Berlin. If you look closely at the ground, you will see the marker.' A pause. 'If the lady at the back could please be seated…'

Several passengers tittered. Others craned their necks, trying to see out the bus. A boy switched on his music; some kind of alt metal poured out of the speakers, loud enough that the boy would be deaf by the time he was thirty.

Kurt slowed the bus a little to accommodate traffic. His mic buzzed, like it always did when he received an SMS. He flicked his gaze to his phone, reading the notification. Just the weekly schedule coordination update. He looked back at the road.

And slammed his foot on the brakes.

A man was standing in the road.

'AUS DEM WEG! VERDAMMT—'

It all happened very quickly. The brakes squealed in protest. Kurt clutched the wheel, but there was nowhere to go except into traffic. They collided with a thud, and an almighty groan of bending metal rent the air. The windscreen shattered, and Kurt threw his arms up to shield his face. When he lowered them, the bus was stationary, the engine cut, and the man was gone.

Alarmed, he undid his seatbelt and leaned forwards. A human-shaped lump lay on the tarmac.

'Scheiße, scheiße, scheiße!'

He pulled himself out of his seat on shaky legs, already operating the door mechanism. It was jammed, but with a groan and a hiss it eventually engaged. Air whooshed past him as it opened.

Someone screamed. Kurt jumped and spun back towards the bus. Nothing amiss.

'Please remain seated!' he called. 'I will make sure it's safe to evacuate—'

Another scream.

Thud!

Someone collapsed into the aisle in a dead faint. A shiver ran down Kurt's spine. He turned back to the road.

Empty.

The body was gone.

Was zum Teufel...?

Behind him, all hell broke loose. Several people were screaming at once. He heard, 'SHE'S DEAD! SHE'S DEAD!' and 'RUN!'. A woman was praying in Mandarin. A man jumped up, sprinting towards Kurt. Before Kurt's eyes, he watched a figure come out of nowhere—a flash of blond hair and terrifyingly long teeth—the figure latched onto the man's neck. After that, Kurt stopped understanding. He watched in horror as the man went pale and limp and sank to the floor.

The figure dropped the body and sauntered towards Kurt. Kurt took a step backwards.

'I—ich—Sie—bitte—ich habe Kinder—'

'Close the door,' it said. It was a man, and yet not. Its eyes were red. A monster in human form.

With shaking hands, Kurt reached out and pressed the button. The door slid closed.

TO BE CONTINUED

SEE MORE BY THIS AUTHOR.

COMING IN JULY 2022...

WICKED BLOOD

Cynthia has never met her father. She only knows one thing about him: he's a dangerous mage with a track record of killing shapeshifters like her.

Finished with school and struggling to figure out what to do next, Cynthia boards a plane to Berlin, following a mysterious postcard from her father. She hopes to find him and finally solve the mystery of her origins. But then Nathan, her vampire hunter ex-boyfriend, asks for a favour. Look up the hunters in Berlin and find out why there's been radio silence from the supernatural community of Berlin for the last eight months.

What should have been a simple request leads to unimaginable danger.

The more Cynthia digs into the whereabouts of Berlin's supernatural community, the more she uncovers secrets that threaten her life. Something is going down in Berlin, but who is behind it? She finds herself torn in two directions: should she be loyal to her people, the shapeshifters? Or should she follow her heart? Which choice will keep her safe when everyone seems to be out for her blood?

It's a dangerous time to be in Berlin... and the answers to Cynthia's questions might just strike closer to home than she realises.

ACKNOWLEDGEMENTS

This book would not exist without the small, but dedicated team who helped me pull everything together. I'd like to express my sincerest gratitude to each of them:

To Debra, my beta-reader and cheerleader, who was the first person to read my writing and tell me to go for it.

To Pierre, my proof-reader, who helped me fix my silly little plot holes and corral randomly disappearing characters.

To Joshua, who created the artwork for my website and the inside cover of the book.

To the team at E-book Launch, who created the gorgeous cover.

And lastly, to my mother: beta-reader, formatter, accountant, cheerleader, emotional support, researcher, and proof-reader all rolled into one. Without her, there would simply be no book. There aren't enough words in the English language to express how I grateful I am for her support. I couldn't have done it without her.

AFTERWORD

I hope you enjoyed reading Nathan's adventures as much as I enjoyed writing them. If you want to discover more about Nathan's world, sign up for my newsletter at www.margotdeklerk.com/landing-page. Subscribers will get a free companion guide to the Vampires of Oxford Universe.

I also share deleted scenes, exclusive content, and previews of what I am working on in my newsletter which comes out every second month.

If you have time, please also consider leaving a review on Amazon.com or Amazon.co.uk and on my Goodreads page. Reviews are the best reward an author can receive.

I hope to see you again when the next book launches.

Sincerely,
Margot de Klerk

ABOUT THE AUTHOR

Margot de Klerk is a young adult fantasy author from the UK. She read German at Oxford University, and currently works as an editor and copywriter. When not writing, she enjoys travelling, photography, and sewing.

Follow her on social media, subscribe to her mailing list, and get information on new books:

Printed in Great Britain
by Amazon

28687413R00182